W9-BJR-590

Confessions of A Little
Black Gown

By Elizabeth Boyle

CONFESSIONS OF A LITTLE BLACK GOWN
TEMPTED BY THE NIGHT
LOVE LETTERS FROM A DUKE
HIS MISTRESS BY MORNING
THIS RAKE OF MINE
SOMETHING ABOUT EMMALINE
IT TAKES A HERO
STEALING THE BRIDE
ONE NIGHT OF PASSION
ONCE TEMPTED
NO MARRIAGE OF CONVENIENCE

Coming Soon
MEMOIRS OF A SCANDALOUS RED DRESS

ELIZABETH BOYLE

Confessions of A Little
Black Gown

AVON

An Imprint of HarperCollins*Publishers*

This is a work of fiction. Names, characters, places, and incidents are products of the author's imagination or are used fictitiously and are not to be construed as real. Any resemblance to actual events, locales, organizations, or persons, living or dead, is entirely coincidental.

AVON BOOKS
An Imprint of HarperCollins*Publishers*
10 East 53rd Street
New York, New York 10022-5299

Copyright © 2009 by Elizabeth Boyle
Excerpts from *Tempt the Devil* copyright © 2009 by Anna Campbell; *Devil of the Highlands* copyright © 2009 by Lynsay Sands; *Bride of a Wicked Scotsman* copyright © 2009 by Sandra Kleinschmit; *Confessions of a Little Black Gown* copyright © 2009 by Elizabeth Boyle
ISBN-13: 978-1-60751-940-9

All rights reserved. No part of this book may be used or reproduced in any manner whatsoever without written permission, except in the case of brief quotations embodied in critical articles and reviews. For information address Avon Books, an Imprint of HarperCollins Publishers.

Avon Trademark Reg. U.S. Pat. Off. and in Other Countries, Marca Registrada, Hecho en U.S.A.
HarperCollins® is a registered trademark of HarperCollins Publishers.

Printed in the U.S.A.

To Jessica Burtt,
whose bubbly spirit and bright eyes
have lit up our home and our lives for so many years.
Where would we have been all this time without you?
May you continue to grow and flourish
and bring the same joy to the children you teach
as you have to my children.
They are lucky to have you.

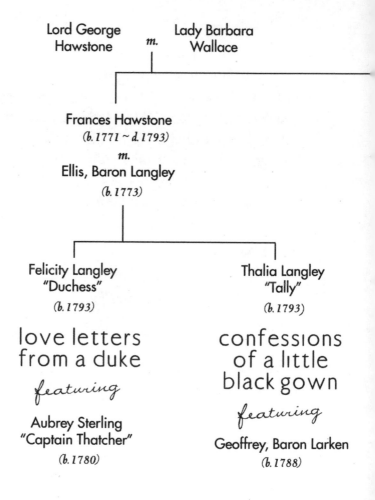

Lord George Hawstone   *m.*   Lady Barbara Wallace

Frances Hawstone
(b. 1771 ~ d. 1793)

m.

Ellis, Baron Langley
(b. 1773)

Felicity Langley
"Duchess"
(b. 1793)

love letters from a duke

featuring

Aubrey Sterling
"Captain Thatcher"
(b. 1780)

Thalia Langley
"Tally"
(b. 1793)

confessions of a little black gown

featuring

Geoffrey, Baron Larken
(b. 1788)

For the complete Bachelor Chronicles Family
Tree, please visit www.elizabethboyle.com

the
BACHELOR
CHRONICLES
family tree

Frederica Hawstone
(b. 1771 ~ d. 1800)

m.

**Bertram Knolles,
Earl of Stanbrook**
(b. 1765 ~ d. 1812)

**Lady Philippa Knolles
"Pippin"**
(b. 1793)

**Carlton Knolles,
Earl of Stanbrook**
(b. 1796)

Also featuring

Lord & Lady John Tremont
"Jack & Miranda" from
something about emmaline
&
this rake of mine

The Duke & Duchess of Setchfield
"Temple & Diana" from
stealing the bride

London
June 1814

"Come to bed, my love," called a rich, sultry voice from the doorway of the parlor.

"Yes, yes, Lizzie, I am nearly done here," Horatio Thurber said, glancing up from the script he was reading.

His wife sauntered into the small room, a gauzy silk nightgown draped over her lush form. An actress right down to her toes, his Lizzie never made anything but the most elegant of entrances.

"What is that you're reading?" she asked, her hand resting on his shoulder, tempting him with her light, teasing touch to come to bed. To bed her.

"A play," he said. "*Lady Persephone's Perilous Affair.*"

"You look quite engaged. Who wrote it? Beadle?

Or was it that Wilson fellow—his plays are such good fun."

"Neither. Two ladies penned this."

She laughed. "Ladies? Oh, Horatio! Not some morality play about a sniveling governess and her overbearing employer."

"No, not at all," he murmured, engrossed in the action on the pages. "These chits can write."

He handed her the first page and she began to read aloud. Actresses never read anything silently when there was an audience to be had.

"By Lady Philippa Knolles and Miss Thalia Langley." She paused. "Sounds to me like a pair of spoiled Mayfair misses if ever there were."

"Most likely," he muttered.

"Is it good?" she asked skeptically. Lizzie, the daughter of a carter and a seamstress, had never had much use for the upper classes. Their gold, yes. Their ability to actually produce something other than bastards, no. "Horatio," she repeated. "Is it good?"

What she meant was, would it earn them a pretty penny.

He nodded, still reading away.

"Whatever is it about?" she asked, climbing into his lap and gazing at the pages he held, and after she'd scanned a few paragraphs, she groaned. "Not another pirate tale. You promised me—no more pirates. They are wretched to stage and you'll have to cast Piers as the lead—that scene-stealing, difficult pri—"

"Ah, but this play is the exception, Lizzie."

She huffed a sigh and began to read as well, and

eventually she was wiping tears from her eyes. "Harrumph! I do so hate being proven wrong, but this is engaging. You must secure it before someone else does. Am I to play Miss Potter?"

He grinned. "Exactly. And Angeline is our Persephone."

She leaned over and dug through the discarded pages for the first one she'd dropped earlier. "Lady Philippa Knolles. *Knolles*," she said. "I remember now. She was with that privateer—Captain Dashwell— the one who got nicked at a ball. I heard tell she was his . . ." Her mouth fell open and a light of pure avarice illuminated her eyes. "Think of it, Horatio. If she really could do this—break her pirate out of prison, save him from the hangman's noose—and us with the entire plot in production."

He laughed and kissed his greedy wife soundly. "'Tis only a play, Lizzie-my-love. It would be nigh on impossible for two Bath misses, a spinster and a servant to free a man from Marshalsea."

"Harrumph," Lizzie sputtered as she led him from the parlor to their bedchamber. "God bless them if they tried—they'd make us richer than the King if they succeeded."

Chapter 1

Sometimes when a Season fails to secure the happiness of a young lady or two, say one's sister or cousin, then the next course of action is to organize the perfect house party.

A notation found on the back page
of *The Bachelor Chronicles*

"Tally, whatever are you doing there clutching your writing desk like someone is about to steal it?" Lady Philippa Knolles asked.

"Someone is, Pippin," her cousin, Miss Thalia Langley, replied, nodding in the direction where Tally's sister, the former Miss Felicity Langley, now the Duchess of Hollindrake, stood in the posting inn yard, ordering the harried footman about with military precision.

"She's rearranging the luggage?" Pippin looked askance at the melee of boxes and trunks.

"Yet again," Tally sighed, sharing a commiserating glance with her dog, Brutus, who was ever at the hem of her gown. "She used to do this to Papa when we were traveling on the Continent. Order the trunks and bags rearranged over and over again. Don't you recall how she harried those poor fellows when we moved to London last winter?"

"Oh, yes," Pippin mused. "I had quite forgotten. Perhaps Hollindrake could suggest—"

"I've already advised him not to waste his breath. Papa and I learned never to argue with her over it, for she only fusses all the more until it is all put to her liking."

"Is there such an arrangement?" Pippin asked, her face a mask of innocence, but her eyes sparkling.

Tally laughed. "No, but she is determined to discover one."

There was barely room for the Duke's procession of carriages and wagons in the small yard, let alone the luggage now stacked in every remaining bit of space. And worse yet, the untimely arrival of a crowded mail coach, as well as a post-chaise, had only added to the chaos as the passengers and postilions jostled for room. Add to that, the luggage from the mail coach was being divided, as some of the passengers departed and others waded through the confusion to gain their appointed seats.

"I'll not lose my sketchbook and jewelry case," Tally complained, clutching her writing box closer. "And one of us had best stand guard over our carriage, lest we find her over here ready to send our trunks to the wagons beneath a crate of dishes and insisting Aunt Minty be moved as well."

"She wouldn't!" Pippin declared, nonetheless taking a nervous glance at Felicity. "I do think she's far too busy to notice our poor possessions."

Tally's reply was an arched glance.

"Oh, dear, you're right." Pippin's brow furrowed. "Look she's sending some fellow over here now."

Muttering her favorite Russian curse under her breath, Tally planted herself firmly before the carriage she and Pippin were sharing with their aged chaperone, Aunt Minty.

The footman's pace slowed as he neared them and found himself facing the two young misses.

"And just what do you think you are doing?" Tally asked, handing her desk over to Pippin and scooping up Brutus.

The young man hung his head. "Well, miss, 'tis Her Grace's orders. I've come for the trunks and your aunt." He stretched out his hand toward the carriage door, and Tally sidestepped into his path.

"Bother Her Grace! You're not to open that door!"

Brutus aided her cause by letting out a menacing growl. Well, as menacing as one could be when you were a dog that could fit easily into a hatbox, and a very small hatbox at that.

Still, it was enough to get the footman to draw back his fingers, for Tally's little dog had gained a reputation amongst the duke's servants as being "a nasty bit of trouble."

Tally shot a heated glance toward her sister, who was right now arguing with the wagon driver over the proper balancing of trunks, before she turned her glare on the hapless servant. "Our Aunt Minty is sleeping. She is not to be disturbed."

Yet the footman persisted. "Miss, I can't go back there without something in hand." He lowered his voice and pleaded, "She'll have my hide."

Oh, dear. Poor man. He was right. Felicity would have his hide.

Tally heaved a sigh and wished her sister's fondest desire had been to marry a tailor or a butcher, rather than a duke. Quite frankly, her twin had become a regular tyrant since she'd married Hollindrake. Not that she wasn't still loveable, it was just that . . . well, now that Felicity actually was a duchess, she'd become utterly intractable, more so than when they'd been mere paupers living on Brook Street.

If such a thing were possible to believe.

"Please, miss," the fellow begged. "Isn't there something you can spare?"

Tally glanced around the back of the elegant barouche. "Take the larger one there—that ought to satisfy her, and it should help balance out that mess she's creating on the wagon."

The man doffed his cap and practically wept in relief to have some offering to take back to his difficult mistress.

As he happily lumbered away, struggling under the weight of Tally's belongings, Pippin leaned over and said, "You needn't have made quite that much of a sacrifice."

"What do you mean?" Tally asked, watching her sister's lips fan out in a smile of glee at the arrival of yet another trunk to move about.

"Giving up your clothes to keep Felicity at bay."

"Not really," Tally said, putting Brutus back down on the ground and retrieving her desk from Pippin.

"How so?"

"For if she loses it, then she'll owe me a new wardrobe."

Pippin laughed, her blue eyes crinkling in the corners. "And here I thought you had placed yourself on the altar for my sake." She tucked a stray strand of blonde hair back beneath her bonnet.

"Hardly so," Tally said, waving one gloved hand, her gaze flitting over the jumbled luggage and landing on a woman who stood in the shade of a large tree across the yard.

About Tally's height and slim build, the lady wore widow's weeds—in black from head to toe. It was nearly impossible to discern her age, shadowed as her face was by the large brim of an elegant hat, but Tally found herself intrigued by the aristocratic line of her nose, and the point of the lady's chin, which lent her angular face a unique distinction.

The artist in Tally loved unusual faces, and immediately she began to memorize and catalogue the lady's features until she had time to sketch them.

But as she studied the woman, something struck her as odd. Instead of the dour, mournful expression one expected from a woman in weeds, the mysterious lady was watching the proceedings in the yard as if she were calculating something, her gloved hand gripping the gnarled, thick bark of the chestnut tree she stood beneath.

Most likely keeping her hawklike gleam on her luggage, Tally mused.

Just then the widow turned and said something to a large man behind her—a servant, from his dress—snapping her fingers and speaking quickly, then pointing at the post-chaise.

Tally glanced at the dark carriage as well, then back at the lady, unable to shake the notion that something wasn't quite right here—that she was concealing more than grief beneath her black bombazine.

Besides, there was something vaguely familiar about the lady. As if Tally had seen her face before. Somewhere. But before she could place the widow, Pippin nudged her in the ribs.

"Tally, are you listening to me?" she asked. "Do you want me to get you some tea or not?"

"Um, uh, no," she said, momentarily distracted from her musings.

"Are you sure?" her cousin insisted.

Tally glanced back at her. "Oh, sorry. Yes, I would love some."

Pippin opened the door of the carriage, caught up both of their tea caddy baskets, and made her haphazard way into the inn, while Tally remained behind to stand guard.

What she would really love, she would have liked to tell Pippin, or anyone who would listen, was not to be part of this circus. Not to have to spend her summer at Hollindrake House.

She nudged a stone loose with her slipper and huffed a little sigh.

A house party. Tally begged to differ. A party implied an event filled with gaiety and amusements. What her sister had planned was nothing more than an opportunity for Felicity to lord over everyone who had naysayed her grand notions of marrying a duke.

Tally snorted in a very unladylike fashion. If that were the end of her sister's machinations, it wouldn't be so intolerable, but she knew what Felicity had truly planned—this house party was nothing more than another way for her to work her matchmaking evil.

Oh, I should have burned that wretched Bachelor Chronicles *of hers when I had the chance.*

For that horrible journal of Felicity's, the one she'd kept for years now, recording all the attributes and material wealth of the lords and gentleman of society, was everything that was wrong with the notion of marriage—at least in Tally's estimation.

Whatever had happened to love at first sight? With finding a man who ignited one's imagination, one's heart, one's soul?

No, instead Tally was going to spend the next fortnight surrounded by perfectly eligible *partis*. Men specifically chosen by Felicity for their breeding, wealth and social ranking.

Like Lord Dalderby or Viscount Gossett.

This time Tally shuddered.

She knew she should be excited and grateful for this opportunity, for what unmarried chit of one and twenty wouldn't welcome the chance to be favored with an invitation to an exclusive house party stocked from the rafters to the cellar with unmarried and eligible men?

Not Tally. For the men Felicity invited were hardly the sort she desired. Someone dark and mysterious. Who'd seen the world that existed beyond England's quaint and quiet green shores.

Unfortunately for Tally, her father's globe-trotting ways ran deeply through her veins, and the staid, predictable life her twin had chosen seemed more a prison sentence than the veritable pot of gold most viewed such an unlikely and lofty match.

No, there would be no mysterious suitors for her, no affairs of the heart, no heart-wrenching choices between the pinnacles of love and death.

She glanced once again across the frantic yard at the huge chestnut tree anchored at the corner of the stables, but the widow had gone—most likely to rescue her luggage or seek refuge from Felicity's battlefield.

Envy, sharp and piercing, stabbed Tally's heart. This widow, for all her dark and searching glances, had the one thing Tally would never have—at least not until she was lucky enough to don a widow's weeds.

Her freedom.

Three days later

"Oh, Thatcher, there you are," Tally said, coming to a stop in the middle of her brother-in-law's study, not even having bothered to knock. She supposed if he were any other duke, not the man who'd once been their footman, she'd have to view him as the toplofty and unapproachable Duke of Hollindrake, as everyone else did.

Thankfully, Thatcher never expected *her* to stand on formality.

The room was cast in shadows, which perfectly matched her gloomy mood over being a pawn in her sister's outrageous plans.

"One of the maids said she saw a carriage arrive," she began, "some wretchedly poor contraption that couldn't belong to one of Felicity's guests, and I thought it might be my missing . . . "

Her voice trailed off as Brutus came trotting up behind her, having stopped on the way down the stairs to give a footman's boot a bit of a chew. Her ever-present companion had paused for only a second before he let out a little growl, then launched himself toward a spot in a shadowed corner, as if he'd spied a rat.

No, make that a very ill-looking pair of boots.

Thatcher had company? She tamped down the blush that started to rise on her cheeks, remembering that she'd just insulted this unknown visitor's carriage.

Oh, dash it all! What had she called it?

Some wretchedly poor contraption . . .

Tally shot a glance at Thatcher, who nodded toward the shadows, even as a man rose up from the chair there. Immediately, the world as Tally knew it tilted, because this man had the bearing and grace of an ancient god, like watching one of the Greek sculptures Lord Hamilton had been forever collecting in Naples come to life.

A shiver ran down her spine, like a forebear of something momentous. She couldn't breathe, she couldn't move, and she knew, just knew, her entire life was about to change.

It made no sense, but then again, Tally had never put much stock in sense, common or otherwise.

If only Thatcher's study wasn't so bloody dark!

Then again, Tally didn't really need to see the man, whose boot Brutus had attached himself to, to *know* him.

Hadn't their Nanny Jamilla always said it would happen just like this? That one day she'd come face to face with the man who was her destiny and she'd just know?

Even without being able to see his face, she supposed.

Perhaps it was because her heart thudded to a halt just by the way he stood, so tall and erect, even with a devilish little affenpinscher affixed to his boot.

Heavens! With Brutus thus, how could this man ever move forward?

"Oh, dear! Brutus, you rag-mannered mutt, come away from there," she said, pasting her best smile on her face and wishing that she weren't wearing one of Felicity's old hand-me-down gowns. And blast Felicity for her tiresome meddling, for if she'd just left well enough alone and not insisted the trunks be changed around, Tally's trunk wouldn't have become lost.

"You wretched little dog, are you listening to me? Come here!" She snapped her fingers, and after one last, great growling chew, Brutus let go of his prize and returned to his usual place, at the hem of her gown, his black eyes fixed on the man, or rather his boots, as if waiting for any sign that he could return for another good bite.

"I am so sorry, sir," Tally began. "I fear his manners are terrible, but I assure you his pedigree is impeccable. His grandsire belonged to Marie Antoinette." She snapped her lips shut even as she realized she was rambling like a fool. Going on about Brutus's royal connections like the worst sort of pandering mushroom.

"No offense taken, miss," he said.

Tally shivered at the rich, masculine tones of his

simple acceptance of her apology. It swept over her like a caress.

Then to her delight, he came closer, moving toward Thatcher's desk with catlike grace, making her think of the men she'd imagined in her plays: prowling pirates and secretive spies. It was almost as if he was used to moving through shadows, aloof and confident in his own power.

Tally tamped down another shiver and leaned over to pick up Brutus, holding him tightly as if he could be the anchor she suddenly felt she needed.

Whatever was it about this man that had her feeling as if she were about to be swept away? That he was capable of catching her up in his arms and stealing her away to some secluded room where he'd lock them both away. Then he'd toss her atop the bed and he'd strip away his jacket, his shirt, his . . .

Tally gulped back her shock.

What the devil is wrong with me? She hadn't even met the man yet, and here she was imagining him nearly in his altogether.

Until this moment, she'd never understood her sister's obsession with Hollindrake or Pippin's for Captain Dashwell, but she'd joined their ranks in the blink of an eye and even before she'd spied more than a hint of this incomparable stranger.

Oh, dear heavens, she prayed silently, *please say he is here for the house party. Please . . .*

"I daresay we have met," she continued on trying to lure him forward, force him to speak again, "but you'll have to excuse me, I'm a terrible widgeon when it comes to remembering names."

The man stepped closer, but stopped his progress

when the door opened and Staines arrived, a brace of candles in hand, making a *tsk, tsk* sound over the lack of light in the room. The butler shot the duke a withering glance that seemed to say, *You are supposed to ring for more light.*

Poor Thatcher, Tally thought. He still had yet to find his footing as the Duke of Hollindrake and all that it entailed.

As the butler and the two footmen traveling in his wake went about the room lighting candles and illuminating the corners, Tally held her breath. Oh, just a few candles more and she's see her future. . .

"Have we met?" she asked impatiently, and to further her cause, she shifted Brutus to one hip and stuck out her hand, which must compel the man, if he was a gentleman, to take the final steps into the circle of light.

"No, I don't believe we have ever met, Miss—"

Oh, heavens, his voice was as smooth as the French brandy she and Felicity used to steal from their teacher's wine cabinet. And it would be even better if he were whispering into her ear.

Tally, my love, what is it you desire most . . .

Oh, now you are being a complete widgeon, she chided herself, closing her eyes, for she couldn't believe she was having such thoughts over a perfect stranger. A man she'd never met. She only hoped this ridiculous tumult he was causing on her insides wasn't showing on her face.

Taking a deep breath, she unshuttered her lashes and gaped in horror at the stranger before her. This was her future? Her destiny? No! It couldn't be.

Certainly not this ordinary, rather dowdy-looking

fellow blinking owlishly at her from behind a pair of dirty spectacles, his shoulders stooped over as if he carried the burden of the world upon them.

Where had he come from? She leaned over to peer past him, searching for any sign of the man she'd expected, but there was no one else there.

Tally swayed a bit. Heavens, she was seeing things. If she didn't know better, she'd say she was as jug-bitten as their London housekeeper, Mrs. Hutchinson.

But no, all the evidence was before her, for instead of some rakish character in a Weston jacket and perfectly polished boots, there stood a gentleman (well, she hoped he was at least a gentleman) in a coat that could best be described as lumpy, cut of some poorly dyed wool, with sleeves too short for his arms. Far too short, for his cuffs stuck out a good four inches. Then she glanced at his cravat, or rather where his cravat should be.

For in its place, to her horror, sat a vicar's collar.

A vicar?

Tally's heart stopped for a second time, and not for the same reasons as earlier. She looked at his throat again, convinced she'd been mistaken. He couldn't be a . . .

Oh, gads, she'd nearly made a cake of herself over a . . . a . . . vicar.

She gulped back her mortification. *How could I have been so mistaken . . . ?*

And how so, for he stepped forward just then to take her hand in greeting—heavens, she'd forgotten she'd been holding it out now for what seemed like an eternity—and his fingers wound around hers in a limp grasp, and he smiled patronizingly down at her as if she were some sort of simpleton.

In truth, she rather felt like one, and it was all she could do to return his greeting with a wan smile.

At this point, her brother-in-law rose abruptly, like a nervous cat. "Tally, how rude of me! This is my cousin . . . uh, um, Mr. Milo Ryder." He paused for a second. "Mr. Ryder, this is my sister-in-law, Miss Thalia Langley."

"Miss Langley," he said, "a pleasure to meet you." Then for just a moment, his fingers wound around hers, his grasp tightened and an unsettling shock of desire raced through her.

Tally glanced up at him and found herself looking into a pair of deep, brown eyes, a color akin to a pot of Turkish coffee like their Nanny Rana used to make for her and Felicity when they were children.

Mr. Ryder's eyes held that same mysterious hue—a color that was rich, subtle, and tempting.

And as she looked again into his eyes, she found him searching her face, examining her, as if he sought the answer to some elusive question as well.

Tally trembled. Actually shivered, for she swore she felt him peer into her very soul. His fingers went from being flaccid to warm and hard, as they suddenly held hers with a steely determination that belied the meek collar around his throat.

Oh, dear heavens, whatever is happening? she wondered, closing her eyes and trying desperately to still her beating heart, keep herself from babbling something completely ridiculous.

And then all her romantic imaginings were gone. His fingers dropped hers, and when she looked up again, she found to her dismay that his features were now masked over, the mystery in his eyes had vanished, and he had turned to ask Thatcher something about the stabling of his horses.

Yet the moment still held Tally in its grasp.

She shook her head over Nanny Jamilla's advice. That a woman just knows when she's about to fall in love.

Given that Jamilla, having been at the French court, had fallen in love enough times to fill the advertisement page of the *Morning Post*, Tally had to assume she knew of what she spoke, but this couldn't be!

In love? With a vicar?!

Tally's hand went to her mouth to cover the gasp that was about to escape, not that Mr. Ryder noticed overly much for he was blandly nodding at something Thatcher was saying about the pastures.

So he was staying? And for some time, by the sound of it.

Tally pressed her lips together. Oh, she could only imagine Felicity's reaction to this uninvited guest. Even if he was Thatcher's cousin.

Tally almost felt sorry him. Without even an "Honorable" or a "Sir Charles" or a "Sir John" attached to his name. Felicity would be cross as crabs over his arrival.

As if on cue, her sister, the Duchess of Hollindrake, breezed into the room. "Oh, Thatcher, there you are! I was about to call you to dinner, but I was delayed by—" She stopped in mid-sentence at the sight of her husband's guest, and to her credit, she smiled widely, that is until her sharp gaze landed on his less-than-fashionable cuffs.

"Felicity, how perfect. I was just about to send for you," the duke said. "Look who has arrived: my cousin, Mr. Ryder."

Tally took a step back, not that Felicity would make a scene in front of a guest, but, well, it was just best to be out of the line of fire where Felicity was concerned.

But to Tally's shock the wide smile continued to spread across her face and she held out her hand in greeting. "Cousin Ryder! What a charming surprise! I must say, I thought you were going to arrive next week—"

Tally looked in shock at her sister and then back at Mr. Ryder. *He had been expected?*

He moved forward without any measure of grace, nearly treading on Tally's toes in the process. "Well, I—I—I—I . . . that is to say, I—I—I," he stammered. "I hope my early arrival isn't an—an—an inconvenience, for I arrived in London a week past, with the idea of staying with our cousin, Lady Bethsheba, but I discovered her suddenly out of town—imagine that! And with the costs too dear to stay on my own—for you cannot believe the prices associated with a stay in London and though I have inherited of late, I daresay parting with funds at such extortionate rates taxes my sensibilities unduly—so I made the unpardonable decision to impose myself upon your kindness earlier than I had been expected."

Tally cringed. *Oh, goodness, he's quite the mushroom, and a pinchpurse.*

Good luck matching him, Duchess, she thought, using not her sister's title, but the childhood nickname Felicity had carried into adulthood.

Meanwhile, Felicity had wound her arm around Mr. Ryder's and was leading him from the study. "Perhaps your early arrival is most fortuitous, sir. Since you are intent on finding a wife"—she looked him over again—"Yes, well, perhaps it is best you've come early, for I believe we do have our work cut out, if you don't mind my saying. And there is no time like the present to begin."

"Um, I . . . that is to say . . ." he stammered anew, glancing over his shoulder at Thatcher as if he expected the duke to step in and save the day.

Tally nearly smiled. Mr. Ryder had asked Felicity to find him a wife? Oh, the poor man. But she wouldn't have been in a rush to pity Mr. Ryder if she had known what Felicity had in mind next.

The duchess glanced over at her sister. "Tally, I'll need your help with Mr. Ryder."

"*Me?*"

"Of course, you!" Felicity's smile widened, which was never a good sign. Like a cat about to pounce. "Unless you have something better to do?"

She could think of a thousand things, quite frankly, for this situation had all the early warnings of an impending shipwreck. "I was actually about to—"

Not that her sister was listening, having already launched into her plans, explaining them in depth to her unlikely *parti.* "Now, Cousin Ryder, I'll see you settled in your room and then once you've had a chance to clean up, please join us all for dinner." She smiled at the poor vicar. "I'll have you seated next to me, so we can discuss which of the ladies I've invited might suit you best. Though I think you will be quite pleased with the one particular lady I have in mind. Have you heard of Miss Esmerelda DeFisser?"

Tally's head spun. Miss DeFisser? Was her sister mad? Whatever made Felicity think that an heiress of rank and privilege would look twice at a vicar? And a scruffy one at that? Oh, he might be one of Thatcher's relations, but the connection was hardly enough to entice Miss DeFisser into becoming a country parson's wife.

But there it was, that look of unholy determination on Felicity's face, and Tally knew there was nothing that could stop her sister from promoting the improbable match.

She glanced heavenward. She didn't know who she pitied more. Mr. Ryder or Miss DeFisser. And further, for some odd reason, she found the idea of Mr. Ryder being matched to any woman quite disconcerting.

And why, she knew not, for it wasn't as if she had the least bit of interest in him.

None whatsoever, she told herself as she followed him and Felicity out of the study. That is, until he passed through the shadows, and for a moment, she spied him as she had earlier—rakish and mysterious. Perhaps it was the ragged cut of his hair falling past his collar or the way for the tiniest second his shoulders straightened and he looked so much taller.

Then she blinked and the rake was gone, leaving Tally wondering for once at her own sanity more so than her sister's.

Chapter 2

The Reverend Milo Ryder
b. 1789
Current residence: Eveling House
The vicar of Bindley-by-the-Way in Lincolnshire, Mr. Ryder received his ordination five years ago. Truly if the man wasn't Hollindrake's cousin on his grandmother's side and hadn't had the good fortune to inherit from an even further removed great-aunt, he would never have made it into my Chronicles. But alas, now that he possesses a house and a respectable fortune, he must be matched.

The Bachelor Chronicles

"Miss, where do you want your trunk?" the footman asked as he and another fellow, recruited from the fields by the look of him, entered the suite of rooms that Felicity had set aside for Tally, Pippin, and Aunt Minty.

Tally glanced up from the desk where she'd been sitting sketching. The spot afforded her the last bit of evening light and a pretty view of the maze below. Over the past few days, she'd spent much of her time (when Felicity didn't have her running a thousand and one errands over the ducal estate) trying to sketch from memory the widow from the posting inn.

Pippin sat up smiling, for she'd been hunched over a letter to her errant brother, and wiped the ink from her fingers.

Finally , Tally thought as the pair set the large black trunk down in the middle of the room with a heavy *thud*. Her luggage had been found.

Pippin and Tally both shot a hurried glance in the direction of Aunt Minty's room, which adjoined theirs, hoping the noise hadn't awakened their sleeping companion.

"Thank you both," Tally whispered as the men left, and then opened her writing desk to fetch the trunk key. When she turned around, key in hand, she looked again at the trunk.

"Oh, heavens, that is not mine," she said to Pippin, pointing at the battered piece now taking up a good part of the parlor they shared.

Certainly hers was similar—for didn't all traveling trunks look alike?—but this one was not hers, of that she had no doubt.

Tally groaned. Of course it wasn't Felicity's trunks that had gone astray, but hers. Her only trunk. With all her new clothes.

"Do you want me to fetch them back?" Pippin asked, moving toward the door.

As much as she wanted to order the footmen to take it back downstairs and drop it on her sister's head, she doubted there was much chance of them doing that. So instead Tally said, "No. Sit and finish

your letter. We'll leave it be for now, and after dinner
I'll ask Thatcher to send someone back to the posting inn—yet again—and see if my trunk has been
returned there." She paced around the well-worn
piece. "I could just strangle my sister," she said.
"Now I haven't anything to wear tonight."

Pippin glanced over at her. "What is so special
about tonight?"

"Nothing!" Tally said, a little too adamantly, and
even as she heard the note in her voice, she turned
away from Pippin for fear her astute cousin would see
the blush on her cheeks.

So that wasn't the entire truth, she conceded silently. *He* was going to be there. In the hour since
Mr. Ryder had arrived, Tally had been unable to
shake a niggling notion that there was more to the
man than met the eye.

No, she knew what she'd seen—a rakish, mysterious man. It wasn't just what she thought she'd
seen, but also what she'd heard. His voice. Not that
tremulous stutter he'd fobbed off on her sister, but
the one he'd used earlier.

No offense taken, miss.

He'd spoken like a man who'd been in command.
Or was used to getting his way. Then there were his
eyes, that searching, penetrating glance he'd cast
over her like a net. He'd taken her measure in that
moment, and she wondered down to her toes what
he'd thought of her.

If he'd found her as maddeningly perplexing as
she found him. Or worse, if he thought nothing
more of her than Hollindrake's very ill-mannered
sister-in-law.

"Whatever is wrong, Tally?" Pippin asked.

"Nothing," she said quickly. Then amending that to add, "It's just that I am tired of wearing Felicity's old gowns. I find it very vexing she won't share one of her new ones and I am stuck wearing these old things." She held out the fine muslin as if it were rags. "My sister is a wretched, interfering, pestilent—"

"Eh, eh, eh," Pippin said, shaking her finger. "Remember, we agreed to go along with this . . . this . . . "

Tally knew exactly what her cousin was about to say, so she offered the kinder description. "House party?"

Pippin smiled. For privately they referred to it as "Felicity's Infernal Folly."

Tally paced a few more steps around the trunk. "If only Mr. Thurber would agree to produce our play— then we'd have money of our own and wouldn't have to depend on her wretched charity."

Or her meddling matchmaking.

"Well, he hasn't," Pippin said, with her usual practicality. "And so we must make the best of our situation."

"Harrumph!" Tally replied as she sat down on the beast of a trunk that had started her tirade.

"I wonder whose that is?" Pippin murmured as she eyed the large piece of luggage. "They are probably as unhappy as you are to have their belongings missing." She paused for a second. "Perhaps we could try to discover who owns it and reunite them.

Tally glanced down at it. "There aren't even any initials," she said, shaking her head. "But there is another way to find out." She returned to her writing desk, tucked her own trunk key away and set to work rummaging around inside, eventually smiling as she discovered what she was looking for amidst the pen nibs, bits of charcoal, sealing wax, and other treasures she kept tucked inside.

When she held up her set of lock picks, Pippin's eyes widened.

"Tally, you mustn't!"

"Why not?" she said eyeing the thick lock on the front of the trunk. "I don't see how else we can discover who this belongs to." She knelt before it and took another gander at the lock before setting to work.

While the exclusive Bath school, Miss Emery's Establishment for the Education of Genteel Ladies, that Pippin, Tally, and Felicity had attended was known for producing some of the most accomplished young ladies in Society, there were a few students whose . . . *ahem* . . . unusual upbringing had brought them to Bath with some scandalous skills, ones that they were all too happy to share with their fellow schoolmates, who welcomed the diversion from lessons on proper table settings and dance steps.

Always curious, Tally had learned how to pick locks from their former classmate, Miss Kathleen Escott—albeit only to open Miss Emery's wine cabinet on occasion. Ironically, the skill had turned out to be handy over the years in getting past the occasional secured door, a jail cell padlock, or in this case, a mysterious trunk. A talent far more useful than Miss Emery's countless lectures on subjects such as how long one must wear black upon the death of a second cousin once removed.

"Do be still," she admonished as Pippin paced behind her. "I can't concentrate with you fluttering about."

"Tally, this is wrong! What if the rightful owner takes offense to you having searched through their belongings? They might accuse you of stealing something."

She paused and glanced over her shoulder. "You're going to lecture me on larceny? Besides, it was your idea to find the owner. How else are we to discover who it belongs to if we don't open it?"

Pippin had the good sense to blush and then held up her hands and backed away.

Tally laughed and went back to work. After a few more seconds of concentration the tumblers clicked into place, and the lock opened. She leaned back, grinning at her success. "You'd best leave if you don't want to be part of this."

Pippin glanced at the door, her lips pursed together. "Oh, bother. In for a penny, in for a pound."

"So I thought," Tally said, getting up and tugging open the lid.

Pippin peered over her shoulder. "How disappointing. I had rather hoped for something exciting. A gentleman's secret treasure trove, or at the very least, an elegant lady's collection of shoes and fans."

Instead, the only thing that met their eyes was a length of jet bombazine that made up a standard widow's gown.

"Hmm," Tally said. "I wonder if this is *her* trunk."

"Whose trunk?"

"The widow at the posting inn." Tally ran her hand over the bombazine, and the silk wasn't the cheap sort she'd expected, but a rich, dense fabric that was far too dear for just ordinary mourning, meant only to be donned for a few months.

"I don't recall seeing a widow," Pippin said, before an awed "O-o-oh" escaped her lips as she touched the silk. "This must have—"

"Cost a fortune," Tally said, holding up the bombazine, and realizing it was about her size. Carefully she laid it on the bed, wondering what sort of woman would invest so much in a gown that would only be worn temporarily. "She must have loved him very much," she said, more to herself than to her cousin, but Pippin, with her sharp ears had heard her.

"Maybe, or mayhap he left her a very rich portion."

Tally giggled. "Then she's honoring his memory quite splendidly by throwing away his fortune on elegant gowns." She traced her hand over the silk again, only to whirl around when she heard Pippin gasp. "What is it?"

Then Tally gasped as well as she beheld the dress Pippin was holding. A gown the likes of which neither of them had ever seen.

Tally's mouth fell open. "Golly sakes. Why I've never—"

But before she could say more, a voice that stopped them both in their tracks interrupted their search.

"Yes, yes, I know dinner is in a half hour. Please tell Staines to set a place for the duke's cousin, Mr. Ryder. I would like him seated next to me."

There was a murmured, "Yes, Your Grace," before

Felicity's determined footsteps echoed anew down the hall.

"Oh, dear, she's coming," Pippin whispered.

Without another word, they stuffed the priceless silk and the gown Pippin held back into the trunk, and closed the lid just as the door to their room swung open.

Felicity walked into the room with all her usual authority. It wasn't as if becoming a duchess had made her this way, she'd been born to the role. "Tally! Pippin! You aren't dressed!"

"Felicity, I hardly see why we must go to all this fuss when it is only family—" Tally began.

Her sister's brow rose only a fraction but it was enough to stop her twin. "Yes, that may be so, but tomorrow it won't be. Our guests will start arriving first thing in the afternoon and I want to make sure the staff and"—she shot a reproving glance at her sister and cousin—"everyone else is up to the task. I have too many hopes attached to this house party—aspirations for all of us . . ."

Which Tally knew meant finding them husbands. Eligible ones. Lofty ones. Dull ones.

Felicity, meanwhile, continued on, blithely ignorant of the anarchy brewing in her sister's heart, "—and if this house party is a success, as I am sure it will be, imagine next Season, when we return to London—"

Tally and Pippin shared a glance. They both had other plans for next year—as long as Mr. Thurber bought their play——and those plans did not include spending their days being foisted upon Society by Felicity.

And they certainly didn't involve finding themselves entangled with some dull viscount or . . .
vicar . . .

Tally shook that wayward thought of Mr. Ryder
from her mind and tried hard to concentrate on
what Felicity was nattering on about.

Not that it was hard to discern—for Felicity had
only two subjects on her mind of late: making her
house party a blazing social triumph, and success-
fully mining her *Bachelor Chronicles* for likely mari-
tal candidates for Tally and Pippin.

But even Felicity could be diverted on occasion,
and this time she paused mid-sentence, tipped her
head and spied the trunk behind Pippin and Tally.
"Well, that is good news. Your trunk has arrived."

"But it isn't—" Pippin started to say before Tally
nudged her sharply in the ribs to stop her from finishing.

"—isn't too late for my clothes to arrive," Tally
said. "How fortunate for me."

Pippin nodded wordlessly in agreement, flicking
a sideways glance at Tally as if she wasn't too sure
what her cousin was up to.

Or that she wanted to be any part of it.

"Well now you can dress appropriately for dinner
and I'll hear no more complaints about you not
having anything to wear," Felicity said, waving her
hands at them and turning to leave. "Don't forget
to include Mr. Ryder in your conversations, Tally. I
expect your help in getting him up to snuff before
Miss DeFisser arrives. Perhaps you can invite him
to play cards after dinner or take him for a walk
and see where his interests lie, so I can decide how

best to proceed with him." Her sister heaved an aggrieved sigh. "I fear he is not the man I expected.
I had thought that a cousin of Thatcher's would be
more . . . more . . ." She paused, for Tally knew exactly what she meant.

More promising.

Felicity sighed and continued by saying, "There
is nothing to be done now except to make do. And
for that, Tally, I need you to be most attentive to Mr.
Ryder."

"Me?!" Tally began to protest, but was cut off by a
tsk, tsk from her twin.

"I am not asking all that much," Felicity said. "Just
discover if there is anything interesting about the
man so we can use those details to entice Miss De
Fisser into marrying him."

Interesting . . . the word brought images of her first
impressions of him. Of a rake who could seduce a
woman with barely a glance. A pirate out to steal a
lady's heart. A highwayman . . .

Even as she began to imagine him in a black coat
and atop a dark stallion, Pippin nudged her out of
her reverie.

" . . . and then tomorrow," Felicity was saying, "we
must see how capable Mr. Ryder is at riding and
bowling, and of course, dancing."

"You want me to dance with him?" Tally sputtered, not so much as a question, but more of a protest.

Felicity paused and stared at her as if Tally had
just begged off in favor of deportation to Botany
Bay. "But of course you are to dance with him.
Tally—whatever is wrong with you? Can't you see

how important this is to me? I'm only asking you to make an impression upon Mr. Ryder so he will trust you and listen to you, so that when you make a few well-meaning and very necessary recommendations as to how he could dress better, and appear more, shall we say, gentlemanly, he'll listen."

Tally's list of protests as to the madness of her sister's plan grew so long, they bottled up in her throat, leaving her speechless.

Felicity, of course, failed to notice. "Dinner is in half an hour. Please don't be late." She left as quickly as she'd arrived, and even before the door was closed, they heard her issuing orders to whatever hapless servant happened to be in the hall.

"Wellington's troops had an easier time of it," Tally managed to choke out. "She's impossible!"

Pippin chuckled, pushing off the trunk. "She is determined, I will say that."

"You are only smiling because she isn't tossing you toward that wretched Mr. Ryder." Tally pressed her lips together and set to work getting the trunk lid propped back open.

"You've met him?"

Tally nodded. "When I went down to ask Thatcher about my trunk, he was there."

Pippin paused, her hand resting atop the black silk. "And?"

Wrinkling her nose, she replied, "He's a veritable country parson. Not unlike Vicar Vials in our play."

Pippin laughed. "Say no more. No wonder Felicity is in such a state." She plucked the black silk out revealing the real treasure inside, the one they'd hidden from the duchess so hastily—a black velvet gown, bejeweled and bedazzling with silver embroidery and pearls sewn into intricate designs.

The two of them stood gaping at the elegant confection, Felicity and Mr. Ryder utterly forgotten.

"That is the most beautiful gown I have ever seen," Tally finally whispered, as if speaking of it aloud would somehow make it disappear.

Pippin glanced at her. "Truly?"

Tally nodded. "I don't think even Jamilla has ever had anything close to this."

"Heavens, Tally," Pippin said, eyeing the silk on the bed and the velvet in the trunk. "I daresay they would fit you!"

Tally glanced down at the black velvet and in a moment saw herself enrobed in it, jewels in her hair and silver slippers on her feet.

In her imagination, she was no longer under Felicity's social guidance, but a lady on her own, free of Society's constraints.

And there was a man. Well, if one had a dress like this, there had better well be a man. And he wore a half mask—making him just as dashing and handsome as she was elegant. He would have no need to ask her to dance, for he'd claim her hand against all takers, and he'd sweep her into a waltz. Then, just as suddenly, the room would empty, until it was only the two of them, with no need for music and only scant candles for light . . . He'd lower his lips to hers and . . .

"Tally! Are you listening to me?" Pippin said, nudging her from behind, having set a perfume pot and a small case to one side.

Gads! So lost in her woolgathering, she hadn't even

noticed that her cousin had gone back to rummaging through the trunk. So much for Pippin's arguments against invading someone else's privacy, for she was now digging about like a rag picker.

"None of this makes sense," her cousin was muttering.

"How so?" Tally said, laying the velvet down next to the bombazine.

"A widow with a dress like that? And there's a maid's gown in here as well." Pippin held it up. "I would love to see Felicity's face if you wore that down to dinner. It would make quite an impression on this Mr. Ryder of hers."

Quite an impression . . . the words struck Tally like a well-shot arrow. But her gaze wasn't on the worn and ragged woolen gown, something one might see on a serving maid in the local public room, but on the black velvet.

Oh, yes, she'd make quite an impression wearing that. A gown so scandalous, the sight of it would be enough to send Felicity up into the boughs for a week, mayhap an entire fortnight.

But it might also change her sister's mind about using her to gain Mr. Ryder's confidence. A lady in such a gown would most likely give a bumbling country vicar apoplexy.

But not him . . . a voice whispered. *Not him.*

The highwayman. The spy. The dark, dangerous man who haunted her.

For one long, wicked moment, she wondered if this gown might be enough to rouse the man she'd spied behind Mr. Ryder's façade.

Well, it would certainly prove or disprove her theory about him.

"Good heavens," Pippin was saying, pulling out leather breeches and a small, masculine-cut coat, both in the darkest black. "Look at this riding habit— why, it could belong to a highwayman."

"I doubt the lady is a highwayman," Tally said, her eyes still fixed on the velvet.

"Care to wager?" she asked, holding up a pair of pistols.

"Lawks!" Tally said as Pippin thrust them into her hands.

"I do believe this trunk *could* belong to you," Pippin joked. "Why this has all the makings of mystery. I do hope we can discover who owns this trunk, for I have to imagine she'll leave Jamilla in the shade."

Tally was still staring down at the pistols in her hands. They were finely wrought and well-used, for the grips were worn and smooth. What sort of lady had such an odd assortment of clothes and belongings? "Perhaps she is an actress and these are her costumes, her props," she suggested.

"I doubt it," Pippin said with firm conviction.

"Why?"

"How many actresses find these necessary?" Pippin said, holding up a set of lock picks exactly like Tally's.

Chapter 3

Mayfair, London
Four nights earlier

The mists that swirled around Larken as he walked down the street were hauntingly familiar. As were the cobbles beneath his boots.

He'd walked here before. Of that he was certain.

Waving his hand before him, he hoped in some way to be able to clear the fog so as to see a path before him, but it was as futile as the sense of despair tugging his chest into a knot of dread.

Everything was about to go terribly wrong.

Somewhere ahead of him a woman was saying, "My lord, you must help me. I cannot stay in Paris another night."

"I cannot. I will not help you," came a reply just as adamant and angry as the lady's request—nay, order—had been.

Larken's gaze flew up. He knew that voice. It was his father's. But it couldn't be. His father was . . .

Meanwhile, the pair continued to argue.

"If you will not help me, I will ruin you. *Your family.* I have more than enough evidence to destroy everything you hold dear," she threatened. "You have no choice but to help me."

"Your evidence is as false as your heart," his father shot back. "And you'll not ruin me or harm my family. *Ever.*"

Larken tried to shake off the urgency behind these words.

This has nothing to do with me, he argued to himself. He needed to escape this place. This night.

This has everything to do with you, the swirling fog seemed to mock back.

"You have little time, my lord. Have you forgotten the child?" the woman brazened. "I believe that alone leaves you no choice in the matter."

There are always choices.

Larken's father had taught him so. Always choices. Good and bad.

And this was going so very bad.

"If you don't take me, take both of us, it will be your ruin," she prodded, pushing his father to make a terrible choice.

" 'T'would be treason, and I'll have none of it. Madame, our partnership ends tonight," the elder Larken told her, with a finality that his son knew all too well. There would be no changing his father's mind now.

Larken stumbled forward, but the mist grew thicker as he neared something . . . He inhaled and smelled the stench of sewage and garbage. The river?

No. Not the Seine.

"Father, watch out," he tried to shout, but his words ended up a tangled mess at the end of his tongue. He reached inside his jacket for his pistol, yet it wasn't there.

"Ends? You think you can end this?" A dark, deadly laugh rippled through the night. "The only one who is going to find an ending tonight is you, my lord. You have crossed paths with the Order for the last time."

The *crack* of a pistol ripped through Larken as if the bullet had struck him. Somewhere there was a splash.

An icy sting surrounded him, as if it were him falling into the Seine's murky depths. And then he was, the water filling his mouth, his nostrils, his ears. He was drowning, sinking into the river, darkness closing in on all sides around him. He was dying, unless he could . . .

Larken's hands flailed over his chest to find where he'd been hit, then reached for the water's surface, his lungs bursting for want of air.

And then there was a shaft of light. It blinded him and yet carried him out of the water, out of the darkness.

He shielded his eyes, trying to discern where he was and what was happening.

Or more important, who was coming for him now.

"My lord? Are you awake?" The man held the candle higher, up next to his face so he was clearly discernable. " 'Tis me, Royston. I hate to disturb you, but now that you are *awake*—" he paused and let his words sink in.

Awake. Larken took a deep breath. Yes, he was awake. Not in Paris, not in France. But here. In London. And this was Royston, his butler.

And he was no longer eleven years old and wandering the streets of Paris trying to stop . . . well, stop Fate.

Larken heaved a sigh. He'd been sleeping. Dreaming. And now he was awake. He didn't know what was worse. The nightmares or awakening and finding his life was no different than it had been when he'd sought out his bed.

"Yes, Royston," he said, stirring further away from the haunting dream. "What is it?"

"My lord, I wouldn't have disturbed you, but I fear you have guests downstairs."

"Send them away," Larken told him, rolling back over and dragging the coverlet with him, though with one eye he stole a glance at the mantel clock. Five in the morning? Christ, he'd only fallen into bed an hour before.

"I fear I cannot send them away," Royston said. " 'Tis His Grace, the Duke of Setchfield, and that gentleman who calls on occasion. The one who never leaves his name."

Larken groaned. He didn't need to know who that was. Pymm. The Foreign Office's spymaster. Pymm never left his name. Left any trace of his presence behind.

And he never called directly on one of his . . . *associates* . . . unless . . .

Unless something had gone terribly wrong.

"Christ!" Larken muttered as he tossed back his drenched sheets and shook the last vestiges of sleep from his weary body. There was nothing to do but get up—and to do his best to ignore the way the floor beneath his feet felt—if only for a second—like the rough cobblestones of Paris.

"You look like hell," the Duke of Setchfield called out in greeting as Larken entered the room.

"I was asleep, Temple," he replied, using the duke's nickname. "Remember sleeping? The thing intelligent people do at night."

"You don't look like you were sleeping," Temple persisted. "Nightmares?"

"None of your concern," Larken replied irritably, walking past the brandy tray. He'd been sent home from the Continent six months ago because he'd become too much of a risk, his superior had claimed. *Dangerous and unpredictable,* one officer had written in a coded missive to Pymm.

One Larken had not only intercepted, but also decoded easily.

Too much of a risk. Larken wanted to laugh. Pymm and his ilk had made him this way. Restless and suspicious of everyone. And coming home hadn't improved his mood—only emphasized how he no longer belonged amongst the elegant Society into which he'd inherited his standing.

He glanced down at the bottles beside him and knew he should offer his guests a libation, but then again it was five in the morning, and they'd roused him from his bed. He wasn't feeling overly hospitable.

That didn't mean that Royston wasn't above such manners, for he arrived in the room with a tray of cold ham and bread. Coffee steamed in a pot, filling the room with its sharp aroma.

Larken let Royston set it down and depart before he said, "Now I don't mean to be rude, but what the devil brings the two of you to my home at such an hour? I'm retired, am I not?"

Pymm's eyes narrowed and he took in his surroundings with a brief flick of a glance before he spoke, quietly and firmly, "Dashwell escaped two nights ago. From Marshalsea Prison."

Escaped? From Marshalsea? Impossible.

Ignoring the way the two of them were studying him, Larken took in this information with a mix of emotions that he dared not show. Dashwell, free? He knew he shouldn't be, but part of him was elated that the American privateer, the man who'd mocked the English navy and bedeviled her merchant ships without remorse, had escaped.

Because before their two countries went to war, Dashwell had been one of the Foreign Office's best assets. A captain daring enough to slip past any blockade, plucking English agents off the Continental shores and bringing them back to safety. Those dangerous adventures and more than a few nights drinking and gambling had made Larken and Dash boon companions.

But that was before the Americans had thrown their lot against the English. Before friends turned, in the blink of an eye, into enemies.

And then last winter, just after he'd been brought home, Pymm had prodded Larken into helping the

Foreign Office capture Dashwell—the foolish bastard having snuck into London to spy out the best prizes before they left the merchant pool.

The entire situation hadn't rested easily with him, but what could he do? Pymm had been right to search him out and order his arrest. Dashwell knew too much about the Foreign Office's operations. Knew too many of the agents. He was a risk to them all.

And so Larken had agreed to help capture his friend.

He'd done worse in war, he told himself. Certainly he had, he'd told himself in the months past. Worse than betray a friend.

"Escaped? Two nights ago, you say?" he asked, trying to sound casual even as he felt a bit of a thrill. He should have known the wily devil would somehow slip free. "So why are you coming to me now?"

"It was by chance that we even discovered the fact," Temple told him. "Overheard it at White's earlier. Seems the Admiralty is in quite a stir but doesn't want to reveal that they've lost England's prized prisoner." Temple didn't stand on ceremony, but went over to the tray and caught up a thick piece of bread, topping it with a slice of ham and took a hearty bite, as if he hadn't eaten in days. "Been a busy night, calling in favors," he said almost apologetically.

None of this made sense to Larken. "How the hell could Dashwell escape? And from Marshalsea, for Christ sakes."

"He had help," Pymm said, reaching inside his coat and pulling out a bundle of papers. He handed the packet over to the baron and let him read what they had gathered so far.

Meanwhile, Temple had another serving of ham and poured himself a cup of coffee, tossing several lumps of sugar into the strong brew. Pymm followed suit, but without the sugar.

"Demmed good organization and perfectly executed," Larken muttered as he read the hastily written report. *Surrounded as they exited the gates . . . Overcome in the mist . . . Carriage found in Mayfair later that afternoon . . .*

"Good God," Larken muttered as he finished up the last page. "Whoever this is, they outwitted the Admiralty at their own game. How the devil did they find out that Dashwell was being moved?"

"We have no idea," Temple said. "Only a handful of people knew." He nodded at Pymm. "We didn't even know."

Larken set the papers aside and raked his fingers through his shaggy hair. "What the hell was the Admiralty thinking, moving him?"

Pymm answered this. "They were going to hang him at Newgate at first light."

This brought Larken wide awake. Hang him? Well, he'd always known that would be Dash's end, but he'd never liked the notion.

For the truth of the matter was that Dashwell was his friend. American or not, no matter what the politicians said.

Demmit, he hated how honor and duty had put them in opposing camps. How many times had Dashwell sailed into French coves and smuggler's haunts to slip Larken in and out of France? Certainly his friend's previous heroics hadn't stopped him from turning Dash in, from seeing him locked up.

But someone else hadn't been so cold hearted. They'd set him free . . . which left another wrinkle in all this. If Dashwell had escaped, then he'd need to be recaptured. Larken shivered and moved closer to the fireplace, pacing in front of the grate, the carpet worn from the many nights he'd spent before it, just like this, striding back and forth trying to make sense of some problem or another.

No, he didn't like the implication of where this all was going.

"There's more to this," Temple said. "Which isn't in the report."

Larken stopped mid-step and glanced over his shoulder at the duke. *Ah, so now they are going to get to the heart of this.*

Temple motioned for him to sit, which Larken did, more than willing to listen if it meant that they would then leave him be.

"While the report describes this as the work of a large, well-armed gang of dangerous thugs, that isn't the truth," the duke said. "I had drinks just a few hours ago with a fellow by the name of Dobbins who claimed it was no gang, but two women who freed Dashwell, with the help of an ox of a man who *is* mentioned in the official report, as well as an unknown fellow they'd substituted for the regular one who drives the gallows wagon.

"The leader was dressed in a red gown, or as the most eloquent Mr. Dobbins said, 'a gel with the finest set of tits I've e'er seen. And hair! Blond, it was. Shone like a lamp, it did.' " Temple paused. "A regular poet, our Mr. Dobbins. But apparently the lady in question was young and fair. And adept at handling a pistol, because she drew before the lieutenant in charge was able to twitch." Temple paused again, letting his words settle down, before he added, "The hag was most likely no old woman, for apparently she moved just as smoothly, and was also well-armed." Again he took a breath and glanced at the coals in the hearth. "I suspect the driver was a woman as well, but I have no proof . . . just . . . "

His words trailed off, but Larken knew exactly what he meant. *Just a feeling.*

After years in the field, there were times when only instincts could draw a line between facts and uncertainties.

Larken's chest tightened as he came to the only conclusion he could see. And now he understood why they had awakened him.

At least he thought he did. "That's why you came here . . . because you think it was the work of the—"

Pymm groaned. Loudly. And then vented his protest in a sharp burst of spleen. "If you say this is the work of the Order, I will have you both sent to Bedlam," he declared, his finger wagging sharply. *"L'Ordre du Lis Noir*! Bah! Nothing but centuries of rumors and deceit by the French to keep fools distracted. Women spies! Bah!"

Temple and Larken shared a glance, the duke's brows tipped at a rakish angle. It was rare they agreed on anything, but this, the Order of the Black Lily, was no fiction to them.

Pymm, while arguably the mastermind who kept England's enemies at bay, wasn't a field officer and had spent most of his years behind a desk. It was nigh on impossible to convince him of anything that couldn't be proved with good evidence.

And evidence of the Order was just that—impossible to discover.

A league of female spies, founded by Mary of Guise, as most tales attested, that had continued, through the centuries, guarding and serving the various French queens and protecting them from the intrigues at home and abroad.

Men like Pymm scoffed at the notion that any woman could hold her tongue long enough to keep the Order's workings a secret—let alone three centuries of French tarts staying mum.

To Larken, however, the Order was no mere conjecture, no fiction spun by the French to keep the English looking over their shoulders. Yet, to confess he knew the truth would risk revealing *how* he knew the French coven of spies existed.

That his father had been involved with the secret organization, fallen in love with one of them and aided her, until the vindictive lady had made it look like he'd committed treason . . . then murdered him when he sought the evidence to clear his name . . .

Hadn't that been what Larken himself had been doing for years—covertly uncovering the Order's workings while away on his missions for England? Something he doubted Pymm would have approved of.

Chasing after ghosts . . . a fool's errand, he'd call Larken's self-appointed mission.

Now he saw he'd been right all along in his attempts to discover their leader, their followers, their mission. Because obviously, they'd brought their mischief to London.

They'd freed Dashwell to put him back on the high seas, so he could once again bedevil England's navy.

But Larken's hypothesis was about to find another skeptic.

"Actually, I don't think this is the work of the Order," Temple said, jolting him out of his reverie. "I have another theory."

There was yet another snort from Pymm, but no outburst, and with this less-than-sterling endorsement, the duke continued, explaining his suspicions of what had happened in the shadow of Marshalsea's protective walls.

And what a theory it turned out to be. For when Temple was finished, Larken gaped at him. "You think this was the work of a pair of Mayfair chits?" He threw up his hands and began pacing again.

And the Foreign Office called *him* unpredictable?

"You're mad if you think two misses barely out of some Bath school could hatch such a plot." Pacing a few steps more, Larken stopped and said, "And I suppose the driver still had her dancing shoes on?"

Pymm sat back, and for the first time in quite possibly the history of his career, he smiled. Well, his lips twitched upward.

"You haven't been listening to me," Temple argued, rising in front of him, putting a stop to his frantic striding across the carpet. "Thalia Langley and Lady Philippa aren't your usual debutantes. Tally grew up in the shadow of her father, Baron Langley, whom you know."

Larken nodded grudgingly. Lord Langley, under the guise of a diplomat, had been gathering intelligence for England for over thirty years. His unorthodox methods, notorious love affairs, and unwillingness to foster out his daughters—dragging the girls from pillar to post across the Continent— had made him a bit of a pariah in the Foreign Office. But there had been no arguing his results.

"This wouldn't be the first time Thalia Langley has broken a man out of jail," Temple said.

Larken's gaze flew up. "What?"

Then to his shock, Pymm nodded in agreement.

"She broke Lord John out of prison," Temple explained. "When he'd been arrested by the local magistrate for smuggling—so don't let her fair sex and Mayfair address fool you into thinking she isn't a devious and resourceful handful."

"But why would Lord Langley's daughter want Dashwell freed?"

Temple shook his head. "She wouldn't, ordinarily. It has everything to do with her cousin, Lady Philippa Knolles. The gel is, much to the dismay of anyone who knows her, quite smitten with Dashwell." He paused, and sighed. "Nay, the girl's head-over-heels in love with him, and she'd go to any length to see him rescued."

"Wasn't she the one who—" Larken began.

Temple cut him off with a curt nod, for he knew exactly what Larken was asking.

Lady Philippa had been there the night they'd

captured Dashwell, and a vision of the girl flitted through his memories.

"She's blond, isn't she?"

"Both of them are," Temple said. "Tally and Pippin are very similar in appearance. And Dobbins was quite specific in his description of our mysterious lady in red. I have no doubt our primary suspect is Lady Philippa—whether or not Tally was this hag or the driver is yet to be discovered."

"I remember the Knolles chit, but I don't recall Miss Langley at all," Larken said, sifting through his memories of that cold January night for some image of the lady in question.

"That's good," Pymm said. "For if you have no recall of her, then it is unlikely she will remember you." He studied his coffee for a moment. "You were masked at that ball, correct?"

Larken nodded. "We all were. It was a masquerade."

"Even better," Pymm said, more to his cup of coffee than to either of the men before him. But he was like that. With an answer in hand, he was already plotting his next maneuver.

Larken still didn't see what this had to do with him, but Pymm's tone and their arrival on his doorstep at this ungodly early hour suggested they already had a scheme in the works.

One that he wasn't going to like.

So, better to cut to the chase and get this over with. Or better yet, get them out of his house.

"Why not go search their residence?" he suggested. "They can't have gone far. Probably tucked him away in the attic."

Pymm heaved a disgruntled sigh and crossed his arms over his chest. "Go barging into the Duke of Hollindrake's house?" he asked. "You want me to go over to Grosvenor Square with a raft of officers, and tell His Grace that his wife's sister and cousin are harboring an American privateer under his roof? If he didn't have my head, Wellington would—he regards the former major as one his most brilliant officers."

Hollindrake? Oh, that put a different wrinkle on it. Larken glanced over at Temple.

The wry look on the duke's face suggested he had another plan. "Dashwell isn't in London. I know exactly where he is."

Then what the hell are you doing here? Larken stopped himself from asking aloud, instead glancing up at the ceiling where above them his bed sat. Where he'd be right now if he wasn't stuck down here listening to Temple's utterly mad theories and probably just-as-cock-brained solution to this mess.

"How can you be so sure?" Larken asked as he started across the carpet again, his agitation growing with every step. Whether it was left over from the dream of Paris or the news of Dashwell's escape, he didn't know.

And as much as that reckless shiver had run down his spine, baiting him with a need for adventure, the thought of going back out on assignment left him rife with fear. *Rash. Dangerous. Reckless.* The words in the report to Pymm haunted him. His fingers curled into a tight fist.

Bloody hell, Dashwell, why couldn't you have just stayed put?

Temple rolled back on his heels, hands behind his

back. "Hollindrake and his entire household left for his estate in Sussex the morning after Dashwell's escape. And I have no doubt Dashwell was with them—"

Larken spun around. "You aren't suggesting that Hollindrake—"

Temple shook his head. "No! I doubt he's any notion of what they've done. That's why I think it was just Tally and Lady Philippa behind this . . . If they had involved Felicity . . ." he paused. "No, Felicity loves Hollindrake too much to risk treason at his doorstep—she probably has no more idea what her sister and cousin have done than the duke. And she's unlikely to notice, for she's got a house party about to commence and knowing the chit, she's got eyes only for the details of making her first big social foray a stunning success."

"So what has this to do with me?" Larken glanced over at Pymm and then Temple. "This seems more your sort of venture, house parties and the lot." He didn't mean this as a compliment, for he'd spent his years on the Continent in some of the harshest conditions, most dangerous spots, while Temple always seemed to be gadding about luxurious salons and palatial courts. "Trot on down to Sussex and search the place," he told the duke, walking over to the door. His hand went to the latch. "Use your infamous charm, Temple, and leave me to get some sleep."

"Under normal circumstances that is exactly what I'd do," the duke agreed. "But I cannot."

The shiver running down Larken's spine turned into a warning tremble. "Why not?" he asked, against his better judgment.

"If I set one foot in that house, Tally and Lady Philippa will know we suspect them," Temple replied.

"They know?"

Temple nodded. "Far too much. The night they broke Jack out of jail, those girls also saved my neck—'tis how Lady Philippa met Dashwell, as a matter of fact. Unfortunately, that leaves only you."

Larken looked up at him and saw the regret and caution in his eyes. So Temple thought him as mad as the rest of the Foreign Office. He shook his head, telling himself yet again that he no longer cared what the world what thought of him. "Send Clifton, send anyone. I have no intention of leaving London. Not now. Besides, I'm retired, might I remind you."

"You'll go," Pymm said. "That's an order."

Larken opened his mouth to argue, but knew better and pressed his lips together in a tight line. The dark, dangerous gleam in Pymm's eyes suggested it was no matter that one was deemed "a danger to himself and others." When King and Country called, there was no choice.

Yet there was a small wrinkle in their plan. The sort of impasse that might save him from their plans.

"This will never work," he said, leaning against the door. "I can't simply show up uninvited and not arouse some sort of suspicion." He took a deep breath and tried to sound every bit as convincing that he'd need to be to extricate himself from this folly. "Especially if these chits are as smart as you say."

Pymm glanced over at Temple, nodding at him in a none-so-subtle cue to get on with it.

"We've been able to identify one of the guests,

and well, Elton has been dispatched to detain the fellow," Temple said, mentioning his resourceful batman. "In the meantime," he began, slowly pulling an envelope from his coat pocket. He held it out, and the last thing Larken wanted to do was take the damned thing. For, once he did . . . well, he'd be trapped into their mad scheme.

And madness was exactly what it was. A man didn't need instincts to know that.

Heaving a resigned sigh, Larken took the folded paper and glanced down at the name and directions written in a woman's perfectly elegant script.

The Reverend M. Ryder
Eveling House
Bindley by Way, Lincolnshire

He shook his head and went to hand the invitation back to Temple. "This isn't for me. This is for some vicar."

And then he saw what they wanted only too clearly when Pymm said with a rare bit of humor, "How is your recollection of *Fordyce's Sermons*?"

Temple waited for Pymm outside Larken's town house. It wasn't long before Pymm concluded whatever private matters there were to seeing Larken on his way to Sussex, but he was suspicious nonetheless.

Pymm had insisted on sending Larken, a notion Temple was dead set against.

And he repeated as much the moment he turned

in step with Pymm as they walked down the quiet street. "I don't like this." Temple paused and then lowered his voice. "He's too rash."

"I've heard the same said of you."

True enough, Temple might agree. *But I've never killed as he has had to.*

"He's dangerous," he argued instead. "Done too many errands for you, Pymm. Don't think I don't know about Madrid. Or what he did in Marseilles." Temple shook his head. "A man can take only so much before he loses his soul."

"He's the best man for the job," Pymm asserted.

This stopped Temple cold. "You don't mean you intend him to—"

Pymm's heels dug to a halt. "Dashwell must be stopped," he said in the same ruthless, determined way a terrier might eye a rat. "He knows too much."

Temple's heart hammered. "You don't mean . . ."

"I won't have Dashwell sailing away from these shores a free man," Pymm said stubbornly. "Oh, don't look at me like that. Justice will be served. Mark my words. But we have to catch him first, and if anyone can do it and leave Hollindrake's name unsullied, it's Larken. Like I said, he's the best man for the job."

"The best man? Why he's spent the last six months roaming about Town at all hours. Can't sleep for the nightmares his work has left on his conscience, and now you're sending him into a house party? Demmit, man! Think of what you are doing! What if he harms one of the guests? You've let a caged tiger loose in a house full of lambs."

Pymm waved his hand dismissively. "Lambs who got the most wanted man in England out of Marshalsea Prison. If you are so worried for their welfare, go along with Larken. But keep your distance from the house, mind you."

"I plan on it," Temple told him.

"Good. I told Larken you'd be near to take his reports."

Temple stumbled for a second, and then caught up with him. "You know this could ruin him. You've sent him out one too many times with promises that you'll restore his father's honor, offering him posts with the diplomatic corps. When he discovers you've used his intractable sense of duty for your own ruthless means, and cannot, or will not help him, he may just turn on you."

Hollindrake House, Sussex
Four nights later

I should have stayed in London, Larken thought as he entered the dining room. Here he'd planned to arrive well ahead of most of the guests and be done with this fool's errand before the house was filled with people, but he hadn't anticipated that there would be family in attendance . . . and so much family.

He glanced up to find the Duchess of Hollindrake smiling at him like a cat eyeing a bowl of cream.

Demmit! Didn't the woman take a break from her matchmaking schemes to eat her dinner?

When she patted the chair next to hers, he had his answer. *Obviously not.*

Blast Temple to hell. The man had never mentioned anything about Ryder coming to this party to seek a wife.

A wife?! Oh, yes, he'd have quite the report for Pymm when he got back. That is, after he got done shoving Temple into the path of an oncoming mail coach. Accidentally, of course.

"Mr. Ryder," the duchess called out, "there you are, just in time to meet everyone." She moved forward, weaving her way through guests and chairs, and caught him by the elbow, latching on with a determined air and glancing up at him, her brows drawn in a quizzical arch. "Mr. Ryder, are you well?"

Oh, demmit, she means you, Larken, he thought, prodding his features into a bland smile for the woman.

"I hope you don't find our manners too dull," she was saying. "With just family in attendance, well, it didn't seem necessary to have a grand, formal meal."

This was how family dined? Larken glanced at the gleaming white cloth, the array of perfectly polished silver, and the shimmer of wineglasses and thought of his own usually hastily gobbled meals. This was quite the contrast to a tray in his study, or some greasy fare from a motley inn in Portugal, or even the hardtack he oftentimes managed to scavenge and tuck away in his saddlebags when his travels for Pymm took him so far afield that his dinner might cost him his life.

Why, even after his father died, he'd lived with his Aunt Edith, and though she'd been married to an earl, she always adhered to the belief in plain fare.

The duchess continued towing, well, guiding him

to his honored place at the table. "My mother-in-law, Lady Charles Sterling," she said, introducing him to an elegantly attired matron. "Lady Charles, this is the cousin I was telling you about, Mr. Ryder."

"Madam, it is a pleasure to meet you," he said, offering her his worst bow. The lady's reply was a polite nod and an air of sympathy to her glance.

Meanwhile, they continued down the endless table toward his chair, which was starting to look something more akin to Puritan stocks than a Chippendale masterpiece.

"This, Mr. Ryder, is Lady Geneva Pensford, Hollindrake's aunt and your cousin as well, I believe," the duchess said, a bit of a tight note to her voice. "I don't recall if you have met."

Larken's throat caught. For Temple had assured him, no one on the invitation list had ever met Mr. Ryder.

Not that he had to worry for overly long.

"Of course not," Lady Geneva corrected, having taken one look at his coat and his ragged hair and dismissed him as too far beneath her notice. "Mr. Ryder is a very *distant* cousin."

Thus dismissed, Larken was able to draw a breath. Thankful that Lady Geneva belonged to that exclusive club of matrons who held breeding and lineage as the primary measure of a person. And even though he was supposedly related, without the Sterling moniker, he certainly did not belong in her frame of reference.

He wondered what she would think of him if she knew who he really was.

Geoffrey, Lord Larken. Son of the disgraced Baron Larken.

Traitor Larken, as some at White's liked to refer to his sire, implying that his son was cut from the same cloth.

No, better that Lady Geneva think him just a poor relation, for if she knew the truth, she'd probably demand such a person be cast from the hallowed halls of this house without a second thought.

His attention was returned to the matters at hand, as the duchess introduced him to the last guest. ". . . Minerva, the Marchioness of Standon," she said, pausing before a tall, redheaded lady.

Egads, not one of the three dowager Marchionesses of Standon! Every man in London knew to cut a wide berth around the trio of ladies who had each married the various Hollindrake heirs only to see their husbands die before inheriting the prized title of "Duke." Now, according to Temple, the widows gave Hollindrake no end of trouble over their settlements and the various Hollindrake households they could use, quarreling amongst themselves and with anyone who crossed their path.

The Black Widows, they were called, at the various clubs about Town.

"Lady Standon," he murmured in greeting, and then deliberately tripped on the leg of a chair to reinforce his charade as the bumbling vicar.

And it worked, for the lady's lips turned into a forced smile and she immediately began straightening the silverware setting before her.

"Now if only my sister would arrive," the duchess said, followed by an impatient huff.

Larken's gaze now locked on the chair next to him. Which happened to be vacant.

Miss Langley.

Now there was a puzzle indeed. For while Temple had described Baron Langley's daughter as a smart and capable adversary, all he'd seen was a hoydenish piece who couldn't keep her wretched dog in order, let alone drive a team of horses or aim a fowling piece straight and steady. Temple had to be mad if he truly thought *she* could be behind such a daring escape.

"I fear my cousin Lady Philippa won't be joining us, for she is staying upstairs with our Aunt Aramintha, who hasn't been well of late. Our trip from London took a terrible toll on the poor dear, but a few days abed ought to have her back in rare form."

Larken smiled, wishing he could make the same complaint and flee to the safety of his room. Besides, with everyone at dinner, he could search the house and be done with this madness.

Yet before he could come up with an appropriate case of the grippe or even a claim of sudden, crippling gout, there was a gasp from Lady Geneva. At least he guessed it was from her, given the moral outrage now coloring the lady's cheeks.

He turned toward the door and the vision he saw standing there, half in the shadows of the hallway and half in the light from the wealth of candles in the dining room, left him wondering if his eyes were deceiving him.

His ears surely were, for he swore he heard the Duchess of Hollindrake mutter something in Russian. And while Russian wasn't his best language he could still translate her muttered words.

"Oh, shit."

But surely the Duchess wouldn't say such a thing, no more than her sister would appear in the door the very vision of what he'd always thought one of *them* would look like.

A mistress from the Order of the Black Lily.

For Miss Thalia Langley was no longer the errant, bumbling chit who'd clung to his fingers earlier, but a creature of the night. Alluring and intoxicating to gaze upon, and stirring his senses into a dangerous, rakish mood that hardly resembled the sedate tastes of a country curate.

By God, he swore, she'd drive a hermit out of his cave for such a sight.

A black velvet gown hung from her shoulders, clinging to her every curve. Nor was there, even here in the opposite corner of the dining room, any way to ignore the deep *V* of the dress. Her breasts nearly spilled out, and when she moved forward, he thought they would, if he hadn't been instantly mesmerized by the sleek undulation of her hips.

It was the sway of the most expensive courtesan, the most practiced seductress. Dobbins's dockside eloquence aside, he could have been describing Miss Langley to the letter.

"Tally," the duchess said, bustling past him and cutting off her sister before she got any farther into the room.

"I think you misunderstood my instructions for

dinner," the duchess said in a whisper loud enough to be heard by all.

Miss Langley sidestepped her sister as if she'd been doing it all her life.

Probably had been, Larken guessed, looking at the twins and seeing not their striking similarities, but the obvious differences between them.

Oh, a mirror would call these two nearly identical— for they both had the same blond hair, the same lithe figures, even moved alike to some degree, but Miss Langley's eyes were alight with a tantalizing mischief that he doubted ever lit the duchess's sharp gaze. Nor had she the duchess's air of authority, the sort of manner that wasn't simply a consequence of her wedded rank, but was as much a part of her as breathing.

And right now, Her Grace's authority was being challenged by this scandalous dress. Glancing at the lady in black, Larken would have wagered his best pair of dueling pistols that Thalia Langley had dressed as such deliberately, but for what reason, he couldn't say. Perhaps the gown was meant only to annoy her sister.

He certainly knew it annoyed him, but for other reasons.

"Where did you get that dress?" the duchess was asking as she followed her sister down the long line of the table.

"It was in my trunk," she said over her shoulder as she continued toward her chair, her gaze locking with his.

She waved aside the footman who moved forward to help her with her chair, and stood elegantly posed, smiling at him like a cat. For a few mesmerizing seconds he could only gape at her, until, that is, he realized what she wanted: for him to help her.

Him and alone.

Larken drew a deep, steadying breath, but found himself inhaling a waft of her perfume and it nearly knocked him over.

Lilies of the valley.

Lilies for a lady in black.

As he arose, she shot a glance at him that nearly knocked him out of his shabby boots. The tip of her lips, the arch of her neck, and the hooded whisper of her lashes as they blinked ever so slowly, offered a promise of something no innocent miss of twenty and then some should have any knowledge of.

His blood coursed through his veins in an unholy fashion. Whatever did she expect him to do? Ravish her right there before the first course?

His heart took a double thud. *For now he knew.*

The reason for this dress. Her late arrival. Miss Thalia Langley had made him her mission. For whatever reasons, she was after him, onto him, would be on him . . .

Suddenly his thoughts were of just that . . . *Miss Langley with that glorious gown in a velvet puddle around her trim ankles and the gel gloriously naked, reaching for him, pulling him to her, and they were lost in a deep, dangerous kiss . . .*

"A-hem," she coughed, her brows tilting above sparkling blue eyes.

He dared another glance at her and watched as she nodded toward the empty chair beside him.

Her chair.

Oh, yes. He was supposed to be getting that for her. Not standing here lusting after his host's innocent sister-in-law.

Innocent? Hardly. Enticing? Entirely.

Distracted, he pulled her chair out, scraping the legs over the polished floor, the sound like a razor being dragged across a strap, a *scrape* that dug into every ear and only called more attention to him.

He didn't even dare another look into those dangerous blue eyes of hers, or the other pairs around the room that he had to guess were now boring into him.

If only to have somewhere to look (other than at Miss Langley's bounteous bosom) he haphazardly glanced up at his host.

Hollindrake had his lips pressed together, dabbing his napkin at them to hide the trembling of his chin.

The ruddy bastard thought this was funny!

Of course he would, for he'd thought Larken's arrival nothing more than an amusing jest as well. Yes, he'd been more than willing to help apprehend a wanted man, but like Larken, thought it highly unlikely that Lady Philippa or Miss Langley had freed Captain Dashwell from prison, let alone brought the man to Hollindrake House. While it was a large house, it would be nigh on impossible, he assured Larken, to hide someone from the servants.

"Thank you, Mr. Ryder," the chit said in a purring voice. "But you are allowed to sit down now," she urged him, politely of course.

"Yes, of course, Miss Langley," he managed, then stumbled on the leg of her chair as he came around to his, nearly bumping into his hostess as she returned to her place.

He felt the sudden stillness of the room as everyone glanced at their place setting or their wineglass rather than witness more of his clod-handed manners.

Really, Larken, he told himself, *you don't have to play the chaw-bacon quite so utterly. Besides, you're here to determine if Miss Langley or Lady Philippa had a hand in freeing Dashwell.*

And given the glances she continued to toss in his direction, she seemed so . . . *willing* . . . to be friends, perhaps it would be . . . well, prudent, to go along with her, gain her trust and then unearth her secrets.

Like how exactly she kept that dress up . . . a rakish part of him whispered.

Oh, yes, that would be entirely in character with his disguise. Like some bad Covent Garden three-act comedy.

The Uncouth Vicar and the Innocent.

He took another glance in her direction and there it was again, that look of hers that left him rattled out of his senses. Make that *The Righteous Vicar and the Ruinous Vixen.*

"There now, we are all here," the duchess said with a regal composure and a serene smile that belied the determined glint in her eyes. "Mr. Ryder, will you favor us by saying grace before we begin?"

Saying what? Larken glanced up at her. Surely he hadn't heard her correctly.

"Grace?" she said, in a nudging sort of way.

"Yes, oh, yes, grace," he stammered. "Yes, of

course." Then he paused and tried to remember what it was one said, for it had been a long time since he'd prayed.

Then for some reason he glanced to his left and looked at Miss Langley.

Rather Miss Langley's breasts, which from this angle were displayed like a pair of doves on a platter.

Lord, help me . . .

Chapter 4

There is hardly a man in England with a secret I cannot unearth with the exasperating exception of Geoffrey, Lord Larken. The baron has proven to be a vexing mystery, but I refuse to give up.

A recent addition to The Bachelor Chronicles

After dinner, the ladies made their requisite departure for the green salon, and Tally found her elbow in the viselike grip of her sister.

Well, she'd known there was going to be hell to pay for coming down to dinner dressed like this, but really, she thought as she glanced at her sister's tight expression, it was Felicity's own fault. Not that her twin would accept the blame.

Still, knowing the best course was to wait out the first wave of complaints, Tally dutifully let herself be led along the long hallways, teetering atop her borrowed high-heeled shoes.

Oh, the dress fit splendidly, but the shoes pinched and were far too high for her less-than-graceful gait.

Though that bit of pain didn't keep her from smiling over Mr. Ryder's obvious discomfiture—not that Felicity had noticed. No, her sister had remained blissfully unaware of the man's distress over her pestering questions, while Tally saw all too clearly he had no desire to marry.

Not when every time her sister mentioned the word "bride," he'd twitched as if he'd been stuck with one of Aunt Minty's knitting pins.

So what the devil was the man doing here if he didn't want to be matched? Surely if he'd grown cold feet over the prospect, he would have merely sent his regrets and not set a foot into the duchess's house party, family obligations or not.

The question became: *Why had Mr. Ryder come here?*

That was the mystery, one that piqued Tally more than she cared to admit.

Having waited patiently at the foot of the stairs throughout dinner, Brutus came trotting up to his mistress, giving her a sharp salute in the form of a single *yip*, and then fell in step alongside her, his little tail wagging happily at their reunion.

When they entered the salon, Lady Charles and Minerva made a discrete beeline to the card table in the far corner, while Lady Geneva sat down in a solitary chair near the fire. Without even looking, she reached down and picked up her embroidery, most likely having been positioned precisely by her maid, who was rumored to be as exacting as her mistress.

With similar efficiency, Felicity ordered the tea tray, waited patiently the four seconds until Staines removed himself and closed the door, before turning to Tally quicker than Brutus after a squirrel.

"What am I to do?" she asked in a hushed voice.

"Well, I—" Tally began, a little confused, for she'd expected a harangue over her choice of gown.

"He's a dullard!" she declared, throwing up her hands and pacing in front of Tally. "Did you listen to him at dinner?"

"Well, I—I—I—"

"I thought not. Good gracious heavens, Tally, you could have at least tried to converse with the man?"

"Yes, well—"

"Were you attending at all?" Felicity asked, not really looking for an answer, for she continued with the next breath, "The weather, Tally! The weather! All the man could speak upon was the weather. Cumulous this, and some nonsense about rain all next week. Rain!" Felicity shuddered. "What a terrible thing to be saying to a hostess on the eve of her first house party."

Tally closed her eyes to try and get this all straight. Felicity was upset about the weather?

At her feet, Brutus made a snuffling sound and when she glanced down at him, the little dog shook his ruffled head as if he were just as confused.

Her sister's pacing came to a quick halt, her foot a mere hair's breadth from Brutus's small paw. Tally reached down and plucked him up to keep him from being trod upon. In her current state, Felicity could mow down an entire battalion of affenpinschers and probably not notice.

"He's not at all what I expected," her sister said, her finger wagging at Tally as if this was all her fault. "A bit sedate, barely affable would be acceptable. That I could work with, but this? This boring, shabby fellow! What will *we* do? However can *we* match Mr. Ryder with Miss DeFisser now?"

Three words finally resonated in Tally's whirling thoughts.

Mr. Ryder. And *we.* As in Felicity *and* Tally. Not Felicity's ridiculous, solitary scheme to play matchmaker, but *their* plan.

She shifted Brutus onto her hip, only thinking for about two seconds that she was going to have dog hair all over the velvet, but that was hardly the most vexing problem before her.

No, her real problem was right in front of her.

Her sister.

We, indeed! As if Tally had had any say in any of this. In this house party from Hades, in the invitation list, or even in her inclusion, which quite frankly, she would have been just as happy without and more than content to remain in London with Aunty Minty as chaperone, where she and Pippin could have continued writing their new play in peace.

"If my house party is an utter failure, what will people say next Season?" Felicity whispered. "If I don't make at least one, nay two, brilliant matches in the next fortnight, I will be deemed a fraud."

Tally heaved a sigh. Of course, it was all about Felicity and her place in Society as the premier matchmaker. No amount of assurances could make her sister believe that just being the Duchess of Hollindrake was enough. She had gotten it in her head that if she were known for making matches, *good* matches, her place amongst the *ton* would be guaranteed.

A cold chill ran down Tally's spine as she saw

herself spending the next two weeks being shoved before every aging, albeit rich and respectable, marquess or earl Felicity could muster from within a fifty mile radius.

She glanced down at Brutus, who with his large, soulful eyes seemed to be pleading, *"Save yourself . . . save us."*

"I hardly think you need to start worrying about Miss DeFisser just yet," she told Felicity hastily. "I do believe Mr. Ryder was merely nervous at being seated so far up the table. You made too much of him and embarrassed him."

Felicity paused, which was a feat in itself, since her twin rarely relinquished the field when she was plotting. "Do you really think so?"

"Yes, for I believe there is much to recommend Mr. Ryder," Tally lied. Truly, she almost felt guilty sending her sister after the man. *Then again, better him than me . . .*

Felicity studied her through narrowed lashes. "What do you mean by saying he has much to recommend him? Have you looked at the man? He's dressed no better than a rag merchant."

It was on the tip of Tally's tongue to remind her sister that they hadn't been much better off not six months earlier, living on Brook Street in a nearly empty house they had "borrowed," and wearing gowns three Seasons out of fashion, but Felicity took great exception to being reminded of their first tenuous weeks in London.

"If he were encouraged," Tally prompted, like a co-conspirator.

"Properly so," Felicity added, latching on to the idea as if it were a lifeline, and beginning to rally. "Yes. Yes. I see what you are saying. Some lessons in conversation, a trip to the tailor, perhaps a dancing master . . . I wonder if he must wear those spectacles? Well, no matter. All of it must be done immediately if he is to make an acceptable candidate for Miss DeFisser. "

"I don't see how you could fail," Tally told her. "Why in the right light, Mr. Ryder might even be handsome. You may even find a Corinthian lurking beneath the surface."

Felicity laughed. "Oh, Tally, if I didn't know better, I'd say you've had too much wine! Mr. Ryder? A Corinthian? I doubt even I could manage such a deception. Hollindrake is handsome. His cousin is . . . well, he certainly isn't what one would expect from the Sterling family."

Tally smiled and then opened her mouth to argue the subject, but snapped it shut just as fast, realizing that in doing so, she'd have to confess her own mistake about the duke's cousin.

That when she'd met him, she'd thought him the most rakishly handsome man she'd ever seen.

"Oh, yes, I do think you are onto something, Tally," Felicity said, with far more enthusiasm. "And I am so relieved that you have finally come around. I daresay when I saw you in that dress, I bore an ill suspicion that you were . . . well, never mind that now. I am so glad you are willing to help."

"Help?" Tally sputtered. And here she'd thought she'd escaped her sister's machinations.

"Well, of course." Felicity sighed, a loud aggrieved huff that suggested Tally was losing her wits. "I need you to oversee Mr. Ryder's transformation."

"Felicity—"

Her sister waved her hands, "I would do the same for you. And it is as Nanny Rana always said, 'as two of one, we must always be of one mind so as to live in harmony.'" Felicity smiled brightly, as if that was the end of the argument.

But Tally didn't think their former nanny meant for Felicity's way to be the only mind that ever mattered. Yet, before she could open her mouth to argue the point, the door opened and Hollindrake came strolling in. And much to her dismay Tally found herself looking for *him*.

Oh, not the mild-mannered, dull Mr. Ryder who'd come to dinner, but the rake she swore she'd seen in the study. Was it madness to believe there was a Corinthian behind his vicarly façade?

That didn't mean she wasn't shocked by the keen sense of disappointment that tugged inside her when she looked again for him and found Hollindrake was indeed alone.

Not her heart, certainly, but somewhere inside her longed to see the man she'd spied in the study once again.

Oh, yes, that was all well and good, she told herself. *But if you found him, then what would you do?*

This was Hollindrake's cousin . . . a country vicar. Hardly the sort of man she dreamed of sharing her life with.

Best stop tempting the Fates, Thalia Langley, she told herself. *Or else you'll find yourself living in*—shudder—

Lincolnshire with a houseful of children and your days mapped out carrying baskets to the poor and ironing shirts, without a hope of ever venturing one foot past the next village.

"Where is Mr. Ryder?" Felicity was asking in that very direct and so utterly unnonchalant manner of hers.

"He went for a walk in the garden," the duke told her. "Something about it being good for the digestion."

Felicity groaned. "Oh, gracious heavens. I do hope he hasn't any ailments. Did he say he was dyspeptic?"

Hollindrake laughed. "No, I believe it was just an excuse for some fresh air."

"Then you needn't have frightened me unnecessarily," she said, taking hold of his arm and smiling up at him.

Hollindrake's eyes sparkled mischievously at his wife, and then he waggled his brows at her and nodded toward the door, as if asking her to depart with him.

Tally glanced away. Really! Sometimes, her sister and her husband were far too intimate in public. She had never thought of her sister possessing a passionate nature, but around the duke, she was quite indecent.

"Which garden?" Felicity asked, returning with her usual single-minded determination to the problem at hand.

"The upper terrace," he offered.

Felicity shot a significant glance at Tally. "Well, what are you waiting for?"

"That wouldn't be proper," Tally whispered in return.

"He's a vicar," Felicity shot back. "I hardly think your virtue is at risk." She followed this with a not-so-subtle nudge in her back. "Tally, dearest, you are the only one I trust to do this."

Oh, demmit! Why me? Her jaw worked back and forth. Yes, cursing, even in her thoughts, was utterly unladylike, but botheration, whoever had made up such a rule hadn't a sister like Felicity.

"Please, Tally," Felicity pleaded, giving her that sad-eyed ploy that said, *We have only each other.* Unfortunately it worked, for despite all her complaints about Felicity, Tally loved her sister fiercely.

"Fine, I shall help. But remember, you'll owe me."

But even as Tally left the salon, with Brutus at her hem, she had no doubts that the moment she was out of sight, Felicity would consider the favor quite forgotten.

Tally paused at the doorway to the gardens, halfway inside the shelter of the house and halfway out, lured by the spice of roses and the soft summer breeze whispering in the night.

It was so utterly romantic, she wished she was slipping outside for some illicit tryst, not this mercy errand for Felicity.

Sighing, Tally glanced up at the moon shining over the fouteenth duke's infamous Terrace Gardens. But instead of being inspired by the vista, she felt altogether foolish.

She'd worn this gown to see if she could rouse Mr. Ryder—a vicar, for heaven's sakes. Not that he'd shown any recognition of her beyond asking her "to pass the salt."

Glancing down at Brutus, who sat on the close-cropped lawn, she said softly, "I fear Felicity's opinion is altogether correct. He's a rather dull fellow, and I've let my imagination run away with me."

Brutus tipped his head and shook it, the mane of hair around his face flying about furiously.

"And worse yet, this evening was an utter waste of my new gown." She held out the velvet for his examination. "But at least I haven't ruined it by spilling on it or tearing it."

But Brutus was already sniffing the air for something to chase after, velvet gowns barely worth his notice.

Something he had in common with Mr. Ryder, Tally thought, smiling slightly.

She stepped down onto the lawn, avoiding the gravel path. It was an odd thing to do, but she smiled as she did it, for her father had always said it was better to go silently into the night.

Then again, he'd taught her and Felicity how to "skulk about" at an early age, neither of them realizing he was merely practicing his own skills in subterfuge. But, she had to admit, this velvet dress was perfect for slipping about unnoticed, for it made not a sound as she walked, and the black fabric melded with the growing darkness as if it had been chosen for just this sort of assignation.

Of course the shoes were another matter, and she glanced down at them, her ankles wobbling beneath her. What an utter shame that such lovely shoes should be so terribly painful.

She glanced across the lawn to the low wall that was the first vista on the fabled walk through the gardens, assuming that Mr. Ryder would be standing there, watching the moon rise over the three perfectly clipped lawns below.

But he was nowhere to be seen. She glanced around the rest of the upper portion of the garden, and found the place deserted.

How odd.

But then Brutus helped her out, his ears pricking up before he set off toward the other side of the house, where the eighth duke's crowning glory sat—the Hawthorne Maze. Planted, legend held, in honor of Queen Elizabeth coming to visit.

Whatever was Mr. Ryder doing wandering over there?

Then she had a wicked thought as she crossed the lawn. What if he is out walking for his digestion? As dyspeptic as Felicity feared? Oh, wouldn't that be perfect.

My dear Miss DeFisser, I would like you to meet the Duke of Hollindrake's cousin, Mr. Ryder. He'd be here to greet you, but I fear his poor digestion has left him terribly indisposed.

Tally smiled to herself, but when she turned the corner, she faltered to a stop, the sight before her putting a complete halt to her foolish musings. For there before her stood a man. Oh, not some poor fellow with ill digestion, but the man she'd spied in the study.

Her heart hammered beneath her breast with a staccato tempo that seemed to announce, *That is him. Him, Tally. The one you've been waiting for.*

Perhaps all her years of traveling with her father, of writing romantic plays, of sketching strangers and friends alike had had another purpose. To fix in her mind her ideal man.

Tall and mysterious. Tense and aloof. And now here he was, standing across the lawn, no longer the esteemed and respectable Reverend Milo Ryder, but an entirely different sort of man.

She blinked to make sure this time her eyes weren't playing tricks on her, but when she opened them, she found him still there, pacing a bit, his quick, hard stride like a passionate tempo to her ears.

But as suddenly as her awe had come over her, another question struck her.

Whatever was he doing?

He'd forgone the infamous Hollindrake vista, and didn't appear to be contemplating a trip into the maze. And he certainly wasn't walking for his health.

No, instead the man was taking a survey of the entire south side of the house. Studying the windows, one by one. He wasn't just studying them, nay, he was counting them, as if he was trying to discern which rooms were which.

As she watched his finger wagging at the second-floor rooms, she saw him pause on the middle suite, where the curtains were drawn obscuring the interior.

Whatever was he doing studying those rooms?

Her rooms, to be exact. The ones she shared with Pippin and Aunt Minty.

It was as if he was looking for something. *Or someone.*

Tally covered her mouth with her hand, cutting off the gasp that threatened to give her away, for suddenly she found herself being tossed into something too akin to the second act in her and Pippin's play, *Lady Persephone's Perilous Affair.*

Too close, indeed.

Stooping down to catch up Brutus and make for the house in all due haste, her hands discovered only grass and an empty spot. Her vexing little dog had caught a whiff of something, or rather the sight of a familiar boot, and had taken off like a hare. A noisy, barking one.

Tally had no choice but to follow her errant dog, but when Mr. Ryder whirled around, startled out of his silent reverie by Brutus's noisy entrance, she came to a stumbling halt.

The man she faced looked ready to do battle, alert and dangerous, his face deadly with murderous intent.

Good God, Tally, she thought, *leave Brutus to his fate and run for the house.*

Then she looked at the man again and shivered. Not because she was cold. No, because his wild gaze awakened a dangerous part of her heart. A wildness she'd always held closely in check. She should be terrified, but Thalia Langley found this man's deadly scrutiny thrilling to her very core.

Wavering and teetering atop her high-heeled shoes, she tried to breathe. Tried to find a voice to call Brutus back, not that it ever worked, but it might be enough to break the spell that held her in this man's mesmerizing thrall.

Go closer, a wicked voice whispered to her. *'Tis him. And he's no vicar, no saint.*

As she took her first step forward, she nearly stumbled over her shoe, the strap having come loose, and so she knelt down to fix it, and when she arose, everything was different. Everything had changed.

Oh, dear, goodness. I am going mad. To her horror, the only thing left of her rake was the bland features of Hollindrake's dull cousin staring at her coldly.

No. It couldn't be, she told herself. *Where did* he *go?*

Yet her next glance left no doubt that the man before her was a rather annoyed, yet dull-witted vicar with an overly-attentive Affenpinscher attached to his heel.

"Off, you. Off!" he was saying in a wheezing voice, waving his hand in a motion akin to a benediction.

And while she knew what she'd seen and she'd swear to anyone who would listen that there was more to Mr. Ryder than this unhappy vicar before her, who would believe her? It was as if the rake inside him had slipped into the night like the most expert of thieves, or most deadly of . . .

Spies.

A spy? Oh, now her imagination was getting the better of her. Though what was it her father had always said? The best veneer is one of congenial blandness.

No one suspects the happy fool . . . or perhaps, Tally thought, *a vicar.*

She glanced up at her window, the one he'd been studying, and then back at Mr. Ryder. Could he be a . . . ? Oh, such a notion was ridiculous. He was

Hollindrake's cousin. A vicar, for goodness sakes!

Or was he?

Startled by her own question, she pasted a smile on her face and did her best to still her trembling heart.

"Oh, how fortuitous! We found you," she said, trying to sound exactly like the other debutantes in London, as if nothing ever entered her head other than gossip or fashions or polite comments about . . . well, the weather.

And not what he was doing spying on her rooms.

"I daresay you should be honored," she continued, beaming down at her dog as if he were the most brilliant of creatures. "Brutus doesn't chew on just anyone. He obviously likes you."

"He needn't," Mr. Ryder said, in that soft, mild-mannered voice he'd used to answer Felicity's barrage of questions at dinner.

But to Tally, his dull tone sounded forced, and she imagined his real voice coming forth in the deep rich tones of a man used to being in command of his own destiny.

He shook his boot, but Brutus clung to him with all the tenacity of his terrier forebears.

Tally smiled apologetically and reached down and tugged the dog off. "At least your boots don't look as if they are very dear. As a puppy, Brutus ruined the archduke's best riding boots. Papa always said that was why the good man gave Brutus to me and Felicity as a birthday present."

"Yes, a most gracious gift," he replied, glancing down at the now pitted heel of his boot.

Tally blithely went on not caring that she sounded

utterly vapid. "Hollindrake avers that Napoleon should have considered the same course, and just shipped crates of these little devils to England, and infested us all with them." She laughed, tousling Brutus's head and tickling the little fellow's ears. "I hardly see what he means, for truly I think the breed adorable and a most excellent lady's companion."

When she glanced up, she found him studying her, much as he had when they'd first been introduced. His scrutiny coiled into her belly like a smoldering fire. Oh, heavens, what should she do?

A dangerous part of her wanted to nudge the rake she'd spied moments before back out from behind that dull collar. Brutus squirmed in her arms—as if to remind her that this was no game she was playing— that is, if her instincts were correct. She took another furtive glance up at her windows. No, there was only one way to determine what Mr. Ryder was about.

And so she continued, "Brutus's grandsire belonged to Marie Antoinette. I don't like to brag about his royal connections, but I think it gives him a certain distinction over other dogs."

He stared at her for a moment, then replied, "So you said earlier."

"Did I? Well, yes, I suppose I did," she said, smiling up at him as if such a thing happened all the time.

But she shouldn't have looked at him, for she found herself caught again by his measuring gaze—one that now said she was being dismissed as hardly worthy of any further scrutiny.

And that ruffled at her far more than the fear of discovery.

Dismiss me, will you? her injured feminine wiles railed.

Remember, Tally, you want him to underestimate you, a more sensible voice argued.

But not to dismiss me entirely . . . that wicked part of her whispered, the part that found this gown, these shoes utterly irresistible.

That desired a man as rakish and devilish as the one she swore she'd seen before.

Meanwhile, an uneasy silence lingered on as she searched for something else to natter about. Oh, if only she were as feather-witted as Miss Sarah Browne and had a knack for filling any void with useless chatter.

"Did you see the terrace?" she asked, resorting to her Bath education and offering a polite, safe subject for discourse.

Yes, that was it. Gardens. The weather. Fashions.

"Yes," he replied, shuffling his boot over the grass.

Well, certainly not much to work with there.

"Not a devotee of gardening?" she asked brightly, tamping down the temptation to take a more dangerous course. Like asking if he knew the prison sentence for committing treason.

"Um, no," he murmured, still staring over her shoulder and not paying her the least bit of attention.

"Then you must prefer architecture," she said, pointing at the house, and taking the conversation into a little deeper waters.

"Not really—" he began to say, and then he stopped himself, and his gaze returned to hers, once again searching.

Well, it didn't hurt to test him a little . . .

"Ah, yes, architecture," he agreed. "This house is considered quite unique."

"So I am told," Tally demurred. "And you were out here . . . ?"

"I thought perhaps to gather some ideas for the estate I've recently, um, inherited . . . Renovations, I believe, are in order, and I found this vantage of the house quite inspiring."

Tally glanced over at the plain south face of Hollindrake House, which was nothing more than a plain brick wall with the predictable, classical arrangement of windows. Either Mr. Ryder was as dull witted as they came, or he thought her foolish enough to believe him.

"Yes, I can see where, perhaps, the window sashings might be inspiring." Tally replied. *Oh, yes, that was good. Imply that you don't believe a single word of his lies.*

He straightened slightly, and then took a few polite steps away from her, as if continuing his review of the, *ahem*, window sashings.

Then again as Nanny Bridget always said, the closest way to discover the truth was by using it.

Well, as close to the truth as Tally dared.

"I fear, Mr. Ryder, I've come here under false pretenses," she said, returning to a more sunny, Mayfair tone.

"Pretenses, Miss Langley?" he replied his brows arching regally over his brows. "Such as?"

She flinched at his apparent disapproval. "Yes, I fear I am not out here for a love of gardening or architecture, but . . . well . . . well . . . "

"Because your sister sent you?" he suggested.

Tally's shoulders sagged with relief. "Oh, yes! Exactly. I am so glad you understand. I told Felicity that my presence out here, alone with a gentleman, could be misunderstood, but now I see that you haven't misinterpreted my arrival as anything untoward." She turned slightly and tossed that last bit over her shoulder in the most provocative manner she could muster.

"I would so hate to be thought of as *improper*," she told him, letting the last word slide off her tongue with just the right hint.

"Not in the least, Miss Langley," he replied quickly in the most vicarly and brotherly of tones, glancing at her and then just as quickly looking away. "No one would ever think you anything but a proper young *girl*."

Tally froze. A what? *A proper young girl?* Clad in a black velvet dress that clung to her like a mermaid's skin?

That confirmed it. He was a vicar and she was going mad, for no self-respecting, dishonorable, utterly unrepentant rake would call a lady wearing this gown "proper," or worse, refer to her as a mere "girl"!

Gently she set Brutus down on the grass and turned to face Mr. Ryder.

And it didn't hurt that she rolled her shoulders back a little and let her breasts rise up to the very top of her very improper bodice.

"My sister has consigned me to discover your likes and interests to better assist you in finding a bride." Tally tried to look contrite, while at the same time coming closer with the same fluid movements Jamilla had taught her all those years ago when their father had been assigned to Paris during the Peace in '01. "I fear Her Grace is rather like . . . like . . . "

Oh, bother! How could one politely describe her wretched sister?

And then the unexpected happened.

"Brutus?" Mr. Ryder offered, with a bit of a dark glint to his already black gaze.

They both laughed, and their gazes caught.

To Tally it felt magical . . . and far too intimate, for his deep, rich laughter drew her to him like she'd never been pulled to any other man.

They stood there for several moments, mayhap two more than was proper, staring at each other, and each struggling with a silent battle.

Oh, goodness! What is happening? Was he actually coming closer to her?

She envisioned him as she'd seen him before, rakish and incautious, taking her in his arms and pulling her close. For wasn't a night like this, a situation such as this, the perfect setting for seduction?

At the hem of her gown, Brutus ran in circles, trying to catch her attention, but before she could catch him and keep him from mischief, the little dog took off after some unseen foe—shooting like an arrow into the maze, disappearing into the shadowy confines of the clipped hedge, his sharp bark growing fainter and fainter as he ran deeper into the thorny hedges.

"Brutus!" she called after him, dashing along the edge of the maze. "Brutus, you wretched beast!" She started into the opening, but Mr. Ryder caught her by the arm.

"Miss Langley! What are you doing?"

"I must get Brutus," she said, trying to pull free. But for a vicar, he had the hands of a coach driver, steady and strong.

"You'll get lost in there," he told her, holding her fast. "Just call to it again."

She shook herself free, taking a steadying breath. Not so much in indignation over the fact that he'd stopped her, but over the way his touch had felt.

So strong. So warm. So dangerously tempting.

It was almost enough for her to consider using Jamilla's "look"—the one that was supposed to drive men wild—on him again—not that it had worked at dinner, but she could hope . . .

No! No! and again, *No!* her sensible side declared. *You are not going to do that. What the devil would you do if it* did *work?*

She pressed her lips together and tried to focus on what it was Mr. Ryder was saying and not her fanciful desire for seduction.

Oh, bother, what was it? Just then a sharp *bark* from the maze steered her back on course. Oh, yes. Brutus.

"Miss Langley, if you would just call out—"

"Call him?" she asked. "Whatever for?"

"So he'll come back."

She shook her head. "Brutus never comes when you call to him. 'Tis too far beneath him."

He gaped at her as if she was as addlepated as they came. "Then just wait for him to come out," he ground out.

"Oh, that will never work. Brutus has a terrible sense of direction." Tally reached out and put her hand on Mr. Ryder's sleeve. She shouldn't, but she couldn't resist. This man, this ungodly man, was so very tempting. "Will you help me?"

"Help you?" He gaped at her as if she'd said it in Russian. He took another glance at her. Perhaps she had.

"Yes. Help me rescue Brutus," she insisted.

"I daresay your dog is perfectly safe."

"Oh, no. He's not a country dog. He may think this is just a park squirrel or a smallish rat. Why he could be chasing after a badger or something truly dangerous! And while he may be a formidable foe to a pair of boots, Brutus has not a bit of understanding that he's not much bigger than my sewing basket."

"This is foolishness . . ." he began to say, glancing first into the shadowed depths of the maze and then back at Tally.

So Tally did something she'd sworn a few moments ago she wouldn't do again.

She cast the "look" up at Mr. Ryder, using every wile she possessed and the advantage of having a dress designed for distraction and other things . . . then looked right into his dark, unforgiving gaze and said, "Please, sir. Will you help me?"

Chapter 5

$\mathscr{G}$ood God! Larken had eluded Napoleon's best agents. Slipped in and out of Abbaye Prison in Paris to aid English agents who'd been captured. Tramped across the Pyrenees not once but three times, alone and unaided, to carry English intelligence out of France to Wellington, and eventually Pymm, at Whitehall.

And now he was being asked, in the name of King and Country, to rescue an addlepated Affenpinscher?

Why hadn't Pymm just left him, pensioned off and forgotten as he was, so he could spend his nights doddering around his empty town house with only his nightmares to keep him company?

He reached out and caught hold of her, stopping her from following her dog into the maze. "Miss Langley, I don't—"

His stern words fell away as the demmed chit tossed him a look, exactly like the one she'd dealt him at dinner. The sort of glance that sent his sensibilities scattering across the grass as if picked up by a sudden gale.

One flutter of those lashes, the come-hither flash of her blue eyes and the tilt of her lips was enough to drive him wild.

Lord! The promise behind such a glance. Did the minx have any idea what that look had him considering?

Taking her into his arms and kissing her. Letting his hands explore what he had been trying all night not to look at—her divine breasts, which her gown displayed without any propriety. He'd kiss her and tease her until she was panting and trembling with the same sharp, aching need her glance awakened in him.

Larken closed his eyes and took a deep breath. He'd been without female company for too long. That's all this was. It wasn't that he hadn't had his share of mistresses and midnight adventures, but in his work for Pymm, he never lingered long enough to discover more than a passionate interlude.

And yet . . . this was no ambassador's wife, no mistress of some German prince whose secrets could turn into his success.

Miss Langley was (at least to the world at large) an innocent, not one to be dallied with and deserted when the time came for him to leave.

Still, that didn't stop his blood from running hot when she fluttered her demmed lashes at him . . .

And even though he held her fast, she still struggled against him, revealing a fiery spirit. He wasn't wearing gloves and her dress ended with capped sleeves, so it was his bare hand on her soft skin, and he'd never felt such a fire from a woman.

As if her very heat invaded his blood, teased him to explore the rest of her.

Larken took a deep breath. What the hell was he thinking?

"Mr. Ryder, are you going to help me save Brutus?" she pleaded.

Help her, indeed! Who was going to save *him*?

But even so, he dared another glance at Miss Langley, only to find her soft lashes fluttering once again, and he swore as she shifted her shoulders back a fraction more, he was going to find himself having the distinction of being the first gentleman in the *ton* ruined by a mere debutante.

Ah, yes. That would add nicely to his family's already tattered honor. He could hear his defense now.

She followed me into the garden and I was overcome by her seductive glance . . .

He had to imagine such feeble excuses wouldn't save him from some scandalous entanglement, the very least of which would entail meeting Hollindrake with pistols and seconds at sunrise.

Another round of frantic barking erupted inside the maze, and the next thing he knew, Miss Langley had taken flight, dashing out of his grasp and into the maze, heedless of the dark and the unlikelihood of her finding the little mutt amongst the twist and turns of the hawthorn hedge, for he had a view of it from his fourth-floor room and its pattern was ingenuous but not forgettable.

Not for him.

"Miss Langley, come back here," he snapped, yet his order was met only with the retreating sound of slippered feet moving farther and farther into the maze and not a word of acknowledgment from the lady.

Apparently she responded to orders as well as her monkey-faced dog.

"Demmit!" he muttered under his breath.

He glanced back at the part of the house he'd been surveying, where he should be at this very moment searching for Dashwell so he could report to Temple on the morrow that the task was completed. Then, if he rode hard enough, he could be back in London before the midnight supper was laid at Brook's.

And yet . . .

Go after her, the wind whispered. *She can help you.*

Help me? Help me the last two paces I already stand from Bedlam, he argued with himself. *The chit is a demmed handful. And Hollindrake's problem. Not mine.*

Unless . . .

What if Temple was right and she'd had a hand in freeing Dashwell? Larken shook his head. She was a chattering, witless example of all that was wrong with Mayfair misses. The theory that she could have masterminded Dashwell's escape was madness . . . utter madness.

As unbelievable as how you find her completely and utterly breathtaking?

"I do not," he muttered. But oh, that was a lie.

For one moment she might be as foolish as his

Aunt Edith's pug, but the next—well, the next there was a sharpness about her that had him feeling like he was matching wits with Pymm.

The chit was an enigma.

A mesmerizing one.

He glanced into the darkened maze and felt a pull that tugged him toward something greater than any mission he'd ever set out on.

Even clearing his father's name.

Hardly more important than that, he told himself. Nothing would deter him from that. *Nothing.*

Except a pair of sparkling blue eyes full of mischief and passion.

Larken shook his head. Gads, this is what happens when one starts gadding about good Society and house parties. A fellow risks becoming as corkbrained as Templeton or that ridiculous friend of his, Stewie Hodges.

No, there was only one thing to do.

"Find Dashwell, get the hell out of here. Find Dashwell, get out of here," he muttered to himself like a vow.

While he could return to the house and send the gardener after her, which is most likely what the duchess would expect Mr. Ryder to do, his host was another matter. Hollindrake's expectations of him would be more exacting, for he knew exactly who Larken was.

And he'd expect Larken to do the honorable thing.

Larken's jaw worked back and forth. If it was any other man than Hollindrake . . . for the duke was one of the few men in the *ton* who didn't look askance at him. Avoid his company. Then again, the duke had served in the field under Wellington and shared, Larken guessed, many of the experiences war left upon a man's heart and memories.

They might not have ever spoken of it, but they didn't have to. Each knew. And would expect nothing less than doing the right thing from the other. The honorable thing.

Shaking aside his annoyance as he stepped inside the maze, Larken set to work. For wasn't lurking about and finding unsuspecting people what he did best, as he had in Madrid or Marseilles?

Yes, and this time he wasn't even expected to kill anyone, though Miss Langley was certainly stretching his patience.

Taking a deep breath, he closed off the regular sounds of the evening, the hum of the insects, the whisper of a light summer wind, the lowing of a beast in a far meadow, and Brutus's barking. Finally he settled in on the sound of Miss Langley's determined tread, trying to discern exactly where she was, recalling the twists and turns he'd memorized from his bedchamber window earlier, while trying to avoid going down to dinner.

As he marched forth, he made his list. First, he'd find her (and to hell with her little dog) and drag her back inside. Then, he'd deposit her in the care of her sister and brother-in-law and make his excuses to escape them all. Finally, he'd find Dashwell, even if it took him all night.

Then, as if the Fates had ruled in his favor, he heard her gasp and tumble over.

"Bother!" came her exasperated sputter, and he couldn't help himself: he grinned.

That was all he needed, for as he listened, he *saw her*, head over heels in the grass, and knew without a doubt which direction he needed to go—for she hadn't stopped muttering her complaints.

He wound through the hedges, following the paths the best he could, listening for her complaints and threats—directed toward Brutus, thankfully—each one like a bread-crumb trail, until he thought he was very close. "Miss Langley?" he said as calmly as he assumed a vicar might.

"Mr. Ryder!" she huffed from the other side of the hedge, as she tiptoed along. "Do be quiet. I'm trying to find Brutus."

"You would do well just to leave him out here overnight—"

"Overnight? Are you mad?"

Larken glanced up at the moon above and shook his head. "I wager by morning you'd find a contrite and well-behaved dog awaiting you."

There was an aggrieved *harrumph* from the other side of the thorns, and still she continued along. *Stubborn chit.* "I do wish you would be still," she whispered. "I think I know exactly where he is."

Oh, yes, now she was the expert in these matters. Then again, he had a good reckoning where the mutt was as well—as would anyone within the Hollindrake parklands, given the little beast's growling and yapping—Brutus was far deeper into the enormous maze than Larken wanted to venture. He had no intention of spending the night hunting for a spoiled dog or the exit when he had more important matters to attend to . . .

Yet this time, when he closed his eyes and tried to recall the pattern of the maze, all he saw was her.

Miss Langley. In that dress of moonlight and shadows. With her blond hair curling down in reckless tangles from its pins, her arms outstretched, her lips parted.

There were no more secrets between them, just the two of them on this moonlit night, and no boundaries, no rules to keep them apart.

Come to me . . . she'd whisper through the hedges. *Take me, my lord . . . if you can catch me.*

"Oh, heavens, no!" she gasped.

Larken's eyes sprang open. Though his blood pounded in his ears, the very real sound of Brutus growling as if he'd caught the largest rat in England wiped away the last vestiges of any thought of passion.

"Do you hear that? He's in terrible trouble," she said. "We must save poor Brutus!"

Poor Brutus, indeed! *When this assignment is over, Larken,* he promised himself, *you are going to take a long holiday in some quiet seaside resort. That or spend a week in London's most expensive brothel and get every recollection of this assignment out of your memory . . . Every thought of her.*

He shuddered and contained the very rash and thorough curse that nearly sprang to his lips.

Vicars, as he recalled, were not prone to using profanity, or even the occasional obscenity.

No wonder they always looked so miserable.

"Oh, heavens, I do hope he hasn't caught anything

too filthy. But at least I know exactly where he is," came Miss Langley's excited whisper. "Stay here while I go get him."

This time he couldn't stop himself. He cursed as he listened to her take flight yet again.

And Temple has the nerve to call me *rash.*

He chased after her, turning one corner, then another, until he was ahead of her. He wheeled sharply around the corner of a hedge, thinking he was enough ahead of her to cut her off.

Not so.

Miss Langley was closer than he thought and she ran straight into him, their collision complete.

In so many ways.

She barreled into his chest, and they fell together, her atop him, her hands grappling to catch hold of his lapels.

And onto the grass they tumbled, a tangle of limbs, one hand winding around her and pulling her closer, even as his other reached out to brace their fall. And while he shielded her from the worst of it, he found himself branded with every curve of her body, the fullness of her breasts, the feminine line of her hips, her long legs wound with his, her breath hot and indignant upon his neck.

It happened in the blink of an eye, but from that moment on, Larken knew he'd be marked by this troublesome bit of velvet, this woman who confounded him at every turn.

In the soft moonlight, he gazed up at her, struck to his very heart by the unlikely hold she cast over him.

Everything around them faded into the background. There was only them. It was a magical sort of thing, one that left a practical man like Larken utterly confounded.

And when she looked back at him, her fingers still clinging to his jacket, her eyes widened with the same passion, he'd wager, that was enveloping him. Her lips opened to say something, but the words escaped her and instead, they parted only enough to form the sort of invitation that needed no explanation.

She glanced at him warily, but the curious desire in her eyes caught him, lured him closer. Made him forget that he was supposed to be Hollindrake's eunuch of a cousin, not the rake this lady brought out in him.

Kiss me, her half-parted lips seemed to whisper. *Kiss me now before this moment ends.*

Against every bit of sense he possessed, which quite frankly, most would argue wasn't much, he pulled her closer and caught her lips with his, tasting the sweet softness she offered.

It was like something so ethereal, so heavenly, he almost stopped—for the purity and innocence of her response was in such contrast to her glances and gown. Then those first tentative moments melted away as she opened up to him, letting him explore her lips and then more so . . . as his tongue swept them open further and a heady, earthy sigh arose uninhibited from within her. That sigh, that sweet sound was like a siren call, and he deepened the kiss, exploring her, tasting her, going quickly mad with desire. He caught hold of her, rolling the two of them over so he covered her, so he could feel her beneath him.

Instead of maidenly protests, she sallied back, arching her hips to meet his, her body coming alive beneath him, her fingers going from their tight grip on his lapels to fanning over his chest, one of them twining into his shirt right over his pounding heart, where something else was awakening inside him.

Something so deep, so primal, it made him all the more hungry for her—like a man starved, he wanted to devour her.

He'd never been so rash, so reckless. Larken, the spy who never needed a map, who could find his way out of the most artful of traps, was utterly lost in her kiss.

Tally had no idea how this all had happened. One moment she was racing through the hedges in search of Brutus, and the next she was in his arms, in his embrace, tangled up with the man she'd never thought to find.

Oh, not Mr. Ryder, but *him*. The one she'd spent countless hours imagining.

The rakish sort of devil who wouldn't stand on ceremony, who wouldn't wait until they stood on the parson's front steps to take what he desired.

A man who would catch hold of her and make her his without any hesitation.

Without so much as a "by your leave, milady."

And no matter, that she'd imagined this moment more times than she'd be willing to admit, she'd never in her innocent thoughts envisioned it like *this*.

Oh, heavens, but when he'd looked into her eyes, and she'd seen the stormy desire afire there, the conflict in those dark, dark eyes of his, she'd wanted only to discover every secret he possessed.

He'd gone from being her brother-in-law's stuffy, ridiculous cousin to the most desirable man in England.

Ever imagined.

Kiss me, she'd silently willed him. *Kiss me now before this moment ends.*

And he had, much to her delight, to her thrill, to her absolute panic, which then gave way to a passionate fire the moment his lips touched hers.

She was lost and nothing else mattered.

Not Felicity and her relentless matchmaking. Nor Pippin and "Aunt Minty" and all their problems.

There was only this man and she never wanted his kiss to end, for it awakened her to a new world of unknown passion.

As his firm, hard lips covered hers, his tongue teased over her own, she felt herself opened, carried into an extraordinary awareness. Her body thrummed to life, giving voice to all the desires she'd held in check for far too long.

Oh, good gracious, if he was kissing her lips, stroking her hair, whyever did her thighs tremble, her body tighten down there?

Because, she thought wickedly, she wanted him to touch her there, to tease her there, in the same way he was gently plying at the loose tendrils of her hair, and as he did, her hairpins fell free; the soft *plunk* as they landed on the grass sounded like the tumblers of a lock clicking open, freeing her.

He continued to kiss her, moving from her lips to

her neck, to the lobe of her ear, which he teased and nibbled at.

His hands roamed over the velvet of her gown, the skin beneath coming alive in a blazing trail of fire.

Touch me, touch me again, she wanted to plead. *Oh, yes, there*, she nearly cried out as his fingers brushed over the rise of one of her breasts, her nipple growing taut beneath.

Both her nipples going taut. How utterly wicked she felt, reveling in his touch . . . how wicked this man made her feel. Made her think of things so ruinous . . . so sinful . . .

Oh, just a moment. Sinful? Her? With Mr. Ryder?

Tally's eyes opened wide, the sound of Brutus's angry barking and growling piercing her desire-befuddled senses.

Heavens! She was kissing a vicar.

Having sensed the shift in her attention, Mr. Ryder stopped his delicious nuzzling, her neck tingling as the cool evening breeze replaced the warmth of his lips. He rose up and for a moment there was only passion in his dark eyes, and then recognition set in, followed closely by the selfsame shock, she had to imagine, that she was feeling.

"Miss Langley, I—I—I—"

She put a finger to his lips, as much to stop the stammering apology about to come forth as for another reason. "Please, sir, not another word," she whispered.

"But Miss Langley—"

This time she covered his mouth and glared at him, the sort of look that Felicity used when she discovered Brutus gnawing on yet another priceless piece of Hollindrake furniture. "Will you be still, sir!" Her voice dropped lower and she paused. "For I don't think we're alone out here."

Larken's gaze narrowed. *Not alone?* What the devil did that mean?

Exactly as she said, for as soon as he did still, he heard not only Brutus, but the crunch of grass, the rustle of clothing a few aisles away.

They weren't alone.

There was someone else in the maze. A silent, unknown intruder. Just as she'd said.

In a fit of pique, Miss Langley wrangled her way out from beneath him, even as he struggled to his feet.

Now if he were a vicar, or even a gentleman, this sort of discovery would have him in a panic over having ruined the chit before a witness, but Larken's thoughts were far from that.

His instincts, already thrumming with desire, now rose in an unholy howl. Who the devil was out here? Lurking about Hollindrake's estate like a thief?

And only one name came to mind.

Dashwell!

Larken started to lean over to retrieve the knife he kept tucked inside his boot, but another fit of furious barking stopped him—and worse, at the sound of Brutus's complaints, Miss Langley shot off again.

How the hell had she gotten untangled so quickly? Let alone gotten away from him? He cursed under his breath even as he dashed down the narrow grassy path after her.

Christ, how was he supposed to stop Dashwell with Miss Langley between them? And what if that bastard caught her first? He'd possessed no scruples about using Lady Philippa as a shield when he'd been trapped at the Setchfield ball, so who could say what he'd be capable of doing with Miss Langley in his grasp?

A red-hot, unanswerable anger swelled up inside him at such a thought. *He wouldn't dare.*

But Dashwell would, Larken knew, and that was enough to spur him on so he was right on her heels, close enough to catch hold of her. Then as luck would have it, right as he reached his hand out, Miss Langley tripped again in her elegant slippers and he hadn't time to avoid her, falling and tumbling over her a second time.

This chit is going to be the death of me. Either by breaking my neck or driving me mad with passion. But before he could decide which it would be, there was a new spate of barking and growling from Brutus.

This time near the entrance of the hedge.

The entrance? How the devil had the fellow found his way out so quickly?

Miss Langley must have been of the same opinion, for she cursed, in Russian no less, much as her sister had done before, and while a vicar would probably admonish her for such a sin, along with a host of other indiscretions, his focus was on a more pressing problem.

Dashwell was escaping. For once the wily fellow gained the park, he could hie away to just about any cubbyhole on the duke's vast estate, escaping like a fleet-footed fox eluding the hounds.

He leaned down, and ignoring Miss Langley's hand which she held outstretched for help in getting up, plucked his knife out of his boot, ignored her surprised gasp and spun around to retrace his steps.

To hell with gentlemanly obligations, she could untangle herself and get to her feet without him, he thought, as he sped away.

"Mr. Ryder, what do you intend to do?" she whispered after him, as he turned the corner and headed for the opening, where Brutus was growling as if he had the entire French army on the retreat.

And in retreat his unseen adversary was, for when Larken reached the opening, whoever it was had escaped.

Near the shadowy trees at the edge of the lawn, the thunder of hooves betrayed that whoever it was, they were making their speedy escape, and would be long gone before Larken could call for his own mount and give chase.

But they hadn't gotten completely away, for Brutus sat there with a prize of his own.

A boot, which he proudly held by the heel.

And when Larken knelt down to examine it, he had his second shock of the evening.

The boot was no Hessian. No worn, rough shoe of a sailor.

Rather the low-heeled sort worn by a woman.

A woman? Whatever would a woman be doing lurking about Hollindrake's house party?

"Madness," he muttered.

"Pardon?" Miss Langley said from behind him. She came forward and looked around. "Oh, how inconsiderate! You let them get away."

"Not by choice," he told her, ignoring the urge to throttle his hands around her throat. Let them get away, indeed! If it weren't for her and those demmed ridiculous, ungainly shoes of hers, he would have caught the devil. "However, Brutus managed to steal this." He held up the boot for her.

"Oh, dear heavens," she gasped, staggering back from it, her hands coming to cover her mouth.

" 'Tis only a boot," he said.

"Yes, I know that, Mr. Ryder. That just happens to be *my* boot."

Chapter 6

*W*hat do you mean Hollindrake's cousin was watching our windows?" Pippin whispered the next morning as she and Tally moved along the sideboard, selecting their breakfast from the well-laden platters of food before them.

A bountiful change from their days on Brook Street, Tally mused, as she followed behind her cousin.

"You heard me correctly. Mr. Ryder is here to spy on us," she whispered back, glancing over her shoulder at the rest of the room and realized how so much had changed in the last six months. Here they were, huddled over the sideboard, whispering in secret because now there was always company and servants about at mealtimes. A vast change from taking trays in the salon of their empty house off Grosvenor Square—the only room they could afford to heat—or down in the kitchen with Mrs. Hutchinson near the stove.

"Bah!" Pippin sputtered, drawing the attention of the other occupants, Lady Charles, Lady Geneva, and Lady Standon.

Tally shot her an aggrieved look and lowered her voice further. "He is not who he appears to be. When you meet him, you will see what I mean."

Pippin looked to argue the point, but one more glance around the room and she wisely held her tongue.

Lady Charles was kind and well-meaning, enjoying her repast and smiling over at the girls. However, the same could not be said of Lady Standon or Lady Geneva, both of whom were this bright sunny morning seated at the far corner of the grand table, sharing gossip and tidbits from the piles of letters that had arrived earlier.

Staines and several footmen stood at the ready, completing the crowded picture.

Hollindrake and Felicity had broken their fast earlier and then gone on to their various tasks that needed attending—Hollindrake to the business of his vast estates and Felicity in full flutter over the pending arrival of so many guests this afternoon.

That left only one other person missing, but Tally only felt relief at his absence.

For once she'd snatched her boot out of his hands, she'd been at a loss to explain how it had gotten out in the hedge, or who might have been wearing it. But if that had been astounding, so had the transformation of Mr. Ryder.

His knife tucked hastily back into his boot, he'd glanced up at her. "I—I—I didn't frighten you, did I?" he asked. "I am so thankful I forgot to take that knife out. Put it there so I would have one lest the silver at the posting inns was scarce." He shuddered a bit and then added. "We must inform His Grace that there are ruffians about."

Before she could protest such a ridiculous assumption, he'd caught her by the elbow and towed her toward the house, looking back over his shoulder several times as if he expected an entire brigade of thieves to come after them. It wasn't until they'd reached the house that he let her go, and even then, only once they'd got to the doorway of the salon.

The heat of his fingers burned at her skin and she kept glancing up at him, hoping to discover the man she'd kissed holding her, but his expression was one of bland fortitude. As if he'd just passed the dullest of evenings, having done naught but play whist with her.

"Good night, Miss Langley," he'd said in a tight voice, and then gone over to Hollindrake to make his report in a low whisper. That done, he'd departed with nary a bow and gone up the stairs with restrained, measured steps.

She'd stared after him for some time, clutching her slippers and solitary boot in her hands trying to make all the tangled, discordant notes of the night come together.

As she had most of the night, lying awake in her bed, torn between recalling that kiss and then his cool dismissal. And to her dismay, none of it made sense—only fanned her curiosity to new heights.

Who was this cousin of Hollindrake's? This stranger?

Pippin reached across her, fork in hand, and

stabbed at several sausages, piling them on her plate, and then after a moment of consideration, she selected a few more for Aunt Minty's plate. "Surely you were mistaken," she added, while helping herself to a second scone and a large pat of butter. "I hardly think Mr. Ryder came here to spy on his cousin."

Tally glanced over at the overflowing plates in Pippin's hand and shook her head. As if Aunt Minty could eat all that. Then lowering her voice even more, she said, "He was surveying the house . . . as if he was looking for *something* . . ." She paused, her brows arched, for she dared not even say it aloud.

"Or someone," Pippin finished for her.

Tally nearly sighed with relief. Of course her cousin would see the situation as she did. Glancing around the room to see if anyone noticed—well, mostly Lady Geneva, who held Brutus in horror—she nudged a sausage off her plate for Brutus, who had been sitting on his hind legs begging quite sweetly. But instead of picking up his breakfast, her dog let out a low growl. And if that wasn't surprising enough— for Brutus loved sausages—then Pippin all but overturned her with a single question.

"That man over there?" she asked tipping her head slightly to the doorway. "That is the man I am supposed to find so fearsome?"

Tally followed Pippin's direction and discovered Mr. Ryder shuffling about in the doorway as if he couldn't decide if his hunger outweighed the formidable female audience inside. From behind his spectacles, his eyes blinked owlishly as if he wasn't even sure where he was.

She glanced over at Pippin, who wore an expression of pure amusement. And when Tally looked back at Mr. Ryder, searching for any sign of the man she'd encountered in the garden last night, had glimpsed in Thatcher's study, she found nothing, other than the same ill-cut jacket and breeches he'd worn the day before.

Tally's gaze fled back to the plate in her hand. How could she be so mistaken about him? Where was the man she swore she'd seen in the garden last night?

The rakish devil she'd kissed. Or more to the point, kissed her.

Behind her, she cringed as she heard him stumble over one of the chairs and offer a mumbled apology for his clumsiness to the other ladies.

Pippin shook her head. "That is the man who you think was spying on our rooms?"

"Well, yes, Pippin, but——"

"Hollindrake's cousin?"

"Well, yes."

"An ordained man of the cloth, a vicar, is here at Felicity's house party to spy on us?"

Well, when she said it like *that* . . . "I know it sounds far-fetched, but Pippin he said he was looking at the architecture," Tally argued. "Believe me, that side of the house has little to recommend itself for study. And whyever would he do such a thing at night?"

"Ah, Miss Langley, good morning," came his familiar grating voice. "I see you are having breakfast."

Pippin slanted a glance at Tally, one that said, *He noticed your breakfast. How observant of him.*

Tally pasted a smile on her face and turned to greet him.

Across the room, he'd looked, well, just ordinary, but up close, he appeared quite rumpled—as if he'd slept in his clothes. And his collar wasn't at all straight. Though he had taken the time to comb his unruly hair to one side, he'd finished the process by applying a pomade to it, which gave off an odor that had Pippin's nose twitching and Tally's eyes watering.

It was hard even to look at him when he smelled so . . . vile.

"Yes, breakfast," she managed to say, now having completely lost her appetite. This was the man she'd kissed last night? Why, it was too mortifying to believe! For however could such a fellow stir her heart, her passions, so utterly?

Last night, hidden in the shadows and mystery of the maze and moonlight, she'd been convinced she was being ravished by a pirate, a spy, a man more dangerous than any she'd ever met.

Oh, but the light of day was a horrid reckoning indeed.

And one more thing was for certain: she'd rather die than admit to Pippin—not even if it reinforced her suspicions that Mr. Ryder wasn't quite what he appeared—that she, Thalia Langley, had fallen into this man's arms like a practiced Cyprian.

And found her first taste of rapture from his lips.

"Mr. Ryder," Tally managed to say, not even willing to look him in the eye. "This is my cousin, Lady Philippa Knolles."

"Lady Philippa, my sincerest pleasure," he wheezed, wiping his hand on his breeches before he took Pippin's in his limp grasp.

Pippin slanted a bemused glance at her. *Him? A spy? Oh, Tally!*

Doubts landed in Tally's stomach with the same disheartening thud of one of Mrs. Hutchinson's infamous scones. Meanwhile, Mr. Ryder was studying the two laden plates Pippin was balancing in one hand.

"My! You have quite the appetite, Lady Philippa! I didn't think young ladies ate so much," he said in a loud, disapproving voice, even as he piled his own plate with extra helpings from every platter. "While I fear my experience with the female persuasion is sadly lacking, I've always heard it said that a bird-like appetite is considered *de rigueur*," he said, mangling the French phrase with a terrible accent.

Tally, who spoke five languages, nearly groaned. What next? Was he going to point out the finer points of female dress?

As he'd nearly undressed her last night with expert ease . . . She shivered, and he glanced over at her.

"Are you taking ill, Miss Langley? I suppose it was the damp last night. I find it has thoroughly invaded my bones this morning. I quite creaked when I awoke."

Tally wanted to stop up her ears with two of Pippin's sausages. Oh, heavens! He creaked when he awoke? How old was this man? She knew for certain Mr. Ryder was just eight and twenty (for she'd stolen a peak into Felicity's *Bachelor Chronicles* this morning before coming down) and yet to hear him talk, one would think he was nigh on fifty!

He glanced again at Pippin's plate and clucked his tongue disapprovingly. "Gluttony, Lady Philippa, is a dreadful sin."

Tally's gaze flew to him, while Pippin could only gape at such rudeness. "My cousin is taking up a plate to our Aunt Aramintha, who, as you know, is not well."

"Oh," he sniffed, as if put out by this act of charity. "I suppose that puts a different light on the matter. You'll understand my mistake, since I've thought ladies of your ilk above such demeaning works of charity."

Ladies of their ilk?

Tally watched Pippin's brows furrow into a furious line and wondered, despite her cousin's love of a good breakfast, if Mr. Ryder wasn't about to find himself with a new pomade—of sausages, toast, and marmalade.

Luckily for them, Felicity came bustling into the breakfast room. "Mr. Ryder! There you are!"

The man nearly jumped out of his skin. And as he whirled around to greet the duchess, the contents of his now laden plate went flying up, depositing his breakfast over the two of them.

A shocked silence held the room for about three seconds, before Mr. Ryder began stammering an apology. "Your Grace! How could I—I—I be so . . . so . . ."

Witless? Clumsy? Ridiculous? Tally would have been glad to fill any of them in for him. For truly how could a man be such a fool?

As Felicity accepted his rambling apology, and Staines and the other footmen rushed forward to help, one of them bumping heads with Mr. Ryder as he, too, tried to clean up the mess, Tally discovered her answer. To her shock, and in the blink of an eye, his lips tipped in the very slightest smile as he tugged at a sausage that Brutus had decided to claim.

How could a man be such a fool? Not easily, she wagered. Not unless he was trying. And that would explain the moment of triumph she'd just witnessed.

But to her chagrin, no one else had noticed, and she doubted anyone would believe her, not given the performance Mr. Ryder was offering at this moment.

"Dear me!" Felicity said, glancing down at her ruined gown. "I will have to go change. Mr. Ryder, I would suggest you do the same."

Thus charged, the man muttered something about his breakfast, but a stern glance from Felicity sent him scurrying from the room.

With him dismissed, Felicity shook out her skirts, mostly to disengage one last stubborn strip of bacon. "Tally, don't forget what we talked about yesterday. The situation is far worse than I supposed. He's a veritable disaster. This is going to take all our wits." She huffed out a sigh. "Oh, how I wish Jamilla was here. She might inspire that man to well . . . be a man." She gave another frustrated sigh and then spotted the housekeeper. "Dear me, there is Mrs. Gates. I must speak to her. I'll be right back," and she hurried out of the room in all her ruined ducal glory.

A strained silence overtook the room, and dear Lady Charles took charge by saying, "Oh, Geneva, Lady Standon, you must hear the news from Lady Finch . . ."

As the duke's mother began to read aloud from

the letter in her hand, Pippin took a deep breath and went back to the sideboard for one more scone. "Tally, I do hate to sound like Felicity—"

"Then don't," she advised her, tossing another sausage to Brutus.

"I must," Pippin insisted. "Tally, you're being ridiculous." She lowered her voice. "Mr. Ryder a spy? I think we've been writing too much of late if you believe an ordinary man"—she paused and shuddered as if she'd caught a lingering whiff of his pomade—"and I do mean *ordinary*, is some sort of spy. Really, you've let your imagination run away with you this time. And for me, of all people, to say such a thing should signify."

But not to Tally it didn't. For there was nothing ordinary about Mr. Ryder. Nothing in the least.

He'd kissed her last night and left her rattled right down to her silk stockings. What sort of vicar kissed innocent young ladies in the garden at night?

And kissed them with such skill . . .

Her toes curled up at the very thought of his lips on hers. Her lashes fluttered shut and Tally spent a dreamy moment reliving every second of it.

How his lips had covered hers, hard and firm, demanding. The heady sweep of his tongue teasing hers. His tempestuous conquest bringing her body to life.

Even this morning, she could feel her thighs clench, her heart beating a little faster as she recalled how he'd touched her, explored her. The touch of a rake, of a man used to claiming what he wanted.

And never would she forget the sound of her hairpins falling away, as if he'd set her free, awakened her . . . to something beautiful and dangerously tempting.

Dangerous . . .

"Tally!" Pippin was whispering. "Whatever are you thinking?"

Her lashes fluttered open, and she found Pippin staring at her. No, gaping at her.

Oh, dear goodness! She was woolgathering over Mr. Ryder. And not the vicarly one. The one she had every reason to tremble over.

"Pippin, I do believe we should go to town this afternoon," she said in a voice loud enough for the whole room to hear. "Isn't Aunt Minty out of red wool for those stockings she is knitting?"

Pippin stared at her as if she had gone mad.

So Tally continued on, "I think it is high time our dear aunt took some air, don't you? A ride into the village might be just the thing for her."

Her cousin shook her head. "No, that won't do. I don't think she is ready for such a venture."

"Perhaps you could have one of the footmen bring her down into the gardens," Lady Charles suggested. "She might improve with some sunshine and fresh air."

Pippin and Tally both forced smiles on their lips. "Yes, ma'am," they murmured politely, before turning and shooting each other furious looks.

It is time, Tally would have said aloud if there hadn't been an audience around them.

Not yet, Pippin's eyes pleaded. *It is too soon.*

"I think Aunt Minty is well enough for a jaunt to the village," Tally said. "A short ride this afternoon will go a long way toward improving her spirits."

"The village? This afternoon?" Felicity exclaimed from the doorway, having poked her head in after having most likely bedeviled the housekeeper with her poxy lists. "How can you suggest such a thing, Tally? Most of the party is arriving this afternoon. You can't possibly run off on some foolish errand just to please yourself. Haven't you a care for how it would appear if you and Pippin were gone?"

It is because of this demmed party of yours that we must get out of here, she wanted to say to her sister, but she dared not.

"Besides," Felicity continued, having paused only long enough to take a deep, aggrieved breath, "we no longer have to run our own errands. It is unseemly. If you have need of something, one of the maids can go along with John Coachman when he takes the tailor back to Tunbridge Wells, and she can fetch whatever you need."

" 'Tis only some wool for Aunt Minty," Tally said before clenching her teeth together.

"Wool? Is that all? Good heavens, I am sure Mrs. Gates has some to spare," she said. "Now come along and let us find Mr. Ryder and lay out our plans for the day. We have so little time before Miss DeFisser arrives."

With that, Felicity turned on one heel and left, and Tally cast one last glance at Pippin, who grinned back as she too made her escape upstairs with her breakfast, having slipped by Felicity's machinations.

Or so she thought.

"Pippin!" Felicity called after her.

Their cousin froze on the stairs, and then turned slowly. "Yes?"

"Please don't come downstairs to fetch Aunt Minty's breakfast for her. Send a servant to do it from now on. You have your reputation to consider."

"But I prefer—"

"Pippin! Did you not listen to what I just said to Tally? We are no longer fending for ourselves on Brook Street." Felicity drew closer and lowered her voice. "We are ladies now, with a position in Society. Send a maid down for your trays, or I will post one in your room to see that you don't stir as much as a single finger."

"Yes, Felicity," Pippin acquiesced, not daring a glance at Tally.

For Tally would have shot the look that said it all.

Whether you like it or not, Pippin, it is time.

The parklands surrounding Hollindrake House were a thick tangle of ancient pines and oaks, enclosing the ducal lands and cutting it off from those who would invade upon his privacy. Inside was another matter.

Over the centuries, the various dukes had gone through spates of gardening and inspiration, including the previous duke, who had been an overbearing, arrogant tyrant in his old age, but in his youth had come home from his grand tour having fallen in love with an ancient Roman ruin, and commissioned one built on his estate.

Very carefully and at great expense, a collection of marble columns and rough stones were laid out to appear as if they had tumbled over more than a thousand years earlier. Even the grasses and weeds were allowed to grow up around them, so that anyone who happened on the place had the sense of wandering into some hidden glen of antiquity.

Hollindrake had suggested it might be an excellent spot for Larken to meet Temple, for it was well out of sight of the house and off the usual tamed paths that the guests might stroll along on a morning walk. And so Larken beat a hasty course there to make his report, gladly slipping free of the duchess's grasp.

Still, that Pymm had sent Temple—of all people—to take his reports (watch over him was more likely) burned in his gut.

Least of which was, how was he going to explain last night?

He shook his head and took a deep breath of the cool, woodsy air, and hoped it would nip away the heat that still burned in his veins. He'd spent a good part of the night, when not pacing his floor, chiding himself over *her*.

Miss Langley.

Kicking himself for kissing the chit. And worse, when he'd finally been able to find some respite in the wee hours of the morning after a fruitless search of the duke's house, it was only to find her wandering through the mists of his nightmares like a tempting beacon—her long blond hair unbound and falling in great waves down her back.

And her lips . . . parted just so and teasing him to come taste their intoxicating allure once again.

Larken took another deep breath. What had he been thinking last night—kissing her? That was just it. He hadn't been. One minute he'd been minding his own business, spying as he'd been trained to do, and the next he was rolling around in the grass with the delectable little minx in his arms.

Tasting her. Exploring her curves. Rashly, impulsively. Without any thought as to the consequences. Without the least bit of concern that she was a lady and most likely an innocent.

Without any thought, whatsoever. Just a bolt of passion and desire that had driven him beyond control.

It was as if she had seen inside his very soul, seen that part of him that longed for . . . oh, hell, he didn't know. Longed for something. No matter the cost. Even if it meant his mission.

He raked his hand through his hair and then regretted the motion entirely, for his hand came back reeking of the pomade he'd put there. When he looked up, he found that he'd gotten to the faux ruin, and Temple was there waiting, his horse nowhere in sight.

"Lawks!" he exclaimed, as Larken entered the circle of fallen stones. "Whatever is that stench?"

Larken grinned. "My new pomade. Do you like it?" He held out his hand.

"I do not!" Temple told him, his roman nose wrinkled in dismay. "What are you trying to do, discover Dashwell by having the entire house fumigated?"

He laughed, pulling a handkerchief from his pocket and wiping his fingers with it. "An excellent suggestion. Do you suppose it will keep that meddlesome duchess and her sister at bay? Keep her from finding me a bride?" Larken took a rigid stance, arms crossed over his chest, and looked

Temple directly in the eye. "You didn't tell me the most Reverend Milo Ryder was coming to this house party to be matched."

Now it was Temple's turn to laugh. "Did I forget to mention that?"

Larken's gaze rolled upward. "Yes, quite."

"How utterly irresponsible of me," Temple said, trying to sound the sincere repentant, but the twinkle in his eyes told another story.

"You rotten bastard," Larken said, wagging a finger at him. "I should have you hung in Dashwell's place."

"Tsk-tsk. Now that would be hardly sporting. 'Sides, seems to me you've grown quite soft from being at home these six months past, if you can't outwit the Duchess of Hollindrake's little schemes." Temple paused. "Without resorting to such a wretched pomade, that is."

"Little schemes!" Larken went back to his agitated pacing. "That woman would have had Napoleon routed in a fortnight."

"Pity the prime minister didn't think of that."

Larken groaned. "And that sister of hers. Oh, now there's a miss who is nothing but trouble."

"Oh, so now you agree with me that she's more than just a bit of a prattle, do you?"

Grudgingly, Larken nodded. "Last night she came down in a dress that was like something you'd expect one of them to wear."

"One of whom?"

"One of *them*," Larken repeated. When Temple continued to stare at him, he expanded on his slim theory by saying, "One of the Black Lilies."

"Thalia Langley? A French spy?" Temple laughed again. "That pomade is clouding your wits. She's naught but a willful chit who's in over her head. Why I've known her since she was just a child. Still is, in many ways."

Now whose vision was clouded?

Miss Langley a child? Hardly, Larken would have liked to point out. More the sort of woman who could tangle a man up like the most experienced courtesan.

Yet given the almost paternal look on Temple's face as he spoke of the troublesome bit of muslin, Larken thought better of correcting his friend's estimation of the minx by relating his encounter with her . . .

How she arched upward, her body coming alive beneath him, her fingers going from their tight grip on his lapels to fanning over his chest, one of them twining into his shirt right over his pounding heart, where something else was awakening inside him . . .

Larken took a steadying breath and paced a bit. No, if he told Temple that he'd compromised Miss Langley, albeit in the line of duty—at least that was how he preferred to look at last night's entanglement— he'd end up having to explain to his hostess how it was he'd gotten both his eyes blackened while out on his innocent morning walk.

But he couldn't keep everything from Temple, for they were supposed to be working together to discover Dashwell's whereabouts. At least those were Pymm's outward orders.

"Were you anywhere near the house last night?" he asked, not only because it had occurred to him in the wee hours of the morning that it might have been Temple, not Dashwell, lurking about in the maze.

"No, not at all."

"Thank God," Larken muttered.

"What was that?" Temple asked.

"Nothing," Larken hurried to say. "Well, not entirely. There was someone else watching the house. I thought it might have been—"

"No, it wasn't me." Temple tilted his head slightly and studied him. "How is it that you didn't catch them?"

"Well, I . . ." Larken couldn't quite tell the truth—that he'd been slightly, no utterly, preoccupied with Miss Langley at the time. So instead, he dissembled a bit. "I tripped on my way out of the hedge."

"You tripped?" Temple laughed. "Daresay that won't go in the report." He paused for a moment. "What did you trip over?"

Oh, yes, Temple would have to ask that. Always one for the details, Temple. Well, there was no way to hedge it over completely.

"Miss Langley," he admitted. "I tripped over Miss Langley."

Temple started to chuckle and then abruptly laughed. "Tally? What was she doing out in the garden with you?"

"Following me," he told him. "On order of the duchess. Like I said before, Her Grace is determined to see me—well, not me, but this Ryder chap—matched." Larken wagged his finger again. "That fellow owes me, for I am saving him from a most determined female."

Temple rubbed his chin. "Felicity can be a bit obstinate when she sets her mind to something. This could become a problem."

It already is, Larken resisted telling him, thinking not of the duchess but her sister. Her irresistible, entirely breathtaking sister . . .

"After you untangled yourself from Miss Langley, did you manage to search the house?" Temple asked.

Larken blanched from a guilty flinch that hit him at Temple's nearly perfect description of the night before.

Tangled . . .

"As much as I could," he told him. "I have a suspicion of where he might be." A vision of Lady Philippa crossing her room and closing the curtains flitted through his thoughts. He'd been watching her when Miss Langley had come upon him.

"Are you positive?" Temple asked.

Larken shook his head.

Cursing, Temple continued, "We can't go in until you are positive where Dash is hidden. We need to go in and get him out, without any fuss or anyone seeing us do it."

Larken looked away, studying the arrangement of the stones, for he didn't want his astute companion to see the conflict in his eyes.

Luckily, Temple had continued blithely on, ". . . if Lady Philippa and Tally are involved in any of this, I won't have them ruined over it."

Their ruin was the least of Larken's concern. Certainly his behavior last night proved that. For his orders were quite another thing. Orders given to him directly from Pymm after Temple had been dismissed.

He wasn't here to extract Dashwell, as Temple believed.

Pymm's orders had been quite specific, and given to Larken alone so as not to be contradicted. England's ruthless spymaster feared (and rightly so) that Temple's close association with the Langley family could cloud his judgment.

So, Larken hadn't been ordered to just recapture Dashwell, but to eliminate the reckless American privateer once and for all.

Larken had come here to murder his friend.

" 'Go after Mr. Ryder,' she says," Tally muttered to herself as she followed the path through the woods. " 'Bring him back,' she orders. 'The tailor will be here before two. Mr. Ryder must have a new jacket for the ball.' Bah! I hope he falls down some old well and stays there." She paused for a moment and spoke to a little squirrel up on a branch. "And if I could contrive to push Felicity down it after him, there would be much rejoicing."

The squirrel seemed unimpressed, chattering and scolding her before scampering off through the close-knit branches.

"Ah, yes, everyone has to have their say in my life," Tally muttered. "Even the Hollindrake squirrels."

So here she was, tromping through the forest, on Felicity's orders to "find Mr. Ryder, immediately." She'd been about to protest, but Felicity had then added if "she" (meaning Tally) "wouldn't do it, then she would scare up Pippin and send their cousin to do it."

Well, they hardly needed Felicity nosing about their suite, so she'd agreed to go.

Of course that hadn't been enough for Felicity. "Encourage him to confide in you," she'd admonished Tally as she followed her down the front steps. "See if you can discover his likes and dislikes. For we must know what he favors so we can encourage him to acquire a liking for Miss DeFisser."

He likes kissing, Tally had almost told her sister, if only to see the shocked look on Felicity's face.

And he's no vicar. I am even starting to doubt that he's truly Hollindrake's cousin.

Of course if she had said anything at all like this to Felicity, then she, Tally, would most likely have found herself being dispatched to the nearest asylum, *ahem*, resort, for her, *ahem*, health.

No, she would have to unmask this faux cousin all on her own and at the same time convince Pippin that it was time to move "Aunt Minty."

She followed the trail toward the folly, which, Staines had told her, was the one that Mr. Ryder had taken for his walk.

A walk, indeed! *Harrumph.* The man had fled from Felicity's machinations like a coward.

A smart one, though.

Tally paused on the pathway, watching the dappled light fall on the forest floor, her mind threading her thoughts together in another way—certainly a man seeking to be married wouldn't be fleeing Felicity's endeavors but welcoming them.

So whatever was he doing here? she asked herself for about the thousandth time. And when she looked up, the sight before her came into focus.

For there at the foot of the folly paced Mr. Ryder, just as the butler said he would be. It wasn't so much the sight of Mr. Ryder that surprised her, after all she'd come this way to find him.

No, it was the way he was walking. Nay, striding. Tall and purposeful. His legs moving with steady grace, and his hand gesturing with strength and meaning.

No stumbling man of the cloth. No bumbling would-be gentleman. But a man arguing his point with vigor.

The vigorous part didn't surprise her. She knew already he was a man of passion.

It was rather the "who" he was arguing with that had Tally slipping into the shadows of the trees and tiptoeing along so she could not only discover who he was meeting in secret, but to what purpose.

For now she suspected, only too well, that she and Mr. Ryder held something else in common.

A heart full of secrets.

Chapter 7

$\mathscr{L}$arken felt Miss Langley's presence long before he heard the *crack* of a twig. He told himself it was years of living under the threat of detection that had heightened his senses, made him as wary as a tomcat in the Dials.

But that wasn't entirely true, for the sense that she was close left him rife with other feelings . . . ones that had no place in his life.

Like a cacophony of wishful desires . . . especially when he heard the rustle of leaves behind him again and could feel her coming closer, an awareness that was more unsettling than the threat of discovery.

Temple heard her as well, and without a word, slipped silently behind the half-wall of stones that made up the back of the folly, hiding himself completely.

Larken looked around, hunting for excuses to explain his presence here, so far from the house.

Lord, what am I going to tell her?

That was it! *Lord* . . . A sly smile tipped his lips as he reached into his coat pocket and retrieved his glasses, along with the slim volume he'd tucked in there for just this sort of emergency.

Flipping open the book, his gaze scanned the page until he came to a most fortuitous line. Larken wanted to laugh.

Oh, yes, this is perfect. Let's see how Miss Langley likes Fordyce.

He struck a stiff pose and began to read aloud, letting his voice carry. "I would exhort and even enjoin Christian women always to dress with decency and moderation; never to go beyond their circumstances and, nor aspire above their station—"

This time it wasn't the crack of twigs, but Brutus who announced her. The little mutt came bounding up the pathway, barking and growling as he approached.

Larken had enough sense to leap up onto one of the stones, even though what he wanted to do was give the mutt a good shake and remind him who was the master and who was the dog.

However, that would mean picking up the damned bit of fluff. Given how the little vermin was about sausages, and from the hungry glint of his squinty little eyes, Larken suspected that to Brutus, fingers and sausages looked quite alike.

And Larken liked all his fingers more than proving his point to a dog.

"*Woof, woof*," Brutus snapped, running around the stone, vexed at being deprived of yet another chance to chew the heels from Larken's boots.

And that was exactly why he was up here, not just to pretend to be this harebrained, innocuous fellow he'd invented, but to save his boots. This was the only pair he'd brought with him, and he wasn't about to find himself padding about Hollindrake House in his stocking feet while the duchess "insisted" on sending his ruined boots off to London for a proper repair—leaving him at her disposal, not to mention complete and utter mercy.

"Ah, Miss Langley, imagine you out here," he said, as blandly as he could from atop his ridiculous perch. In truth, he felt anything but dull looking down at her.

For even in her plain morning gown, Miss Thalia Langley was a sight to behold. Perhaps it was the blue of her pelisse, for it matched the color of her eyes, brightening their sparkle. Used as he was to his own dark, dull pair, her eyes reminded him of the sparkle of the Mediterranean Sea, or the sight of cheery bluebells in an otherwise gray London garden.

Gads, Larken! Pull yourself together. You're thinking in poetry. You're one step away from reciting Byron.

No, looking at her, poetry paled. Especially with the memory of that demmed kiss he'd stolen from her in the maze still fresh in his thoughts.

That was exactly why he should never have done it. For having felt her curves, explored just a hint of her lithesome body, it was impossible to see her as that prattling bit of muslin he'd met in Hollindrake's study.

She approached him slowly, looking one way, then the other as if she were . . . searching for someone. But quite clearly from the perplexed tip of her brows, she hadn't exactly seen Temple, perhaps had only thought she'd seen Larken with someone.

"Yes, good day to you, sir," she said politely. "My, it is a fair walk all the way out here. Whatever are you doing?" She continued into the circle of the folly and scooped up Brutus, glancing at Larken's perch atop the rock and then down at her dog as if she couldn't see what he was making such a fuss over.

Then again, she most likely had more than one pair of boots, as evidenced by the one Brutus had found in the maze.

"I was practicing a sermon," he offered, climbing down from his faux pulpit and remembering to do it with less agility than he'd used to get up on it.

"What on?" she asked, a teasing twinkle to her blue eyes. "The wages of sin?"

Sin. The way the word tripped from her tongue was a sin in itself.

"Yes, well—" he stammered along, and not because he was trying to play the bumbling vicar, but because this bit of muslin had him at sixes and sevens. He glanced quickly over his shoulder, where Temple was hidden, and then lowered his voice to say, "Miss Langley, on that subject, I fear I owe you an apology."

"Whatever for?" she asked, moving like a nymph across the grass, weaving her way artfully through the arranged stones.

"For last night. My, um, my behavior. My behavior was boorish."

"It was?" she asked, smiling at him. "I thought quite differently. For if that was you behaving boorishly, I daresay I wonder what you would be like if you chose to be wicked?"

Wicked. Another word that sent a ripple down his spine, as if she'd thrown down a gauntlet and issued a challenge. One he could ill afford to take, no matter how tempting it was.

Demmed flirtatious chit.

Her fingers toyed with the lionlike mane around Brutus's head. "Well, I suppose if you are going to apologize, then I must as well. I could make excuses like Mrs. Hutchinson used to do and blame the brandy bottle for leaving me quite bosky—"

Bosky? He hardly expected such a piece of cant to come out of the mouth of a Mayfair miss, let alone hear her make such a reference to someone she was obviously familiar with. Intimately so.

"Mrs. Hutchinson?" he asked.

"Oh, yes, our housekeeper and cook when we lived on Brook Street." She paused for a moment and then lowered her voice. "She drank shamelessly, but as Felicity said, it kept the dear lady from noticing that we couldn't pay her. Happily, she's taken up with the duke's batman, Mr. Mudgett, and she's become quite a puritan of late—well, if you don't count the fact that they are, oh, how shall I say it?" She tapped her fingers to her lips, and then smiled. "Living together without the benefit of marriage. Mrs. Hutchinson avers she won't be married again, and Mr. Mudgett doesn't mind as long as she stays away from the bottle. Actually, they are quite content, though no doubt Felicity will see to it that they marry before long. Bad example for the other servants and all."

Larken coughed as her shocking speech sunk deeper and deeper into his head. Certainly he'd spent no time at Almack's and very little in the gilded drawing rooms of London, but he doubted this was the sort of conversation one heard bandied about like the weather or the next evening's invitations. It was almost as if she was trying to . . .

He glanced up at her as the realization hit him. Why the demmed little minx!

She was deliberately trying to tempt him. Vex him. Get him to slip out of character.

Just as he had done last night when he'd kissed her.

Ignore her, Larken. You have done this for years and can easily outwit an inexperienced chit.

But she wasn't done yet.

"Listen to me prattle on," she was saying. "Since I can't really blame my poor showing last night on Hollindrake's wine cellar, then I will blame that dress. Have you ever seen such a creation?" She sighed. "How I wish it was truly mine."

This caught his attention. "Not yours?"

She shook her head. "No, not at all. You see my trunk went missing—'tis a long story, and once again, all Felicity's doing—and another trunk was sent in its place. The dress belongs to someone else, and what an interesting lady she must be to have had such an elegant gown made up. Not to mention the shoes. You remember the shoes, don't you?"

He did. How he wished he didn't. Attached as they were to her feet which led up to her ankles and shapely calves . . .

"Yes, well," Miss Langley was saying, "once I

got the trunk opened—no easy feat, mind you, the lock was devilishly tricky—and discovered that dress—"

"You broke into someone else's trunk?" he sputtered.

"Heavens, no! I merely picked the lock, but like I said—" She stopped and glanced up at him. "Oh, dear, I've shocked you. Why is it I keep forgetting who you are?"

Larken felt the weight of her gaze pierce all the way past his collar, past the bad pomade, back into that place she'd teased open last night. "You picked the lock?" he managed to ask, returning to the safer subject of her litany of crimes. Breaking into another's property. Absconding with their clothes.

Tempting vicars with her ankles and come-hither glances.

"Yes, but it was a rather tricky one. Probably French made. The French are a very suspicious people. They make their locks far more difficult to open than English locks." She set Brutus down and the little mutt went off to sniff away at the rocks and fauna. "I fear the real crime was those shoes. They were divine, weren't they?"

She parted her lips and smiled at him and it was clear it wasn't her shoes that she was referring to, but the kiss they'd shared.

Larken took a deep breath. Then another. *Steady, my good man. Remember you're a vicar.* "You mean the pair you tripped in?"

"Oh, yes, they are the devil to walk in, but as Nanny Jamilla says, 'Women must endure all sorts of trials to be fashionable.' And those shoes were too tempting. Have you ever been tempted by a pair of shoes, Mr. Ryder?"

Yes, he had. Last night, as a matter of fact. But he wasn't about to admit it to her. He took another breath and glanced down at the volume in his hand, trying to remember the dull and lofty-minded passage he'd been reading.

"Oh, what is that you are reading?" she asked, pointing at the book.

He held it up for her to see. *"Fordyce's Sermons.* I was just memorizing a pertinent passage."

Her nose wrinkled. *"Fordyce?* You intend to preach from *Fordyce* on Sunday?"

"Why, yes," he said, all ready to launch into his planned prating speech on the edifying qualities of the dull reverend's sermons when her words finally connected.

You intend to preach from Fordyce *on Sunday?*

As in *this* Sunday? His gaze swung momentarily over toward where he knew Temple was hiding. And was now most likely doubled over in laughter.

Oh, this assignment just kept getting better and better.

"Preach? This Sunday? Well, I hadn't thought—"

"Of course, you probably didn't," she rushed to say. "But with the duke's old vicar doing so poorly of late, and with all the bother of the party to organize, I daresay Felicity forgot to tell you. She plans to have you replace Mr. Roberts this Sunday, if only to put you to your advantage before Miss DeFisser."

Yes, she did indeed mean *this* Sunday. Which meant he had no choice but to find Dashwell before

Saturday night and be long gone before the church bells tolled Sunday morning.

Still, he shook his head. Adamantly. "I couldn't . . . that is to say, I would be . . ." This time he struggled to find the right explanation as to why he'd rather be drawn and quartered than get up before the entire house party, the Hollindrake servants and the nearby village, and make a complete fool of himself.

Not that he'd ever worried overly much as to the state of his immortal soul, but he had to imagine there was a slight distinction between being Mr. Ryder in the line of duty during the week and offering spiritual advice . . . unless it was how to be damned for all eternity.

"Oh, you'll do very well." Now it was her turn to smile slyly. "However, I would advise you not to quote from *Fordyce*. He tends to put Felicity in an ill humor."

"And you, Miss Langley? What is your opinion of the good reverend?"

"Me?" She shook her head. "I don't think . . . "

"Certainly you have an opinion—" he said, thinking he sounded quite convincing as the concerned vicar.

"Oh, yes, but I don't think you will think too highly of my opinion of Mr. Fordyce."

Larken glanced down at the volume in his hands. "I would be honored to hear your thoughts."

She made an amusing little snort of disbelief. A *harrumph* that suggested otherwise. "Remember, you insisted."

"I'll remember. Pray, go on."

"There are his views on marriage for one thing," she said with a shudder.

"Marriage?"

"Yes, marriage," she said, this time with a bit more vehemence. And then she let him have her opinions. "Gracious heavens! It is a wonder any lady marries after listening to him describe such a union. Marriage, indeed! More like transportation to some heathen colony." She wagged her finger at him. "Nanny Rana said marriage should be a blessed union of joy and pleasure."

He knew better than to ask, but he couldn't help himself. "Nanny Rana?"

"Oh, yes, our dear nanny in Constantinople."

"And she was married?"

Miss Langley laughed. "Oh, heavens no. She was a concubine the sultan gave to Papa after my mother died."

"A wha-a-at?"

"A concubine," she repeated. "Do you know what one is?"

He raised his hand to stave her off. "Yes, I know what one is. But I can't imagine your father leaving such a woman to . . . to . . ."

"Care for his daughters?"

"Exactly," he said with a snap of his fingers. Even if he weren't supposed to be shocked over the moral implications of such a situation, a very British part of him was truly taken aback.

"He hadn't much choice. A fever swept through the city. My mother died, as did her maid who had come with them to Constantinople. And there was Felicity and I, but infants to be cared for. Papa was bereft without Maman, and we were so small . . . What could he do? Besides, it would have been an insult to the sultan to refuse. As it was, Nanny Rana turned out to be a lovely woman. She had the most expressive eyes and a light, pretty laugh." She looked away, as if the memories were too dear to share, too intimate.

"And you don't remember your mother at all, do you?"

She glanced up at him, as if his question had startled her. It had him, for he'd asked it before he could stop himself.

She shook her head. "Not at all."

"Neither do I," he told her. "My mother died when I was born."

Whatever was he doing? This wasn't his life he was supposed to be telling. He was Milo Ryder, Hollindrake's godly cousin. Christ, he hoped like the hell Ryder's mother was dead—not an entirely charitable thought, but necessary.

Larken took a deep breath, trying to shake off the way her wistful speech had lured him into making such a confession, tugging from his heart his childhood memories of loneliness and longing for something he never had.

"Oh, I am so sorry," she said, reaching out to put her hand on his sleeve. Her fingers curled around his arm and squeezed him. The sudden warmth of her touch, and the intimacy of it, was disarming.

And this time he didn't feel that she was trying to test him.

No, this was a gesture from Miss Langley's heart.

And it curled into his chest like a warm ribbon.

The darkness, the anger, the dangerous black void that had followed him home from the Continent, threatening to swallow him alive, lessened, if only a little. Like the first bit of sunlight that pierces a deep morning fog.

"There is nothing to be sorry about," he told her, pulling away. "It is hard to miss what you have never known."

If he'd been trying to break away from her, he was failing utterly, for she looked up at him with a sense of understanding. He'd never shared this with anyone else, but telling her opened up a part of him that he'd kept hidden away for years.

Apparently French locks weren't the only thing Miss Langley could open.

For his part, Brutus broke the spell between them, scratching and barking up a nearby tree. At least the little mutt hadn't found Temple's hiding spot.

"A squirrel, I imagine," she said over her shoulder as she went over to pluck up the spunky dog. "I daresay he'd have no idea what to do with one if he ever caught it."

Larken laughed. "Rather like chasing after a husband. What does a lady do after she's caught the poor fellow?"

"Well you won't find me barking up any trees, if that is how it looks," she said. "I have no intention of falling prey to Felicity and her *Bachelor Chronicle* schemes—no matter how many earls and viscounts she scatters about the grounds like acorns."

"*Bachelor Chronicles*?"

Her nose wrinkled up. "Felicity's journal. More of an encyclopedia of eligible men. She's been gathering intelligence and keeping notes on just about every nobleman in England for years. Well, I want none of it. None of her carefully chosen gallants."

The duchess kept a journal of eligible men? Why didn't that surprise him? Poor Hollindrake. The man had never stood a chance.

And neither did it seem would Miss Langley. Despite her protests. Her sister would bully her into a lofty marriage.

He choked back a shocked laugh and managed to ask, "I thought it was the aim of every English miss to seek an advantageous union." He rocked back on his heels and tried to look as pompous as he sounded.

"Not mine!" she exclaimed. "I have no desire to be wed."

Now this was not the opinion he'd been expecting. Some Wollstonecraft-inspired speech on the education of women and the equality of the sexes, perhaps. But this? No desire to wed? He'd never heard a woman so adamantly declare herself without any intention of marrying.

At least not one who wasn't over sixty. And even then, only those who were widowed with a dower large enough to keep them in solitary comfort.

Not want to get married? Something ruffled up inside him, almost as if his vicar's collar tightened to force the words to his lips. "But you must marry."

"Bah!" she replied. "If marriage means what Mr. Fordyce declares—all that submitting and obedience and meekness—then I shall remain blissfully happy as a spinster for the remainder of my days." She shot a scathing glance at the book in his hand.

"What a bothersome fellow, Fordyce. And truly, take my advice to heart. Don't let Felicity see you with that book. She'll ring a peel over your head you won't forget easily."

"Yes, thank you," he said. Then again, if he was unable to find Dashwell before Sunday, he could always hold a Saturday-night reading from the volume to ensure he was packed off without further ado.

Meanwhile, Miss Langley smiled up at him. "That's why I'm out here. Her Grace sent me to find you. I fear she commands you to attend her immediately. The tailor is due to arrive, as is the dancing master."

A tailor and *a dancing master?*

"But I don't—" He glanced back over his shoulder at the rocks and considered dragging Temple out and finishing his earlier thought of hanging the wily bastard in Dashwell's place. "No, I really don't think I—"

"No, I don't suppose you do," she said, coming up and curling her hand around his elbow and starting to tow him down the path. "But you haven't any more choice in the matter than I."

He shot a glance over his shoulder, aiming it in Temple's direction. *I will get even with you for this . . .*

Miss Langley continued on, "If I had any say in my life, I would spend my day here, sketching this wonderful place. Why, it is like happening upon some little bit of Italy." She clapped her hands together and gazed at the stones a bit starry-eyed, but then she sighed and nudged at a tuft of grass with her shoe. "Or I would find a handful of wildflowers and spend the afternoon with my watercolors trying to capture their hues. But it is not to be. We are both, I fear, subject to her tyranny at present." She paused and glanced at him, and for a tenuous moment he understood the dismay to her tone, could sympathize with the light of uncertainty in her eyes.

It wasn't that far from his own feelings, for if he were to tell the truth, his preference would have been to remain in London and not be sent on this fool's errand. Stayed home to brood in solitude and roam about the city at night in search of . . . well, what he didn't know.

She would . . . a voice nudged insistently.

Larken ignored it as best he could. "Is there anything else Her Grace has planned for today?" he asked, as he led her from the folly toward the pathway. "Forewarned and all."

"Well, if you survive the tailor and we pass muster with the dancing master—"

"We?"

He would never have thought it possible, but the cheeky minx blushed. "Yes, we. I daresay she merely suspects that you cannot dance, whereas she knows I am rather . . . well . . . " She looked away, as her cheeks pinked to a bright shade of red.

"Miss Langley, are you telling me you cannot dance?"

She pulled to a stop. "No, I cannot. I can do many things, sketch, write a play, manage a decent tune on a pianoforte—at least so I've been told. I can even darn a sock, and make toast if it is necessary—"

"Then I will know whom to call if the cook becomes desperately ill and I require toast," he offered, smiling at the very notion of her in the kitchen.

"It isn't funny in the least, Mr. Ryder. I'm a terrible dancer. You'll never believe this, but when I try to dance, my feet go one way, and I go another."

He would have told her she needn't go to great lengths to convince him, when the image of her teetering along in her high-heeled slippers across the grass, and tripping in them not once but twice, rather proved the matter.

"And now," she continued, "Felicity is insisting on throwing a ball the evening after next, and expects me to make a good show of my 'accomplishments,' as she calls them."

"Haven't you been to other balls?"

"Yes, to one last winter, but I was able to cry off the rest of the Season . . . for the most part, because of Pippin, but Felicity has declared that we will rise above our disgrace and make our first public outings here and now."

"Disgrace?" he murmured, guiding her along the path and steering her around a muddy spot.

"Well, yes," she replied, picking up her skirt and frowning down at the mud that now decorated the hem despite his efforts.

Could one steer this sort of woman?

"Pippin . . ." she began, then corrected, "I mean, Lady Philippa, whom you met this morning, fell in love with a man Felicity did not favor." She said it as if her cousin was over the moon for a shoemaker or a butcher, rather than one of England's foremost enemies. "And when it was discovered that she found him preferable to any other man, well, Society was not kind." She paused before she finished. "There was a bit of a scandal."

A bit? A hurricane, more to the point, but he wasn't going to stop her from sharing her confidence with him. "Yes, I suppose Society isn't as forgiving as one might hope."

Miss Langley nodded. "This house party is as much about seeing us put back in those elevated circles as it is to renew Felicity's place as the *ton's* best matchmaker."

He stumbled a bit when she said that and this time she steadied his pace. "The wha-a-at?"

Miss Langley glanced up at him. "The *ton's* best matchmaker. I assumed that's why you wrote to her, to enlist her services."

He quashed the questioning light in her eyes as quickly as he could. "Of course, yes, her skill as a matchmaker. I didn't realize she was as well known as you say. I just merely—"

"Merely? There is nothing 'mere' about Felicity. You've unwittingly engaged the most determined woman in London. England, even," Miss Langley replied. "She's made, oh, now, let me see . . . " She tapped her fingers to her lips as she counted.

With each one, Larken felt as if he were being struck by arrows.

"One, two, three, four, five," Miss Langley paused. "Shall I count her match with Hollindrake? For that was all her doing."

"I suppose you must," he told her faintly. What did he care after the third tick of her fingers? By the second one he'd been nearly overcome by the usual panic that every unmarried man felt at the mention of that word.

Matchmaker. And here Larken had thought himself made of sterner stuff. Yet this assignment was suddenly taking on the sort of hazard that one usually associated with breaking into a Paris prison.

"Oh, yes, I suppose I must include Hollindrake," Miss Langley was saying. "Well, that makes six then. And she means to have an even dozen to her credit before the summer is out."

"A do-do-zen?"

Miss Langley nodded. "Yes. And over the course of this house party."

"So soon? So many?" he gasped. Was it he, or had his collar suddenly tightened, cutting off his air? Even though they had just left the woods behind and were now coming to the wide meadow that ran up to the formal gardens, the bright sun sparkling down on them, Larken had the sensation of being thrust into a deep, dark cave.

"Of course," she was saying. "For what is the point of going to all the bother of this," she waved her hand at the line of wagons coming up the drive, where the guests and supplies were coming in a steady stream, "if not to make as many matches as possible?"

But six matches? Before he could stop himself, he asked the inevitable. "How are so many possible?"

"Well, there's you, me, Pippin, Miss Browne, Miss De Fisser, the Elsford sisters, and of course, Lady Standon."

"Which one?" he remarked dryly, forgetting himself momentarily.

"Minerva, I suppose, since she was invited." Then

she smiled. "I daresay having all three of the Lady Standons bickering amongst themselves is bedeviling Hollindrake, and Felicity in turn. Mayhap I should suggest to her some way of getting the three of them married off, if only to divert her for a time." She sighed. "Not that it would work for long, I suppose. She's bound and determined to make her dozen before winter and return to Town quite triumphant."

Or rather unbearable, her tone implied.

Oh, yes, Larken could sympathize with Miss Langley. For while he was only here until he found Dashwell, the chit beside him was trapped. Truly, he pitied her, for his sentence was only temporary. Miss Langley's would be a lifelong commitment.

He plucked the copy of *Fordyce* out of his pocket and held it up. "I suppose a lesson on meekness and discretion would be lost on Her Grace."

"Utterly."

They both laughed and even as he slipped the book back into his pocket, Larken spent a spellbound moment trying his best to forget the whys of his coming to Hollindrake House.

That he was here to find Dashwell.

He glanced down at her. That this miss may have had a treasonous hand in freeing him seemed a rather staggering notion. In many ways she looked like any other English lady, with her simply dressed hair, her fair skin and innocent blue eyes, walking alongside him as if this were an ordinary morning walk.

He glanced around and realized with no small measure of shock that this was how others lived.

Every day. While he'd been mucking about in the mire of Europe and her wars, England had carried on in this bucolic splendor.

He had missed nearly all of his youth—one that was usually spent gambling, and horse racing, and whoring, to restore his family's lost honor. Had it been worth it? For he'd lost so much time, so much of himself, and now in many ways he was trapped by those years, in the darkness they'd drawn over his heart, his very soul.

He rather felt like the bumbling fool, for to most men this walk across a meadow was a completely normal pastime, but for him, the beauty of it, the glorious peace and simplicity of it left him speechless. He who had spent nearly ten years of his life living in the hell of war. He had forgotten the dear and priceless pleasures of simply living.

Even Brutus seemed to have curbed the worst of his ill behavior and trotted alongside his mistress like a veritable lamb.

Suddenly, for some inexplicable reason, he found himself wishing to discover a way out of all this. For both of them. He and Miss Langley.

Oh, demmit. Dash was one problem, but however could he save her from one of her sister's "gallants," as she put it?

You know how . . .

Larken paused to hand her over a stile, the stark blue of the sky just as bright as the twinkle in her eyes. The color was enough to make a man forget everything.

To become as treasonous as the lady before him might possibly be.

And for the first time in his life, he knew, as his father before him had known, what it was to have a heart divided. If only he didn't also know the consequences.

For it had killed his father, as surely as it may hold the same fate for him.

Chapter 8

*W*hatever had Larken thinking such thoughts?

He had nothing more to do than to look at Miss Thalia Langley to know the answer. This minx's openness, her complete lack of practiced propriety, had him bewitched.

Even as she prattled on about a visit to the gardens at Versailles with her father and someone by the impossible name of Nanny Jamilla, all he could think of was Tally's lips.

That was what her sister and Temple called her, wasn't it? Tally. The nickname fit, for it suggested a winsome spirit, a blithe and almost ethereal quality.

Even her lips held a sort of come-hither tip to them, one that begged to be kissed.

Certainly they begged him, as proved by last night. Good God, he'd behaved like the greenest lad, rolling about in the grass with her . . . and yet . . .

After spending the better part of a decade lurking

in the shadows of the war torn Continent, she was a beacon of something he didn't quite understand, but how it filled him with longing.

And that look she tossed at him with the same ease one might throw a stone into a pond, left him delirious with need, as if she were casting a spell over him with some secret, ancient magic that couldn't be dispelled with reason or duty.

Cowhanded she might be in the ballroom, but he suspected in the bedchamber, Miss Thalia Langley would move like the most elegant Viennese waltz.

An image of her in that glorious black gown, her bare feet padding across the thick carpet in his room tripped through his fancy. Of that dress falling to the floor and her joining him in his bed, joining with him . . .

Steady, my good man. Remember, you're a vicar. Try to behave like one.

Larken stifled a laugh. Quite possibly his masquerade as a vicar was on par with her dancing.

At his side, she glanced up. "Pardon. Did you say something? I fear I was nattering on."

"Uh, no," he managed. "Just enjoying the peace of the countryside." They both looked over the meadow, having climbed the low rise, and were now standing just at the edge of the "wilderness" before they crossed over into the formal gardens that surrounded the duke's grand house.

The countryside lay out before them in all its pastoral glory, lofty clouds floating by lazily, while the green of the grass was only interrupted by the lines of hedges and the occasional thatch of a crofter's roof.

"The calm before the storm?" she suggested.

"Something akin to that. I had quite forgotten how I love the country."

"You make it sound like you've been away," she said, so offhandedly it left him unguarded.

"I—I—" Then he looked down at the intelligence behind those deceptive blue eyes of hers and checked himself.

I have, he'd almost said.

Careful, Larken, he admonished silently. *You're better than this. She's no more than a chit of what . . . one and twenty? It isn't as if she can outwit you.*

Care to wager on that? he could almost hear Temple saying.

Down at his feet he spied a little knot of wildflowers. The same sort that had grown in the meadows near Aunt Edith's home, where he'd tramped and wandered after his father's death.

The purple-blue blossoms reminded him of her eyes, so he reached down and plucked several stems, and when he arose, he found her watching him.

Oh, good God. What did he do now? For never in his life had he given flowers to a lady. What the devil had possessed him to pick them in the first place?

The words she'd said earlier . . . The longing within them still echoed in his heart. *". . . Or I would find a handful of wild flowers and spend the afternoon with my watercolors trying to capture their hues."*

Her sweet lament had prodded him into doing this ridiculous, impetuous thing. And not knowing what else to do, he jerked his hand out toward her like a foolish youth.

* * *

Tally tried to breathe. And not because she'd caught a whiff of his pomade.

Flowers? Her knees started to wobble.

Here she had tried everything and anything she could think of to trip Mr. Ryder up and now he'd left her upended with this simple gesture.

Wildflowers . . . in his trembling grasp.

No, her shocking revelations about her unconventional upbringing, her denunciation of marriage, not even her story about Mrs. Hutchinson and Mr. Mudgett had ruffled his cool façade.

And yet here he was making this offering of flowers, and quite frankly, appeared to be ready to toss up his accounts over the entire thing.

What sort of man was he?

The sort who kisses like a rake and now wants to charm you with wildflowers . . .

Tally reached out, their fingers tangling together as she gathered the stems from his grasp. Her gaze jerked up, for his touch, that moment, that brief second as their hands entwined sent a lightning bolt of desire between them.

"Thank you, sir," she managed, wishing she could be more eloquent, say something . . . ask him if he had felt that tug as well.

"They are called *Succisa pratensis Moench*," he said.

"They are?"

"Yes. They even grow in—" his words fumbled to a halt.

Was it her imagination or was he leaning toward her? She searched his eyes for some clue, some hint, eyes so dark and black, she wondered if his mother had been a Spanish princess or gypsy queen.

Of course, that wasn't the sort of question one asked a gentleman.

Then again, she suspected he wasn't entirely a gentleman.

"Grow in where, Mr. Ryder?"

"Um, uh, Northhamptonshire. They grow there as well."

"I imagine they grow just about everywhere. I believe I remember seeing them in Germany when I was young. I don't remember what they are called there."

"Well, you can also call them Devil's Bit," he added. "That's the more common name." He glanced down at his boots. "I had a tutor for a time who was quite the botanist."

She smiled and leaned a little bit closer to him. "Mr. Ryder, you are a wealth of contradictions."

"I am?" He glanced up at her.

"You are," she said. "You read from Fordyce, yet you—" *kiss like a rake*, was what she wanted to say, but finished instead by adding, "have a rakish nature."

But he knew what she meant. "Miss Langley, I protest—"

"You shouldn't. I quite like that part of your character."

He laughed. "Now it is you who are teasing."

"I am not. For in addition to those qualities, I find you have not only a romantic side—" she held up her flowers as evidence— "but a practical one as well." She glanced down at the flowers in her hands. "*Succisa pratensis Moench*, indeed."

"Now see here—"

"Oh, don't bother heaping more of your protests on me. Your secrets are quite safe with me. But I must say . . . "

"Yes?"

"You quite perplex me."

He nodded, his hands folding behind his back. "Then we are even in that regard."

"We are?" Tally tipped her head just so, wishing his rakish nature would give him a nudge.

Kiss me, please kiss me again, so I'll know if last night was a dream or truly real.

He gazed at her, and she swore he heard her silent plea. "Why yes," he said, leaning forward, then starting to walk again. Right around her and up the meadow path.

Tally nearly toppled over. But once she regained her footing, she set off after him. "However are we even, Mr. Ryder?"

He paused as she caught up. "For you, Miss Langley, are without a doubt the most perplexing lady I have ever met."

She came to a tumbling halt before him, and he reached out to steady her. She felt anything but perplexing. Hardly the vixen she'd been last night in his arms. But one glance into his dark eyes and she knew what he meant—he saw her "rakish nature" as well.

"Thank you," she replied.

They both laughed, and he held out his arm to her,

and for a moment she hesitated before putting her hand on his sleeve and they walked again along the fence, up the hill toward the house.

He might, she thought as she took a sly glance up at him, be quite tolerable with a little help.

A new suit, most definitely. A haircut? She glanced again. No. She rather liked his wayward locks. When they weren't stinking of . . . she sniffed ever-so-slightly and ever-so-discretely and was rewarded with *eau de* rancid lard and . . . what? She sniffed again and gave up.

If only he had a valet.

Tally nearly tripped over her own feet. That was it. *A valet!* Felicity just happened to have a spare one, Claver. The one Felicity had hired and the duke found so very annoying. Poor Claver, with no one to fuss over.

And Claver would never let Mr. Ryder come downstairs smelling like he'd been wallowing with the hogs. Tally bit her lips together to keep from grinning, for something else occurred to her. "Do you need your spectacles to see?"

"Pardon?" he murmured, coming out of whatever reverie she'd just roused him from.

"Your spectacles? Are they necessary?"

He *hemmed* and *hawed* a bit before he admitted, "No. Not unless I'm reading."

"Are you reading now?" Tally asked, coming to a stop, hands at her hips.

"No, I suppose I'm not," he said. "But they give me a more vicarly air, or so I've been told."

She studied him. "Yes, but you have very striking eyes. You shouldn't hide them."

A sly grin turned his lips. "You think I'm hiding them?"

That and so much more, she wanted to say, reveling in the ambiguity surrounding him, moving slightly closer to him. Was this a mystery of her imagination or in truth? She didn't know.

Not that she would with the help of a black affenpinscher, who wove between their legs, barking and bounding up, nearly overturning Tally in his bid to attract her attention.

"Brutus!" she scolded, but her little dog just grinned at her and barked some more, as if he knew exactly what she was about and wasn't having any of her mischief.

Of all her luck, to have a dog with a conscience.

If that wasn't enough, the crunch of carriage and wagon wheels coming up the drive tugged her back to solid ground.

"We'd best continue on," she suggested.

"Ah, yes," he replied.

This time he didn't take her hand, and Tally felt the distance between open up again like a gaping yaw.

After a bit, and out of the blue, he spoke, breaking the unnerving silence between them. She might have felt relieved if his question hadn't held an odd note to it.

"You cousin, Lady Philippa—" he stopped as if he didn't know how to proceed.

"Yes, what about her?"

"Does she share your distaste of marriage?"

The question sent a ripple of caution down Tally's spine.

"Yes," she said, keeping her answer short, but then her tongue got the better of her. "And no."

"Yes and no?" He shook his head. "Your cousin sounds like a lady in conflict."

If you only knew . . .

Then she tried to answer him as diplomatically as she could. She was her father's daughter after all. "Pippin is opposed to marriage if it is only for marriage's sake. She'll only marry for the deepest love."

"To her unsuitable *parti*?"

Tally looked down at the grass. "No. That isn't possible."

"Then I am sorry for her."

"As am I," Tally said, the shackles of responsibility tightening around her, coupled with a fear of what was to come as the house now filled with guests. Rather than dwell on that, she said, "Indeed, Pippin and I are writing a play on that very subject right now. *Tears of Helene, or A Lady's Moral Dilemma*."

He came to a grinding halt, his boots digging into the gravel. "You write plays?"

"Yes, I think I mentioned it before," she said, looking up to find Felicity waving at her frantically to hurry along to help her greet everyone.

For the life of her, she couldn't take another step forward, and it was all she could do not to turn tail and run back to the folly.

"Pippin and I have written several plays," she managed to say. "In fact one of them is being considered for production by a London company as we speak—though we will not receive public credit for the authorship, for obvious reasons."

"Of course," he murmured, his gaze fixed as well

at the arriving guests. There was a calculated light to his eyes—as if he was weighing and measuring each person as they alighted. Checking them off some unknown list.

She'd seen her father do much the same thing on more than one occasion, as if cataloguing one and all surrounding him. Felicity had the same talent, yet for her own reasons.

But whyever did Mr. Ryder care who the other guests were? That is, unless he was looking for . . .

Miss DeFisser! Tally's gut clenched in displeasure. The same feeling she got every time she saw their old schoolmate, Miss Sarah Browne. Which made no sense, for Miss Browne was a detestable peahen and Tally didn't even know Miss DeFisser.

Except that the girl was destined for . . .

"Still, to have written a play, Miss Langley," he was saying. "That is quite an achievement. May I read it?"

She was so lost in her own reverie, of imagining Miss DeFisser and *him* together that she didn't quite discern what he'd asked. "Read what, sir?"

"Your play, of course." He bowed slightly. "I would be honored to read your efforts."

She shook her head. "Heavens, no! It is hardly appropriate for a . . . for a . . ."

"A young lady perhaps?" He rocked on his heels, his brows tilted at an angle that could only be described as teasing.

Teasing! From a vicar. A shiver whispered down her arms, like the portent of gooseflesh.

"Have you been writing something wicked, Miss Langley? Something you fear you will have to repent? Something untoward I might discover about you?"

She did shiver this time. No, tremble. Right down to the soles of her slippers. "Discover?" she managed to whisper. "I doubt it, sir."

He leaned closer. "I don't. I think you have some very distracting secrets, Miss Langley, that I would be delighted to uncover."

Tally felt her insides unravel. Secrets? Uncovered? This was becoming more unnerving than the notion of being a vicar's wife. For suddenly he was no longer harmless, with his Fordyce sermons and horrid pomade.

This was a man capable of uncovering her darkest secrets.

The loose ends inside her coiled into panic, because with it came a realization that as much as she feared discovery, she longed for him to try.

To test her. *To uncover her.*

"I believe my sister needs me," she said, turning to flee and nearly stepping into the path of a carriage.

Mr. Ryder caught her before the distracted coachman ran her over, holding her by the elbow. The grand carriage came to a stop before them, the horses dancing and prancing, the driver setting the brake with a tired arm.

And all the time, Mr. Ryder held her fast. His touch, firm and strong, sent rebellious ripples of desire down her limbs. Whyever did he affect her thusly?

"Tell me, Miss Langley," he asked, "is your play a lesson on the art of love? One that even I could learn from?" His voice teased her, tempted her. Sparked that fire that he'd kindled last night, as if he'd stroked her neck, kissed her lips, touched her . . .

The door to the carriage flew open, and a young lady descended. "Oh, Miss Thalia!" she exclaimed. "Don't tell me! You've been scribbling another of your monstrous plays. Well, you can set your pen aside, for I have the most engaging story for you that will leave all your imaginings in the pale."

Larken glanced up at the young lady making her way out of the carriage and found himself horror-struck that this "gel" might be Miss DeFisser. If that wasn't excuse enough to send him high-tailing it back to the London, he knew of no better.

"Oh, how foolish of me," she said, holding out her hand for Larken to take. "I should say *Miss Langley*, now that your dear sister is married. That makes you the spinster of the family, doesn't it?" Her lips curled into a spiteful smile as she descended, a look that faded as she glanced over at him and realized who held her hand. She plucked her fingers back, her nose wrinkling as a waft of pomade hit it.

"A spinster?" Tally said, her spine going stiff as she spoke. "Something we have in common, wouldn't you say, Miss Browne? Being spinsters, that is?"

Larken had lived through more than one hair-raising incident, but none that spelled more tension than this meeting of misses. Was it him or did this exchange sound like a pampered housecat hissing at a wild stray?

He eyed the pink-festooned creature standing before him and suppressed—as best he could—the shudder that rose up his spine. Well, if there was something to celebrate it was her name. Miss Browne. Not Miss De Fisser. At least he wasn't about to be saddled with this bi—ahem, *miss*—for the next few days.

As it was, Miss Browne struck a commanding pose, glancing up at the magnificent house before her and sniffing, as if it was well and good but hardly up to her standards. "At least you will have your dear cousin to share your days with, for I can't see how she will ever marry. My situation, on the other hand, is quite promising, what with my inheritance and my good name unsullied." She glanced at Larken, and in the flick of a lash, dismissed him.

He would have grinned, but that probably wouldn't have been very vicarly.

Having removed him from her consideration, Miss Browne continued baiting Miss Langley with a look that might have been sincere if her eyes weren't dancing with malice, "Poor, poor Lady Philippa. There are so many who say her disgrace has completely tarnished her virtue." She turned to the matron getting out the carriage behind her. "Isn't that so, *Maman*? That Lady Philippa's disgrace is still the subject of much discussion in Town."

He felt, rather than saw, Miss Langley surge past him, and caught hold of the back of her skirt, smiling over her shoulder at Miss Browne with the blandest expression he could muster as he held Miss Langley fast.

Miss Browne continued unabashed. "Though not I. I find such talk so distasteful, for I feel so deeply over her ruin. So very deeply."

Larken considered releasing Miss Langley and

letting her loose on this harpy, but he had to imagine *that* scandal would only give Miss Browne more to gossip upon—that is once she got out of bed after the thrashing she'd receive.

To his delight, Brutus came to the rescue, darting out from beneath one of the wagons and catching hold of a beribboned confection decorating the hem of Miss Browne's dress.

"A-a-a-h!" the nasty chit shrieked, leaping back and dancing on her toes as she tried to dislodge the little beast. But Brutus, true to his breeding, hung on until he'd torn his prize free, then he raced away, head high and ribbons trailing after him, like a horse that had just won the derby.

"Oh, stop him!" Miss Browne cried out. "He's gone and ruined my gown."

Larken glanced down at her hem and in truth, couldn't discern where the ribbon had come from, since there were so many of the demmed things crowded all over the hem.

"Tally!" the duchess chastened, coming forward to greet her guests and smooth over this less-than-perfect welcome. "Please restrain him, will you?!"

Dutifully, Tally caught hold of her dog and after a bit of a tug-of-war, she was able to get the frou-frou out of his mouth and hand it over to their guest.

It hardly looked the perfect flower now, all wet and mangled, and Miss Browne stared down at it in horror. Whatever protest she'd been about to impart fell away as the crunch of wheels announced the arrival of yet another carriage.

Suddenly Miss Browne was all smiles again, straightening and posing for the new arrivals, that is until they began to alight and she frowned by wrinkling only her nose. "Ah, the Elsfords. How egalitarian of Your Grace to invite *them*."

"The duke and Major Elsford served together," the duchess replied.

Tally stepped closer to her sister. "I find the Misses Elsford delightful, and not the least bit overreaching like other people."

"I suppose you would," Miss Browne replied, eyeing her hem again and having completely missed the slight aimed at her.

Hollindrake and his wife strolled forward to greet their guests, and Larken searched his memory, an alarm ringing through his thoughts.

Major Elsford? Have I met him? He perused the panoply of officers and agents he'd encountered in Spain and Portugal, but no, Major Elsford was not amongst them. Thankfully. The fewer people who needed to be drawn into his deception, the better.

He was having a hard enough time keeping his identity a secret from Miss Langley.

As it was Major Elsford alighted his plain carriage as one might expect a career army officer would, straight and at attention, while his wife, a narrow lady who appeared older than her years—most likely from a life following the drum—exited in much the same fashion, tall and rigid.

The Misses Elsford came bubbling out of the carriage like a pair of frolicking kittens—ready for this grand adventure and delighted to be included. No feigned manners with them, for when they looked up at the house before them, their easy natures turned to openmouthed awe.

But the Duchess of Hollindrake moved in quickly, dispelling their sudden case of cold feet with her easy smile and warm greeting.

Hollindrake shook the major's hand enthusiastically, and there was the usual slapping on the back and jests tossed about in the easy manner of military men who had shared years of adversity.

"Ho there, Major!" Hollindrake said. "Welcome, welcome!"

"Ah, yes! Thank you, indeed, Thatcher," the man blustered and then stopped himself, as if just seeing the house beyond for the first time. "Ah, demmit, I forget myself. Your Grace it is now, and a fine title for a most excellent officer."

Hollindrake took this compliment with a modest nod. "News from London, sir? What do you hear?"

"Hear? Hear? Nothing, sir. 'Tis a quiet and dull place, now that summer is upon us."

"Nothing much? I daresay you quite mistake the matter!" This loud exclamation came from Miss Browne, and all eyes turned toward her. "Nothing much in London, sir? Why the Town is all abuzz, quite rife with talk and speculation." She paused again, preening with importance.

Larken had to give the gel her due. She knew how to draw attention to herself, for she certainly had the floor now.

"Whatever has everyone been talking about, Miss Browne?" the duchess asked politely.

"Why, I would think you of all people would know, Your Grace," she replied. "For haven't you heard? Captain Dashwell has escaped from Marshalsea Prison."

He watched not Miss Browne, but Tally. And to his horror, the flowers she'd held in her hand fell away.

She couldn't have condemned herself more openly, more completely, and for Larken, the petals struck the ground with the same damning finality of an executioner's axe.

Chapter 9

"Tell me you had nothing to do with this," Felicity said, facing her sister and cousin in their suite upstairs.

After Miss Browne's announcement fell like a cannonball on the guests, Felicity had managed to sweep aside the chaos like a general—directing Mrs. Elsford and her daughters to their rooms, the Brownes to theirs, and delegating the rest of the matters of trunks and necessities to Staines.

Then she had caught Tally by the elbow and led her upstairs, where she was now holding her own personal tribunal.

"Tell me you didn't help that . . . that . . . *bounder* escape," she said, shaking from head to toe with anger.

Tally shifted from one slipper to another, for she'd never seen her twin so angry. Ever.

Even Brutus seemed to know that now would not

be a good time for one of his interruptions and made a beeline for furthest spot under the sofa.

"Duchess, I—" Tally began, using her sister's nickname.

Felicity's hands waved frantically in the air before her. "No! Don't tell me. Don't tell me anything. I don't want to know."

Of course, Miss Browne had regaled her audience with a complete account of the night. How an elegant (albeit masked) lady had distracted Dashwell's guards, then with the help of accomplices, freed the American privateer. Shockingly, all had escaped into the Southwark stews, not to be seen or heard of since.

A plot too familiar to escape Felicity's notice.

"But Felicity, I thought you said—" Tally began again.

"Never mind what I said," the duchess replied, groaning and then pacing in front of them. "Oh, this is dreadful. And on the eve of my house party. Of all the times!"

Pippin and Tally shared a quick glance, Tally all too ready to groan, *If I have to hear one more time about her demmed house party, I'll . . .*

Her cousin's eyes filled with agreement. *Yes, but we have other worries . . .*

"Haven't you a care of how this looks?" Felicity exclaimed. "That most likely Uncle Temple will be arriving any moment now to have a look around. Or worse, that horrible Mr. Pymm will send someone to pry about without our knowing it. And then if Dashwell himself were to come here! Or worse, be found here—"

"Will you lower your voice," Tally told her sharply. "Not only will you wake Aunt Minty," she said in a harsh whisper, adding a nod toward the door behind her, "but you might have a care who hears you. If your intention is to have your wild theories aired before all of Sussex, then continue on, for you are doing a better job than the *Morning Post* with your mad ranting."

Her sister's mouth fell open, as if to contradict her, but then Tally's words sunk in and she snapped her lips shut, her hands fisting at her sides.

But at the same time, Felicity's fears came to roost in Tally's chest, her heart hammering.

Send someone to pry about without our knowing it . . .

If only it could be an impossible notion. If only she didn't know the truth.

That he was already here.

For even as Felicity had made her declaration, an image of Mr. Ryder rose up before Tally. No, it couldn't be. He was Hollindrake's cousin.

Wasn't he?

Marching back and forth across the carpet, Felicity fired off her questions, though her register was noticeably lower. "It is one thing for my reputation to be sullied," she said, pausing before them and striking her most ducal stance. "But what of Hollindrake's?"

Tally's gut clenched. *Hollindrake?* Oh, the devil take Felicity. She would have to remind them about Thatcher. Of their obligation to him. Worse yet, the duke had only ever been kind and generous to his wife's collection of relations, odd acquaintances and questionable servants.

More generous than they deserved, Tally was ashamed to admit.

"All of London is going to be speculating who that mysterious lady might be . . . " Felicity was saying, letting her voice trail off and pinning her glance on Pippin.

But their cousin wasn't an earl's daughter for nothing, and she held her own against Felicity, staring her right back with deadly calm.

The duchess glanced at both of them before she said, "Tell me you've had nothing to do with this. Nothing that will draw shame on Hollindrake. I must know."

The desperate note behind Felicity's plea plucked at Tally. *Oh, dear heavens, what a terrible tangle . . .*

"Nothing, Felicity," Pippin told her, calmly and with a sincere note to her voice that would have erased the doubt of even the most cynical of judges. "I am as shocked as you are."

Tally didn't trust herself to speak, so she nodded her agreement.

Felicity let out a large sigh. "Good. Now it is on to my other problem. Mr. Ryder. The tailor and his assistants are attending to him in the second parlor, and I can only hope this Monsieur Gaspard is as good as they say and will have a new suit in order before the ball tomorrow night. I so want Miss DeFisser to be suitably impressed with him." She sighed again and started to leave.

Tally looked up after her, but saw not her sister's departing figure, but rather Mr. Ryder dressed to the nines and entering the ballroom.

Any woman would be impressed, as long as he was . . . Oh, yes! She'd almost forgotten.

"Felicity?" she called after her sister.

"Yes?"

"Consider asking Claver to act as Mr. Ryder's valet. The poor man does nothing for Hollindrake, and it seems a shame to see his excellent talents going to waste."

That, and Claver would take to this assignment with such alacrity and glee, he'd keep Mr. Ryder entangled until Tally found a way to unravel all this.

Felicity brightened. "That is the perfect solution. I don't know why I didn't think of it myself."

Tally smiled in return, but it did little to lessen the guilt jostling about inside her. "And one more recommendation, if you truly want Mr. Ryder to make a good impression—"

"Yes?" Felicity asked eagerly.

"Have Claver dispose of Mr. Ryder's pomade jar."

Felicity laughed. "That will be his very first order of business."

Tally waited until Felicity's sharp-heeled steps hit the stairs before she turned to face Pippin.

"This must end," she told her. "It is exactly as Felicity fears. And worse. We are already under scrutiny."

Pippin shook her head. "Not more of your fears over Mr. Ryder? Tally, you are seeing spies where there are none. That man is nothing more than Hollindrake's odd cousin—"

Tally opened her mouth to argue, but Pippin cut

her off. "I will hear no more arguments on the subject. We are above reproach, I tell you. We have left nothing to chance."

The door to Aunt Minty's room opened and a tall figure appeared in the doorway.

"That, my dear Circe, is why you should be scared," Captain Dashwell told her, using the pet name he reserved for her and her alone. "For when you're convinced your enemies can't outwit you, they'll corner you every time." He paused and held out his hand to her, and she moved quickly across the room to take it, easing into the crook of his arm where she fit perfectly, her head gently resting over his heart. "Tally has the right of it," he told her, his hand smoothing over her hair. "It is time for this to end."

Yet what he didn't say was the one thing they were all thinking.

Before our luck runs out.

They had good reason to be wary, for Miss Browne's announcement hadn't sent only Felicity into a panic, but Larken as well.

Damn that stupid, prattling chit! he thought as he stood in the second parlor, having been caught by the housekeeper and towed down here only to find himself outflanked by an overeager tailor and his flotilla of assistants.

It didn't serve his temper any better that he was being measured and taped and pinned as if he were being fitted for his shroud. And it *would* be his shroud if he let Dashwell escape. Pymm had made that all too clear.

"The bottle green or the mulberry, monsieur?" the tailor asked, holding up two bolts of wool. "I believe the bottle green would look quite handsome with a naccarat waistcoat."

There was a collective outburst of oohs and aahs from the man's help, as if he had just doubled their wages.

Larken stared at the offerings in horror. Orange? This man wanted him to wear an orange waist-coat? He shuddered. Why, he'd look like that utter nincompoop, Stewie Hodges. Didn't anyone make a good black coat and nankeen breeches any more? For that was all a man needed, in his estimation.

"You don't approve?" the tailor said with a little sniff, as if he had never had one of his brilliant suggestions rebuffed. "But Her Grace said you were here to court a lady. And how else does a man charm a woman but with his fine ensemble? You will distract her from all the others, and lure her into your favor." He turned to his assistants. "Is that not so?"

"Of course," and, "Most assuredly, sir," came the assistants' ready chorus of agreement.

"You'll have her utterly deceived," added the youngest of the lot, and his less than sycophantic answer did not serve him well with the others, who glared disapprovingly.

Larken ignored them all but the tailor before him. "My good man," he said. "I am a simple clergyman"— *Not your usual aging coxcomb or Lothario who inhabits Tunbridge Wells because he can't afford London's prices*— "and prefer a more somber selection, befitting my station."

"I feared as much." The man sighed and then

snapped his fingers at one of the assistants. "The Spanish blue."

Larken nodded his approval immediately. It wasn't black, but the dark, deep blue was close enough.

"The naccarat would make an excellent addition—"

"No!" Larken barked at him. "I'm not wearing orange."

"It's more of a tangerine," an assistant corrected, and then slunk away quickly when Larken shot him a look that said while he was a vicar meant to save men's souls, he wasn't opposed to sending one directly to the very fires of hell.

The room grew still, except for the snips of scissors and the occasional sniff from the tailor. All the while, Larken stewed and simmered over having to stand there like a poppet while his adversary was most likely getting away.

If he weren't tied to secrecy and discretion, he'd be blazing through the duke's house like a hound on the scent, and make short work of this assignment . . . *to kill Dash.*

He flinched, and this time not from a wayward pin. *Demmit*, why did he find himself so tied up over this? It wasn't like he hadn't killed before.

But not a friend . . . Oh, it had been an easy enough thing to agree to in the half-wakened state in which they'd found him, for he hadn't really believed Temple's cockamamie theory that two Bath misses had somehow managed Dashwell's escape . . . and from Marshalsea of all places . . . not only that, but out from the very tight grasp of a naval officer and his marines.

That is until he'd met Tally . . .

"I believe we have all we need," the tailor said, with a wide flourish and bow.

"Thank you," Larken said, getting down from the stool he'd been perched on and making a hasty exit from the room before the duchess returned with yet another distraction.

He'd had enough of those for one day. Lord! He'd all but given himself away—twice—to Tally. First, telling her how his mother had died when he was born, and secondly . . . over the flowers he'd given her. What idiotic thing had he nearly said? Oh, yes.

. . . *They even grow in* . . . Portugal, he'd nearly said. Portugal! Oh, yes, most country vicars spend time lolling about the war torn plains of Portugal.

Perhaps he was as 'round the bend as they whispered about him behind his back at the Foreign Office. As dangerous and reckless as his superiors had claimed.

He certainly felt reckless around *her* . . .

Worse yet, he didn't want to discover that Tally— no, he corrected himself—*Miss Langley* was involved in any of this. He didn't want to discover that this miss who intrigued him, enlivened his spirit, who teased him to flirt—*him, flirting!*—was in any way tangled up in this treasonous mess.

He paused in a long gallery and glanced out one of the windows toward the meadow where the wild-flowers grew.

Flowers . . .

What was it that the tailor and his assistants had said?

You will distract her from all the others, and lure her into your favor. . .

That was close to the point, but there had been one other offer of advice.

You'll have her utterly deceived . . .

That was exactly what he had to do. Lull Miss Langley into his favor and deceive her completely.

And in the end, she'll despise you for your deception, your betrayal. Just as you'll despise yourself for killing Dashwell.

Larken shook his head, clearing such sentimental thoughts aside.

He had a task ahead, one that would brook no room for such foolish sentimentality. Held no room for the chance at something he dared not even name.

An hour before supper, Tally left the suite to make arrangements for a carriage for the next morning, on the pretense of taking Aunt Minty out for some air and a little bit of shopping in the nearby village.

They had gotten Dash into the house dressed like Aunt Minty; they should be able to get him out the same way, if they left early enough and had the luck they so needed.

Her thoughts were so awash in plots and plans she barreled right into a solid wall of chest.

Mr. Ryder's, to be exact.

Oh, she didn't need to look up to know it was him.

She just knew. Then she tentatively took a sniff, and found not that wretched stench of pomade, but a hint of something much more elegant, masculine and rich, something akin to the finest scents one might find at Floris on Jermyn Street back in London.

"Mr. Ryder," she said, backing up clumsily and

smoothing out her skirts as she went, looking up to find that the man she'd long suspected lurked beneath his ill-fitting coat and horridly combed hair stood before her.

Egads, what had Felicity done? Or rather the tailor and Claver . . . they'd gone and transformed Hollindrake's rumpled, bumbling cousin into a Corinthian.

"Mr. Ryder?" she whispered, reaching out toward him without even thinking and when she did realize it, she pulled her hand back and tucked it into the pocket of her apron.

What had she been thinking? Oh, she knew. She'd wanted to touch him to make sure her eyes weren't deceiving her.

"Miss Langley," he replied, bowing perfectly, his gaze never leaving hers.

"Um, may I help you?" she asked, fixing her gaze on a vase on a table, the portrait overhead, the yellow curtains on the window. On anything but *him.* "I believe you are in the wrong wing," she pointed out, pulling her wits about her.

"I don't think so," he said, rocking back on his heels and looking at her. Really looking at her, as if he couldn't get enough of her.

"Your room is two floors up and at the other end."

"I wasn't looking for my room. I was looking for *you.*"

She glanced up again. "For me?"

"Yes, *you.*"

The way he said it sent shivers down her spine. Whatever was he doing? Flirting with her?

His eyes narrowed and he glanced at her, a slight smile on his lips. And then he brought out his offering.

An entire bouquet of wildflowers. Pristine white flowers, delicate pink blooms, and more of those blue Devils he'd picked for her earlier. He held them out to her and when she took them, he held her hands.

"You dropped your other ones, so I thought . . ." his words faltered to a stop, but his eyes sparkled with something else.

Egads! Mr. Ryder was flirting with her.

Nay, he was courting her.

For one divine moment, Tally forgot everything. Pippin and Dash. That she was up to her ears in treason. That she was supposed to be going downstairs to ask Staines for the carriage.

Everything but the fact that this man wanted her . . .

But that wasn't it. He wanted something. From her.

Demmit, Tally. He's here to stop you. Trap you.

By any means possible . . .

Truly? Any means? She wished she didn't feel so pleased by that idea.

Tally stepped back, not only from him, but away from the realization that Felicity was so very right. There was someone here to spy on them. And he was standing right before her. She'd wager her black velvet gown on it.

She took a deep, steadying breath. "If this is a bribe to gain my assistance in keeping you out of my sister's path, let me make this very clear: I won't help you."

"You won't?"

Was it her imagination, or was he edging closer to her? She shook her head, both at her desire for him and at his question. "No, I cannot. Felicity rang a peel over my head for dawdling earlier and she already suspects you of avoiding her. 'Dragging your feet' as she put it."

"Me?" He moved as he spoke, not really taking a noticeable step but moving like a great cat with his prey in his sights.

Prey? Her? A shiver ran down her spine. The part of her that delighted in this cat-and-mouse game. If she was the prey, wouldn't it be wickedly fun to discover how he proposed to catch her?

"No, it would not," she said aloud.

"Would not, what?" he asked, moving again.

If he got much closer he'd have her up against the doorway, with the sturdy oak at her back, and nothing but Mr. Ryder covering her.

Tally gulped and gave the first part of her imaginings life, bumping into the door and finding it as solid as she'd suspected.

And what of the other half of this trap?

Oh, yes, he'd be just as hard and unforgiving, she thought, gauging the inches between them and wondering how much courage she could muster. For if she were truly fearless, truly the woman she wanted to be, she'd let herself become as entwined with him as they'd been last night.

"Miss Langley, there is something I would like from you . . ." he whispered, drawing nearer, his words brushing against her neck, her ears.

She tipped her head and shivered at the delicious intimacy of it.

Thalia Langley! What are you thinking? Duck around him. Stomp on his foot. Knee him, for goodness sakes.

"Yes, Mr. Ryder?" she managed to whisper, standing her ground. To run would be cowardly . . . wouldn't it?

"I was wondering if you—"

"If I?"

He paused and looked down at her, hungry, dark desires burning in his gaze. He wasn't even wearing his spectacles, she noticed, and without them, his eyes were even more piercing.

"Miss Langley, I would be so very delighted if you would indulge me—"

"Indulge you?" she repeated, while her thoughts ran wild yet again. *Mr. Ryder, I would indulge you anything at this moment. . .*

"Yes, indulge me," he repeated, "with a small favor."

Just a small one? Tally felt flushed from her head to her toes, her body trembling with the same sort of wild desires she'd discovered in the maze last night.

Just a small indulgence? Nay, sir. I would have you entirely indulge me . . .

"If you would but allow me into—"

His dark, passionate eyes held her gaze with a hypnotic power. Tally's hand closed over the latch on the door, about ready to pluck it open and tow him inside the suite by his cravat. One she hoped he wasn't overly fond of, for she wasn't going to waste any time in removing it.

For there was nothing between them now, nothing to stop them except . . .

Pippin and Dash.

Tally shivered and came to her senses, glancing up at him and catching sight of something else in his eyes—something she hadn't noticed before in her desire-plagued distraction.

Triumph. At the idea that he was about to gain entrance to her suite.

He'd played her like the greenest of innocents.

Tally's passion turned in another direction—something more akin to rage—and she was about to put both hands on his chest and give him a hearty shove onto his ass, when from behind them, she heard a voice she hadn't welcomed in some time.

Felicity's.

"Mr. Ryder! There you are! I have been searching high and low for you," she called out from the end of the hall, the sharp click of her heels like the staccato beat of a drum.

Thank heavens for her busybody ways, Tally thought, sagging against the door.

Felicity marched to a halt before them. "Mr. Ryder, whatever are you doing with my sister?"

Chapter 10

$\mathcal{L}$arken nearly leapt out of his skin at the sound of the duchess's voice behind them. And if he wasn't off his mark, Miss Langley looked relieved for the rescue.

Demmit. He'd nearly had her where he wanted. Seduced and willing to help him.

"Mr. Ryder, I will ask you again," the duchess was saying. "What are you doing with my sister?"

Holy mother of God, it was like looking his Aunt Edith in the eye when she'd suspected him (and usually rightly so) of some misdeed.

"I um, I was—" he stammered. "Your sister—"

The duchess tapped her toe, her impatience prodding him to find a suitable answer.

Other than the obvious one. *I was attempting to seduce her so as to discover what she knows of Dashwell's escape.*

The duchess's blue eyes narrowed.

Eyes . . . that was it.

"I discovered Miss Langley out here in the hall with something in her eye and I was assisting her in removing it." He hastily reached inside his jacket and retrieved a handkerchief, handing it over to Tally with all due haste. "Perhaps that will manage the task better than my blundering," he offered.

"Might help if you wore your spectacles," the duchess observed.

"Yes, yes, quite so," he said, fishing them out of another pocket and sliding them on his nose. "Ah, yes, that would have made the task much easier."

For her part, Miss Langley obviously didn't want to draw her sister's attention too close to her portion in their interlude, and covered for him nicely, dabbing her eye and exclaiming with some conviction, "Oh, I believe it is gone, sir. Thank you." As she handed him back the linen square, their fingers touched for the briefest second, and when they did, she drew hers back as quickly as if she'd touched a hot grate. "You must have gotten it out," she added, glancing away.

"Harrumph." The duchess wedged herself between him and his quarry and sent him a withering look. "Mr. Ryder, is there a purpose for you to be in this wing?"

As in, what the hell are you doing lurking about my sister's room?

"Most certainly, Your Grace."

"And that reason is . . . ?" the duchess pressed.

Oh, hell, what good reason could he give that

would wipe that look of suspicion off the duchess's face?

He had to come up with some reason as to why he was skulking about her suite of rooms like some Lothario in a Covent Garden tragedy.

Covent Garden! That was it.

"Her play," he blustered. "Your sister promised me the most delightful diversion of reading her play."

Behind the duchess, Miss Langley gaped at him as if he'd gone mad.

"Are you sure you want to spend your time thus employed?" the duchess asked, her brows arched skeptically. "I fear you might find it rather—"

"Lacking in moral foundation," Miss Langley said. "Yes, Felicity. I warned him that it wasn't the most proper of stories."

"I have problems sleeping," he confided in an aside to the duchess. "I had rather thought—" He made a show of yawning, the implication clear: such silly drivel would surely put any sensible man straight to sleep.

Glancing over at Miss Langley, he found her nostrils flaring. Oh, he'd gotten her in a fine temper.

But then again passion and anger were but two sides of one coin. One that could be easily flipped.

"Well, Tally? What are you waiting for? Please fetch your play for Mr. Ryder, so I can take him with me to go over the entertainments for the week." She smiled up at him. "For Miss DeFisser's benefit as well as yours."

"But Felicity—" Tally protested.

The duchess turned to her sister. "I daresay, if you

promised the man he could read it, you can't change your mind now. Besides, isn't that what you and Pippin want? An audience for your scribblings?"

Tally's jaw worked back and forth, as if she were mulling just the right retort.

However, the duchess wasn't finished yet. "Well, here is Mr. Ryder. Willing and able to read it—"

"Quite willing, ma'am," he offered.

"Yes, so there you have it, Tally. Go get the play for Mr. Ryder."

With no way out, Tally huffed and went back inside her rooms.

He smiled at the duchess, who returned his offering with a furrowed brow and an aggrieved glance.

Ah, Aunt Edith, you live on.

Miss Langley was back in a trice, a bundle of papers in her hands. "Please do use care, this is our only copy."

He nodded, and took it carefully, thinking that it would be quite safe on his nightstand, for he had no intention of reading the melodramatic musings of a ramshackle pair of misses.

"There now, you have your entertainment and I have nearly completed my errand." The duchess turned to her sister. "Do you recall Pippin having a cousin on her father's side by the name of Hartwell?"

"Hartwell? No, I don't believe—" Miss Langley replied, just starting the shake her head, when she froze, her gaze flying up. "Did you say Hartwell?"

"Yes, Tally. Hartwell. If you would but stop wool-gathering for two seconds put together I wouldn't have to repeat myself all the time." She sighed and continued. "Mr. Hartwell arrived and is downstairs requesting to see Pippin. He was traveling nearby and knew that she intended to summer here and took the chance of seeing her." She sighed again. "I don't remember the connection, but he does look vaguely familiar."

"The Knolles all have that look," her sister offered quickly. "Oh, I have no doubt Pippin would be delighted to see him. Most likely he carries news of her brother."

"Oh, yes," the duchess brightened. "Of course. I just couldn't place him, but now you've put it all together for me. Should I put him in the Winter parlor?"

"Why not just send him up here," Miss Langley suggested. "We still have a good portion of our tea tray left and the servants are most likely stretched to their wits ends with dinner in an hour."

The duchess nodded. "Yes, yes. Perfect suggestion. I'll have Staines show him up. Will you tell Pippin or shall I?"

"I will," the chit offered quickly. "For didn't you have plans for Mr. Ryder?"

"Yes, I did! Thank you for reminding me." The duchess turned and took his arm. "Mr. Ryder, come. I have a long list of possible entertainments. Come tell me what you are best at."

What was he best at? After years in the king's service, he'd become quite talented at a number of things, and yet right now, only one thing came to mind.

Murder.

* * *

Staines brought up Mr. Hartwell a few minutes later and Tally only hoped that Felicity wouldn't remember why he looked familiar . . .

He walked with an elegant stick, angling it as he stopped before the ladies. After the door was shut and Staines had retreated down the hall, he glanced at Pippin and then at Tally and bowed, low and perfectly.

"Ladies, I am honored," he said in a cultured voice that didn't hold a note of Bruno's Cockney legacy. "Tarleton Jones, at your service."

Tally and Pippin shared a stunned glance.

This was Tarleton? The brother of their good friend, Bruno Jones? When Bruno had said he would send his "little" brother if there was trouble, they hadn't thought he meant that literally.

The two men could not be less alike. And though there was a resemblance around the nose and the forehead, where Bruno still claimed his pugilist physique, and was more like a walking bear than merely a man, his brother was, well, more of a mere man.

Short and thin, to the point of being diminutive, "Mr. Hartwell" wore the clothes of a dandy. A pea green jacket, lemon waistcoat and striped trousers were only usurped in grandeur by an elaborately tied cravat that nearly swallowed the small man alive.

"I come bearing a gift," he said, pulling out a coin from his pocket and handing it over to Pippin, who glanced down at it and then nodded to Tally.

For Tally and Pippin hadn't broken Dash out of prison alone, but had enlisted the help of not only their former schoolteacher, Miss Porter (now known to the world as Lady John Tremont, or by the unkind moniker "Mad Jack's wife") but also Jack's trusted servant, Bruno Jones.

Before they'd parted in Southwark, Lady John had shown Tally and Pippin a clipped coin, and said she would give it to anyone she sent to them—so they could trust her messenger implicitly.

"Thank you, sir," Tally said. "Please be seated. May I offer you some tea? You must be tired after your journey."

"How kind, how kind," he said enthusiastically, settling down onto the settee and taking the cup Pippin poured for him with all the manners of a perfect gentleman.

"I must say, Mr. Jones," Tally said, "you aren't exactly who we expected."

"Ah, I suppose you imagined I would be a large brute, on the order of my brother. If you are disappointed, imagine my father's dismay. However, our dear sainted mother saw my short stature as a chance for a different profession." He moved his hand with a flourish from the top of his head to his polished boots. "The results are the gentleman you see before you. As it turns out, having one in the family helps when there is a need to move in more, shall we say, illustrious circles."

Tally smiled. She liked the conniving Tarleton already. But then again, she had a soft spot in her heart for Bruno as well. But the arrival of Tarleton did not bode well. "Something has gone wrong, hasn't it?"

For the plan all along had been for Lady John to bring Aunt Minty along with her when she and Jack came for the house party. Then they'd make the switch, with Pippin and Dash riding for the coast during the hullabaloo of Felicity's elaborate entertainments.

"Has something happened to Aunt Minty?" Pippin asked, handing him back the coin.

"No, no, Aramintha is well," Mr. Jones said. "As incorrigible as ever. Actually, I've got her stashed nearby and we need to find a way to get her into the house."

"So something has happened," Tally pressed. For none of this was as they had planned.

"Yes. I might suggest, if it is possible, to bring your 'Aunt Minty' out so he can hear this as well."

Pippin rose to her feet and nodded, before she went into her room and whistled softly, giving Dash the signal that all was clear.

He came out and introductions were made, with Dash bowing to Mr. Jones and expressing his appreciation. "My sincere and everlasting gratitude, sir."

"I shall not forget your offer, Captain, if I ever have need to leave England in a hurry."

They all laughed and then Tarleton's face turned serious. "Miss Langley, your apprehension is well-placed. Lady John has discovered some very grievous news."

The room chilled around Tally, as if an ominous reckoning was about to bind them into an impossible knot. It wasn't that she regretted helping Pippin free Dash, or even driving the carriage, which at the time had seemed more a lark than dangerous, but now . . . well, suddenly their play brought to life was coming to an end, and she feared that the lines being played out would be starkly different from those they'd written, despite their success so far.

Tarleton continued. "Her ladyship insists Mr. Dashwell be taken to the coast without any further delay. It has become imperative that he make it out of the country as soon as possible."

"What has changed?" Tally asked. "Other than that the news of his escape has become the talk of the countryside."

"It is far worse than that," Tarleton said, leaning forward, hands folded over the top of his walking stick. "They mean to find you out, Captain, without delay."

"Wouldn't be the first time they tried to catch me," Dash said, as cavalier as usual when it came to his safety. "But even if they do, they will only jail me again, and by the time their courts have sorted out all my offenses, this war will be over, and I will be free—they'll have no choice but to release me."

Brash and daring—it was why Pippin had fallen in love with him, but right now, Tally wished the man were a little more temperate, cautious.

"No, sir, there will be no more jails, no more reprieves for you, for you will be dead. You know too much to be let free. They've sent an agent after you to see you finished."

Pippin gasped, and to his credit, Dash turned to her and wound his arm around her, holding her close. "Never happen, Circe. Mr. Jones is here and I assume he has come with a plan from your Lady John."

"That I have, Lady Philippa, never you fear," their guest assured her.

"What does Lady John have in mind?" Tally asked, still reeling from Tarleton's news.

"They've sent an agent . . ."

Oh, dear heavens. It was true. Mr. Ryder!

"I must get you out of here as soon as possible, sir," Tarleton was telling Dash. "You will travel as my valet—I have the necessary clothes and papers, so no one will suspect your identity." He paused for a moment. "I overhead some of the maids mention there is to be a ball tomorrow night, yes?"

Tally nodded, suddenly seeing the convenience of the ball that she'd been dreading and what it was Tarleton was asking. "My sister has invited most of the countryside and a good part of our friends from London." She paused, envisioning the overflowing house. "In the chaos, who is to notice if you were to leave with a valet when you arrived without one?"

"Exactly," Tarleton said, slapping his knee and winking at her. "You are as sharp, Miss Langley, as Lady John warned me you would be."

But one key point to the plan hadn't escaped Pippin. "But how will I—"

Tarleton shook his head. "My lady, you cannot come with us."

"But I won't—"

Mr. Jones was just as adamant. "Her ladyship was firm on the point, you are not to travel with us. It is too dangerous." Then he looked directly at her. "All the stories in the papers and on the lips of every coachman from London to Hastings is of a lady in red. The fair beauty who rescued her pirate lover. You, my lady, are the real risk of Captain Dashwell being discovered. With him traveling as my valet, no one will look twice, so intent is everyone in finding you."

Pippin shook her head furiously, her fingers twining around Dash's strong, broad hand. "Dash, tell him. Tell him we won't be separated."

Dash glanced up at Tarleton, who just simply shook his head.

The answer was clear. There was no escape with Pippin in their company, and Tally could feel her grief cut like a knife even before she started to cry.

Dash drew her closer. "Oh Circe, it is only until the war is over. Before the end of the year, I'd wager. Then I shall be back for you and nothing will ever keep us apart again."

Yet even as he made his assurances, Tally felt the hand of Fate come down and touch their lives.

It wasn't going to be as simple as Dash made it sound, and their plans were not going to work. Not with Mr. Ryder already poised to strike.

She glanced up at Tarleton. "Did Lady John say who the Foreign Office sent? Which agent?"

Tarleton nodded. "Lord Larken. They've sent Lord Larken."

Larken? Not Mr. Ryder. Tally let out a breath she felt as if she'd been holding for hours, relief in her every bone.

But not so Dash. He sat up, his brows furrowed together. "Larken? No, you must have it wrong. Larken is—"

"You know him?" Tally asked.

"Yes. He's a friend. At least I thought he was." Dash got up and paced back and forth before the fireplace, then paused. "Is Lady John positive? It's Larken they've sent?"

Tarleton nodded.

Tally looked from one man to another. "But if it is how you say, and this Larken is a friend—"

Dash paced anew. "You don't understand. Larken is no mere agent. He's the one they send when there can't be any mistakes. When it must look like an accident or so that there is nothing left to leave a trail. He's the most determined, dangerous man I've ever met." He raked his hands through his hair. "Don't you remember—he was there the night I was arrested—"

"He was?" Tally asked, shocked to discover that she'd had seen him before—or at the least been in the same room. Yet even that, it was Dash's description of him, for it left her utterly rattled.

"He's the most determined, dangerous man I've ever met."

"Yes," insisted Dash. "It was his pistol your sister took and shot me with."

That night was such a blur of memories, and for the life of her, Tally couldn't recall the man, so worried had she been for Felicity and moreover, Pippin, who had been in the line of fire.

"That is why I took you in my arms," he said to Pippin. "I knew Larken wouldn't shoot. Not you. Not me. Oh, I know much of what he's done—on the Continent, for that wretched Pymm—and what he's capable of doing, but I never thought . . ."

"But this is good, isn't it?" Pippin asked, rising to her feet as well. "And if he is, as you say, a friend, then he can't possibly want to . . ." She couldn't finish the sentence.

. . . kill you.

Sadly, Dash shook his head. "The man I knew, the one I called friend a few years ago, before the entire world plunged into this mad war and made us enemies, *he* wouldn't have . . . but the man I saw last winter, the man who was recalled home, isn't the same person I knew."

"How can that be?" Pippin asked. "He's your friend. You've saved him, haven't you?"

This time Dash grinned. "Aye. Several times." Then he laughed. "Plucked him off a beach near Le Havre once with half the French army after him. Nearly got shot myself trying to get him through the surf." His eyes glittered as if the memory was that of a fine picnic, but then just as quickly they clouded over and he sighed. "But none of that matters now . . ."

"But friendship," Pippin insisted. "His life—"

"Oh, Circe, my dear, good-hearted Circe," Dash said, reaching out and toying with a strand of her hair. "War can do that to a man. One who's been asked to do too much. Things he can't take back or ever forget." He looked down at his boots and shook his head. "That is the man they've sent. Why, he's feared by even his own."

Pippin sank down into the sofa, as pale as her muslin gown, and Dash stalked back and forth across the room.

Tally's gaze followed Dash's haphazard pacing. "You know what he looks like? You could describe him for us, couldn't you?" Inside she was making her own sort of plea. *Please say he's fair and blue-eyed. Slight of build and a jovial sort.*

Describe anyone but . . .

"He'll be disguised," Dash said. "The man is capable of being anyone. A Swiss jeweler, a Portuguese banker, even a priest." He paused. "His eyes. You'll not miss his eyes. Black as night. Like looking into the heart of the devil."

Tally swayed, barely able to listen to the rest of what Dash was saying. *Black as night.*

"Teased him once about 'em," he joked. "We were both drunk, quite pissed actually, and I asked him if he had some Spanish blood to him or if his mother had been a gypsy. Blackened my eye, the ruddy bastard. But I never poked fun at his honor again. Takes it quite seriously. Father was tangled up in some disgrace and Temple said Larken had nearly gotten himself killed ten times over to restore his family's honor. 'Twas what made him so dangerous, so ruthless."

"He's here," Tally whispered. And once she stopped trembling, she managed to repeat it. This time louder. "Lord Larken is already here." Everyone turned to her. " 'Tis Mr. Ryder, he's Larken, come disguised."

Dash's words rattled about inside her like a discordant melody. *Dangerous. Go to any length.*

Even seduce me to gain my confidence, she guessed. *And I nearly gave in.* She couldn't stop the shaking that ran through her.

"Tally, you can't be certain—" Pippin argued.

"His eyes, Pippin, his eyes." Tally's hands fisted at her sides. "You saw them. You know I'm right. I said as much—from the first moment I met him, something wasn't right."

That wasn't entirely the truth, it was more that there was something *too* right about him. Something beneath his vicarly veneer that called to a dangerous vein in Tally's heart.

"Mr. Jones, dare we wait until tomorrow?" she asked, panic pushing her to see this over, and quickly.

"I don't see how we can do it earlier," Tarleton said. "Still have to get Aramintha in and my horses are demmed tired. But tomorrow night it must be and no later."

"So soon?" Pippin said, as if the plans were finally registering with her. "And then what? How can you ask me to wait again? I cannot, Dash. I cannot."

"But you must." He returned to the sofa and tried to cheer her spirits. "Think of this as just another act in your play."

"Yes, Pippin," Tally added. "This will give us time to finish *Helene*."

But Pippin was too lost in her own misery to listen.

Yet even as she tried to cheer her cousin, something about the mention of their play tugged at Tally. She glanced at the empty spot on her desk and then uttered a thick curse in Russian. Words that would have curled the hair of every matron in London— that is, if they spoke the language.

The vehemence behind her exclamation was enough to bring Pippin out of her misery. "What is it, Tally?"

"Our play. Our foolish, ridiculous play!" she complained, rising and rushing to her desk, seeing one manuscript but not the other. "I gave Mr. Ryder—oh, drat, I mean Lord Larken—our play."

"I thought you said he wanted to read it," Pippin replied.

"Yes, *Tears of Helene.* But oh, Pippin, I've done something dreadful." She turned from the desk, her hands knotting into her skirt. "In my haste, I gave him the wrong play. Lord Larken has *Lady Persephone's Perilous Affair.* He has our entire plot and plan on his nightstand."

Miss Browne stood in the middle of the large parlor holding court as if she were royalty.

"I truly loathe her," Tally complained in an aside to Pippin, who stood beside her. After dinner, the entire assemblage of guests had arrived in this stately room for an evening of light entertainment. The doors to the garden were open and twilight gathered outside, leaving the roses and rich lawns in romantic half-light.

Felicity's party now included not only the family, the Elsfords, and the Brownes, but also Lord Cranwich, Sir Robert Foxley, and Lord Grimston, a trio known for their love of sport, excellent lineages and, most important, fine estates with good incomes. How Felicity had managed to induce them to come, Tally couldn't imagine, but she suspected that her sister intended Sir Robert, who sat next to Cranwich on the settee, for one of the Elsford sisters, and either Cranwich or Grimston for Miss Browne.

Most likely because their holdings were close to

the Scottish border, about as far as one could get from Felicity's domain in Sussex.

Mr. Jones, under his guise as Pippin's cousin Mr. Hartwell, sat in the corner trying to entertain a less than amused Lady Geneva.

Over by the pianoforte, leafing through the music sheets with the youngest Miss Elsford at his side, stood Lord Boyce, a shy sort of fellow who had warranted a starred entry in the *Bachelor Chronicles* for his gentle disposition and good income.

And the final bachelor was Brent, Viscount Gossett, who stood on the other side of the room with his gaze cast on one lady, and one lady only. He came from a line as old as the Domesday record, and Tally knew exactly whom he was slated for: Pippin. Not that the viscount appeared to mind, for his interest hadn't moved away from her cousin all night.

And then there was Mr. Ryder. Or rather, Lord Larken. Tally sighed, unable to look at him and not feel . . . guilt mostly, for even though she knew who and what he was, she couldn't shake her desire for him.

"You asked how it is that *Maman* and I are still in England, what with our countries at war, did you not, Lord Cranwich?" Miss Browne asked the man seated before her on the couch.

"Yes, Miss Browne, you were saying at dinner that it was a most thrilling tale."

"It is, if I may modestly say." The chit preened and posed a bit, waiting for the prompt from her audience to begin.

Pippin leaned over and whispered, "*Modestly*! I daresay she'd be hard-pressed to spell the word."

Tally laughed out loud, and then covered her gaff by coughing and making a great show of pulling a handkerchief out of her sleeve.

"Do tell us, Miss Browne," Lord Grimston called out. "I love a good adventure."

The girl smiled at him, favoring him with a coy glance before she began. "You see, we had first set out for Havana on a British ship with every intention of transferring there to a ship bound for an American port."

"If they could get past the English blockades, that is," Sir Robert boasted.

Miss Browne's eyes narrowed, but her smile never wavered, "Yes, quite," she replied. "However, our difficulties arose shortly after we left London . . . "

Tally drew a deep breath and glanced around the room, caring not a whit about the girl's prattling tale, only to find her attention pulled in Lord Larken's direction.

She cursed silently in Russian and dragged her gaze toward a vase on the mantel.

". . . and can you imagine our despair when the captain struck the colors and surrendered to the other ship?" Miss Browne was saying. "*Maman* and I were in despair over our fate."

"What is she going on about?" Tally whispered to Pippin.

"Her ship was stopped at sea," she replied, her gaze fixed on the door, her thoughts most likely occupied with the plan for tomorrow.

"Turkish pirates?" Tally suggested, nudging her cousin in hopes of cheering her up.

"Oh, how I wish," Pippin said. "Do you think it is too late to hire some?"

"Unfortunately so," Tally replied in a soft whisper, shifting from one foot to another. "I need to find a way out of here and get upstairs and get our play out of his room."

Pippin nodded in agreement.

Mr. Jones had tried earlier to slip into Lord Larken's room, but the man had locked his door. A locked door would present no problem to Tally, however. Still, there was no leaving with Lord Larken's ever watchful gaze upon her.

From the settee, Lord Grimston sat up, blustering as he went. "Don't tell us you were left to fend for yourselves against this bounder?"

"Yes, Miss Browne," Lord Cranwich added, always in competition with his good friend. "However did you escape?"

"You must remember, we are American and luckily it was an American privateer who captured the ship."

Grimston guffawed and coughed over this. "Luck? Those bastards—if you'll excuse me for saying so—are no better than gutter rats. Take that Dashwood fellow—"

"Dashwell," Cranwich corrected.

"Is it, now? Well, that Dashwell devil then. There's a ruddy fellow who would have sold you to the East Indies and slept well with his pouch of gold under his pillow."

"Harrumph!" Pippin sputtered and would have

moved forward to defend her lover, but Tally caught her by the arm.

After a slight shake of her head, Tally whispered, "Remember, we are being watched."

Pippin settled back, but with a look that said she wished she could sell Lord Grimston to Eastern traders.

"But my lord," Miss Browne said, her voice tinged with a triumph that caught Tally's attention and rang with a malevolent note that could only spell ill for them all. "It *was* Captain Dashwell who took us captive."

Chapter 11

*E*very conversation in the room stopped and nearly all eyes pointed at Miss Browne. Why, she couldn't have outdone herself with anything less than the announcement that she was carrying Prinny's bastard.

But Tally's attention was drawn elsewhere, for utterly different reasons.

The moment the overblown American had made her brazen speech, Tally had immediately turned her gaze toward Lord Larken and to her shock found him not gaping at Miss Browne like the rest of the room, but studying the corner where she and Pippin stood.

More to the point, gauging Pippin's reaction.

The calculated light behind his spectacles and the measuring weight of his glance sent a chill down Tally's spine.

What was it Dash had said? Oh, yes.

". . . the Larken who was recalled home isn't the same man I knew. War can do that to a man . . . He's the most determined, dangerous man I've ever met."

She shivered and glanced away from him, but not for long, her gaze flitting back toward him. Wasn't that exactly how she had seen him the first moment she'd clapped her eyes on him?

Darkly dangerous? Mercurial? A man of mystery and deception?

Was the man who'd awkwardly given her a hastily picked handful of blossoms in the meadow today, truly capable of killing Dash or anyone else who stood in his way?

She shivered, and forced her gaze back to Miss Browne, and listened as the girl regaled one and all with her story.

"Captain Dashwell is quite infamous as you all know, as evidenced by his terrible treatment of my poor, dear friend, Lady Philippa, taking her hostage last winter at the ball where she was very nearly shot." Miss Browne paused and struck a tragic pose, but lest anyone's attention turn toward Pippin and not stay riveted to her, she continued quickly. "But I can tell you quite a different story about the man, for *Maman* and I spent an entire sennight aboard his ship, and he quite lived up to his name, for he is a *dashing* sort of man."

She smiled at her quaint play on words, the Misses Elsfords sighing in unison, while their mother, Felicity, and the rest of the older women in the room frowned with disapproval.

Not so Pippin. Tally glanced over to find every bit of color had drained from her cousin's cheeks.

"But Miss Browne," the eldest Miss Elsford said, "he didn't, he wouldn't have . . ." She blushed a bright pink and looked as if she wished she'd never opened her mouth.

"Of course not!" Miss Browne exclaimed. "Being an honorable man—"

Grimston snorted, and Tally would have done so as well, if Miss Emery hadn't spent three years drilling it into her students that "ladies never snuffle about like hogs."

Miss Browne ignored him. "Captain Dashwell would never do anything untoward to me. He treated me as a lady. He said he would rather surrender to the British than compromise his principals to use any woman thusly. He once called me his 'Circe'—"

Pippin gasped, her hands covering her mouth, and Tally thought her cousin was going to be sick right there and then, but her sound of astonishment went unnoticed for it was well covered by another chorus of sighs from the Misses Elsford.

Damn Dash, Tally thought. Tossing about endearments like ha'pennies to urchins. She didn't dare look at Pippin, but she could feel her cousin's outrage, her anger. But whether it was at Miss Browne or Dash, Tally didn't know.

Miss Browne preened a bit more. "When we came within sight of the English coastline, he set us ashore in the dark of night, with all our belongings and even some gold to see us safely back to London. I daresay I will never forget his kindness as he handed us up onto that lonely beach . . . " Her hand went to her lips for a moment, as if recalling something so private, so intimate, she didn't dare reveal it.

Oh, great heavens, Tally thought. *If Pippin isn't going to be sick, then I am.*

"How it distresses me so to think of him being hunted, like an animal," Miss Browne said, shaking her head.

Beside her, Pippin swayed, as if about to faint, but this time it was Lord Gossett who intervened and cut Miss Browne off before she could add to her story.

Or rather, embellish it further.

"Miss Mary, did you not say at dinner you would be delighted to play for all of us, so we could have some dancing?"

The younger Miss Elsford glanced up at the viscount, a bit befuddled. "Why yes, my lord, I did offer."

"Excellent!" he said, crossing the room in long strides, his tall, elegant figure drawing all eyes away from Miss Browne. "And Lady Philippa, I believe you promised me the first dance, did you not?" He held out his hand to her.

"I don't believe I—" Pippin began to say, that is until Tally prodded her.

"Appearances," she reminded her with a low whisper.

Pippin shot her an aggrieved look, but nonetheless took Lord Gossett's hand, slipping her slim gloved fingers into his broad grasp and favoring him with a smile. "How kind you are, my lord, to remember."

"It appeared you needed a diversion," he said softly, so that no one else could hear him.

Pippin blushed, putting some color back in her cheeks, while Tally took another look at the viscount and considered him closely. He'd seen Pippin's distress and turned the tables on Miss Browne.

Honorable *and* kind, Tally thought as he led Pippin out to dance and waved at the other gentlemen to claim their partners. As he turned to take both Pippin's hands, he smiled at her, and Tally thought him quite handsome.

How unfortunate Pippin's heart was already taken, for the viscount would have made her an excellent husband.

Egads! Whatever was she thinking? Tally shook her head. Matchmaking, indeed! She was getting as addled as Felicity.

Miss Mary, with the able Lord Boyce hovering at her shoulder and turning pages for her, struck up a merry tune.

Sir Robert sought the elder Miss Elsford's hand, while Grimston and Cranwich jockeyed for Miss Browne's favor, with Grimston winning the match—he was an earl to Lord Cranwich's mere barony. Amiable in defeat and unwilling to be left out of the field, Cranwich turned and asked Lady Standon to dance.

Tally dared a glance over at Mr. Ryder, only to find Felicity nodding at her.

Get over here, her sister was saying silently.

Tally smiled and shook her head slightly. *Not for your life.*

What? And have her sister foist the *faux* Mr. Ryder on her as a dancing partner? No, she was going to maintain her cowardly vigil over here in this corner, thank you very much.

Yet when she looked again, it was to find her sister

beside her, taking her by the hand and leading her over to Lady Charles and Mr. Ryder. "You looked so lonely over there, Thalia," Felicity said sweetly. But her use of Tally's full name belied that—she only called her "Thalia" when she was truly and thoroughly vexed.

Tally sighed and resisted the urge to bolt from her sister's grasp, for there was too much at stake over the next day to raise Felicity's ire. "I daresay I was quite content," she offered. "But thank you for taking me under your wing, dear sister."

"Mr. Ryder was just regaling us with tales of . . . of . . . " Felicity faltered and it was obvious she hadn't been listening to a word the man was saying.

"Ornithology," he offered. "The study of birds. I saw a most engaging lark this afternoon. Why it was so unique—"

"Perhaps you would like to dance, Mr. Ryder?" Felicity suggested. "I know my sister would be delighted to favor you with her company."

Tally pasted a smile on her face, but at the same time, pinched her sister under her arm. *Hard.*

"I do not approve of such intimate dancing, Your Grace," he said.

"You don't approve—" Felicity began.

Suddenly Tally glanced up. Perhaps Felicity was the key to all this. "I didn't think a man of your convictions would," she said, jumping into the discussion, "given your fondness for *Fordyce* and all."

"*Fordyce*?!" Felicity sputtered, glancing first at her sister and then Mr. Ryder.

"Yes, didn't you know?" Tally asked her. "Mr.

Ryder plans on giving a lengthy sermon from *Fordyce* on Sunday, don't you, sir?"

Lady Charles's lips twitched and she covered her mouth to keep from laughing out loud.

"Mr. Ryder, I do believe I've made an error in judgment—" Felicity began, looking ready to show him the door. Hollindrake cousin or not.

Out of the house and out of our way, Tally wanted to crow. *Find your way out of this wrinkle, Lord Larken*, she thought, as she glanced up at him, not opposed to letting a sly smile tip her lips.

But the man hadn't been one of the Foreign Office's most successful agents for nothing.

"As have I, Your Grace," Mr. Ryder said. "I fear I should never have come down for dinner." He wavered on his feet and to Tally's amazement the man actually managed to look ill.

And Felicity fell for it, leaning forward to steady him.

Tally stood stock-still, with her arms folded across her chest. Oh, the wretched devil! Of all the . . .

"Dear heavens," he managed to say faintly. "I fear I must beg your indulgence and allow me to retire for the night. My dyspepsia. I am quite overtaken."

"Mr. Ryder, no!" Felicity said, as the man looked about to faint. "Please, please, sir, go on upstairs. I shall make your excuses."

He brightened a little. "Where I will redeem myself to your kind regard by resting up for the rigors of tomorrow."

"When there will be dancing," Tally offered, completely unrepentant and for which she received a pinch back from her sister.

"Good evening, ladies," he said, bowing off-kilter and making a course through the dancers that nearly upended the eldest Miss Elsford.

"Oh, heavens, what am I to do?" Felicity moaned as he left the room.

"Invite more gentlemen," Lady Charles suggested, leaving the sisters to seek out the company of her son.

"Tally, he is awful! He's been going on and on about . . . oh, what it was I can't recall."

"Ornithology," Tally reminded her, though she was only half-listening, for she was busy watching Mr. Ryder going up the stairs two at a time—rather agile for a man with delicate digestion. Too bad his illness was as feigned as the rest of him.

"Ornithology, indeed! Dreadful subject!" Felicity said with a shudder. "And now to discover that he's dyspeptic! Why, if it becomes known I tried to match Miss DeFisser with such a wretched, dull man, I will be ruined. We'll all be ruined."

"True enough," Tally said with a sad shake of her head. "Too bad he's just slightly ill and not completely overcome."

Felicity froze. For it wasn't hard to see that her sister was thinking exactly what she was. "You aren't suggesting—"

"Just a slight illness," Tally said, holding up her fingers just an inch apart. Hadn't Nanny Brigid done the same thing to their father when he'd been reassigned to the Russian court? It had kept them trapped at the Viennese court for nearly an extra fortnight.

"He's Hollindrake's cousin," she protested, but not

as vehemently as someone who was completely opposed to the idea. "I can't deliberately—"

"He's a very distant cousin," Tally reminded her. *How distant, you have no idea.*

Felicity shook her head. "It would be wrong. I couldn't."

But Tally knew exactly what that meant. "But I could."

"If you don't mind . . ." Felicity rushed to say. "The blue packets of powders will give him just a slight case of the gripes, Tally. But only two packets, nothing more."

"Of course. I'll do it right now, before anyone questions a thing," Tally assured her, going to move past her sister, her eyes already set on the staircase.

But Felicity stopped her. "Don't mistake the packets. The other ones are for my megrims. I would hate for you to give him those. Why if he drank too much, he'd sleep right through the entire house party."

"Oh, don't worry," Tally told her. "I have no intention of making a mistake."

Larken suspected that if Dashwell was anywhere, he was in the suite of rooms shared by Miss Langley, Lady Philippa and the as yet unseen Aunt Aramintha. He had his suspicions about this "Aunt Minty" of theirs. He moved silently down the hall toward the wing where their chambers were, smiling to himself that the duchess would keep her sister and cousin occupied downstairs so he could . . .

Eliminate the man and then get the hell out of here, he

told himself, steeling his gut against the pang of guilt that prodded him.

Leave and never look back.

Not even to see Miss Langley again.

Larken stumbled over the edge of the carpet. His clumsiness, he vowed, wasn't over that blue-eyed, troublesome romp, but because the hallway wasn't well lit. Yes, that was the problem.

Miss Langley, indeed! With her plays, and sketching, and curiosity and travels . . . She'd drive a man mad.

Can you imagine seeing Venice with her at your side? Or Lisbon? Being stuck listening to her as she prattled on in awe at some crumbling ruin, smiling with joy just for being there to share the sight with someone who . . .

. . . who loved it as much as she did.

He shook such fancies aside. Trying to convince himself that he found her chatter maddening.

But the truth was, he didn't.

She was like a breath of spring cutting a swath through his dark existence. She saw the world with the eyes of youth and innocence, carried sunlight into the dark reaches of his heart. He closed his eyes and tried yet again, as he'd done for months, mayhap years, to blot out the nightmares, his years of service. The events and deeds that he'd tamped down inside himself so tightly, he feared the day they'd break free and would rule his mind.

The prison in Paris. The stench of the cells. The haunted, desperate faces of the men inside them. Knowing he could only free one of them.

The look on the fat Spaniard—the one who'd been

selling English secrets to the French—just before he'd died.

Finding his contact in Lyon dead. Her throat cut—and that had been the only merciful part of her death—her gown in ribbons and her blood everywhere else.

Dash's face, his expression when he realizes you've found him, not as a friend, but as his deadliest and final foe . . .

That was his existence. His nightmares. Not wildflowers and fanciful ruins.

But today . . . remember this afternoon, how it had felt. How for a time, with her at your side, you'd forgotten.

Forgotten his duty. His honor. His obligations.

There would be no spring for him. There couldn't be, he told himself.

Larken drew out the pistol he had tucked inside his boot, and began moving silently down the hall toward their door. With everyone downstairs, that left only Dashwell, alone in the room.

He'd . . . he'd eliminate . . . Larken stumbled yet again over the point of his being here.

Damn it, he'd finish Dashwell off, toss his body out the window where he could retrieve it easily, and no one would be the wiser.

Drawing a steadying breath, he nodded at this simple plan. What could Miss Langley and Lady Philippa do once they discovered Dashwell missing? Raise an alarm that their illicit guest had met with foul play?

He smiled to himself, yet felt none of his usual satisfaction over outwitting an adversary, his steps leaden, his heels dragging as if he were being towed into Almack's instead of toward a duty that was his and his alone.

Oh, there was Pymm's promise of seeing his father's name cleared, but hadn't Larken heard that promise before? Empty promises and duty. As empty as his soul.

Perhaps it was just that. That this had become so routine to him, that a man's life meant nothing more than duty, that he'd become as cold and unfeeling as the bitch who'd killed his father.

Suddenly the carpet beneath his feet was no longer some Turkish treasure but cobblestones, and the air murky with the thick scent of the Seine.

"How can you kill me, Aurora, when we have shared so much?"

"What have we shared but time, you fool?"

"You cannot kill me, the child . . ."

Larken froze and shook his head, for it wasn't the voices in his head that haunted him, but something else. Footsteps coming from behind, and he whirled around, ready to shoot.

"Goodness gracious, Mr. Ryder, what are you thinking?" Tally exclaimed, shocked to find her quarry aiming a gun at her. "Is that a pistol?"

The man before her was hardly the bird-loving, bird-witted fool Felicity had been bemoaning just a short time earlier. Here was the formidable Lord Larken Dash had warned them of.

And as much as she was terrified right down to her slippers that he was about to shoot her, there was something dangerously thrilling about the murderous look in his eyes.

Tally shivered, and for all the wrong reasons. "Sir, would you please put that down," she said, nodding at the pistol. "I am certainly no cracksman here to take the silver."

He finally came out of the trance he seemed to be in and glanced first at her, and then at the pistol in his hand. "Oh, dear, oh, my. I fear you startled me, Miss Langley," he managed, retreating into the guise of Mr. Ryder, bumbling vicar, his arm going limp and the pistol dropping to his side.

But it was too late. She'd seen him. Seen right through him. To the dark, dangerous man behind the collar.

"Startled you, sir? Whom did you expect to find?" she asked, her heart beating wildly. She should despise him. Hate him for what he'd been sent to do, was so willing to do.

But something about Dash's description reached past that.

". . . the Larken who was recalled home isn't the same man I knew. War can do that to a man. One who's been asked to do too much. Things he can't take back or ever forget . . ."

But what if Lord Larken could? a gentle voice nudged at Tally. *What if he could find a way out of the darkness surrounding him?*

"I fear all this talk of Captain Dashwell has me in a state," he was saying.

I imagine it does. "How so?" she asked instead.

"He's a murderous fiend, I hear, and as I was coming upstairs, I thought I heard someone—"

"All the way down here?" she asked, glancing in

the direction of the stairs well behind her and the long hall that led to where they stood. "How odd. And whyever would you assume it was Captain Dashwell?"

He heaved a sigh and looked ever so downcast. "I fear there was talk . . ."

Really, he was quite good at what he did, Tally conceded. If he ever lost his position with the Foreign Office, she would recommend him to Mr. Thurber. He'd make a great actor.

"Talk?" she prompted.

"At dinner," he added, then lowered his voice. "As to Lady Philippa and her association with that American. That he may be coming here to find her."

Tally was no poor thespian either. She laughed, loud and thoroughly. "Captain Dashwell? In search of my cousin? Hiding in our rooms?" She reached out and leaned against the wall. "Mr. Ryder, I fear more than your dyspepsia is out of order."

"I suppose when you put it that way, it does sound foolish," he said, looking more aggravated than embarrassed.

Tally let that bit of success go to her head, a feeling of confidence nudging her into deeper waters. She pushed off the wall and stepped closer to him, to this dangerous man who had her heart pounding in her chest.

"Would you like to come in my room and search it?" she offered, tossing him the look that Nanny Jamilla had said would make a man, your one true love, follow you to the ends of the earth.

And for a moment, for a whisper of a second, she

thought he might . . . and to her shock, her body quaked with unmet needs, desires he'd awakened in the garden.

Had it been just last night? No, for it seemed like a lifetime ago, and that made the ache left by his passionate touch only more piercing.

Kiss me, sir, she wanted to whisper. *Kiss me and take me inside my room. Undo me. Uncover me.*

He seemed to hear her silent plea, for his hand reached out and took hers, pulling her slowly, gently closer to him.

But his careful touch belied the truth. She was tempting the very devil.

"Your room, Miss Langley? Whatever mischief would I find in there?" he said, his head dipping down as he whispered the words over her ears, his breath like a kiss, teasing her senses.

She teetered on her heels, and he tightened his grasp, drew in his web, as he brought her closer still.

When she glanced up at him, she found his gaze masked by those wretched spectacles he wore. Without thinking, she reached up and took them off, setting them down on the table beside her door.

Make love to me through the night. I care not who you are.

Nor I you, his dark eyes seemed to say as he leaned closer, about to . . .

"Uh, hum," came the jolting sound from behind them. "Miss, sir, I've brought the tea you requested," Claver intoned from the end of the hall, maintaining his discrete distance as they made themselves more . . . respectable.

Mr. Ryder released her as if she'd grown as hot as

a fire iron, and Tally felt her color rise from her toes to her cheeks.

And it wasn't just from being caught thusly, but from the realization of what she'd been thinking . . . willing to do. . .

Betray Pippin. Twice now. She'd let him nearly seduce her. And in this same wretched spot. She'd been willing to give herself to this man in exchange for one dangerous night in his arms. And at what a price.

"Claver?" Mr. Ryder asked, backing away from her.

"I brought your tea, sir," the valet replied.

"Tea? I didn't order—"

Tally took a deep breath. There was no escaping what needed to be done now. "I ordered the tea. Or rather my sister did. For your health, sir."

There was a slight sound from him, rather like a groan, but she knew she had him caught in the crosshairs.

Would the vicar protest? She thought not. But Lord Larken, with his quarry in sight, might continue to put up a bit of a fight.

So she put up a little one of her own. "It is a brew our Nanny Brigid was famous for—why, it cured the Archduke's dyspepsia, and Her Grace thought it might aid you. I gave it to Claver so you wouldn't suffer any longer than necessary from your distress."

"I don't think—"

Tally didn't let him finish, for she had a weapon on her side not even he could boast. "I daresay if Claver reports back that you didn't drink at least two cups, you'll find my sister up here spoon-feeding you back to health."

And neither of us wants that, Tally thought. *For Felicity will know immediately I've given you the wrong packets.*

He glanced first at her, then at her door beyond, before acknowledging her check to his latest sally. "My apologies, for earlier, Miss Langley," he murmured. "I seem to forget myself around you."

This took Tally entirely aback as she watched him walk down the hall, toward a determined Claver and a fate he had no idea awaited him.

Much worse, she felt a twinge of guilt. Not that she was about to poison him. No, not that little sin.

But because it was the first time he'd honestly revealed something about himself to her.

I seem to forget myself around you.

A truth they shared.

Chapter 12

Larken got to his room, his anger over his failure held in tight check. Barely.

Behind him, Claver fluttered about, having placed the tea tray on the table, and now setting the room to rights and fussing over "Mr. Ryder's ill health" and "Her Grace's kind and thoughtful regard."

"Sir, how would you like your tea?" the man offered, the teapot in hand, poised over the delicate cup.

Poured over Miss Langley's pert head, was his first thought. "I really don't—"

This was met with a stubborn *tsk-tsk*, and a muttered, "Her Grace's benevolent concern" and so Larken had no choice but to nod at the man to pour the demmed witch's brew.

No wonder Hollindrake refused to suffer this fellow's company.

"One lump or two?" Claver asked, in that perfectly ingratiating valet's tone of his that was getting on Larken's nerves more than Miss Langley's constant interference.

No, nothing could rank higher than the way that chit seemed to knock the wind from his sails and plans with her wide blue eyes and the flirtatious tip of her lips.

A pair of very kissable lips.

Ones he'd been about to plunder thoroughly before Claver's untimely arrival. He didn't know if he should thank the man or toss him out the window.

"Sir?" the man asked, sugar tongs in hand and innocently unaware of his tenuous fate. "How many lumps?"

"Two," he said, considering the time in his childhood when Aunt Edith had dosed him with some perfectly wretched posset—the bitter concoction had curdled his stomach for a week.

And considering the Duchess of Hollindrake was coming in at a close second to Aunt Edith, he probably should have asked for a third lump.

Instead he paced about the floor, his need for action driving him mad, even as Claver gently stirred the tea, placed the cup perfectly on the saucer, and then nodded toward the bed.

"Why not take some rest, sir? Have your tea, and I am certain you will be fit come morning."

Larken suspected the only way to be rid of the fellow was to do as he was told, so he put himself atop the bed, tried to look properly relaxed and gulped down the tea in three hasty swigs.

And even as the cup rattled down in its saucer,

there was Claver, pot in hand, pouring a second cup. "Her Grace said two cups should remedy what ails you."

Dashwell dead and a night with a willing wench beneath him would be more to his liking, but he wasn't about to tell poor Claver that.

Larken took the second cup and tossed it down in all haste, handing it back to the astonished valet. "That is all, Claver. You can tell Her Grace I shall be a new man in the morning."

Just after I remove an unwanted guest from her house—if he's even here—and I'm well on my way back to London.

However, Claver didn't move. "Shall I fetch the chamber pot, sir? In case your bowels—"

"Yes, yes," Larken told him, completely unused to being fussed over, let alone having someone so involved in his life. Demmit, he thought as Claver rushed to bring the porcelain pot close enough for an invalid. He wasn't going to get rid of Hollindrake's underworked valet until he gave the man something of substance to do—so he waved at the new jacket the tailor had done up, as well as a wrinkled cravat. "Can you give that a brushing and the cloth a press? I am going to just"—he glanced around for something solitary to do—"read Miss Langley's play until I fall asleep," he said, plucking it up from the side table and making a great show of settling in. "I fear it shan't take long." He even yawned for good measure.

"Ah, excellent idea, sir," Claver said, catching up the coat and throwing it over one arm. "I'll leave the tea in case you have need for more."

The only thing he was going to do was drain the pot into the rose garden below.

"Good night, Claver," he said, trying to sound pleasant, so the man's report to the duchess would be favorable enough to keep her occupied elsewhere.

"Good night, sir. Pleasant dreams," the valet said as he closed the door.

Larken shook his head. "I wouldn't know what that would be like," he said softly, getting up and locking the door so he wouldn't have the well-meaning Claver disturbing him again.

He glanced back at the manuscript on the bed where he'd left it and was about to push it aside, when a sleepy sort of lethargy stole through his body.

Perhaps he'd settle down and read a line or two and then take another shot at finding Dashwell.

As he did just that, he glanced at the title and groaned. *Lady Persephone's Perilous Affair.*

Oh, good God. Some ridiculously tragic romance between an innocent miss and her ne'er-do-well guardian, most likely. And Temple and Pymm thought this pair of chits capable of masterminding the greatest prison break in English history?

Fool's errand is what this was, all it ever had been. He groaned again and opened the collection of pages about halfway through and started to read.

Setting: Dark prison yard. Captain Strike in chains, surrounded by guards.
LADY PERSEPHONE
Good sir, you are making a mistake. Captain Strike belongs to me and I shall not let you hang him.

CAPTAIN STRIKE

Don't do this, my love. I will not have you harmed.
    Flee now while you have a chance. My poor life
    is hardly worth yours.

LADY PERSEPHONE

I will not leave you to hang. For what is my life
    without you?

CAPTAIN OF THE GUARDS

Madam, get away from here. This is none of your
    concern.

LADY PERSEPHONE

I will not leave without my true love.

She draws a pistol from her red gown, as does the
    old hag, the carriage driver, and a large looming
    man who steps from the shadows.

CAPTAIN OF THE GUARDS

Are you all mad? This is treason. Put your weap-
    ons away before you come to harm.

LADY PERSEPHONE

If you think my fair face belies a steely nature, you
    are wrong, sir. The far greater crime would be
    my dear heart's death, for it shall be mine end
    as well. Now, good sir, surrender your prisoner
    or die.

Larken gaped at the pages before him. Why, he
could be reading Pymm's report of Dashwell's
escape . . . right down to the lady in red and the
substituted driver.

But how could Miss Langley and Lady Philippa
have written this, unless . . . unless . . . He blinked
and shook his head, for his thoughts were growing
more and more disconnected. Trying to concentrate,

he found he couldn't even remember where he was or what was he doing. The unfamiliar room . . . the odd buzzing inside his head.

Reading the top of the page he held in his hands, it all became clear again.

Lady Persephone's Perilous Affair, my ass, he thought, this was Dashwell's escape done up as a tidy little adventure.

And there were only two ways Miss Langley could have written this: one, if she'd obtained a copy of Pymm's private report, or two, if she'd been there.

Helped execute it, just as she had written it.

That realization brought him awake, fully awake, enough to realize that Temple had been right all along.

He went to get out of bed, but found his limbs unresponsive, and as he tried to move, he couldn't even remember why it was he needed to get out of bed. Larken glanced around the unfamiliar room until his gaze fell on the tea tray.

The tea.

Then it all came back to him and his anger roiled up inside him, betrayal piercing the heavy fog quickly overtaking him.

She'd drugged him. That dizzy Mayfair miss and her flirtatious glances. She'd outwitted him and even now was most likely seeing Dashwell and Lady Philippa spirited away.

Not that they'd get far—for between Hollindrake's extra footmen and Temple keeping watch, the estate was well surrounded.

Then again, so had been Marshalsea Prison . . .

Larken struggled to get out of the bed, to warn

Temple, to reveal all to Hollindrake, but it was too late, the drug had him in its thrall, his limbs unresponsive, his lids refusing to open.

Yet as the darkness descended upon him, he clung to one thought. *Of making her pay . . .*

Sometime well after midnight, Tally crept down the hall toward Lord Larken's room. The house was quiet now, as the dancing had been a great success and all had sought their beds tired and sated from a day of travel and the vigorous playing of Miss Mary.

Soft snores arose from some chambers, while others were as still as graves.

Taking to heart her role as furtive spy, Tally had donned the black velvet to move down the halls, but left the high-heeled shoes behind, sticking to the surety of her bare feet padding across the carpet.

As she approached Larken's room, Tarleton slipped from the shadows of a long curtain. She nearly jumped out of her skin, for even though she knew he was near, she never would have suspected him of being *that* close.

"I've been here since that valet fellow herded our friend inside," Tarleton whispered.

"Thank you for doing this," Tally replied.

"My pleasure," he said, bowing elegantly. "Besides, your cousin and her companion are having a bit of a row." He shrugged. "That pretentious bit downstairs really sowed some sour oats."

"That she did," Tally agreed, thinking of Pippin's hurt over Dashwell's having been with with Sarah, calling her by the same pet name he used for her. *His Circe.* Even if it were nothing but tarradiddle—having come as it were from Miss Browne's boasting—it had, as Tarleton said, done its work.

He nodded at the door. "He hasn't gone nowhere, I assure you."

"Did he lock the door after Claver left?"

"Yes, but I ain't heard a peep out of him. What did you put in his tea?"

She just smiled, drew out her set of picks, and set to work, opening the door seconds later.

He bowed, a grin of pure appreciation on his pixie face. "Her ladyship said your were a most excellent rum dubber. Here I thought she was pulling my leg." He leaned over to admire her work. "If you ever decide to give up being a fine lady—"

"I think I am well on my way on that account," she replied softly, glancing into the room, which was mostly cast in shadows.

"So it seems," he whispered. "I'll stay and keep watch, while you finish this."

Tally shook her head. "No, sir, it will do our plans no good if I am caught and you are near at hand. Best you finish our work by seeing Aunt Minty put in place. This is my folly now."

He looked about to argue, when the mattress behind them creaked as the large figure atop it tossed and rolled.

Tally and Mr. Jones froze. Tally out of utter fear of discovery, and Mr. Jones from his long years of "assisting" in the family business of thievery.

Then Tally seized the opportunity and slipped inside the room, closing the door gently and turning the lock, cutting off any further discussion over the matter.

This was her mess to tidy up, and hers alone.

She'd come without a candle, and now she wished she had one, for the room was nearly pitch-black. As it was July, there were no embers in the fire to offer even a meager bit of light.

But outside the moon shone brightly, offering her the help she needed, so Tally carefully and slowly dragged one of the curtains open ever so slightly.

A thin beam of moonlight slanted across the room, ending at a large battered valise, which sat propped against the wall.

Tally glanced at it, a wicked suspicion coming over her. *I wonder what's inside that?*

Remembering her task at hand, to find her manuscript and get away before she was discovered, she set aside her curiosity. Though not for long, for all too quickly she discovered her prize atop the nightstand, the ruffled manuscript pages ripe for the plucking.

Oh, heavens, this is too easy, she thought, glancing first at the sleeping form of Mr. Ryder and then, much to her consternation, back at his valise.

Really, what harm would one small peep be? She bit her lips together. No, she shouldn't, but even so, she found herself tiptoeing over to the valise and kneeling beside it.

Taking a deep breath, she tried to open it, but found it locked.

She glanced over at the bed and said softly, "Now, now, Mr. Ryder, or rather, Lord Larken, what secrets do we have here?"

Retrieving her pick, it took her a bit to open the little lock on the valise, longer than the door had taken.

A rather complicated lock, my lord, she mused, taking another furtive glance at the bed.

Staring again at the valise, a rare bit of reason prodded her. *This is folly, Tally. Utter folly. Snatch up those pages and flee.*

But I must know the truth, I must know who this man is.

And not for the obvious reasons.

No, Tally had no desire to discover this man was some country vicar.

Felicity had her duke. Pippin her pirate.

And I want my spy . . . a dark, unpredictable man who will complicate my life, tangle up my heart and kiss me insensible . . .

Her hand slipped inside the valise and she felt around, only to find the bag empty.

She sat back on her heels, utterly disappointed. But not quite deterred. Looking at the bag again, this time she picked it up, and its weight gave away its secrets.

It was far too heavy to be empty.

She grinned and opened it again, this time her fingers examining the seams, pockets and finally the bottom. She remembered a case her father had, one that he used while traveling on diplomatic missions, one she and Felicity had often played with, carrying contraband sweets or trifles into their room hidden inside its secret compartments.

Closing her eyes, she concentrated until she found the subtle latch and tripped it open.

"Sir, you've been to Mr. Stennet's shop on Vigo Lane, haven't you?" she whispered. Well, she should have known as much from the Swiss lock.

Taking another deep breath, she opened the compartment. The first thing she touched was the cold steel of a pistol, the icy shock drawing her hand back as if she'd been shot. Again she glanced at the bed and this time drew an unsteady breath as her heart hammered wildly, just as it had when he'd aimed it at her earlier, the pistol a dark reminder of why he was here.

Gingerly nudging the pistol aside, she ventured deeper, her fingers fanning across a packet of papers tied with a ribbon. These she retrieved, quietly untying the ribbon.

Tally, you shouldn't snoop, Nanny Brigid had chided time and time again. *A nosy person is just a thief in disguise.*

Hardly a thief, Tally argued to herself. *I have no intention of taking anything. Just reading the words and carrying a bit of information away. Hardly my fault he left these so easily accessible.*

To someone with lock picks and a penchant for hidden compartments.

Even as she tiptoed over to the window to read by the light of the full moon outside, another of Nanny Brigid's lectures rang in her ears.

A light is still a light—even though the blind man cannot see it.

Tally pressed her lips together. Of course, she could always live by Nanny Tasha's favorite Russian proverb. *Unless caught, one is not a thief.*

She always did have a fondness for their practical Russian governess. So that settled the matter. She wasn't going to take the papers, and she had no intention of getting caught.

Leaning against the casement, she tipped the papers to take advantage of the light and started to sort out what she had found. And what a treasure trove she'd unearthed.

Identity papers. For an Esmond Ferrand, a French trader. Ambrogio Martinello, an Italian gemsmith. Benedicto Neves, a Portuguese banker. All stamped and ready to move a man easily from one country to another. A man such as Lord Larken.

Tally leaned her forehead against the cool glass and tried to breathe. Oh, what a dangerous tangle. Before her eyes she saw Pippin and Dash's lives hanging in the balance, and her heart broke as she realized what she must do.

Stop him. Thwart him. Outwit the king's most dangerous agent.

And in due course, he'd discover her deception and hate her for it. Despise her for her treason and treachery.

Barely breathing, she stowed his belongings back in the traveling bag and closed it, paying special attention to locking it precisely. Then she did what she should have done instead of snooping about— she gathered up the *Persephone* pages as quietly as she could, doing her best to ignore the momentary thrill of elation at having succeeded.

"No!" he growled in his sleep. "Stop now. I won't let you."

· She froze, the only thing moving was her heart hammering wildly in her chest. He hadn't come awake, had he?

She peeped over her shoulder at him through her

shuttered lashes and watched as he tossed again in the sheets, calling out as he went, "No, I say! You cannot do this! Father, be careful!"

Yet his eyes were closed and he tossed again, rolling over wildly, fighting the unseen demons who held him captive.

A nightmare! The man was having a nightmare. She would have sighed in relief, if it hadn't been the tormented twist of his face, the way he fought and twisted beneath the coverlet.

What have you done to him, Tally?

She turned back to the bed and moved closer to inspect, finding his forehead covered in a fine sheen of sweat and his lips set in a grim line.

He twisted again, calling out, "You've killed him! Killed him, I say."

Oh, dear, perhaps three packets of Felicity's megrim powders had been too much. She reached out, thinking to soothe his brow, when she spied something else in the bed. *Pages.*

Goodness, no! He'd been reading her play before he'd succumbed to the doctored tea.

Carefully, she managed to pluck one page after another from the bed, until she thought she had them all. That is until she spied one more, pinned beneath his elbow.

She weighed her choices—leaving it and hoping it was some innocuous scene, like Lady Persephone's and Captain Strike's wedding, or worrying that it was one of the more damning scenes.

Like the one where Lady Persephone and her friends free the pirate from his prison.

Taking a deep breath, she leaned over the bed, slid her hand along the mattress, and caught the corner of the page, ever so carefully pulling it free.

And it very nearly was, until suddenly his other hand snaked out from beneath the sheets and caught hold of her wrist.

"Did you think I wouldn't catch you?" he whispered in a voice filled with a dangerous and deadly rage.

The fog descended upon Larken like a dark, winged creature, enclosing him in her evil talons.

This is a dream, he tried to tell himself. *This isn't real*. And yet . . .

Beneath his feet the damp cobbles chilled him right through the soles of his boots. The mist cut him off from everything, the buildings around him, the surrounding city, even the night sky.

There was nothing but the thick fog, the dim haze of a lamp hanging from the post above him, and voices in the distance.

"Aurora, everything has changed," his father was saying.

Larken lurched toward the familiar sound of his voice. "Aurora," he'd called the woman. *Aurora*. Had he heard this name before? He didn't know. But he clung to it, desperate not to forget it.

Aurora. The name of his enemy. The name of the woman who'd changed the course of his life, his family's honor with her treachery. This clue sparkled before him and he clung to it as if he'd found a chest of gold.

"I will not help you," his father was telling her. "We are finished."

"This doesn't have to end, *mon chère*," she replied in purring French tones, words that lulled the senses, the soft seduction concealing the woman's true nature. True intent. "You still love me. You'll always love me."

"I can't. I won't. If I had known . . ." His father's struggle came through with every word.

Known what, Father? Of her deception? That she's a mistress of *L'Ordre du Lis Noir*? A sworn enemy of England?

Your enemy . . .

That you would never have fallen in love with her?

But there was something else in his father's anguished words that struck Larken. An underlying message that came to close to his own heart.

That you can't always choose those you love. And his father did love this Aurora. As much as he denied it, the elder Larken still wanted to love her . . . to trust her.

Don't! Larken tried to call out, fighting the fog that held him in its icy grasp. *Get away from her. Now!*

And yet it was too late, for the shot rang out, but this time instead of jerking him awake, it tore through the fog, opening a path for him to follow, to pursue his father's killer.

He didn't hesitate at this chance to catch her. For there she was before him, gowned in black and standing over his father's body.

"Aurora," he called to her.

She looked up at him, and for the first time, he

saw her face, the evil light of triumph in her eyes, the tilt of her nose, the thin twist of her lips. But it was just a glance, for she turned and fled, as fleet as a she-wolf.

So it's to be a hunt, is it, madame? He leapt after her, the fog plucking and pulling at him, trying to close in around him, yet he continued on, headlong into the darkness until there was nothing but an inky void before him.

Where the devil had she gone? He stopped and tried to listen for the fall of her feet, but all he heard was the whisper of words that were both disjointed and out of place. One voice in particular.

This is my folly now, a young woman whispered.

Folly. The word teased at him, tempted him to go in another direction.

Follow her, it teased.

Was it her? Aurora? He turned, pulled by something he couldn't see, but he could smell. Lilies of the valley.

The fog fell away as he stumbled forward, the cobbles giving way to a rich Aubusson carpet, which cradled his feet in luxury. Somehow he'd gone from the byways of Paris into a house, a vast mansion; and what had been a street was now a long gallery.

And at the end of it a woman stood poised by the window, papers in hand, a stricken look on her face. And when she glanced up and spied him, she turned to flee.

For a moment, Larken stilled. It wasn't *her*, his father's murderer, but someone else. How had he let Aurora slip away yet again? Still he couldn't shake his gaze from this lady before him.

Catch her. Don't let her get away. She holds the key to everything.

He struggled forward, his feet so clumsy it was hard to keep up with her as she dashed down the hall and turned swiftly around a corner. If he could just move a little more quickly, he could catch her.

He followed her headlong into a bedchamber, and just before she slipped through another doorway, he caught her hand.

Caught hold and refused to let go, tightening his grip around her narrow wrist, crushing her soft skin beneath his fingers.

"Did you think I wouldn't catch you?" he said.

It didn't matter that this wasn't Aurora, this was more important. He could feel it. His instincts came awake in startling clarity, as if he were now the wolf and she his prey.

She struggled against him, which only made him more furious, and so he hauled her closer until she slammed against him, the force carrying them back onto a bed. He rolled quickly, trapping her beneath him, catching her hands together and pinning them over her head. She continued to resist, bucking at him, but he held her fast, refusing to let go.

This is her. . .

But as her wild strands of hair fell away, it wasn't the dark-haired French mistress he expected, but a face he knew. . .

No, it couldn't be. Not her. Yet the curves beneath him said otherwise. He'd explored them before, desired her as he'd never wanted another woman.

The fog swirled around them, and it was only he and her, and the bed beneath them. He inhaled deeply, smelling her perfume and the unmistakable soft, sweet scent of her arousal.

Hunger and desire filled his veins. Oh, yes, and the overwhelming passion to take her. Bury himself inside her.

Larken shook his head, tried to climb out of this dream that held him captive. This was impossible. He didn't want *her*.

Liar.

And as if to make the point even further, his body responded so quickly it stunned him. His shaft hardened. He ached for her.

She's yours, Larken. Always has been. Take her. 'Tis naught but a dream.

A dream? It seemed so demmed real. He could feel the quick thud of her heart, feel the waves of her breathing washing over him like stormy waves rushing and falling.

"Release me. You know not what you do, my lord," she told him in an angry whisper. The wild light in her eyes said she knew exactly what he was considering.

Release her? Was she mad? Just when he'd finally found her? Captured her . . .

"This isn't what you think," she told him, as his hand reached down and pulled at her gown, tugging it up so he could trace his fingers over the smooth, sleek skin of her legs, her thighs.

Oh, God, how he wanted her. Desired her.

She sucked in a deep breath as his hand skimmed over her undergarment, reaching beneath the lace-trimmed silk and finding his way to the other silk—the curls beneath. So it seemed she felt the same fire, the same passions, for her hips swayed at his touch, invited him to continue his reckless exploration.

How wrong is this? he wondered. Was he as fool-hardy as his sire?

To desire a woman bent on his destruction.

"You're dreaming, sir," she whispered, now sounding more desperate than angry. "You must stop." But even as she said it, her hips arched up as he touched the folds hidden beneath her undergarments, slick and wet with need.

She desired him as much as he did her, for even now her fingers clung to his shoulders, and a soft moan escaped her lips as he teased her further.

He inhaled her perfume again, let his touch explore her, let the dark passion she invoked inside him come boiling to the surface and surrender to it every bit of caution he possessed.

A dream? If only every night held dreams such as this. Yet what else could it be but a dream?

"You know not what you do," she whispered, her struggles less anxious, her body moving with his.

"I disagree, my little minx. I know exactly what I am doing," he told her before his mouth crashed down and his lips covered hers.

When Lord Larken's lips covered hers, Tally knew she was lost. His kiss sent any bit of restraint she possessed scattering for higher ground.

Restraint had no place in his rakish bed. Not the way he touched her.

His tongue grazed her lips, inviting her to open up to his exploration, pleading with her to tangle with him, taste him, as he was enjoying her. And she did, God help her, she couldn't stop herself.

Every swipe of his tongue, the hard, unforgiving strength of his lips atop hers, the torture of his fingers on her sex, it was like being swept into the same sensuous dream that held him in its clutches.

He had an excuse for this scandal, but what was hers?

That she'd desired him from the first moment she'd clapped eyes on him?

Yes. Yes, she had.

He released her hands as if he could feel the change in her mood, that her fight had now turned to acquiescence, to a desire to burn with him.

His kiss deepened, and she clung to him, for it swept her along in this rising tide of madness. He kissed her thoroughly before breaking away and moving his mouth to her neck, her shoulder, down the front of her gown.

Beneath the heat of his lips, her skin burned. Her fingers raked through his hair, the wild tangle of dark strands falling to his shoulders.

He'd gone to sleep in only his shirt and breeches, and she brazenly ran her fingers beneath the linen and traced her nails over the solid wall of his chest, explored the crisp triangle of hair there, rough and tumble beneath her fingers.

Again he plied at her sex and it tightened and ached beneath his touch, her thighs quivering, tightening around his hand to hold him there. The torment as he stroked her made her breathless and restless and anxious all at once.

Was it possible to desire a man so completely? Want what only he could give you so utterly?

"Yes, yes," she whispered as he loosened her gown and pulled it from her shoulders, his lips following the velvet down, until he caught hold of a newly freed nipple.

Taking it in his mouth, he sucked on it until it hardened and pebbled beneath the rough pad of his tongue, sending a new frenzy of passion through her veins.

As her body awoke beneath this sweet torment, he continued to pull and pluck at her gown, her undergarments, her chemise, until she found herself naked.

She should have been embarrassed, but she rather felt like a Venus she'd once seen in Lord Hamilton's house in Naples, ripe and willing.

Far too willing.

And this rake knew it. For when he'd removed her clothes, he'd done the same to his, hastily divesting himself of his shirt and breeches, which now lay entwined and rumpled with hers on the floor, even as their naked bodies melded together.

Hard and long, the head of his member rode against her sex, his hips flexing as it went further and further between her legs.

For a moment, Tally panicked. If she did this, there was no going back.

Going back to what? she thought, as he caught hold of her hips and drew her closer, his fingers teasing a path down over her curls, her legs opening to him, the cleft wet with need, ready for him.

She'd longed for one night with a rake for as long as she could remember. It wasn't as if she'd ever cared for Society's conventions . . . all she'd ever desired was to follow her heart. Her passions. And this man seemed to know exactly how to unleash them.

Slick and ready, he slid himself over her, rubbing her with his shaft, kissing her deeply, touching her, and bringing her to the brink of need, tempting her to take this one last leap into the unknown.

"What do we do now, my little minx?" he whispered in a ragged voice.

As if there was any other choice, for her body thrummed with desire, her breath caught in her throat, even her heart seemed to still.

"Take me, Lord Larken," she told him, taking hold of his hips and pulling him closer.

Release me from this prison.

Chapter 13

$\mathscr{S}$omewhere in the madness of passion, Larken began to awaken.

Enough to realize that he was enveloped in no dream. That the lady beneath him was Miss Langley. *Tally.*

No, he mused. Her name should be Trouble.

But it was all too far gone by the time he'd found some semblance of reason, some inkling that he wasn't dreaming. Perhaps it was the heat of her skin. The taste of her as he sucked at her nipples. Hard, round pebbled peaks beneath his tongue that were as sweet as heaven.

The wet, slick feel of her cleft beneath her fingers. A slippery slope if ever there was one.

He shouldn't be doing this. Not with her. Treacherous, dangerous minx. And yet . . .

How he ached to be inside her, to drive himself

into her and stroke her until she cried out his name in her release.

Vaguely he thought of the consequences . . . that she was his enemy. Hollindrake's innocent sister-in-law.

He kissed her again, and her tongue danced wickedly over his.

Perhaps not so innocent, he mused, his shaft growing even harder as she touched him there. Stroked him, explored him as he had done to her. Had he taught her all this?

Of course he knew the answer . . . yes, he had. For the other night, she'd been tentative and shy, but that was now lost, ruined by his need for her.

Her fingers wound around him, running slowly over his head and down the shaft, sending need so rife he thought he was going to spill himself all over her hand.

Did she know what she was doing to him?

In a daze he glanced at her face and found a feline smile tipping her pert lips.

Oh, yes. She knew.

"What do we do now, my little minx?" he asked her, nestling her beneath him so he was just above her, poised to fill her.

She answered with a reckless whisper, her hips rocking upward. "Take me, Lord Larken." Her legs opened for him, wrapping around him, leaving him a course no man could refuse.

He didn't hesitate, and began his plundering, thrusting inside her, sweeping aside the barrier that told the truth.

She was an innocent.

Or rather she had been.

He heard her gasp, and covered her mouth with his, kissing away her surprise and stroking her slowly, gently to rekindle the fire.

Larken had made love to countless women— widows, courtesans, even a princess once, but never had any of them done this to him.

Unleashed a desire inside him that drove him to such heedless need. And with it came an unsettling notion that no woman would ever satisfy him again. No one but this one.

This impossible, treacherous minx. His Tally. His Trouble.

Her hips met his, and she clung to him. What she whispered to him, he couldn't hear through the roar of blood in his veins.

He wanted her. Wanted to spill his seed inside her, and feel her release twist and shudder around him.

"I—I—I—" he stammered as he felt himself gaining that peak. He continued to stroke her, kiss her, taste her, feel every bit of her lithe, lush body come alive beneath him.

And then it happened.

She came, her body dancing with release, her channel stripping him of the last of his control, pulling from him a wave of passion that sent him reeling back into the darkness from which she'd awakened him.

Tally had known that there might be pain the first time she made love. Every nanny from Rana to Tasha had told her that, but what she hadn't expected was how fleeting it would be, or what came next.

Larken filled her with his sex, driving inside her, and all she could do was answer with her own ragged thrusts of her hips.

How she wanted him to continue. To push her further and further up this course. It was as if he were carrying her into the night sky, the stars and clouds and darkness giving way to a black void that called to her.

"Oh, please," she whispered to him, clung to him as he stroked her toward this impossible madness. She was going mad, for all she wanted was to have him inside her, and every time he pulled away, she clung even harder to him, strove to regain the feel of his length.

Her body tightened, her nipples grew harder as they brushed against the hair on his chest, the thick masculine smell of him filling her senses.

Her heels dug into the mattress as she tried to get closer, get more from each stroke.

She looked up at him, and saw the very same need in his dark gaze. Wild and ready, filled with hunger.

His lips came crashing down atop hers and he kissed her, sealing their future. For even as his tongue entwined with hers, his rock-hard length dove even deeper into her, she found what she had been seeking.

For the night sky through which he'd been carrying her opened up suddenly in a hail of fireworks: ravishing, quaking explosions that drove a deep moan from her.

"Oh, yes, oh, yes," she exclaimed, even as he thrust one more time inside her, and he found his own release, his body shuddering and driving even deeper inside her as he sought to discover every last bit of passion there was between them.

And even after the frenzied explosion passed, and her body continued to tremble and quake, she clung to every indecent wave as it washed over her, for she never wanted this night to end.

Why would she? She was in heaven.

And in that moment, Tally knew she would never be the same.

Never be complete without him.

Without this man who would come to hate her when he discovered the truth.

Then again, as she looked up at him, spied the grin on his lips and the devilish cast to his eyes, she knew she needn't worry about that just now.

For his lips sought hers, and their dangerous chase began anew.

The next morning, well, rather in the early afternoon, Larken made his way downstairs. The breakfast dishes had been put away long ago and the servants were carrying trays outside to the gardens, where a grand picnic was being laid out.

He followed one of the heavily burdened footmen down the hall and through a drawing room where the double doors to the terrace were thrown open. Yet he stopped short of venturing outside, into the sunshine, into the clear light of day.

No, right now, he preferred the shadows, a dark cloud having settled over him.

Larken had awakened alone in his bed, the sheets a tangled mess, and for a while wondered if his memories of Miss Langley, his troublesome, impossible Tally, had been naught but dreams.

Dreams he could manage.

Yet the red stain on his sheets, the evidence of her lost innocence, pushed his doubts aside. As had her chemise, which, in her haste to slip away from him, she'd forgotten.

So his night of passion in her arms had been real. And that scared him more than any Paris prison, any covert trip into Spain. His fears weren't from the fact that he'd ruined her—though he didn't relish meeting Hollindrake over a misty lawn with pistols and seconds, nor how such an encounter (the duel, not the lovemaking) would look in his report—no, his anguish came from how she'd made him feel.

She'd done something to his heart last night in those final wee hours they'd spent together. The tenderness of her touch as she explored his body, the sweet temptation of her lips, and the soft sighs as she found her release that last time.

Larken raked his fingers through his hair and gazed at the terrace and lawn beyond the doors.

Tally was out there and he'd have to say something to her.

But what?

Tell her how she made you feel. That you care not what she's done. That you find her impossible and dangerous and too tempting to resist. That you want her by your side always, for her smile and curiosity and bent for trouble would bring a light into your dark life that you can't afford to live without.

He shook his head. He could no more tell her

those things than he could give up his pursuit of Dashwell.

But he must. For the first time in his life, he felt drawn to a world outside the espionage and subterfuge he had lived in for far too long. And all because of her.

With the war in France now over, and the fight with the Americans waning, where would he be when it was all over? A diplomatic post, as his father had held? Not likely. Not without Pymm's help. And that he wouldn't have without Dashwell's capture . . . and end.

But there was another sort of life out there for him. And Tally's bright eyes and smile were like a beacon into that world. This world. The one he'd been born to and had so studiously avoided.

Larken went to take a step outside, to seek her out, to tell her . . . tell her everything, when a dangerous, dark voice stirred doubt into his soul.

Who's to say she hasn't been doing her job, as you have yours? That she cares naught for you . . . that's she twisted your heart as Aurora did to your father's . . . only to free Dashwell, to see you stopped?

There was enough truth there to still his boot, hold him fast. For he had no doubt she knew who he was—or rather who he wasn't—for his valise had been rifled through while he slept.

Larken couldn't help himself. He smiled. And here he'd thought her boast about being able to pick a lock had been naught but her attempts to rouse him, to get him to break his vicarly veneer.

Well, she had now.

An image sifted through his thoughts. *Of a lady standing by a moonlit window, a handful of papers in her hand, and a stricken look on her face as she read them.*

And while he'd thought it merely part of his dreams, he knew now that somehow in that drug-induced fog he'd seen her as she'd studied his papers. The ones he'd thought were so cleverly hidden.

He'd have to speak to Mr. Stennet the next time he was in London about considering a new design for his traveling valises. They were not as impenetrable as the man claimed. Not if an ordinary Mayfair miss could unravel its mysteries.

A Mayfair miss who could pick locks, flirt like a Frenchwoman and curse in Russian . . .

He shook his head. No, Tally was anything but ordinary.

Catching hold of the doorjamb, his fingernails dug into the wood as he tried to find a way to untangle this mess. But no, there was nothing left to do but go upstairs, root Dashwell out—damn Pymm's orders to do so discreetly—finish off the American and leave.

Leave this house. Leave England. Travel as far from her and his past as he could. There would be someone else. Some other lady out there. There had to be.

One who wobbles about in stolen high heels? A chit who flirts like a courtesan and then innocently tumbles into his arms and steals his heart? Insists on keeping a wretched menace of a dog? And possesses a pair of bright blue eyes that beg a man to see the good in the world.

His chest tightened, and when he tried to breathe, it was like someone had shot a hole through it.

With a cannon.

No, he'd never find another lady like Tally.

Yet, she'd ruined his mission, done everything in her power to stop him. Divert his attentions. Unravel his plans.

Much as Aurora and her *L'Ordre du Lis Noir* had done to his father.

"Demmit!" he muttered under his breath as he tried to put all the pieces together in a way that . . .

No, the only way to end all this was to search this house quickly, top to bottom, starting with Miss Langley and Lady Philippa's suite. Where he would no doubt find Dashwell.

If they hadn't gotten him out already.

Turning on one heel and determined to be done with this business, he found himself running right into his other nemesis.

The Duchess of Hollindrake.

"Mr. Ryder!" she said, pasting a hasty smile on her face, while her gaze scanned him—judiciously, of course—for any sign of ill health or other infraction. "You look refreshed this morning!" she said as if she didn't quite believe it. "Well, there may be hope for you yet. Why, you even look ready for this evening."

"Pardon?" he replied absently, his gaze searching for an escape route. "This evening?"

"Why, the ball, sir! You haven't forgotten, have you?" She made that "harrumph" his Aunt Edith favored when she was cross. "I believe Miss DeFisser should be here by then, though I can't for the life of me understand what might be delaying her, especially when I wrote such promising things to her about you."

Larken pasted a smile on his face. "Your concern and care in all this, Your Grace, has been too kind. Now if you will excuse me, I have some matters—"

But the duchess wasn't really listening. She caught hold of his arm and spun him around and had him outside before he could take a breath. "You must come and join everyone for the picnic. Staines said you did not have breakfast—"

He glanced down at the petite bundle of dynamite beside him. Was there anything she didn't know about her household?

Such as how her sister had spent the night . . .

"Oh, good God," he choked out, tripping over the corner of a tile on the terrace.

She glanced up at him. "It isn't more of your dyspepsia, is it? I can send up Claver with more powders, if you would like. Better yet, I suggest you eat something, sir, to keep up your stamina. I expect all the gentlemen to do their part and ensure there are no wallflowers at my ball."

Stamina? He would have liked to inform the duchess he'd done his part last night, but thought the better of it.

"No, Your Grace," he said, trying unsuccessfully to break free of her grasp. "That would be intolerable."

"Exactly, Mr. Ryder. I knew you would see how important this is. Now come along, for the picnic is about to begin and we have more guests I would like to introduce you to," she offered, giving her hand a flourish over the perfectly tended landscape before them, where tables had been set up, even a tent to shade the ladies.

Nearby, the Misses Elsford, Lord Boyce, Sir Robert, and several others he didn't recognize were bowling on the green, while Miss Browne held court beneath a bright pink parasol, with Cranwich and Grimston on either side of her.

But one lady in particular caught his attention and held it.

Tally. The sight of her fair head bent over a sketchbook sent his heart into a tremulous rhythm. Some young buck stood beside her, making small talk and trying to catch her eye.

Larken didn't recognize the pup, but had an immediate dislike for him. He glanced around for Brutus and wondered where the devilish little dog was. Why wasn't the mutt doing his duty and attaching himself to this bothersome fellow's boot?

The sunlight fell down upon her simple bonnet, and on the single tendril of her blond hair that had slipped free and now lay curled upon her shoulder. His fingers itched to unwind it.

Oh, sweet fair Thalia, he mused, that wretched need for poetry rising up inside him at the sight of her. Make that something else rising, because when he looked at her, he saw her not in her simple gown, but splendidly naked in his bed.

Just then, she looked up and saw him. Their gazes met and Larken's heart stilled. Had it just been a few hours ago when they had been so close, so joined that she'd seemed a part of him?

And yet now they stood so very divided by their loyalties.

The duchess, her attention diverted as she directed several of the footmen, had relaxed her hold on him and he took the opportunity to escape.

Make haste, Larken . . . Go finish this task and be done with the madness . . .

He glanced at Tally again. *Not quite yet . . .* For now that he'd seen her, he knew the least he should do was apologize. That was the honorable thing to do. . .

Honorable? Guilt slowed his pace toward her. Honorable would be to beg her forgiveness. No, offer for her. Honestly, if he truly possessed a shred of honor, it would have kept him from making love to her three times. He paused. No, make that four times, last night.

The foppish fellow flicked a glance at him as he approached and dismissed his plain appearance as hardly worth noting. But Tally's gaze was another matter, and he swore he detected a flush rising on her cheeks.

"Lord Norridge," she said, "would you mind fetching me my drawing case? I do believe I left it in the library."

The young man's brow furrowed, for he looked like he had no desire to yield his place beside her. However, good breeding prevented him from refusing a lady's request, so the hopeful Corinthian bowed and went off with the haughty air of a knight in search of a dragon.

Tally waited for a few moments and then raised the hem of her gown to reveal the box sitting beside her foot. "Oh, dear, I believe I've sent him on a fool's errand." A wicked smile tipped her lips.

Larken's heart did a double thump. He didn't know what he loved more about her, her conniving wiles or her total lack of remorse.

Loved? His throat nearly closed. He loved her. No, he couldn't. He wouldn't.

"I do believe you've sent the right man for the job," he said instead.

"More than you know," she replied, reaching down into her case and fetching a rag. She wiped at a charcoal smudge and then continued working on her sketch.

He glanced down at her notebook—a drawing of Miss Mary Elsford and Lord Boyce—and marveled at her skill, for she had caught them in a moment that captured both their youth and bright spirits. "You're quite good."

She laughed. "You needn't sound so surprised."

"I'm sorry. In truth, I expected nothing more than a simple landscape."

"Ah, and that was your mistake."

"Mistake?" he asked. "How so?"

"Sir, how long have you known me?"

Her question took him aback. "Pardon?"

"How long have you known me?" she repeated.

"Since night before last."

She paused and glanced flirtatiously over her shoulder at him. "Have you known me to be a woman of simple ideas or talents?"

Touché.

He laughed. "It is just that your skill is of some note. You've captured Miss Mary's likeness exactly as she is, right down to the turn of her nose. I'd know her anywhere with that sketch in hand. 'Tis a rare talent you possess."

Gazing down at her, their eyes met, and no longer was he thinking of her skill with a charcoal, but the way her kiss enflamed him. A talent in and of itself.

One of many, he would have liked to add, but the moment had grown awkward enough without his adding to it.

She glanced away and nodded her appreciation. "You sound like my father. When Papa realized how good I was at capturing a likeness, he had me draw all the people we met and he would include them in his diplomatic pouches home."

"I'm surprised your father never recruited you for the Foreign Office," he said.

She laughed. "I fear my talents were spoken for long ago and I daresay my employer wouldn't allow me to go gamboling off for King and Country. She'd claim I have far more important matters to attend to here."

"Your employer?"

Tally laughed. "Yes, my sister. Duchess latched onto my skills years ago, when we were in school in Bath to be exact. Since then, she's kept me quite busy drawing bachelors for her *Chronicles*."

Tally paged through her book. "Yes, here was my first commission. Lord John Tremont."

"Christ!" he muttered before he could stop himself. The minx had captured the notorious Mad Jack exactly.

"Yes, I suppose you would know his lordship," she said, one brow arched regally. For what agent in His Majesty's service didn't know Lord Jack or hadn't passed through his estate near Hastings on their way to the smuggler's ships he arranged to give them passage to France and beyond.

Ships that had included Dashwell's infamous *Circe.*

Larken stepped back, the ground as unsteady as if she'd just pulled the rug out from beneath him. For here she'd made her point quite clearly—she knew exactly who he was—and gone back to absently flipping through her sketchbook as if it was no matter that he wasn't the duke's cousin, rather a spy sent to uncover her secrets.

No, indeed there was nothing simple about Tally Langley.

Since he'd never been unmasked before, he tried to find something to say. Something to counter her only-too-correct assumption, but instead his gaze fell on the passing parade of drawings in her sketchbook as she turned the pages.

Drawings of Brutus, Lady Philippa, the duchess, an elderly lady knitting, even Miss Browne, though he did his best to ignore the horns protruding from her head and the tail that stuck out from the back of the lady's gown.

"How is it that you can do that?" he asked, grinning at the rendering of Miss Browne. She actually looked more jovial with the horns.

"Do what?" she asked, glancing down at the drawing.

"Bring someone to life like that?"

She shrugged, "Papa always said it was because I see people differently."

"Differently? How so?"

She paused for a moment, as if not sure how to explain. "I don't see the outward lines of a person, but what is in their heart. Their 'essence' is what our Nanny Rana called it." She continued paging through her sketches.

"Stop," he said, pointing at one.

"I thought you might recognize him," she said.

"Dashwell," he said softly.

"Yes, Dash. I drew it last winter, if you must know. Before he was caught," she said quite pointedly as if his capture had been an evil wrongdoing.

He would have liked to remind her that even then, Dashwell had been a wanted man, so her aiding him before the Setchfield ball where he'd been captured had been as treasonous as her help in freeing him from Marshalsea. He was about to ask her which part she'd played in the act—the old woman or the driver—but she countered him by saying, "Hardly the fearsome devil everyone makes him out to be, wouldn't you say? And your friend once, or so I am told."

To his consternation, she'd caught the very essence, as she called it, of Dashwell—that Irish sparkle to his eyes, and the jaunty tip of his square chin that made him look more like a boon companion than England's great enemy.

"That isn't a matter for me to decide," he said stiffly, reverting to his Mr. Ryder persona. The stuffy fellow was handy at times. And to change the subject again, he nodded over toward Lady Philippa, who stood under a tree with Lord Gossett. Tally's cousin appeared quite entertained by the dazzled viscount, who was doing a bit of slight of hand to enchant the lithe beauty.

"Your cousin looks amused."

"She's always been happiest in the country."

"And you?"

Tally's nose wrinkled. "Not I. I love city life. More people, more entertainments. Places to explore." She sighed. "When the wars are finally over, I intend to go back to Paris and Vienna and Naples and see them all over again."

"Alone?" For a very proper, stuffy English propriety reared its head inside him. Tally traveling about the Continent on her own? Never! Not if he had anything to say about the matter.

But that was the point. He didn't. He wouldn't. He shouldn't even be here, dallying after her like that foolish pup had been doing before him.

She shrugged, not answering his question. Flipping a few more pages, she was coming to the end of her collection, when one drawing in particular caught his eye.

"That one—"

"This one?" she asked, flipping to a drawing of Brutus and a boot—of course.

"No, the other one—of the woman."

"This one?" she asked, turning the page. "Do you know her?"

"No," he said almost immediately, that is until he looked at the page again, the image from his dream rising forth like a ghost and blending with the likeness before him. "Good God." *Aurora?* It could very well be. "Perhaps, I do," he admitted. "Who is she?"

"I haven't the vaguest notion," she said, tipping her head to study the picture anew. "I saw her at the posting inn when we changed horses the other day. I thought she had an interesting air about her. But I haven't got her quite right—"

"Her brow," he suggested. "Her brow should be a little more pronounced." He glanced up at the company of other ladies. "Rather like Mrs. Browne's."

She glanced at the lady and then down at the drawing. "Why, yes, yes, that's it." She reached for her rag, rubbed at the lines there and then set to work putting it to rights.

When she'd finished, she looked up at him. "Are you sure you don't know her?"

"No." He tried to sound firm, but inside his head a furious argument ensued.

But you do know her. That is her.

In Sussex? At a posting inn? Whatever would she be doing here?

You aren't considering all the facts . . .

The last voice sounded very much like his father's. He'd always been one to want to weigh everything before coming to a conclusion. But then again, that hesitancy had cost the elder Larken his life.

"No, I haven't the vaguest notion who she is," he repeated.

Tally sighed and studied the drawing. "You know, now that I think about it, I wonder if it is her trunk that I have. She appeared more of the sort to wear those shoes than I."

Larken laughed. Actually he quite liked the way she wore them, but he wasn't to tell her that.

She continued her story. "She arrived by post-chaise just as Felicity had all the baggage in a terrible jumble all over the yard at the inn." She paused for a moment. "Oh! That's it. It must be! I don't know why I didn't think of it before." She grinned up at him. "My lord, I do believe you've solved a mystery."

Larken felt a shiver run down his spine, as if the threads that held this entire case together tugged at him deliberately to pay heed.

To a story about lost luggage and traveling widows? Now he was going mad.

Just as it is madness to continue to stand here, dallying after a woman you cannot have.

"Miss Langley, about last night—"

"Sir, I think it is better if we didn't—" she said, not even looking up from her work.

"But I feel compelled, honor bound—"

She stopped her work and looked up at him. "Honor bound? If you had any honor, my lord, you wouldn't be here."

Chapter 14

Geoffrey, Baron Larken.
(Addendum, dated May 12, 1814)
He was with his father when the man was murdered in Paris during the Peace in '01. I recall this because Papa was summoned from court to hire a proper escort to take him and his father's body back to England. At the time, there were whispers about the senior Lord Larken's associations with the French, and some continue to this day to besmirch his son's reputation. Hollindrake avers Larken served the King admirably and honorably. But sadly, the war took a dreadful toll on his spirit and he is an embittered young man, lost in his nightmares of a past he cannot forget or forgive. . .

The Bachelor Chronicles

*T*ally knew she'd waded into dark, dangerous waters the moment she'd called his honor into question. Hadn't she just read his entry in the *Bachelor Chronicles* this morning? And now she'd put herself in the same league as gossips like Miss Browne and her hideous mother.

But what the devil was she to do? For he'd actually looked quite intent when he'd begun to . . .

She shivered, for it was an impossible notion to even consider. Was he truly about to do the honorable thing and make an offer for her?

"Miss Langley, I hardly see what you mean by that, especially when our circumstances call for . . . nay, demand that we—"

"*Mr. Ryder,*" she said in a sharp whisper, putting every bit of emphasis on his false name that she could, "I have no idea what you are speaking of, for we have no circumstances—"

Egads! He was serious. Serious about proposing and marrying her. Was he mad?

Well, she knew she was . . . for a wild, impetuous moment, she considered accepting him before he discovered the truth about her.

And if Dash does escape tonight . . . if he eludes his hunters and makes it back to his ship . . . and if there is no connection whatsoever to me and Pippin, then . . .

Could it be possible?

No. For Tally couldn't go to him in good conscience.

Botheration, she'd drugged the man last night, and who was to say his impulsive (and incredible) lovemaking, as well as this faltering proposal of his, weren't but reactions to the powders she'd dumped into his teapot?

She glanced up into his dark eyes and wished she hadn't. They burned with a furious light, and guilt tugged at her right down to her slippers.

Look what Miss Browne's story had done to Pippin and Dash. And even though it was that infamous miss's word against Dash's, Pippin was furious with the captain for his gallantries. And Dash? Being as stubborn and unrepentant as any other overly proud man, he'd refused to refute any of it.

And now Mr. Ryder, no, Lord Larken, was one breath away from proposing to her, and she was casting aspersions on his honor and driving him away—the sort of man she'd spent most of her life dreaming about.

Everything was a wretched mess, a dreadful tangle.

"Miss Langley, don't you see what last night meant?"

She knew what it meant to her. She'd discovered a world of unspeakable passion in his arms. How could she tell him that some time in those wee hours, she'd fallen in love with him?

In love with a man her sister described as "lost" and "embittered." How could he not be so, when that dreadful Foreign Office had asked so much of him? Sent him to kill a friend. What sort of honor is there in that?

How could it not eat away at a man's very soul?

Tally, who loved beauty, loved life when it was bright and full of spirit, gazed up at him and wondered what he had seen . . . and done . . . and if there was any way to help him ease the nightmares, give him new memories to wallpaper over the blackness that had marred and twisted his features as he tossed and turned in the sheets.

Yes, how could she help him, when she still had to thwart him? Stop him. Deceive him.

"I cannot fathom what you mean, sir," she said, staring down at her drawing. "Last night? Why last night was rather uneventful. Hardly worth mentioning."

Not unless you want to see my heart break . . .

"As you say, Miss Langley," he said, letting out a long breath, and glancing up at the other guests. "Your cousin looks rather happy," he said, nodding toward Pippin and Lord Gossett. "I thought you'd said she was attached elsewhere—"

"Circumstances change," Tally rushed to say. As hers had the first moment she'd seen Larken. "I believe Lord Gossett has given Pippin's heart a new direction, now that she knows her destiny cannot follow another."

His gaze flicked immediately back from watching Pippin to meet Tally's and so she pressed her point further, since now she had his full attention. Dropped her treasonous crumbs for him to pick up and devour.

"For how can a lady love someone who is lost to her? Gone. Well away and out of her reach."

She didn't know how much more clearly she could state her lie, short of saying, *My lord, Dashwell has left. And there is nothing you can do about it.*

"My cousin inherited a very practical nature," Tally added. *Well, more practical than mine,* she would have amended if she'd felt inclined. "And therefore is able to see Lord Gossett's advantages more clearly than a more romantically inclined lady might. Given her previous entanglement, shall we call it, and that man's less than honorable nature, she's come to a new understanding of what love means."

They both glanced over at the pair, where Lord

Gossett had Pippin giggling as he made a great show of pulling a coin out of her ear with a bit of slight of hand.

"Obviously he is taken with her," Tally said, forcing a smile on her lips. "And in time . . . well, I would imagine if Lord Gossett has anything to say about it, she will find her heart turned. For the best, my sister would say."

"And you, Miss Langley? Do you find your cousin's change of heart for the best? I can't see you putting your heart aside so easily if you were in her shoes." He paused, waiting for her to deny him, to tell him how she felt. And when she remained silent, he finished by saying, "Then again, maybe you already have."

Tally closed her eyes, but she needn't have bothered, for he turned on one heel and walked away. Each thud of his boots as they marched over the terrace tiles shot through her breaking heart. She kept her lashes tightly shuttered, to keep the tears from falling and because she knew if she opened them, she'd look for him.

Call him back. Confess everything. Give him the answers that would give her away.

I must do this, can't you see that, my lord? I must for Pippin's sake.

And yours as well. For you cannot have need of a traitorous wife, when you have worked so hard to redeem your family's honor. And what will killing a friend do to your already troubled heart?

Much to her horror, Lord Norridge came bounding back, full of apologies. "I am so sorry, Miss Langley, for I have been completely unsuccessful in retrieving your drawing box." He paused for a moment. "But ah, there it is, at your feet!"

She glanced down at it, and then up at the dark-clad figure disappearing into the house. "I am so sorry, my lord. What a wretched fool I am."

But she wasn't saying it for Lord Norridge's benefit.

Settling into a comfortable chair, Aunt Minty reached for her knitting, marveling at the rare luck that had brought her to this comfortable existence in her dotage, after having spent most of her life as the finest buzman who'd ever picked a pocket in London. Then as age had crept up on her, and she was no longer nimble enough, she'd taken to fencing pocket watches, gems, and other trinkets for some of the most infamous highwaymen who'd plied the trade. Instead of swinging from a noose like so many of her acquaintances, she was safe and snug now.

Aramintha Follifoot was in some regards a legend amongst her Seven Dials and Newgate cronies. Had probably seen more diamonds and emeralds and fine gems pass through her nimble fingers than the queen herself.

Oh, she'd lived her life well, loved once, been married a time or three, once to two fellows at the same time due to some mix-up with the hangman, but that matter had taken care of itself when one of the blokes had been shot while stealing a horse.

The constable's horse.

"Not the brightest of lads, was Mortie," she was wont to say.

But Aramintha had never had children, never really wanted them, until she found herself taken in and encircled by the Langley sisters and their fair cousin, Lady Philippa. And with these headstrong, unlikely ladies she discovered what all the fuss was about.

While having a former pickpocket and fence as one's chaperone would be deemed scandalous and unforgivable by Society, not so to her "diamonds," as she liked to call them. They loved her as if she were their own flesh and blood.

And in return she loved the three of them as if they were dipped in gold.

"Not like the rest of these rum morts who calls themselves Lady This or Countess That," she would brag to their cook, Mrs. Hutchinson. "Paste is what all those other fancy birds are, next to me diamonds."

And her diamonds were what the lively trio was, and if they wanted to find themselves husbands and chase after odd dreams, then Aramintha was going to do everything in her power to see them find their hearts' desires.

She'd helped Felicity marry her duke, hadn't batted an eye when Pippin had come to her for help, and now, as the door to the large, airy room swung open, and a pale, teary eyed Tally came barreling in, Aramintha sighed.

So it is your turn, is it, child? she thought as she took only a glance at the stricken look on the gel's face.

Red wool laced through her fingers, her knitting pins froze. "Tally-girl! Is that you? Come sit with me, child, and tell me everything."

Tally shot across the room, the door banging shut behind her. She fell into the lady's arms and began to cry.

"Ah, there now, Tally-girl, you shouldn't be crying like that," Aunt Minty told her, carefully setting aside her knitting. Socks were always needed, but even they could wait when one of her girls needed her.

"I've made a terrible blunder of things," Tally confessed.

Aunt Minty sighed, for she'd heard much the same thing from Pippin not a few hours earlier. She should never have agreed to let them send her off, even though it had only been for a sennight. For as their hearts broke, so did Aramintha's—though she would have been hung by her heels and dangled over a bear pit before she'd admit to such a thing.

"Tell me all about it," Aunt Minty said softly.

And Tally did.

By the time she was finished, Aramintha had only two thoughts.

However could this Lord Larken not forgive Tally? And if he didn't, he'd find himself missing his ballocks.

Anyone who doubted she had the nerve or the hand to make such a shot had only to ask her second husband, the ever-randy Bertram Follifoot, whose eye for the ladies hadn't stopped wandering when he'd married Aramintha. But seeing as he was roasting with the devil, the one to ask was the undertaker.

"Poor Bertie," the fellow had joked to the drunken and jubilant crowd at Bertram's wake. "Gone to hell in his best suit, but without his best parts."

And that would be this Lord Larken's fate as well if he was trifling with her wee, dear girl.

Missing his best parts, that is.

Standing before her mirror, Mrs. Browne was putting the finishing touches on her ensemble when the door behind her opened.

"Sarah, dear, is that you? Remember to pay particular attention to Lord Grimston. I have it on good authority his estate in Durham makes this dreary place look quite provincial."

"You always did have expensive tastes, didn't you, Aveline?" came the reply.

The voice sent a chill down Mrs. Browne's spine.

"Aurora," she whispered. Putting down her brush and turning around slowly, for it never did one good to startle her, Mrs. Browne faced the one woman she wished to perdition like no other.

Her sister. Dressed convincingly as a scullery maid, she'd fool anyone with her disguise. Anyone but Mrs. Browne.

"Get out of here," the matron told her sister. "You promised me not a month ago that you would leave me alone and now here you are. You've bled me dry, Aurora. There is no more gold or money to give you. I cannot get any more funds until this war is over."

"Aveline, Aveline, we are sisters. What would *Maman* say if she could hear you?"

"That I was a traitor to our family and our traditions, but I care not. The queen was lost nearly twenty years ago, Aurora; there is no need for the Order any longer. Even Josephine, poor consort that she was, is gone. The France we served no longer exists."

She turned back to her dressing table, her mind adrift with wild thoughts, but not before she spotted in the mirror the sly, wry tip to her sister's lips. A feline smile that was her lure, the worrisome clue that Aurora was quite confident in whatever dreadful scheme she'd dreamt up, and was obviously determined to have Mrs. Browne's help in it.

More money and gold and aid in leaving England, most likely. If only that was what she wanted. She'd happily see her sister and her past sent to the farthest reaches of the world if it meant she never had to see that mad light in her eyes again.

"Aveline," Aurora whispered, "it is time you repaid your debt to the Order. It is due, and due now."

Those cold, chilling words brought Mrs. Browne spinning around, caution cast to the wind. For there was only one way a debt to the Order was repaid— with one's life.

Aurora laughed softly. "Silly woman, I have no intention of killing you . . ." Her words trailed off, but the last part hung between them.

Not yet. Not if you do exactly as I ask.

Wasn't that how it always was with the Order? No escape from the obligations, the duties passed from mother to daughter through all the generations that had come and gone since it had been founded by Mary of Guise to protect her daughter, Mary, Queen of France and the Scots.

There had been shifts and subtle changes in the Order's alliances over the centuries, but always,

France's queens and French interests were to be protected.

And so it had been with Aurora and Aveline, born into an old French family, their own mother one of the highest-ranking members of the Order.

Aveline had been married to a rich American merchant, Mr. Browne, and sent overseas to watch and record the events as they unfolded in the new United States. Beautiful, dangerous Aurora had been married to an Englishman—like so many of the Order's daughters—to slyly spy on France's constant enemy from within the lofty reaches of England's aristocracy.

Aurora had never been pleased with her match, and just before the revolution, her husband had died quite suddenly. And before anyone could look too closely into his unexpected passing, she'd slipped back to France, disappearing into the mists of the Terror, with the help of her English lover.

But Aveline's heart had never belonged to the Order. She'd been rather relieved by the growing disorder of France, for it left her free in the safety and rich comfort of Boston. The revolution, the chaos of the various regimes, and the rising fortune of Bonaparte had ripped the Order apart at the seams, or at least so Aveline had thought. For some time she hadn't even known her sister's fate.

Not until the Peace in '01, when she and Mr. Browne had gone to Paris to extend his trading alliances. And then she'd discovered her sister. Well, Aurora had discovered *her* and dragged her quite unwilling back into the Order's affairs . . . or rather, Aurora's affairs.

"I have no debt to repay, for there is no Order left," Aveline told her sister. "Be gone before you are found. I will not protect you."

Aurora smiled and played the final card between them. "What of the child?"

"Sarah?!" Mrs. Browne gasped. "You cannot mean to—"

"But I do. If you will not help me, then I will take her in payment."

Mrs. Browne crossed the room, her own life no longer an issue. She caught her sister by the arm, her nails digging viciously into her sister's flesh. "You harm her and I will kill you."

Aurora didn't even flinch, only smiled. "So you still have some of your heart left, I see. That's good. It means you will help me or I will take Sarah."

Mrs. Browne released her, as if suddenly her sister's skin burned. "If it is gold you want, take what is left in my purse and go."

Again that laugh, that bitter, hard laugh. "I don't need your money. I have that in plenty."

"But you've—"

"Taken freely from you over the last year? But of course, you offered it, thinking it would free you and because you are a fool. Actually, I'm very rich. You'd be amazed who will pay for the Order's services these days. Wars are profitable for spies and *merchants*. Profitable and *dangerous*."

Mrs. Browne glanced up. Merchants. Like her husband, whose fortune was being made outfitting American ships and refitting captured British ones.

Dangerous because Mrs. Browne knew her sister wouldn't think twice of having Mr. Browne killed in some unhappy accident, the same sort of random act of violence that had claimed any number of those who crossed Aurora.

"Then go dally with your spies," Mrs. Browne told her, "and leave me be."

Aurora moved toward the window. "That is exactly what I have in mind. For there is a spy in this house. Lord Larken."

Mrs. Browne shook her head. "There is no one here by that name."

"He is here. I have seen him in the gardens. He is dressed like a priest."

"The vicar?" Again she shook her head. "No, you are mistaken. That is the duke's cousin, Mr. Ryder."

"He is Lord Larken," Aurora said. "Take another look at the man. Perhaps you recall his father? You do remember him, don't you?"

Years and memories swept past Mrs. Browne like a winter storm, cold and chilling. And suddenly she was in Paris again.

And the name tolled at her, jarring the connection loose.

"Larken?" she whispered. *Oh, good God. Not this. Not now.* She wavered on her feet but did her level best to remain upright. She couldn't show her sister the least bit of fear.

But it was too late. Aurora had seen the panic in her eyes.

"Yes, yes," her dangerous sibling was saying. "Rather ironic *his* son would come to this place, but Fate has a way of bringing these things around for a reckoning, don't you find it so?"

"He's searching for you?"

Aurora shook her head. "No. He has no idea I'm here. He is here for another reason. The same one I am. Dashwell."

This time Mrs. Browne reached out for the corner of the bed and sat down, for she felt as if the floor beneath was about to give way. "Thomas Dashwell? He's here?"

Aurora tipped her head in acknowledgement.

"And you want to help him?"

She shook her head. "No, I fear Dashwell has out-lived his usefulness. If the English had gotten it right in the first place, he would be dead already." She muttered a curse in French, and then went on, "If they hadn't spent the last six months debating who gets to hang him, I could be well and gone from this wretched place. I nearly had him in January, before he was caught, but he slipped past me."

"What do you care for Dashwell? He's been be-deviling the English for years, which I might point out, is right in line with your interests."

"It was for a time, but he knows too much."

"If that is so, who's to say he hasn't talked?"

Aurora, always so confident, shook her head. "He's owed a rather large sum of money, and I believe he's holding out hope of being paid."

"Which you will not do," Mrs. Browne added. Men had always been useful to the Order, until they knew too much or became insistent on being paid for services rendered. Then the debt was "paid" in the usual way of the Order.

"If he is recaptured, he could use the information he has about the Order—"

"To bargain for his life," Aveline finished. She

wouldn't put it past the illustrious captain to do just that. "How can you be sure he is here?"

"He's here," Aurora replied. "I've seen him at the window, though they've done a good job so far of concealing him. They plan to move him tonight."

"Again, I don't see how you are so sure—"

"It is what I would do. Move him during the chaos of a ball."

Mrs. Browne shook her head. "But I hardly see what this has to do with me."

"Aveline, don't be a fool. Dashwell knows who you are. Who do you think paid him to bring you back to England when you tried to return home?"

"You had us brought back here? Saw us trapped on this side of the ocean? During a war?"

Aurora smiled. "It is always good to have family close in times like these. And my instincts were correct. I have need of you. First in helping me find Dashwell. And then there is the matter of my trunk."

"Your what?"

"My trunk. I fear it was mixed up at a posting inn and brought here by mistake."

Mrs. Browne felt as if she were being pushed deeper and deeper into a mire. "Where is it?"

"I believe the duchess's sister has it because I saw her wearing my black dress the other night."

"Miss Langley has your trunk?" Mrs. Browne thought her throat was going to close. Miss Thalia Langley had access to Aurora's belongings? The same Miss Langley that Sarah had complained could pick locks like a common thief? "Aurora, whatever is in there?"

Then her sister said the one word that convinced Mrs. Browne she had no course but to help.

"Everything."

With the commencement of the ball fast approaching, Tally made only hasty preparations for the evening. She had no heart for a night that seemed draped in impending doom.

If only she could shake the notion that something was about to go very wrong.

And she knew just who was waiting, watching, ready to pounce at any misstep . . . Larken.

If only . . .

Tucking a ribbon back into her hair, she heaved a sigh, took one last glance into the mirror before she pasted a smile on her lips and joined the others in the sitting room.

Pippin and Dash, still at odds over Miss Browne's story, stood on opposite sides of the room, each stubbornly ignoring the other.

Dash had donned the plain, serviceable suit that Tarleton had brought up, and Aunt Minty had trimmed his hair into a style befitting a proper valet. He'd even shaved and looked so utterly respectable, it was hard to believe he was such a dangerous pirate.

Privateer, Tally silently corrected.

Tarleton stood by the fire, chatting with Aunt Minty, resplendent in a brightly colored suit, the brocade sparkling in the firelight. The diminutive con artist could pass for a duke, and Tally smiled to herself, for she doubted even Hollindrake would be dressed so richly tonight.

If anything, Tarleton's eye-catching ensemble was an excellent foil to Dash's drab garb. It made the wanted man nearly invisible next to his supposed employer's colorful plumage.

Pippin wore a new gown as well, a pale yellow concoction that clung to her lithe frame. She looked like a fragile spring blossom, and Tally could see, from her pale cheeks and wary glances, that she was no more happy about tonight than Tally was.

As Tally was the last to join the conspirators, there was an awkward moment of silence as they each glanced anywhere but into each other's eyes, everyone weighing their chances for success, as well as the cost that could come if the evening's plans went awry.

"Come, Circe, the hour is upon us," Dash said softly. "Let us argue no more. We have risked too much . . . *you* have risked far too much for me, for us to part in this foolish manner." He paused for a moment. "Besides, I love you with all my heart. You and no other."

Gooseflesh ran down Tally's arm at his honest, heart-wrenching confession, for his words, the ragged catch to his voice told the truth.

He did love Pippin. And in that instant, Tally realized how much she envied her cousin. Envied Felicity and her adoring duke.

If only . . .

Tally shook her head and turned away, as Pippin, who needed no more encouragement than Dash's confession, swept across the room, her pretty face once again alight with love. She flew into his arms and their kiss, so intimate and hungry, drew all eyes away from the couple as they said their good-byes.

"I don't want to part," Pippin said. "I fear we will never find our way back together again."

Dash laughed, his fingers toying with one of the artful curls in her hair. "Don't be foolish, my dearest girl. Of course we'll be together again. Very soon, I promise. How can it be otherwise between us?"

Even as he said those words, Tally swore the dark shadow she'd felt all day passed over them, cursing Dash's promise. It was as if the Fates mocked his confidence.

No, it couldn't be true. They had risked too much for Dash and Pippin not to be together, she wanted to rail to the heavens. But instead, she said softly, "Come, Pippin, it is time."

Pippin followed her reluctantly to the door, as Tarleton laid out the plans one last time.

"After you two go down, Dash and I will go to my room and wait for the drive and the house to become a complete crush. I've got my carriage awaiting us near the old stables—"

"The old stables?" Pippin glanced at Dash. "No one would notice if I went out there and we could—"

"No, you cannot," he told her. "Besides, I don't think I can do this but once."

Part. Say good-bye.

Tally knew her heart was breaking for much the same reasons. For she suspected, nay, she knew Larken to be her heart's match, her true love, and yet the gulf between them was as formidable as the one that was even now opening between Pippin and Dash.

Taking Pippin's hand, Tally led her from the room

and they walked in silence to the stairwell. As they came to the final flight, the din of the crowded house began to envelop them.

Glancing down to the foyer, Tally wasn't surprised to see Lord Gossett there at the foot of the stairs, awaiting their arrival. Well, Pippin's arrival.

But more shocking was the man on the other side of the steps.

Lord Larken. She nearly tripped over her heels at the sight of him.

He looked so handsome in his new dark coat and buff breeches, offset by the white of his shirt and the simplicity of his cravat. No peacock, Larken didn't need the bright waistcoats and brazen displays of lace to attract attention; his sculpted jawline, his very height and the breadth of his chest now that he wasn't hunched over were quite enough.

Add to that, his dark hair—now brushed back and tamed in an unfashionable queue—and those deep, mysterious eyes of his were enough to make any woman take a second, longer gaze at him. To fantasize about what it would be like to untie the cord wound around his hair and unleash the beast within this restless man.

Tally didn't need to imagine what it was like— she'd discovered that pleasure all last night and found herself aching for another such evening . . . and one more after that.

She nearly tumbled again and this time caught the railing before she made a lovely entrance into the ball by falling down the stairs into a tangled heap.

"Tally, are you well?" Pippin whispered.

She tore her gaze away from the aggravating

man—who was now grinning at her, the nerve of that bastard—and glanced over at her cousin. "Yes, Pippin. I am well."

Tally almost felt guilty over her own conundrum when she knew what this night meant to Pippin. And here was her cousin worried about her! How like Pippin.

"Try to smile," she whispered over to her. "It might put some color in your cheeks. You've become dreadfully pale of late."

"I can't help it," Pippin said, her lips making a halfhearted effort to turn upward.

Tally's gaze strayed down the stairs again— honestly she hadn't meant to, but she just couldn't help herself.

And there he was staring up at her with that wolfish hungry gaze. Her heel grabbed into the next step and she wavered perilously.

"Are you are certain you are well?"

Tally straightened. "Couldn't be better," she lied.

"Lord Larken looks much improved," Pippin pointed out.

She sniffed and didn't look in his direction. She had some self-control in that regard. "Don't you mean Mr. Ryder?"

Pippin slanted a glance at her. "I for one prefer him as a baron, don't you?"

"I do not." After another step, she changed the subject. "What of Lord Gossett? I think he is quite the handsomest man here tonight, don't you?"

Now it was Pippin's turn to stumble a bit. "He almost makes me wish . . ."

Tally came to a stop. "Wish what?"

"That I'd met him first," Pippin confessed. "Then all of you wouldn't be taking these risks for me." This took Tally aback and Pippin seeing her shock rushed to explain. "Don't get me wrong, Dash is my heart, my love, but this afternoon, in the garden . . . well, for a moment, I found myself wondering what it would have been like to have met Lord Gossett first."

Tally knew that dilemma.

"Oh, he's everything I ought to love, rich and handsome, and very charming." Pippin sighed, then looked over at Tally. "But he's not a pirate."

Tally laughed. "I daresay he'd take up the profession to win your heart."

Pippin smiled. "Don't suggest it, for I fear he would. And I don't like using him as a distraction to keep Felicity out of our way. He's too good of a man to be used thusly."

"I don't think he minds," Tally told her, as the viscount came forward to meet them.

"Lady Philippa," Lord Gossett said, bowing and then reaching out to take her hand. "May I escort you in?"

"Thank you, my lord," she said, falling in alongside with him and leaving Larken and Tally alone together.

Why hadn't he left? Tally thought she had made her lie convincingly enough to have him believe that Dashwell was gone and that there was no need for him to stay, but obviously the man hadn't believed her.

How utterly ungentlemanly, she mused, feeling only a little bit of pique. Because it also meant that for another few hours, she'd have to keep him from discovering the truth.

It didn't help that the moment he took her hand, the heat of his fingers rushed through her gloves, and her insides melted with desire.

Taking a steadying breath, Tally tried to think of some way of deceiving herself into believing that she didn't care a whit for him.

She could do that. She could lie to herself. Then she glanced up into his passion-filled gaze and knew this night was destined to be a long and dangerous charade, for she didn't believe herself anymore than he did her.

Chapter 15

$\mathscr{L}$arken watched Tally come down the stairs and felt an unfamiliar stir—oh, there was the more familiar rise in his loins, but the one in his heart was like nothing he'd ever known.

Demmit. However could this woman look more beautiful than she had in his arms last night? But seeing her as she stumbled her way down the stairs, blushing with each misstep, he had to restrain himself from rushing forward to help her.

Help your enemy, that wry voice reminded him.

And as much as he wanted to spend the evening shooing off the inevitable horde of admirers about to swamp the duchess's sister, he needed to ensure that she was well out of his way so he could finish his task.

Certainly she'd told him that his services here were no longer needed, hinting broadly that Dashwell was already far from Hollindrake House, but he didn't believe her. Oh, yes, he'd been distracted last night, but the guards and footmen posted to keep a strict, albeit discreet, eye out for the pirate had all been at their posts and none of them had seen anything untoward.

Other than the one who'd spied Mr. Hartwell smuggling in some old bawd. "No 'arm in that, eh, gov'ner?" the footman had said with a wink and a nudge.

No, Larken agreed. No harm in that, not when it meant that Dashwell was still here, and tonight, if his instincts were correct, the American would make his move in all the chaos and confusion.

And to finish his work, Larken needed Tally distracted. He would have liked to have continued in the same manner she had him, taking her up to his bed and spending another night in her arms, but that scenario was fraught with peril.

To his heart.

No, better to see her well engaged all night, so he could slip away. And to that end he'd already set his own plans in motion.

"Miss Langley," he murmured, bowing over her fingers as he took her hand.

He swore she shivered as their fingers entwined, which meant . . .

Nothing, he told himself, as he steered her into the ballroom.

"You needn't hold my hand, sir," she whispered to him, even as they passed their host and hostess. "I know the way to the ballroom."

"Ah, but I insist," he told her. "After your kind consideration of my interests over the past few days, it is the least I can do. Besides, I have a surprise for you."

She slanted a suspicious glance up at him as they entered the crush of the ballroom. Larken pulled to a stop, Tally teetering to a halt as well.

"Here it is," he told her, nodding to a spot just past her shoulder.

She turned and he wished her back wasn't to him so he could see the surprise and fury in her eyes.

For there ready to take her hand was Lord Norridge. And behind him, four other gentlemen and heirs ready for their turn to charm the lovely Miss Langley.

He leaned over and whispered in her ear, "I knew you were a bit anxious about the evening, what with the dancing and all, so I have taken the liberty of filling your card with five of the most cowhanded partners available."

She whirled around, and he thought he was going to have to add pugilist to her list of skills, for her hand was balled into a tight fist.

"No need to thank me, Miss Langley. It was the least I could do for you."

"But . . . but . . ." she sputtered as he handed her off to Lord Norridge and the man led her (well, more to the point, dragged her) out to the dance floor, utterly oblivious to his pretty partner's reluctance.

Larken left the ballroom, ready to be finished with this assignment. Nothing would stop him now, and he'd be gone from this madness before the hired orchestra struck their last note.

The last note. He faltered for a moment, shocked to find himself wishing that he could be there to hear its last echoing refrain, and in his arms would be a fair-haired miss, with stars in her eyes and kisses full of passion even as she apologized for how she'd spent the night trampling his toes.

No, instead, the last note would find him far from here. With blood on his hands, and her undying hatred at his deed.

But there was no choice in the matter. Dashwell had to die, and Larken would never have the sort of ordinary existence that fools like Norridge and the rest of them took for granted.

"Mayhap," he muttered under his breath as he climbed the stairs, "I'm the fool."

Larken's hand closed over the latch of the door and he took a deep breath as he glanced down at the pistol in his other hand. He had no doubt that Lady Philippa and Tally had been hiding Dashwell in their suite of rooms, and now, with everyone preoccupied with the ball, was his chance to finish this mission.

Yet he paused. Captain Dashwell. Privateer. Spy. Scourge to England's merchants and Navy.

Dashwell wouldn't hesitate to kill you, a wry voice nudged him. *Besides, it isn't as if that man hasn't made enemies clear across the Atlantic and then some . . .*

Demmit, it was like having Pymm whispering in his ear.

Yet even as he put his shoulder to the door, something stayed him. A voice. Pure and sincere.

How is killing an unarmed man honorable? He wouldn't kill you if you were defenseless . . . He could almost see her standing before him, hands fisted to her hips. *'Tis murder, plain and simple.*

It was. But this was also war. And he had a duty to mind the king's business. No matter where that took his soul.

So Larken shoved the door open and barreled into the suite, pistol drawn and blotting out any last bit of interfering, whispering conscience.

The hallway had been dark, as was the room, but for a few candles on a table, and the soft glow of coals in the fireplace.

In a wide, comfortable chair beside the grate sat an old woman knitting. And beside her, in a basket, slept Brutus.

"Sssh," she murmured, not even looking up from her work. "I'll not be responsible for your boots if you wake that infernal dog." Her fingers paused, red wool wound around them, and she glanced up at him, her apple cheeks pink beneath her white lace cap. "Ah, I thought I might meet you this evening. Come for him, have you?"

Aunt Minty. So she was real. He was starting to think she was nothing more than a mirage to hide Dashwell behind.

"Well, don't stand there with the door open, I can't abide drafts," she complained. "Been cold since the winter—such a terrible winter, wasn't it? Snow like I can't ever remember. And the river all frozen. It's as if it froze my blood, it did, and it's yet to thaw."

Quite honestly he was a bit taken aback by both this quiet domestic scene, as well as her complete nonchalance over his blustering arrival, but that only stopped him for a moment, and he walked past her and went to work searching the rooms that connected to this main parlor.

"You'll not find him here. He's been gone for some time," she called after him.

He came back to the parlor and watched for a moment as she knit along, her fingers moving with a steady, almost hypnotic motion. "I don't believe you."

She shrugged as if she had better things to do than argue with him. Then she tipped her head and studied him. "Glad you did show up. Got some business to discuss with you."

"With me?"

The knitting fell to her lap. "Well, I wouldn't be discussing it with that beastie, now would I?" she said with a nod toward Brutus.

"I haven't time for idle chatter," he said, turning to leave.

"And what is it you're going to do?"

"Find him," he said over his shoulder, his hand on the latch.

"Harrumph." The needles clicked anew. "Not about him. But about my Tally-girl."

That stopped him. Tally. His head hung and he shook it. "That's difficult. Impossible."

Another "harrumph" told him her opinion of his reply.

Yes, he supposed it wasn't much of an answer. But he wasn't about to start discussing his heart, his desires with a former pickpocket, no matter that she looked like someone's beloved, trusted grandmother.

"I don't have time—" he began, opening the door.

"If you care to listen, I've been sitting here pondering something that I think you could answer."

He glanced over his shoulder. Now she was just stalling. "Madam, if you think to stop me, I—"

She rushed to cut him off. "Because how is it that you found Tally-girl's boot out in the gardens when there's been no sign of her trunk since it went missing? Puzzling, don't you think?"

"Yes, yes, the boot," he said, taking a glance at the trunk tucked in the corner of the room with that solitary boot atop it.

The one Brutus had wrestled from the person who'd been lurking around the maze. And here he'd been convinced it was Dashwell that night. Had assumed it was him.

"A lady, I have to imagine was wearing it before that mutt stole it from her."

A lady? A chill ran down Larken's spine.

Meanwhile, as her knitting pins clicked and chatted away, so did Aunt Minty. "But what sort of lady would be nosing about in the dark of night, wearing Tally-girl's boots, I ask you? I've been sitting here waiting for you and a thinkin' on just that notion."

He shrugged, though he couldn't shake loose the niggle of suspicion that her question planted, taken root. What sort of lady, indeed?

Then again, he knew damn well what sort lurked about in the shadows.

And apparently, so did Aunt Minty. "Now, I ask you, why didn't this bit of muslin just bring the gel's trunk to the front door, as nice as you please, and ask for her own back? Have you thought of that, my lord?"

Again he shook his head, but he also closed the door and leaned against it, listening to her theory as a dark cloud began to settle overhead.

"Heard talk of such women when I lived in the Dials," she told him. "You know about that, now don't you?" He nodded and she continued. "Well, I lived in the Dials a good part of me life and saw a fair amount of things that weren't meant to be seen. Saw strangers pass through those streets, for it's a place where no one is likely to ask too many questions. Not in the Dials. Not if'n you have the gold to silence 'em, that is."

He pushed off the door and walked over to the trunk, picking up the boot and studying it as he listened to her.

"Occasionally there would be a lady come through. Oh, you knew she was a lady, as much as she would try to hide the fact. French, those ones. Can't hide that. They were a dangerous lot. Could slip in and cut a man's throat and be gone better than your best riverside badger." She paused and looked him directly in the eyes. "Ever heard of 'em?"

He glanced over at her. "A badger, or one of your mysterious ladies?"

She grinned. "I can see why my Tally-girl is in love with you. You're a bit of a tease, now, aren't you?"

Larken had stopped listening after she'd said those fateful words.

"*. . . my Tally-girl is in love with you. . .*"

"Is she? Truly?" he asked.

Aunt Minty slowly rewound the wool around her fingers and began knitting again. "So you are listening to me."

"Every word," he told her, frozen in place.

"Aye. She loves you. Fell in love with you the first moment she clapped eyes on you. Knew you were naught but a Covent Garden pater-cove."

He laughed. He'd thought he'd done a better job of impersonating Hollindrake's cousin than that. But as much as he saw the humor in the situation, marveled at Tally's keen instincts, he couldn't laugh for long. "I fear her regard isn't all that well placed."

"Stuff and nonsense," she shot back. "But you'll come to your senses right soon, I wager. Once you catch that Frog filching, murdering mort who's got me Tally-girl's trunk. She's the one who's a danger to us all, as long as she's a sneakin' about and waiting like a cat on the ledge to pounce."

"You think one of these French ladies is after—"

"Didn't say what she's after, just said she's around, mark me words."

He went along with her theory, purely for the sport of it, at least that was what he tried to tell himself. And yet there were too many odd pieces tumbling together one after another—his dreams last night of Aurora, Tally's drawing from the inn, the stray boot and the stranger in the maze.

But it still didn't explain why a member of *L'Ordre du Lis Noir* would be here . . .

That whispering voice returned, echoing what it had been nattering on about earlier.

"*. . . it isn't as if that man hasn't made enemies clear across the Atlantic and then some . . .*"

Dashwell. The Order was after Dashwell. Just as he was. For it was highly likely, given Dash's penchant for gold, that he'd been aiding both sides for years. Lining his pockets with gold and to his detriment, learning too much . . . The Order, with their primary objective of complete secrecy, probably had even more reason for wanting Dash to disappear . . . permanently.

It made sense, it tied everything together so neatly, he couldn't breathe, yet it still wasn't enough to erase all his doubts.

"How can you be so sure," Larken began, "that whoever has Miss Langley's trunk is one of these French morts, as you call them?"

"Cause I took a closer peek inside that there trunk," she said quite proudly, leaning over and digging through her workbasket. She plucked out what looked like a heavy purse, and with a measure of agility that surprised him, tossed it to him. The bigger shock came when he caught it, for the weight of was enough to have him nearly drop it. Nearly, for as Larken caught it, a chill ran across his palm.

"Go ahead, look inside," she said. "Convinced me when I saw them."

He pulled the ribbons open and pulled out a gold coin, one of many, and found himself looking down at the profile of Bonaparte.

"That's not all of it," Aunt Minty told him. "There's enough French gold in there, hidden 'neath the false bottom, to see our good King George himself murdered."

Mrs. Browne stood off to one side of the foyer and waited, dismayed and disgruntled to be caught up in Aurora's plans. Her sister was mad, always had been, but this . . . attempting to kidnap someone at the Duke of Hollindrake's ball, why it was worse than madness . . . it was utterly ruinous.

If she were caught, where would that leave Sarah? Mrs. Browne pressed her lips together, even as her fingers gripped the pistol she held concealed in the folds of her elaborate gown.

Sarah, dear and darling Sarah. She deserved a good marriage—and far from England, Aveline could see that now.

Whatever had she been thinking, bringing her daughter to England in the first place? She should have known Aurora would show up just when everything was going so well.

Mr. Browne had argued against it, and it had been the only time Aveline had crossed her husband. And him nothing but kind and generous and well-to-do. She'd been a fool. And once she helped Aurora, she and Sarah would be on the first Dutch ship she could find and make their way back to Boston if they had to go by way of the China seas.

Behind her, she heard footsteps on the stairs, and glanced up. It was Mr. Hartwell, that odd cousin of Lady Philippa's, if she remembered correctly. She looked again. Ah yes. Mr. Hartwell and his valet.

She would have disregarded the pair completely, but something about the man's servant caught her eye.

When she took another surreptitious peek, shock filled her bones. Though the valet's hair was shorn closely to his head and his face shaved clean, she knew without a doubt the plainly clad man beside

Mr. Hartwell was the usually wildly flamboyant Captain Thomas Dashwell.

Until this moment she'd been hoping Aurora was wrong, that Dashwell wasn't here. She rather liked her brash compatriot, knew her husband and many of her fellow countrymen considered him one of their country's greatest heroes.

Her part in what would surely be his death churned in her stomach, but there was Sarah's future at stake.

As they exited the front doors, Mrs. Browne followed quickly and caught up with them as they made it to the drive.

"Excuse me, Mr. Hartwell, I believe you dropped something," she called out, trying to sound sweet and sincere. It worked, for both men turned and she moved forward, pistol in hand.

"My dear Mrs. Browne," the man brazened. "What is the meaning of this?"

"I must ask you both to continue around the side of the house," she told them. "If you please, just do as I say and we can be done with this business quickly." Then she looked Dashwell directly in the eye. "Sir, I know who you are, and if you try anything, my maid is watching from the windows above and she will cry out an alert that will bring every man in this house running. You'll be hung before dawn."

Not that it matters, she thought miserably, nodding for them to continue into the shadows around the house. *You'll be dead the moment Aurora has her hands on you.*

Just then, out of the shadows, a soft laugh rose. "*Trés bien*, Aveline. You have not lost your touch."

In front of her Dashwell stiffened, as if he had heard a ghost. "Aurora," he gasped as the lady stepped from the shadows, clad in a black riding habit, pistol in hand.

"*Oui, mon chère*. I have come to find you. I should have known you would slip past the English once again, but you shall not find me as easy to evade."

"If you have come to repay me," Dashwell said with his usual flirtatious cheek, "your timing is impeccable. I have need of your gold."

Aurora laughed, a sound that sent a chill of foreboding down Mrs. Browne's spine. Because she'd heard that mocking laugh once too often. Like just before her sister had murdered her English lover in Paris.

"Dashwell, where you are going, gold will be of no use." Aurora waved at her sister. "Go get what I need from my trunk."

"But you said I'd only have to bring—"

Aurora turned on her, pointing the pistol at her. "Go, now. Or when I am done with this business, I will find Sarah and take her with me, where she should have been all these years."

Mrs. Browne turned and fled, praying with each shaking step that the trunk would be exactly where Aurora thought it was and that the gold inside had yet to be discovered.

If I fail, she thought wildly, *I'll find Sarah and be gone from here, before she has time to catch us.*

But that was a foolish notion, for there was no escaping Aurora. Not when she held all the cards.

* * *

Larken entered the ballroom with only one thought. Find Tally.

All the way down the stairs and as he pushed through the crowd, the idea of her being in danger prodded him forward.

What if something happened to her?

It was enough to make him discover the madness inside him.

He loved her. Somehow in the last few days, he'd fallen in love with the madcap, treasonous, impetuously romantic chit.

When he'd confessed as much to Aunt Minty, it had been as if a weight had been lifted from his heart, his life. He loved her. And demmit if he was going to let anyone harm her or those she loved.

"Excuse me, pardon me," he said as he prodded and shoved his way through the crowded ballroom. "Please move aside."

"I never!" murmured one matron as he bullied his way past her to come to the edge of the dance floor.

Before him couples twirled and parted and came together again, but there was no sign of her.

Oh, where the devil was she?

And then, as if in answer to his prayer, he spied her. His relief was immediately replaced by a pang of guilt. She looked positively miserable being paraded down the line by Lord Norridge, who held her hand just so and made sure he smiled and winked at the other ladies he passed.

Gads, what a popinjay! Larken knew he'd owe her more than just a sincere apology for signing her up for what, two dances, with that idiot?

Well, he'd do one better and relieve her of the situation—and he did so, by snagging out his hand, catching her by the elbow and tugging her out of the line and into the crowd.

Larken wondered how long it would take Norridge to realize he was dancing by himself.

Tally, on the other hand, wasn't coming easily, dragging her heels and tugging at his grasp. When that failed, she cursed him roundly. In Russian. Giving a rather colorful description of his parentage. Or therein lack of.

As if he were going to let her go over a barrage of insults. Now or ever. It was the sort of scene that would have had him grinning if the stakes weren't so high.

"Let me go or I shall scream," she threatened.

"Scream," he told her, "and I will toss you over my shoulder and give every man in this room a good look at those ankles of yours as well as your rather delightful backside."

Her eyes widened and her mouth opened in a gaping *O* as if she were about to raise the dead with her complaints, but she must have seen the intractable intent behind his threat, and she said nothing.

Though it didn't keep her from dragging her heels.

Through a doorway and a salon and then through another. And finally into the room where he'd been pinned and poked by the tailor.

Even before they came to a halt, he issued his demand, "You need to tell me where Dashwell is. Now."

Her reply was a loud, indignant *snort*. Arms crossing over her chest, she teetered on her heels and glared at him.

So, this wasn't going to be easy, but she'd see the sense of trusting him quickly enough.

"You don't understand," he told her, "his life is in danger."

Oh, that got her talking. "Yes, I would say so. *From you.*"

He recoiled a bit as if she had struck him. And in that slight movement, she took a chance to dodge past him, but once again he caught her and this time hauled her right up against him, both hands holding her tight.

"Lord Larken, unhand me." Her words came out with such deadly calm, he nearly did so.

Nearly.

"Not until you tell me where Dashwell is. I must know."

She shook her head. "Never."

Leaning over, he stared right into her eyes. "Demmit, this is no game, Miss Langley. None of your Lady Persephone nonsense."

Staring right back at him, meeting him word for word, she said, "And it never has been a game to me, my lord."

Oh, God, this was getting him nowhere. He tried another tact, loosening his grip and trying to smile a bit. "Tally, please. I beseech you, tell me where he is. You must trust me. Your Aunt Minty said—"

"Aunt Minty? What have you done to her?"

"Nothing!"

"Then whatever has she to do with this?"

Larken drew back. The truth was hardly going to help his cause, but he wasn't going to let any more lies find their way between them. Keep them apart. "I was up in your room just now—"

"In my room? Looking for Dashwell, I assume?"

Going from bad to worse, he flinched. "Yes," he ground out. "If you must know, then yes, I was in your room looking for him."

"And if you'd found him, what then, my lord?" The question hung in the air.

Honesty. No lies, he told himself. "I would have killed him."

She reeled back from him, slipping out of his grasp. "Murdered him, you mean."

Larken nodded.

"So why do you think I will help you find him when you have every intention of killing him?" She sidestepped him again and moved so a chair sat between them. It might as well have been the English Channel. "How is it, sir, that you can kill a friend? Is that how you regard those you love? Easily expendable and forgettable in your unending quest for honor? I ask you, sir, where is the honor in murder?"

"Tally, listen to me. Everything has changed. You must believe me. Your Aunt Minty did. In fact it was her reasoning that got me to see the right of things. There is more at stake here than just Dashwell's life. When we opened the trunk—"

"You were searching my belongings?"

Oh, of all the hypocritical accusations. "Just as you did mine?"

"That was different. I haven't been lying about my identity or my intentions."

"You haven't? Does your sister know what, or rather whom, you've been keeping upstairs in your room?"

At this, she had the decency to blanch.

"And I might point out that 'your things' are not yours at all, that trunk belongs to a member of *L'Ordre du Lis Noir*."

That brought her gaze up. "The Order of the Black Lily?"

"You know of them?" Now he was taken aback.

"Papa told us stories of them as bedtime tales, but I never thought they truly—"

"Oh, they exist. And that trunk belongs to one of them, and I suspect she is here for the same reason I am. To find Dashwell."

Her mouth opened in that wide *O* again. "Oh, dear, no!"

"Oh, yes," he said. "And if the Order is desparate to find Dashwell, mayhap the information they want to stop him from sharing would be valuable to England."

"Enough to save his life?"

Larken nodded.

For a second they just stood there, and he could see she was sifting through what he'd told her and trying to come to a decision.

To trust him or not.

Since his pleas had gotten him nowhere, he let his infamous reckless nature speak for him. Coming around the chair, he took her in his arms, before she could barely get out a shocked, "My lord!" he sealed her mouth with his lips and kissed her.

Hungry, naked desire filled his veins, and for a

second he wondered if this was the wisest means of persuasion, because it was taking him down at the knees.

At first her hands balled up in fists against his chest, but as his tongue swept over her lips, opened them to his exploration and swept over her own pert one, her fingers uncurled and wound instead around his lapels, pulling him closer.

It was like falling into heaven to have her like this, and if the entire world hadn't been about to implode around them, he would have carried her to the sofa across the room and made love to her.

And so it was that he reluctantly pulled away from her. "You must trust me."

Her eyes were afire with passion, her breathing coming in ragged gasps. Beneath his hands, she was trembling, for it seemed she felt the same as he did.

And if she did, if it were true that she loved him, then he had to do something. "I give you my word. I will not kill him."

She paused and looked deeply into his eyes. "Truly?"

"Yes. Please, Tally, I must know—" But he never finished his plea, for over her shoulder and out the window in the clear moonlight of the garden was the answer to his question. "Dashwell!" he gasped as he let her go and rushed to the window.

For there indeed was Thomas Dashwell, along with that odd cousin of Lady Philippa's, and a woman . . .

"That's not—" Tally began to protest as she followed him. "What the devil is Mrs. Browne doing out there?" Then she paused. "That isn't Mrs. Browne, but the woman from the inn."

"Not Mrs. Browne?" he repeated, as he looked anew at the lady prodding the other two along. "What is the quickest way out there?"

She shook her head. "I will not let you—"

"Tally, don't be a fool. I will not kill Dashwell. I gave you my word." He paused. "I can't do it now. For if I did, you would never forgive me and I cannot live without your regard." He paused and then found the courage to speak the truth. "Without your love."

This brought her startled gaze up to his. For a tenuous terrible moment, he thought she was going to deny him, deny his heart. But the moment passed and she nodded quickly and waved toward the door. "You need to go to the end of the hall and then through the second parlor. There is a set of French doors in the salon beyond that let out to the corner of the house near the old stables. I would guess that is where she is taking them," she said, nodding toward the window where the three were disappearing around the corner.

"Thank you," he said, kissing her quickly and shooting toward the door. When he got there, he turned around and told her. "Go find Hollindrake and tell him what has happened. He'll know what to do." He opened the door, but then paused again. "And Tally?"

"Yes?

Was it him or did she sound hopeful?

"I love you."

And then he disappeared before she could reply.

Chapter 16

*T*ally started for the ballroom and nearly tripped with her first step. "Bloody wretched shoes," she muttered as she kicked them off and ran in her stocking-clad feet back to the ballroom.

And though Larken had told her to go straight to Hollindrake, there was no way on earth she was going to tell her brother-in-law what had been going on under his roof.

Not that he probably doesn't already know, a rather practical voice chided.

Ignoring it, she made a beeline straight for the only person she trusted on this. The only other person who had as much at stake as she did.

Pippin.

And she found her quickly, for she had only to look over the heads of all the gentlemen to find the tall, handsome figure of Lord Gossett. She slid though the crowd, muttering apologies and trying to ignore the complaints of "poor manners" and "all the shoving and jostling" that followed in her path.

"Pippin, there you are," she said, breathlessly. "I fear I must steal her away from you, my lord. There's an emergency of sorts, um, I, well, that is, I need Pippin because—" Tally searched for an excuse, not that her cousin's face hadn't grown pale with panic. "My shoes," she blurted out. "The heel broke and I wanted to wear Pippin's pair that will go with this gown, but can't for the life of me find them. Would you be a dear, and come with me?"

She'd already wound her hand around Pippin's arm and was towing her from her admirer, so that they barely heard Lord Gossett bidding her to return soon.

"Whatever has happened?" Pippin whispered as they made their way out of the crush.

"I'm not entirely sure, but someone who looks like Mrs. Browne has kidnapped Dash and Mr. Jones. Lord Larken believes she is a member of the Order of the Black Lily, or something like that."

Pippin pulled to a stop. "Are you jug-bit?" she asked, using one of Aunt Minty's favorite expressions. "You're talking madness."

They had made it nearly to the door and were about to enter the foyer, when Tally stopped her and pointed to the stairs beyond. "Look there. What do you see?"

"Mrs. Browne. That hardly gives any credence that she's—" Pippin's arguments failed as she saw exactly what Tally was pointing at.

The pistol in the lady's hand.

"Oh, dear," Pippin gasped as the matron disappeared into the darkness above. "Do you think she—"

"I don't know," Tally said, pushing Pippin forward, a plan forming in her head. "Follow her," she told her cousin. "Just as Felicity and I taught you how to follow someone. Keep to the shadows and if you can find a way to stop her, do it."

Pippin started for the stairs, but then she paused. "And what of you?"

"I am going to save them," she said.

Her cousin nodded and made her way up the stairs as silently as a cat, and Tally had turned to dash down the hall to Hollindrake's office when she came face-to-face with the last person she wanted to find blocking her path.

Felicity. "And where do you think you're going?" she demanded.

Larken made it to the gardens and found his way past the maze and along the grassy lawn toward the old stables. A lantern hanging from a carriage cast a beacon of light that drew him along. The carriage was ready to travel, the horses in their traces, but there was no sign of a groom or driver.

Which didn't bode well.

In fact there was no sign of anyone, which made it even more eerie, considering the crush of carriages, servants, and grooms in the front drive.

Grudgingly, he had to acknowledge it was a good plan. For who would question a stray carriage leaving the house early? A local baron who'd drunk too much, a lady overcome by the heat of the ballroom, a couple arguing over another's indiscreet behavior.

Any of those could be inside, and no servant was going to look twice into such private business.

But that was just the point. There were no servants about, and Larken knew he was on the verge of discovery. He crept closer and closer to the old stables, and as he drew near, voices came into earshot.

"Aurora, be reasonable," Dash was saying. "Forget the debts between us, we are friends, allies. I have to surmise it was you who sent word to Lady Philippa about my hanging, wasn't it? Certainly you wouldn't see me freed just to put me in a grave, now would you?"

"But you've outgrown your usefulness, my love," she purred.

Larken froze. The woman's voice, her very words pulled the past right into the present.

"*. . . you've outgrown your usefulness . . .*"

The exact same words this bitch used before she'd killed his father. It was nearly enough to send him pitching forward, gun drawn, to kill her where she stood, but she was continuing to rail at Dashwell, and her revelations were stunning.

Enough to stay his course, at least for the moment.

"Aurora, I would never betray your confidences. How many years have I helped you?"

"And been paid handsomely."

"For the last two years?" Dash struggled to sit up straighter. "All I've seen during that time is promises. Promises of gold. And still I helped you. Didn't betray you. Why? Out of loyalty."

She laughed. "*Capitaine*, you would sell your own mother to save your neck. Besides, I didn't pass along the news of your hanging to your little English mistress to see you out of jail," she told him. "I had every conviction that she would bungle the entire affair and see you all killed, before you struck some sort of bargain to save your neck. Gave the English something worth letting you live."

"Ah, but my dear Aurora, you overstate your worth. Believe me, I tried to sell your secrets and no one believed me. Didn't want to be peddled old myths. Didn't believe you even existed."

"Liar," she hissed.

He shrugged. "It's the truth. The English don't care about you and your Order. I fear you are a relic from another time. You have no queen to protect, only an upstart Corsican to aid. And now he's off to Elba, an emperor no more. Hardly the noble cause you once defended so admirably."

"Shut up," she cursed, her entire body trembling with rage. "Shut up. You know nothing of my cause. Nothing whatsoever."

"Then why kill me?" Dashwell posed.

Larken would have grinned at the captain's dangerous and reckless statements, but his taunting was going to get him killed if he didn't cease.

"Really, madame, as I've said before, I do believe you've made a mistake," Mr. Hartwell began. And was cut off by the sharp retort of a pistol. Larken heard the man groan his last as he slumped to the ground.

"Christ!" Dash cursed. "Aurora, there was no reason to kill him. He's naught to do with any of this."

"He's naught to anyone now," she said, the sound of a second pistol cocking.

Larken had heard enough, and came around the

corner, pistol drawn, ready to shoot this mad witch where she stood. For a split-second he held her in his sights, his finger poised over the trigger and about to pull it, when suddenly he was pitched forward, a thunderous crash sounding in his ears and stars bursting before his eyes.

Even as he fell, he turned and spied a large man with a shovel in his hand. Dressed in the coat and hat of a driver, it was apparent that while legend held the Order's women worked alone, Aurora had help.

Help that now grinned wolfishly down at him and looked ready to finish his handiwork.

Felicity stood with her hands on her hips and faced Tally. "Where do you think you are going?" she repeated.

"Duchess, there is just a bit of trouble," Tally stammered. "Uh, with my shoes," she offered, holding up the hem of her gown to show Felicity her stocking-clad toes. "Pippin is going to loan me her white slippers. You know the ones—with the bows—that you insisted she buy just after you were married." Tally smiled, hoping it hid the panic welling up inside her bones.

And she thought she'd managed it, for Felicity nodded and turned to return to the ballroom.

Tally breathed a soft sigh of relief. But it was a wee bit early to be celebrating.

Felicity paused, half turned, and glancing over her shoulder asked with quiet precision, "This wouldn't have anything to do with Dashwell being upstairs in your suite, would it?"

It was as if the foundation of Hollindrake House

had been ripped out from beneath her toes. Tally staggered back and caught herself by grabbing hold of the door jamb. "What sort of ridiculous notion is that?" She managed to laugh.

Felicity swept forward and caught her by the arm, towing her into a nearby alcove. "What is going on? Hasn't Mr. Jones gotten him out yet, or have you ruined that as well?"

"How did you know?" Tally whispered back. "How did you know that he was Mr. Jones and not Mr. Hartwell?"

Felicity's gaze rolled upward. "Pippin's cousin is seventy-four years old, and I sincerely doubt he would be pinching the silver as Mr. Jones was doing last night during dinner. Bruno has told me often enough that his brother Tarleton is the finest lift in all of London."

Tally cringed. What had Tarleton been thinking? Pinching the duke's silver! And at dinner, no less. Yet that was hardly the point. "Before that, what gave us away?"

"From the moment Aunt Minty took ill." Felicity huffed a sigh. "Aunt Minty has never been sick a day in her life, and when I questioned her as to what was going on, she told me."

"But . . . but . . . " Tally tried to put the words together.

Meanwhile, Felicity had thrown up her hands and was pacing the carpet. "Why didn't I stop you from trying this harebrained scheme?" She shuddered. "Because I knew Pippin was determined to see Dash freed. And I could have put my foot down, but that would have only prodded her to do something utterly rash. At least your plan had Miss Porter's approval, so I had to assume there was some sanity behind this madness."

Tally nodded. Without their former teacher's help, her knowledge of the Foreign Office operations through her marriage to Lord John Tremont, and Bruno's brute force, none of this would have been possible.

"Oh, Tally, couldn't you see the risk you put us all at? How ruinous this might be for Hollindrake?"

"I knew," she said miserably. "I felt terrible, but Pippin couldn't do it alone. And she—"

"Wasn't going to fail him, yes, I know." Felicity reached out and squeezed her sister's hand. "What has gone wrong?"

"Larken says—" Tally began. "Oh, the man you think is Mr. Ryder is Lord Larken, sent by—"

"Yes, yes, the Foreign Office. Of course I knew, for he was—" She stopped for a moment. "Never mind that. What does Larken say?"

Tally eyed her sister and tried to determine what it was that Felicity had been about to reveal, but shook it off and continued, since time was of the essence. "He claims that a member of *L'Ordre du Lis Noir* has been following us, and with Mrs. Browne's help has kidnapped Dash and Mr. Jones. He's gone off to the old stables to stop them, and sent me in here for help."

"Mrs. Browne?" Felicity's gaze leapt up as if that was the only point that mattered. "What has she to do with all this?"

"I haven't the vaguest notion," Tally said. "We could ask Miss Browne, for there she is." She pointed to their former schoolmate, who was preening and posing between two dangling lordlings, with a glowering Grimston just off her elbow. "I told you not to invite her."

"I wondered when you'd get around to that," Felicity said, glancing back toward the ballroom. "What have you in mind?"

"I was going to get Hollindrake's pistol from his desk and follow Larken. I fear he is walking into danger."

"He most likely is, if the *L'Ordre du Lis Noir* is involved." She shook her head. "I always knew when Papa said they were just make-believe he wasn't telling the truth. I think he feared if we knew they were real, we would have run off and joined them."

"He was probably right," Tally said.

"Indeed," Felicity agreed. "You go fetch the pistol, and I shall bring Miss Browne to help us."

"Miss Browne?" Tally said. "Do you think this is wise?"

"Well, if her mother is involved, then we can use her daughter to our advantage." She straightened her shoulders and turned to get to work.

Tally caught her by the elbow. "Felicity, you aren't just using this as an excuse to get even with Miss Browne for all the times she taunted us and paraded her wealth before us, are you?"

Her sister ruffled, and shook Tally's hand from her arm, then made a polite show of smoothing out her gown for a passerby. When he was gone, she whispered back, "Tally, I would never do such a thing."

But the sly smile on Felicity's lips said something else.

* * *

"Hollindrake," Lord Gossett said, as he moved beside his host. "Have you noticed something odd?"

The former army major looked over and smiled as if there was nothing wrong. "That my wife, her cousin, and her sister are all missing?"

"Yes."

"Actually, my wife is over there," he nodded across the room to the doorway and the foyer beyond. "It appears she is kidnapping Miss Browne and dragging her from the ball."

"Do you think there is more amiss here than meets the eye?"

"Considering Lord Larken is also gone, yes, I do," the duke said.

"Larken?"

"Yes. He's here to find Dashwell."

"So all the talk of his escape—" Gossett's speech came to a halt as he added up all the pieces. "Oh, dear God. I had rather hoped—"

"Well, so had I, but it appears we are both about to be sorely disappointed. Or worse, disgraced." He bowed to a passing matron. "I would appreciate your discretion as I go discover what trouble my wife and her relations have brewed up under my roof. I know you are the local magistrate, but—"

"You have my word on the matter, but only if you let me assist," the viscount said in all earnestness.

He nodded, and they made their way across the crowded ballroom as quickly as they could.

A faraway argument roused Larken from the blackness where he lay. At first he couldn't remember where he was or why his head hurt like the very devil. From the smell of the rough ground in which his nose was stuffed, he knew he wasn't home in London after a long night of carousing.

He took another sniff, and this time the sweet scent of blood filled his nostrils.

He was bleeding, he knew that, for his head had that heavy, thick feeling of being clouted. But it wasn't only his blood he smelled, for when he cautiously opened his eyes, he discovered Mr. Hartwell lying nearby, his blank stare looking heavenward.

Larken didn't need to see the deep, dark claret stain across the man's chest to know he was dead. He'd seen that look on too many men's faces to know they were looking toward a light that only the dead saw.

Beside him, Dash was trussed up like a Christmas goose, and across the stable, just on the other side of the lamplight, stood a woman.

Her.

Suddenly the entire evening came back to him in dangerous clarity.

"Now what do you propose to do, Aurora?" Dashwell was saying with his usual devil-may-care coaxing tones. "Kill Larken as well? Hardly sporting and will most likely bring the entire Foreign Office down on your head."

Larken opened his eyes cautiously, considering the nature of the debate happening overhead.

"If you think to frighten me, Dashwell, with tales of English prowess at capturing their enemies, I and my brethren have eluded them for three centuries. Those pompous fools in London have never believed they could be outwitted by mere women."

"You make an excellent point, Aurora," Dash agreed. "But you have no sisters left to protect you," he said softly, coaxing. "No one to shield you from disclosure. You are the last of your kind, and it is a sorry day to see it coming to an end."

The lady flinched as if she'd been struck by Dashwell's quiet bit of truth, but she rallied quickly.

"An end?" she mocked. "I see the situation rather differently. I have you in my sights, and Larken as a hostage. When my servant returns with the carriage, we'll drive away without any notice—that was your plan, was it not?"

Dash acknowledged her question with a slight nod.

"And then when we are out of earshot, I fear you will become the victim of your own fame. Shot while trying to get to your true love nearby." She paused. "My only regret is that your untimely death will add a sadly romantic twist to your infamy. Give your demise a pitiable, tragic air that you hardly deserve."

Dash shrugged and then looked her right in the eyes. "And how unfortunate your part in the story will be lost in history, as your sacred Order will be naught but dust."

Oh, excellent strategy, Dashwell, Larken thought. *Prod the madwoman into shooting you.*

Not while I still have a breath in my body. He'd promised Tally that Dashwell would live. And demmit, the arrogant bastard would, if he had to give his own life to see his wretched friend live.

With every bit of wherewithal he possessed, he struggled up, his hands bound behind his back. Never had his life hung by such a tenuous thread, but then again, he knew that all too soon, Hollindrake and Temple would arrive.

"I don't believe we've been introduced," he managed to say, as he wrangled his way up into a sitting position beside Dash. "But I believe you are the bitch who murdered my father."

"Well done, Larken," Dash applauded. "With such manners it is a wonder you can even get a whore to pay attention to you, least of all a lady."

"As if you have ever noticed the difference," Larken replied.

Dash managed to look affronted. "Kind words from the man who came to kill me."

"Failed to kill you," he pointed out.

"Ah, but it appears this dear lady intends to remedy your shortcomings."

"Silence, both of you," Aurora said, coming into the light.

And for the first time, Larken looked into the eyes of the woman he'd sought for all these years.

She was a striking beauty still, her hair as black as her heart. And there was something about the way she smiled that was strangely familiar, as if he'd seen that smug turn of the lips before . . . and recently.

"You take after your father," she said. "How unfortunate you will share his fate."

"I'll see you dead before that," Larken said. "You'll pay for your crimes."

"My dear boy, you are as naïve and foolish as your father was. He thought to reform me, and you think you can stop me." She waved her pistol at him. "You are but a hair's breadth from seeing him again, so do not tempt me to hasten your reunion."

But her threat was lost when the carriage drove into the old stables. The great barn of a building had been constructed so that wagons and carriage could be driven directly inside and the horses, harnesses and traces removed under cover.

Aurora's servant sat up in the box, hat drawn down and cloak around his figure.

Was Larken mistaken, or did the man look smaller? And then the driver tipped the brow of his hat just so and winked at him.

Tally! He glanced up at Aurora to see if she'd noticed, but she was too busy opening the door and motioning her pistol at Dash for him to get in.

Larken took this opportunity to get a better look. While at first glance he had assumed it was his Tally, he now saw how wrong he'd been. That wasn't Tally up there, but her sister.

The duchess?

So where the devil was Tally? Larken's heart was nearly wrenched in two. But he didn't let any of it change his countenance. And if Dash had noticed the switch, he gave naught a clue.

Larken struggled against his bindings, furious at Hollindrake that he would let his wife drive into danger like this.

And then he realized what had really happened after he'd left Tally in the study. She'd never gone to Hollindrake. Had ignored his instructions completely.

And whatever harebrained scheme she had in the works, it was putting her life, and that of her sister's, in danger.

All of them in danger.

Larken ground his teeth together, ignoring how that added to his already throbbing skull. When he got out of this mess, he was going to kill her.

That is if Hollindrake didn't beat him to the punch.

Then his nightmare became only too real as Aurora looked inside the carriage and said with gleeful delight, "My, my, my! What have we here?"

Hollindrake, Gossett, and Temple stood in the shadows and watched as the shadowy figure donned the great coat from the man lying at her feet, tucked on his hat, and climbed gingerly up onto the carriage, catching up the reins and driving it right into the open causeway of the old stables.

"Is that who I think it is?" Temple asked.

Hollindrake nodded. "Yes. It's Felicity." The duke would have shouted at his wife, cursed her roundly and soundly, if it wouldn't have alerted whomever she was trying to deceive inside the stables.

"And we have another puzzle," Temple said, nodding behind them, where from the house, Pippin was coming, tramping across the lawn, prodding a furious-looking Mrs. Browne before her. The matron's muttered protests were met with yet another poke from the pistol in Pippin's hands.

Gossett stepped out of the shadows before either Hollindrake or Temple could stop him. "Lady Philippa, that is as far as you go."

The duke wanted to groan, but then again the love-struck viscount had never served his country, either in the war or through the Foreign Office, and hadn't the experience to act with some measure of restraint.

Temple though, was another matter. He acted quickly, pulling the ladies into the cover of the hedge, and then yanked Gossett back out of sight as well.

"Your Grace!" Mrs. Browne said indignantly. "Your wife's cousin has gone mad."

Pippin snorted. "Aunt Minty caught her stealing gold and identification papers from the trunk that Tally got by mistake. She's helping a French agent murder Dash."

"I would never—" Mrs. Browne began to protest, but Hollindrake cut her off by covering her mouth with his hand, and then reaching with his other to take the pistol away from Pippin.

"Mrs. Browne, I would like you to listen carefully to what I am saying. Your daughter is inside a carriage that my wife just drove into that stable—"

The lady's eyes grew wild, rolling in that direction and then turning to beseech the duke. Her words were mangled, but two of them were very clear. "Oh, no."

"Who are you helping?" he demanded, and when he pulled his hand from her mouth, she willingly revealed all.

"My sister."

This made no sense, but then again, neither did Temple's quiet question. "Madame, is your sister a member of *L'Ordre du Lis Noir*?"

She glanced down at the ground, and then nodded.

"Demmit." Temple raked his fingers through his hair. "Larken was right all along. If he's still alive, he'll never let me or Pymm hear the end of it."

"So this Order," Gossett asked. "Are they dangerous?"

"Deadly," Temple said. "At least that is what legend has said."

"The Order is no legend," Mrs. Browne snapped at him. Then she sighed and explained it all. "Aurora is the last of our kind and she wants Dash dead to hide any connection to her. She'll dispose of him later, once they are far enough away. She blackmailed me into helping her, sent me upstairs to retrieve her money and papers from the trunk, but you must stop her. For if she finds she has my Sarah, she will not release her and I'll never see my daughter again."

Hollindrake looked from the stables to Temple, who shrugged and jerked his head in that direction.

The message was clear. *Time to end this. Before it is too late.*

Larken gaped as Aurora pulled Miss Browne from inside the carriage. The girl's hands were bound, as was her mouth.

"Well this is an enchanting surprise. However did you manage this?" Aurora asked her driver.

His heart stilled, as Felicity just nodded to the woman in a servial gesture. *For you, my lady*, it said.

"Excellent work," Aurora replied, barely giving the driver any notice, fixed as she was on her new prize. She was about to pluck the gag off the girl's mouth, when another voice rang out.

"Madame, it is over."

The Frenchwoman swiveled in that direction like a cat, pulling Miss Browne in front of her and prodding her pistol into the girl's head. She'd moved so fast, so quickly, Larken marveled at her deadly instincts, for indeed she was trapped, but with an innocent hostage as her shield.

At one end of the stables stood Temple and Hollindrake, and between them, a pale and drawn Mrs. Browne.

The matron spoke. "Let Sarah go. Please, Aurora, you have no desire to harm her, I know that. Let her go and your life will be spared. I have their word."

Both Temple and Hollindrake nodded, and inside Larken rebelled. They might have agreed, but he certainly wouldn't rest until this woman was on her way to the gates of hell.

At this generous offer, Aurora scoffed. "You think some misplaced maternal wellspring is going to save her, Aveline? I didn't care what happened to her in Paris, why should I now?"

Paris . . . Larken's head nearly exploded with memories, the throbbing from where he'd been struck nothing compared to the cacophony of images as they arose, his father's voice piercing his pain.

What of the child . . .

Larken's gaze wrenched up. Aurora and his father hadn't been talking about him that night, but of another. *Their child together.*

He stared at the frightened, bewildered miss being held against her will, and saw what he'd all but missed before. The resemblance was startling. Miss Browne held an uncanny likeness to a portrait of his grandmother that hung in his London house, as well as to the woman holding her.

This is was his sister. His half-sister.

"You cannot stop me," Aurora said, backing up

and pulling Miss Browne along with her. "I cannot be stopped. Never."

Then out of the shadows behind her came a sight that Larken's heart leapt to see.

Tally. Alive.

But what the devil was she thinking?

For his impetuous, foolish minx held a shovel in her hands, most likely the same one he'd been hit with, and was making her way slowly and silently toward an unsuspecting Aurora.

Everyone seemed to be holding their breath, each one saying a prayer for her success, even as Aurora continued her mad rantings.

"Three hundred years. Three hundred years we've succeeded and we'll continue for three hundred more," she crowed. "See that we don't."

And just then, a sharp crack echoed through the stables. Tally looked down at the broken twig beneath her foot, and then up at Larken, a look of utter dismay and apology on her face.

Demmit, he cursed, *when would she ever learn to keep a watch on her toes?*

Aurora whirled around, a mad fury in her eyes and her pistol well aimed.

As the shot rang out, Larken's heart tore in two.

Chapter 17

*T*ally looked down at her chest, fully expecting to see a crimson stain ruining her gown, but there was nothing there but black velvet.

When she looked up, she could see why. Aurora wavered on her feet. She no longer held Miss Browne, but still she stood, shock having widened her eyes into great, dark pools. The pistol trembled in her hand and she aimed it at Tally again, but before she could fire, she pitched face forward into the ground.

Miss Browne let out a piercing scream before she rushed to her mother's arms.

In the driver's seat, Felicity sat with a smoking pistol in her hand, a dangerous gleam in her eyes.

Hollindrake surged forward. "Are you harmed?"

Felicity shook her head. "Is she—"

"Dead?" Hollindrake glanced over his shoulder at the still form. "Yes."

"She was going to . . . It was Tally's life . . . I had no choice."

"You saved your sister," he said as he helped her down, held her close.

"I had the shot," she said, taking a furtive glance at their fallen enemy. "I knew I was the only one."

"And you did as you should have, Duchess," Temple added. "Your father would be proud of you. Always said we should recruit you—"

"Not ever!" Hollindrake said with firm command. Then to his wife, "And don't you ever consider it!"

Temple smiled as he glanced over at Aurora. "Remind me, Duchess, never to bring unwanted guests to one of your affairs."

Felicity shook her head at her dear, old friend, and then let her husband draw her away from the scene.

Meanwhile, Tally had dropped her shovel and made her way to Larken, cupping his face in her hands, tears spilling down her cheeks. "I thought I'd lost you," she whispered.

He nodded toward the shovel. "So was that to bury me with?"

She sat back and let out a disgruntled sigh. "I was coming to your rescue."

"A most excellent job," he said, as beside him, Temple was helping Dash to his feet. "But you could have gotten killed."

"And you would have been killed if I hadn't helped," Tally scolded as she reached around to untie his bindings. "It seems to me, Lord Larken, you need someone sensible to keep an eye on you."

"And who might that be?"

But before she could answer, Pippin came dashing into the stables, her gaze wild with fright. "I heard the shots—" she began, her shoulders sagging with relief at the sight of Dash, whole and unhurt. Behind her Gossett followed, and he caught her by the elbow and pulled her to a stop, holding her fast.

Once again, the entire assembly paused, for there was only one last piece of business left. Temple stepped forward and offered Larken a hand up. "Shall I?" he asked him.

Tally glanced at both men, momentarily confused by their somber expressions. Whatever was wrong?

Larken shook his head, and began to speak. "Thomas Dashwell, by the order of the King, I arrest you for having committed acts of piracy and" —Pippin's anguished cry stilled Larken for only a moment, but he continued on, his voice unwavering— "murder, wherein you shall be hung—"

Tally stepped in front of him. "You cannot do this. He is your friend," she said, pointing at Dash. "You promised you would not kill him."

"Friend or not, Miss Langley, I must do this," he told her, setting her aside. "I won't be the one to end his life, but—" He paused. "Can you not see why I must do this?"

"No, I cannot," she told him, and rushed over to Pippin, who was now being held back by Felicity.

The three of them turned in unison toward the house, with Mrs. Browne and her daughter in their wake.

The men watched them leave, and only Dash spoke.

"I don't envy any of you bastards," he said. "I might be headed for the hangman's noose, but I dare say it is a better fate than what awaits any of you from those three."

The next morning, Hollindrake house was quiet with an uneasy air.

The arrest of Dash and the death of Aurora and Tarleton had sent a giddy tide of gossip through the crowd and then emptied the ballroom faster than a house fire—especially the news that one of the guests had been murdered.

Pippin sat alone in the parlor of their suite, Tally having hied herself off to who-knows-where and Aunt Minty having gone some time ago in search of the housekeeper for some more red wool, her knitting having assumed a furious pace.

The door behind her opened and closed, and she assumed it was Aunt Minty, but the firm steps on the floor told a different story.

Her gaze swung around, half expecting to find Dash standing there. But it wasn't.

There in the middle of the room stood Viscount Gossett.

And much to her shock, she realized she was glad to see him. She rose to her feet, looked into the sincere depth of his blue eyes and felt a shiver run down her spine.

"I know it is entirely improper of me to intrude," he said, raking his fingers nervously through his golden brown hair, "but I have something I would like to say to you."

She opened her mouth—to say what, she never did know—but he stopped her with two simple words.

"Marry me." It wasn't an order. It wasn't an honorable statement, made out of duty.

It was a man's heartfelt plea.

Marry me.

Pippin wavered, reaching out and catching hold of the back of a chair to steady herself. "I—I—I—" she stammered, before she took a deep breath and found the wherewithal to speak coherently. "You shouldn't have come here. And more to the point, I shouldn't have encouraged you."

"I thought perhaps—"

Pippin didn't know what nudged her to rush in and make the following confession, "My lord, had I never met Dash, and we had come here to this house party, I could imagine—"

"Imagine what?" he said quickly, crossing the room and standing before her. He put his hand atop hers and the warmth of his fingers was intoxicating.

She'd been in a deathly chill since Dash's arrest, and here was Lord Gossett offering her a warm, steady haven. And in his eyes, she saw a depth of regard that tugged at her.

"It isn't possible," she told him, pulling her hand away. "Not now."

"I know, I know, this is utterly the wrong time and place," he said. "But if not now, what of later?"

She shook her head. "No. I have too much regard for you." More than she should. She loved Dash. She had since she was sixteen and her heart was his.

But there was so much at stake right now. And if Dash were to hang?

Pippin turned away and swiped at the tears rising in her eyes.

"Too much regard?" Lord Gossett persisted, coming around her and handing her, without any ceremony, a simple linen square. "That's promising. Too much regard is more than many people begin with. Marry me, Lady Philippa. *Pippin.*"

She almost looked up at him when he said her name thusly. His earnest tone teased her, spoke of something so pure and honest, it wrenched at her. All she could do was shake her head again. "I cannot."

"Whyever not?" he asked. "You'll save your name, your family's good name, from disgrace."

That was a stretch. Her father had been a drunk and a gambler, and her younger brother stood to follow in his father's footsteps.

But Gossett didn't seem to care. "Marriage to me would stop any investigation as to your involvement in his escape from Marshalsea. You'll save your neck."

"And what of yours, my lord?" she asked. "What of your good name?"

Gossett stepped back from her. "My name?"

"It would be ruined." Now it was Pippin's turn to press the point. She must. She had to. *If only I didn't . . .*

"I don't see how my name would be ruined," he said, with all the confidence born of centuries of aristocratic breeding and confidence. It wasn't arrogance with Gossett, but a sense of knowing who he was. An honorable man. "Marriage to me would only—"

She cut him off. "Stop. Please, I beg of you, stop. You are making this so terribly difficult."

"But it isn't difficult," he told her. "It doesn't have to be. I cannot think of what will happen to you if you are not—" he paused. "Married and protected."

"I don't need—"

"But you do, Lady Philippa. You do. You and your child."

Her hands went to the bulge of her belly that would soon press past the careful folds of her gown, which had thus far hid her growing pregnancy. "How did you—"

"Because of that," he said, nodding at her hands folded over her womb. "You did that the other night when you were distressed and I knew right then you were carrying his child." He paused before he continued, "But he is lost to you, and I am not. And, Pippin, my dearest, Pippin, I want to marry you, for your sake and for the babe's sake as well."

She shook her head again. "As long as he is in that cell, sentenced to hang, I cannot—"

Gossett caught her in his arms and held her. His grasp was gentle and reassuring, but his words shocked her as nothing else could have.

"What if I were to see him freed and safely out of England?"

Larken spent the better part of the day closeted away with Hollindrake and Temple, writing reports and comparing notes to ensure that Tally and Lady Philippa's names were well out of the final, official version. There were also the arrangements for Dashwell's safe return to London, as well as unburdening his heart with the truth to both.

Of what Pymm had ordered him to do. How he wouldn't do it now, even if it meant being a failure.

Yet in the light of day, failure seemed a brighter start to his new life than the "honor" and "duty" King and Country had demanded of him.

And now, as the afternoon waned and supper approached, he had one last task. To find Tally. And when he did, then he'd . . .

What the hell are *you going to say to her, Larken, when you do find her?*

There were so many reasons to go to her and beg her forgiveness, plead with her to spend the rest of her life with him, but there were also some very big obstacles that arose between them, as dense and thorny as the hawthorn hedge that made up the maze.

Like the fact that she had committed treason in freeing Dash.

As you *would have, had you not been so blindly stubborn*, she would argue back.

He shook off that thought. What else had Tally said? Oh, yes. How could he forget?

"How is it that you have come to kill a friend? Is that how you regard those you love? Easily expendable and forgettable in your unending quest for honor? I ask you, sir, where is the honor in murder?"

His father had understood what true honor was—placing one's family and heart first, no matter the cost. Larken knew now that his father hadn't gone to Paris to restore his honor, but to retrieve his daughter, lured by Aurora's promise that she'd surrender their child to his care.

And his love for his natural daughter had cost him his life.

Larken shook his head. Honor. Duty. They were all he'd known for so long, and those ideals had nearly cost him his soul. Now it was time to redeem it. To seek the love that was his escape from the prison he'd cast himself into for far too long.

He glanced up at the old stables, where Dash had been locked in a stall and placed under guard—but the guards were nowhere to be seen. Gone. Leaving Dash free to . . .

Bloody hell!

Larken dashed across the lawn, but the whinny of a horse from inside had him pull up short, just before the doors.

He glanced inside and to his amazement spied Lord Gossett guiding his prized stallion toward Dash's cell. It was said the beast was the fleetest animal in England, and one the viscount had refused all offers to sell.

The horse was all that, but the magnificent animal wasn't what stopped Larken. The sight of the sleek saddlebags it wore, as if it and its rider were about to make a fast, hard trip, told all.

Gossett stood before Dash's cell. "Wake up, sir," the viscount said. "I've come with an offer."

Larken slipped inside and hid in one of the stalls. He thought Dash had seen him, but when he looked again his friend paid him no heed.

"Get up," Gossett said. "We haven't much time."

Dashwell stirred and rose from his stool, coming to stand in front of where the viscount stood. "What do you want?"

"That you take this horse, the gold in the saddlebags, this map and ride straight for the coast."

Laughing, Dash sat back down on his stool. "And what? Be shot as I cross the first meadow? I think not, my lord."

"Dashwell, I've risked everything I have to do this," Gossett told him, a deep, emotional note to his words rang with a truth that stilled Larken's heart. The viscount was in earnest.

"I will free you and see that you have safe passage from England on one condition."

Larken edged forward. What the devil was Gossett doing?

"A condition? Let me guess. Has it to do with Lady Philippa?"

Gossett shook his head. "No. It has to do with Lady Gossett. My wife."

It took only a moment for Dash to see what he was saying. Larken as well. *Christ sakes, no!*

Lady Philippa had married Gossett to save Dashwell.

The sheer anguish darkening Dashwell's expression tore at Larken's heart. Gossett could have been kinder if he'd just put a bullet in the captain.

And as the finality of it all sunk in, Dash raged forward, catching the bars with his hands. "What the hell have you done? What did you do to her?"

The viscount stood his ground, and said with just as much intensity, "Nothing more than what you should have done when you had the chance." He paused. "I married her. *She's well and good out of your reach now.*"

His tone and implication were clear. *Pippin had always been out of his reach.*

Dash paced about the cell wildly. "She wouldn't have done this. She wouldn't do this. Not unless . . . " He swung at the bars again, his hand snaking out, and this time Viscount Gossett stepped back.

"If you think I forced her, you're wrong. And I might add, it took very little convincing, for I have much to offer her, and what can you give her, Dashwell? A hanging for aiding you? Having her hunted as you have been? Is that what you offer the lady?"

"I should kill you." Dash's knuckles glowed a ghostly, deadly white as he clung to the cell bars.

"That would be one way of doing it," Gossett said, even as he pulled a long chain from his pocket, obviously having thought of everything, including the key. "But it would not regain the lady's favor." He paused before he set the key in the lock. "Freedom Dashwell, or death?"

Dash nodded, and Gossett let him out.

Oh, Christ, Larken thought. *This isn't going to turn out well.* He would wager his London town house that Gossett had no idea how dangerous the man he'd just freed could be. But Larken did, having seen the captain fight his way out of more than just tavern brawls.

The American stepped out of his prison, paused as he weighed the viscount with his narrowed gaze and then rolled up his fist and punched him with a facer that would have toppled a man twice the viscount's size. As it was, the force sent Gossett flying backward, sprawling on his ass and rolling across the stable ground in the straw and dirt.

But to his credit, he got up, shook himself off and stared at Dash with all the deadly calm of a man who may be bleeding and blackened but still victorious. "I suppose I deserve that."

"I should kill you, you bloody bastard," Dash said.

Gossett ignored him, reaching over and picking up the reins to his horse, tossing them to Dash. "Take good care of him." Then he pulled a packet from his jacket and handed it over. "There is a map inside there, marked with my properties between here and Hastings, as well as a note to my staff with my seal upon it that will see you well fed and aided until you reach the coast. I assume the gold inside will be enough for you to find someone willing to overlook your current situation and aid you in securing safe passage from England."

Dash looked inside and nodded. Then he glanced at the spot over Gossett's shoulder where Larken was concealed.

So he *had* seen him come in.

"I only hope I can get there without any interference."

Larken knew what he meant. That he wouldn't step forward and stop his escape. He tipped his head out of the shadows and saluted him, then turned his back as Dash climbed up on the strong horse.

"Take good care of this animal. He's the best in the land," Gossett said. "And if you would see that he is returned, I would be indebted."

Larken nearly laughed. Gossett! Always the honorable man, thinking everyone else was the same.

But to his credit, Dash nodded. For he understood that a good horse to a gentleman was like a fleet ship to a sea captain. Then he leaned down and said something to Gossett that Larken couldn't hear, before spurring the horse and riding from the stables as if the devil were on his heels.

Still, he couldn't fathom how Lady Philippa could have done such a thing. With her decision, she'd gained Dash his freedom and his life, but at such a terrible cost to them both.

Larken closed his eyes and leaned his forehead against the post, listening as Gossett walked away from the stables.

What if it had been Tally? Married to another? What if he let his obsession with honor and duty, his fears over his dark past, like Dashwell's reckless nature, drive them apart forever?

Once he knew that Gossett was far from the stables, Larken slipped into the gardens, for he knew he couldn't make the same mistake as his friend and lose his heart.

Larken walked down the forest path to the folly carrying a well-laden basket. The duchess had spent the last half hour on his heels, helping him pack it and prodding him over his intentions toward her sister—which, thankfully, he'd been spared from sharing by the timely arrival of Hollindrake, who'd all but dragged his wife away and left Larken in peace to find his own way forward.

As he tromped along, the smell of leaves and

wildflowers blended with the damp air beneath the trees. Dappled sunlight found its way through the thick canopy above.

If only his heart wasn't hammering wildly in his chest. Gads, one would think he'd never faced adversity before.

Of course, adversity hadn't a fair face and a talent for tangling up his heart, like Tally did.

As he came to the folly, he spied her sitting on one of the far-off stones, sketching. With her brows furrowed and her mouth set, it appeared that she was doing more erasing than actual drawing, along with a good bit of cursing.

"Problems?" he asked.

She spun around, nearly dropping her sketchbook and charcoal. "Oh, dear. 'Tis you!"

He didn't know if that was an accusation or her way of saying she was happy to see him.

Since she hadn't set Brutus after him—the little dog was curled up at the base of the stone, watching first him and then his mistress before going back to his sleepy watch—he had to assume she wasn't furious at his invasion of her privacy.

Meanwhile, Tally had hastily gathered her sketchbook and pencils together and set them aside. She chewed at her lower lip, before running a distracted hand over her hair, as if trying to set it to rights.

He would have told her not to bother, for her bonnet had long since been discarded, and the breeze had tousled her fair hair. The soft tendrils fell past her shoulders and she looked as if he'd just awakened her from a long nap.

"I must look a fright," she said, glancing down at

her gown. "You always seem to find me when I am hardly presentable."

"I beg to differ," he said, coming closer. The wind stilled, and the rustle of the leaves died away, and it was as if he'd come into a fairy glen and one wrong move, one errant word could scatter her from his reach forever. The image of a stricken Dash still burning inside him, he didn't want to do anything to lose her. "I find you quite lovely."

She glanced away, a faint blush rising on her cheeks.

Coming closer still, he set the basket down on the stone opposite her.

"Whatever is that?" she asked.

"I believe it is a picnic."

She edged off the stone and looked at the basket. "You don't know?"

"I've never been on one," he told her. He supposed hardtack and cold tea atop a Portuguese plain did not count.

"Never?"

He faced her. "Never. Perhaps you could—"

But she was already off the stone and edging past him cautiously, so that only the briefest hint of her hem touched him. "Never been on a picnic," she was muttering.

Larken grinned at her dismay . . . and her willingness to help.

It was a start. But to what?

Something . . .

In the meantime, Tally pulled out the contents, setting them out in a delicious array on a pair of plates, handing him the bottle of wine to uncork, and sneaking, when she thought he wasn't looking, a perfectly plump and ripe strawberry.

He reached over her shoulder and fetched out a bone for Brutus.

"You'll spoil him," Tally chided.

"Wasn't my idea," he told her. "The cook added it in when your sister wasn't looking. She said it was, ahem"—he cleared his throat and did his best imitation—"to keep that little beastie occupied."

Tally laughed. "And so it is," she said, pointing at Brutus, who dragged his prize up the path and well out of sight so as not to have to share. Then she stilled. "Did you say, 'my sister?' "

He nodded. "She rather cornered me."

"I am so sorry."

"Don't be," he told her. "She was full of advice."

Tally groaned. "Oh goodness. Whyever do I have to have such a sister? Why couldn't I have had an ordinary sort of twin who minded her own business?"

Now he laughed. "Yes, but then we wouldn't have this," he said, holding up the bottle of wine. "And a very good vintage I must say." And to prove his point, he uncorked it and filled the glasses. They settled in atop a large block of marble stone and Tally passed a plate to him.

Was it his imagination, or were her hands trembling?

He glanced up at her and saw her brow as furrowed as it had been when she'd been drawing. "Thank you," he told her, and he began to eat.

They did so in silence, each taking furtive glances at the other, until finally she set down her plate and faced him. "Are you leaving?"

Her question startled him. And after he took a gulp of wine, he answered her. "Yes."

Her lower lip trembled. "And have you come here to say good-bye?"

Good-bye? Larken's heart stopped. Is that what she wanted? For him to leave? And before he could stop himself he blurted out, "Lord, I hope not."

And after that confession, he reached over to take her hand in his and do the most dangerous thing he'd ever done.

Propose.

Tally's gaze bolted up to meet his, even as his hand covered hers. *I hope not?* Could it be possible?

She tamped down the rush of happiness that threatened to overtake her heart. She'd spent the entire day unable to even dare hope that he could forgive her—why, she'd nearly gotten him killed by not going directly to Hollindrake. She'd convinced herself that he must despise her foolish, headstrong ways.

But his eyes burned with a fiery, passionate light that gave her hope. Gave her much more than that.

It ignited her desire for him in a heated rush.

"My lord—" she whispered.

"Geoff," he corrected.

"Pardon?" she asked, glancing up from his hand, from where his fingers were entwined with hers, binding them together. It was such a simple gesture, but it held so much meaning. He hadn't let go of her. Not yet. And he wasn't here to say goodbye.

"Please, call me Geoff."

Tally blushed, the heat rising up from her slippers

at the very intimacy of such a thing. "Geoff," she said softly, letting his name fall from her lips like a sweet confection. "Can you ever forgive me?"

"For what?" he asked, looking utterly confused.

"For everything," she rushed to say, her other hand covering his. "For bringing you here, entangling you in all this. If I hadn't helped Pippin break Dash out of jail, then you would never have been sent to . . . to . . ."

Kill Dash.

The unspoken words stilled the air around them.

He pulled her closer, into his arms, and kissed the top of her head. "Yes, yes, we both know what I was supposed to do. And if you hadn't done what you shouldn't, then we might never have met," he told her. "And that would have been most unforgivable."

"I nearly got you killed," she said, sick to her heart over the memory of seeing him lying on the stable ground, bound and tied, blood on his head.

"Nearly, but I am still here," he said. "And more so because of you."

"Me?"

"Yes, of course you. You've done more for me than you could ever know. I was so utterly lost before I met you. How much so I didn't realize until you tripped into my life."

"Quite literally," she teased, her heart brimming over. "Thank goodness you were there to catch me."

"And I would like to be there for you, to catch you that is," he said tentatively, before looking into her eyes and saying the one word she never thought he'd say. "Always."

Tally knew this was a proposal in his awkward sort of way. No long lofty speech, no direct question, just his own way of saying he wanted her. Always.

And she knew she should say yes, but she answered him in her own way.

With a kiss.

Larken watched her eyes go from tentative to a mischievous sparkle as he posed his question. He held his breath as he awaited her answer, and she gave it, quickly and as only Tally would.

She leaned forward, caught his face with her soft hands, and put her lips to his.

Sealing his offer with her kiss.

The moment her lips touched his, Larken was undone. Lost again. How did she do this? Awaken his body and his heart in this thunderous need for her?

He pulled her close, gathering her into his arms and plundering her lips hungrily. He wasn't going to let her go, ever. Even though his heart knew now, she was his. Always.

His tongue swept past her lips and tasted her, danced with hers. She was ripe and willing, as eager as he was to enflame that spark between them into a bonfire of passion.

He kissed her, then let his lips explore her neck, her earlobe, the pulse at her throat, downward to the edge of her bodice.

His other hand was working its way upward, pulling her hem along even as his hands trailed over the lithe, long line of her legs, up over her hips, towing her dress up and over her head.

She shivered, but not, he thought from a chill, rather in anticipation of what was to come. Larken looked down at her lush, willing body and ached to be inside her, joined with her, seeing her find her release as he stroked her.

He bent down and buried his face in her neck, kissing her, moving down, plying the straps of her chemise from her shoulders so he could free her breasts, his hand cupping one while his lips took the ripe tip in his mouth like a berry, sucking it until he heard the deep throaty sigh that escaped her lips, felt her hips arch upward.

Already hard, he was breathless from her eager response. Picking her up, he held her for a moment in his arms, before carrying her to the soft, thick grass that grew in the middle of the folly, and there he laid her down, divesting himself quickly of his shirt, boots and breeches.

She reached for him, pulled him to her, her legs winding around his hips and her lips on his.

"Please, Larken, please . . . " she whispered breathlessly.

Her sensuous plea nearly left him undone, and he'd barely begun.

Tally lay back in the grass and watched Larken undress. It was like watching a marble statue come to life before her—the thick muscles of his arms and chest, the narrow taper of his waist to his slim hips, and then the corded muscles of his thighs.

And his manhood. His glorious length, long and hard and erect. Just for her. Hers for the taking.

But before she could touch him, before she could taste him, he'd dropped to his knees before her, a wicked smile on his lips. He took her foot in his hand and began to kiss her toes. She squealed with laughter, the delicious feeling running up her leg, even as his lips came higher and higher, kissing her, exploring the curve of her calves, soft turns of her thighs.

And then he was there, at her apex, his breath hot upon her sex and she could barely move, barely breathe, for his fingers brushed over her, parting the way so his lips could taste her.

"Whatever are you—" she began . . . *going to do*, she would have finished, but he was already there, kissing her, running his tongue over the tight nub, nuzzling her, exploring her.

"Oooh," she gasped, her hips arching to meet him, meet this sweet torture. He ran his tongue over her in long, sweeping strokes, and all she could do was cling to his shoulders as her body began to tremble and quake.

He was going to carry her up there, take her over the edge with just his kiss, and then she did, come in a rush of heated desire.

"Larken, oh, demmit, Larken, that is so good," she cried out.

He pulled her beneath him, laughing and kissing her anew, nuzzling her breasts, his fingers finding the spot his lips had tortured, and continued the waves of passion that rocked her until she could take no more.

"Oh, just kiss me," she whispered, and he did, cradling her in his arms, stroking her hair. His touch claimed her, worshipped her and she wondered that anyone had ever felt so wonderful.

And as she gazed up into his eyes, she felt the dark desire there reignite her passion anew.

She moved like a cat, and rolled atop him, nuzzling and exploring him as he had her, right down to his manhood, and without hesitating, she ran her tongue over it, from the base right up to the tip, listening to the ragged groan that echoed from his chest.

"Woman, what are you trying to do to me?" he gasped, as she ran her mouth over him, loving the taste of him, the feel of him in her hands, the sense of power that came with pleasuring him as he had her— and the way it aroused her, bringing her right back to the same breathless, anxious place that begged to be filled.

She continued to suck on him, until he pulled her away, his eyes so dark, so smoky with need, she knew exactly what he wanted, and willingly she lay beneath him, her hands on his hips, and pulled him to her.

He entered her quickly, with a long, thick stroke that filled her.

Tally sighed at the pleasure of it, her legs winding around his hips, her body joining with his.

Larken paused and looked down at her. "You are mine. Now and always, you troublesome, scandalous minx."

All she could do was grin back. He saw her as she'd always dreamt of being seen, as a scandalous woman, full of passion and desire.

And she was his. Now and always.

"Prove it," she whispered back.

So he did, stroking her and bringing her to her release, even as he found his own, sealing their fate and binding them together always in an explosion of passion.

Long after the sun had set, Tally and Larken walked along the cool forest path back toward the house. They had made love until they were exhausted, eaten and drank from their picnic and then found the strength to make love one more time, gently and quietly in the soft twilight.

"I'm not the best man for you," Larken said.

Tally's footsteps faltered to a stop, hands going to her hips. Brutus pulled up as well, pausing beside her hem. "I think I'm the judge of that." She paused and then grinned at him. "I find you quite perfect."

He laughed and caught her hand and pulled her back along the path, Brutus happily following. "Truly though, I've done things—"

"Sssh," was her quick reply. "Dwelling on the past will not serve us. You can't change what you've done."

"What would your Nanny Rana say about all this?" he teased.

She shook her head. "No, I think Nanny Tasha would serve us better. You must find peace with your past, she'd tell you. Fill your heart with new memories and discover the joys that are right before you."

"Like you?"

"Like me," she said with lofty confidence.

They had come to the point where the forest gave

way to the meadow and Hollindrake House rose before them like a great citadel.

Tally groaned. "She'll insist on a grand wedding."

"You don't sound happy about that prospect," he said.

"Not at all," she declared. "For she'll expect us to have banns and wait! Not that *she* did, but she'll want at least one respectable marriage, and I daresay, mine is it."

"Isn't that what you want?" he asked. "I thought all ladies wanted—"

"Not me!" Tally protested. "Lord Larken, have you ever known me to want what is expected?"

He laughed. "No. Never. I don't know what I was thinking." Bringing her fingers to his lips, he kissed them. "So my future Lady Larken, what do you want?"

Her gaze drifted over toward the stables. "I've always fancied . . ."

"Yes?"

"I've always wanted . . ."

"You have but to ask, Tally, my love," he told her.

Taking a deep breath, she made her wish. "Gretna. I want to be married in Gretna Green. I want to make a scandalous dash for the border, Felicity's big Society wedding be damned."

Larken needed no more urging, catching her by the hand and towing her toward the stables, where Aurora's post-chaise still sat. As they ran toward it like a pair of wayward children, he said, "But when we return from Scotland, I expect you to tell your sister this was entirely your idea."

Tally pulled to a stop. "Lord Larken, are you afraid of my sister?"

"Right down to the soles of my boots."

She nodded in agreement and took a wary glance at the house. Really, besides being dark and dangerous and utterly handsome, he was downright intelligent. "Perhaps we can come home by way of Paris . . ."

"Buying you more time before you pay the piper?"

"Yes. And I'm sure, knowing my sister, by the time we return—in a good year or two—she'd be up to her neck in making matches—"

"Good matches," they both said and laughed merrily as they stole away to make their perfect one complete.

Epilogue

Gretna Green, Scotland
A week later

Tally and Larken had made it to the tiny Scottish hamlet on the border and after settling their purloined post-chaise with the innkeeper walked across the village square to the tiny church that served the runaways who sought hasty marriages.

The sennight of traveling had left them rumpled and tired, but Larken had never been as sure of anything in his life as he was about marrying the woman beside him. Their days together had only convinced him further how perfect she was for him.

They'd made love in rustic inns, argued once over something trifling until they had dissolved into mutual laughter over their stubborn natures, and discussed their plans for a fine future.

With their mutual skills and experience, Tally had

no doubt they would be able to secure a diplomatic posting. And Larken agreed—for not only that, with Temple and Hollindrake behind them, not even Pymm could stand in their way.

"One thing still troubles about all this," Tally said, as they walked hand in hand.

"What is that?" he asked.

"Mr. Ryder. I mean the real Mr. Ryder. You didn't . . . that is to say, you wouldn't have . . ."

He glanced down at her. "You aren't suggesting that I killed a vicar, are you?"

"Oh, no! Of course not," she said hastily. Then after a moment, she added, "You didn't, did you?"

"Bloody hell, of course not," he sputtered, much to the chagrin of an old matron passing them.

Tally heaved a sigh. "That is a relief." They walked a little bit farther and Larken bent over to pick a stray flower for her that was coming up beside the road. "Then whatever happened to him?"

Larken laughed. "If you must know, Templeton sent his batman, Elton, to delay the real Mr. Ryder's arrival. I suppose he is arriving at Hollindrake House as we speak, full of apologies to your sister for his tardy appearance and giving her much delight over someone new to match."

They both laughed and climbed the steps up to the church. A serving woman was coming down, bucket in one hand and a broom in another, obviously having just finished the morning cleaning. "Oh, don't you look to be the happy and dearest of couples! And such a fine morning to be wed."

"That it is, madame," Larken said, doffing his hat to her.

"There's a lovely couple in with the master right now being married, but I don't think anyone would mind if you go right in and wait in the back of the church. Just swept it clean, I did."

"Thank you very much," Tally said. "Will the other ceremony take long?"

The lady laughed. "In a hurry, are we? Well, I was young once and know how it is. Just like the fine couple afore you. Anxious to be wed and off on their new life. And such a romantic pair those—met at an inn just last week, the poor wee dear lady having carriage trouble and the kind gentleman there offering to help her, take her along in his carriage. And what would you know, after a day together, he turned the carriage north and here they are. 'Tis a fine story, it is." She paused and rubbed her nose with the back of her dirty hand. "And there I go, nattering on. And you two wantin' to be married. Now in with you and mind the scraper, I just swept and don't want any more of that mud tracked in."

"Yes, ma'am," Larken said, bowing to her and making great pains to scrape his boots to her exacting standards.

When they'd settled into a pew at the back, Tally suddenly sat bolt upright.

"Egads," she gasped. "I cannot marry you!"

All the heads at the front of the church turned to gape at them, and Larken shook his head and waved his hand for them to continue.

He shot a glance over at the beautiful and lithe lady at his side, arching one brow like a question mark. "Rather late to change your mind," he whispered.

"Oh, I suppose so," she said, but the furrow to her brow told another story.

He leaned over. "Out of curiosity, may I ask why this sudden change of heart?"

She turned to him, all earnest and as ruffled as a hen on a windy day. "I just realized that if I marry you, that will make Miss Browne my sister."

He burst out laughing, much to the consternation of the couple being wed, the vicar and a witness, most likely the vicar's wife. The good woman hissed a sharp, *"shush"* at him, and properly chided, he covered his mouth and nodded an apology to the crowd at the altar.

"While I can understand your dismay at gaining such an alliance with Miss Browne"—to which she interjected a sharp *harrumph*—"our marriage does give you the wonderful advantage, if I do so humbly say myself, of making me your husband."

Now it was Tally's turn to laugh, and there was another *"sssh"* from the front of the small church. "Well, when you put it that way," she whispered. "You do have a way about you." She tossed him that "look" that made his insides turn molten and his desire for her send any bit of good sense he possessed on an extended holiday.

He caught hold of her and kissed her. And this time they both ignored the *"sssh"* that followed.

When he was finished, he pulled away and looked down into her passion-filled eyes. "Does that make it better?"

"Almost," she teased. "I think it will take some more convincing for the sting of such a relation to go away."

And so he set to work convincing her some more, kissing her until he thought they'd set the church aflame.

With any luck, Larken mused as his lips teased hers to open for him, it would take a lifetime to finish this task.

So occupied with their kiss, so caught up with their mutual passion, they never heard the vicar pronounce the couple at the altar married, even though he intoned in a loud voice, "Miss DeFisser, it is my deepest honor to declare you married and to be known henceforth as Mrs. Milo Ryder. Sir, you may kiss your bride . . ."

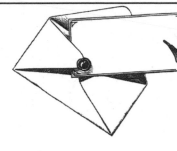

Dearest Reader,

You are in for a treat!

In the coming months we'll read about two sexy devils, one wicked Scotsman, and a little black gown in these four irresistible Avon Romances—all sweeping, sensuous historical romances by four bestselling authors at the top of their game.

Turn the pages
for a sneak peek and be the first
to fall in love with
Avon Books's latest and greatest!

Coming January 2009

Tempt the Devil

Anna Campbell

Olivia Raines has ruled London's demimonde with an iron will and a fiery spirit. Sought after by London's most eligible men, she has never had cause to question her power until she meets the notorious Julian Southwood, Earl of Erith. From the moment he first saw her, Julian knew he must possess her. So when he discovers a secret that could destroy her livelihood, Olivia has no choice than to bargain with the devil.

London
April 1826

Across the packed, noisy salon, Julian Southwood, Earl of Erith, studied the notorious strumpet who would become his next mistress.

He was in the middle of Mayfair on a fine spring afternoon. Yet the reek of sex for sale was as pungent as in the slave markets of Marrakesh or Constantinople.

The crowd was mostly male, although a few provocatively dressed women mingled in the throng. Nobody paid them the slightest attention. Just as nobody but Erith seemed to notice the startling and realistically detailed frescoes of rampant Zeus seizing swooning Ganymede.

From a corner dais a pianist and violinist doggedly plowed through a Mozart sonata. The music came from a different world, a cleaner, purer world untainted by animal carnality.

A world the Earl of Erith would never again inhabit.

Erith shook off the bleak self-reflection and turned to the man beside him. "Introduce me, Carrington."

"Shall do, old chap."

Carrington didn't ask the object of Erith's interest. Why would he? Every man here, including his companion, focused on the slender woman reclining with studied nonchalance upon the chaise longue.

Without being told, Erith knew she'd deliberately chosen her setting in front of the tall west-facing windows. Late afternoon sun flooded her in soft gold and played across her loosely bound tumble of tawny hair. In the clear light, her vivid red dress was like a sudden flame. The effect was worthy of the Theatre Royal.

Even he, familiar to ennui with courtesans' tricks, had felt the breath catch in his throat at first sight of her. One glance and the blood in his veins hummed a deep, dark song of desire, and his skin prickled with the compulsion to make her his.

And she achieved this remarkable effect from half a room away.

Of course, this was no ordinary courtesan.

If she were, he wouldn't be here. The Earl of Erith only bought the best. The best tailoring. The best horses. The best women.

Even by his exacting standards, this particular cyprian was a prime article.

Two extraordinary women had set London on its

ear in the last ten years. One, Soraya, cool, dark, mysterious as moonlight, had recently married the Duke of Kylemore, igniting the scandal of the decade. The other, radiant sun to Soraya's moon, arrayed herself now before Erith like a spectacular jewel.

He assessed her as closely as he'd contemplate an addition to his stables.

Lord, but she was a long Meg. A sheath of crimson velvet displayed her lean body to dramatic advantage. She'd fit his tall frame to perfection, even if his taste usually ran to plumper, more voluptuous bedmates. His memory filled pleasantly with the fleshy blond charms of Gretchen, the mistress he'd left in Vienna a month ago.

Gretchen couldn't contrast more strongly with the jade before him. Where the Tyrolean beauty offered soft, yielding curves, this woman was all spare elegance. The bosom under her gown's low neckline wasn't generous, and her waist was long and supple. He guessed the narrow skirt hid legs as graceful and elongated as a thoroughbred's.

Gretchen had been dewy with youth. This woman must verge on thirty. By that age, most bits of muslin frayed at the edges. But this bird of paradise continued her unchallenged reign over the male half of the ton. Her longevity as the most sought-after courtesan in London made her yet more intriguing.

His gaze slid up to her face. Like her body, it was unexpected. After the rhapsodies he'd heard in the clubs, he'd imagined less subtle attractions. The unmistakable greed he'd heard in her admirers' voices had led him to imagine a brassier, more overtly available bawd.

Her jaw was square, almost masculine. Her nose was a trifle too long, her cheekbones too high. From where he stood in the gilt-framed doorway, it was impossible to tell the color of her eyes, but they were large and brilliant and set at a slant.

Cat's eyes. Tiger's eyes.

Her mouth . . .

Her mouth perhaps explained what he'd heard about her preternatural allure. It might be too large. But who would complain? No man could look at those succulent lips without wanting them on his body. Erith's groin tightened at the decadent pictures rocketing through his mind.

Undoubtedly, she had . . . *something.*

She wasn't a great beauty. She was well past first youth. Nor did she flaunt her charms like tawdry trinkets on a fairground stall. If he'd encountered her at a respectable gathering rather than this louche brouhaha, he'd almost believe she belonged to his own class.

Almost.

After the hubbub, all this was surprising. Disappointing.

But even as he dismissed the wench's heralded charms, his eyes gravitated back to that spare, strangely aristocratic face. To that sin of a mouth. To that luxuriant hair. To that long, graceful body curved in complete relaxation upon her couch while men eddied around her in an endless whirlpool of fascination.

She was the most powerful figure in the room. Even at the distance, he felt the sexual energy sizzling around her.

She swept the room with a contemptuous glance. The raised angle of her chin and the irony that teased the corners of her mouth indicated defiance, courage, challenge.

He tried to deny the sensual pull she exerted. While

his reckless heart kicked into the emphatic rhythm of a drum beating an army into battle.

No, she wasn't what he'd expected, but he didn't fool himself into believing she was anything less than quality.

She lifted her head and smiled at something the effete fellow standing at her elbow said. The lazy curve of those lush red lips shot another jolt of lava-hot arousal through Erith. That smile spoke of knowledge and sharp intelligence, and a sexual confidence he'd never encountered in a woman. Never, even though he'd dealt with the fallen sisterhood for the last sixteen years. Every drop of moisture dried from his mouth, and his interest, wearied through playing this game too long, engaged with an intensity that astonished him. The covetous buzz in his blood notched up a degree.

Oh, yes, she was going to be his.

Not just because she was the elite of London's courtesans and his prestige would accept nothing less as his *chère amie*. But because he wanted her.

More than he'd wanted anything in a long, long time.

Coming February 2009

Devil of the Highlands

Lynsay Sands

They call him the Devil, the most notorious laird in all of Scotland. But Cullen, the new Laird of Donnachaidh, pays them no heed. He cares only about the survival of his clan, and for that, he needs a wife. He wants someone stout to bear him sons. He wants a pliable woman who wouldn't question his dictates. He wants a passionate woman to warm his bed. Then he meets Evelinde . . . one out of three isna bad.

Cullen was the first to see her. The sight made him rein in so sharply, his horse reared in response. He tightened his thighs around his mount to help keep his seat, moving automatically to calm the animal, but he didn't take his eyes off the woman in the glen.

"God's teeth. What is she doing?" Fergus asked as he halted beside him.

Cullen didn't even glance to the tall, burly redhead who was his first. He merely shook his head silently, transfixed by the sight. The woman was riding back and forth across the clearing, sending her horse charging first one way, then the other and back. That in itself was odd, but what had put the hush in Fergus's voice and completely captured Cullen's tongue was the fact she was doing so in nothing but a transparent chemise while holding the reins of her mount in her teeth. Her hands were otherwise occupied. They were upraised and holding what appeared to be a cape in the air so it billowed out behind her above her streams of golden hair as she rode back and forth . . . back and forth . . . back and forth.

"Who do you think she is?" Rory's question was the only way Cullen knew the other men had caught up as well.

"I doona ken, but I could watch the lass all day," Tavis said, his voice sounding hungry. "Though there are other things I'd rather be doing to her all day."

Cullen found himself irritated by that remark. Tavis was his cousin and the charmer among his men; fair-haired, handsome, and with a winning smile, it took little effort for him to woo women to his bed of a night. And the man took full advantage of the ability, charming his way under women's skirts at every opportunity. Were titles awarded by such an ability, Tavis would have been the king of Scotland.

"I'd first be wanting to ken why she's doing what she is," Fergus said slowly. "I've no desire to bed a wench who isna right in the head."

"It isna her head I'd be taking to me bed." Tavis laughed.

"Aye," Gillie said, his voice sounding almost dreamy.

Cullen turned a hard glare on his men. "Ride on. I'll catch up to ye."

There was a moment of silence as eyebrows rose and glances were exchanged, then all five men took up their reins.

"Ride around the meadow," Cullen instructed, when they started to move forward.

There was another exchange of glances, but the men followed the tree line around the meadow.

Cullen waited until they had disappeared from sight, then turned back to the woman. His eyes followed her back and forth several times before he urged his mount forward.

It hadn't appeared so from the edge of the meadow, but the woman was actually moving at high speed on her beast, slowing only to make the turn before spurring her horse into a dead run toward the other side. The mare didn't seem to mind. If anything, the animal seemed to think it was some sort of game and threw herself into each run with an impressive burst of speed.

Cullen rode up beside the mare, but the woman didn't immediately notice him. Her attention was shifting between the path ahead and the cloth in her upraised hands. When she finally did glimpse him out of the corner of her eye, he wasn't at all prepared for her reaction.

The lass's eyes widened, and her head jerked back with a start, unintentionally yanking on the reins she clenched in her teeth. The mare suddenly jerked to a halt and reared. The lass immediately dropped her hands to grab for the reins and the cloth she'd been holding swung around and slapped—heavy and wet—across Cullen's face. It both stung and briefly blinded him, making him jerk on his own reins in surprise, and suddenly his own mount was turning away and rearing as well.

Cullen found himself tumbling to the ground, tangled in a length of wet cloth that did nothing to cushion his landing. Pain slammed through his back, knocking the wind out of him, but it positively exploded through his head, a jagged blade of agony that actually made him briefly lose consciousness.

A tugging sensation woke him. Blinking his eyes open, he thought for one moment the blow to his head had blinded him, but then felt another tug and realized there was something over his face. The damp cloth, he recalled with relief. He wasn't blind. At least, he didn't think he was. He wouldn't know for sure until he got the cloth off.

Another tug came, but this was accompanied by a grunt and a good deal more strength. Enough that his head was actually jerked off the ground, bending his neck at an uncomfortable angle. Afraid that, at this rate, he'd end up with a broken neck *after* the fall, Cullen decided he'd best help with the effort to untangle himself from the cloth and lifted his hands toward his head, intending to grab for the clinging material. However, it seemed his tormentor was leaning over him, because he found himself grabbing at something else entirely. Two somethings . . . that were covered with a soft, damp cloth, were roundish in shape, soft yet firm at the same time, and had little pebble-like bumps in the center, he discovered, his fingers shifting about blindly. Absorbed as he was in sorting out all these details, he didn't at first hear the horrified gasps that were coming from beyond the cloth over his head.

"Sorry," Cullen muttered as he realized he was groping a woman's breasts. Forcing his hands away, he shifted them to the cloth on his head and immediately began tugging recklessly at the stuff, eager to get it off.

"Hold! Wait, sir, you will rip—" The warning ended on a groan as a rending sound cut through the air.

Cullen paused briefly, but then continued to tug at the material, this time without apologizing. He'd never been one to enjoy enclosed spaces and felt like he would surely smother to death if he did not get it off at once.

"Let me—I can—If you would just—"

The words barely registered with Cullen. They sounded like nothing more than witless chirping. He ignored them and continued battling the cloth, until—with another tearing sound—it fell away, and he could breathe again. Cullen closed his eyes and sucked in a deep breath with relief.

"Oh dear."

That soft, barely breathed moan made his eyes open and slip to the woman kneeling beside him. She was shifting the cloth through her hands, examining the damaged material with wide, dismayed eyes.

Cullen debated offering yet another apology, but he'd already given one, and it was more than he normally offered in a year. Before he'd made up his mind, the blonde from the horse stopped examining the cloth and turned alarmed eyes his way.

"You are bleeding!"

"What?" he asked with surprise.

"There is blood on my gown. You must have cut your head when you fell," she explained, leaning over him to examine his scalp. The position put her upper body inches above his face, and Cullen started getting that closed-in feeling again until he was distracted by the breasts jiggling before his eyes.

The chemise she wore was very thin and presently wet, he noted, which was no doubt what made it transparent. Cullen found himself staring at the beautiful, round orbs with fascination, shifting his eyes left and right and continuing to do so when she turned his head from side to side to search out the source of the blood.

Apparently finding no injury that could have blood-ied her gown, she muttered, "It must be the back of your head," and suddenly lifted his head, pulling it up off the ground, presumably so she could examine the back of his skull. At least that was what he thought she must be doing when he found his face buried in those breasts he'd been watching with such interest.

"Aye, 'tis here. You must have hit your head on a rock or something when you fell," she announced with a combination of success and worry.

Cullen merely sighed and nuzzled into the breasts presently cuddling him. Really, damp though they were, they were quite lovely, and if a man had to be smothered to death, this was not a bad way to go. He felt something hard nudging his right cheek beside his mouth and realized her nipples had grown hard. She also suddenly stilled like prey sensing danger. Not wishing to send her running with fear, he opened his mouth and tried to turn his head to speak a word or two of reassurance to calm her.

"Calm yerself," was what he said. Cullen didn't be-lieve in wasting words. However, it was doubtful if she understood what he said since his words came out muffled by the nipple suddenly filling his open mouth. Despite his intentions not to scare her, when he real-ized it was a nipple in his mouth, he couldn't resist closing his lips around it and flicking his tongue over the linen-covered bud.

In the next moment, he found pain shooting through his head once more as he was dropped back to the ground.

Coming March 2009

Bride of a Wicked Scotsman

Samantha James

An ancient curse . . . a deathbed promise. Lady Maura O'Donnell swore to her dying father that she would re-claim the Circle of Light, an enchanted Celtic relic that had brought her clan prosperity through the ages—until the night it was stolen two centuries earlier by a notorious pirate. Now the pirate's descendant, Alec McBride, Duke of Gleneden, holds the key to this treasure. Maura will do whatever she must to recover the Circle from this wickedly handsome Scotsman. But Alec is just as determined to dis-cover what secrets this lovely Irish lass is hiding.

Alec watched as she downed the remainder of her wine. "Why have I not seen you before today? Are you a guest of the baron's?" Lord above, he'd have re-membered those emerald eyes. He'd never seen such brilliant green . . . as green as the landscape of this rocky isle.

"Only for tonight."

"Then perhaps introductions are in order." He wanted to know who she was, by God. "I am—"

"Wait!" She held up a hand. "No, no! Do not say. This is a masquerade, is it not? A night to disguise our true selves. What say we dispense with names?" That tiny smile evolved into seduction itself.

Alec laughed. She was sheer delight. And an accomplished flirt. "As you wish, Irish."

"That *is* my wish, Scotsman."

Alec settled down to enjoy the thrust-and-parry. "May I get you something? A plate perhaps? The desserts are quite exquisite." God help him, the dessert he had in mind was *her*.

"I am quite satisfied just as I am."

He was not, thought Alec with unabashed lust. "Well, then, Irish, perhaps you would care to dance?"

Alec didn't. But manners dictate he ask. Beneath her eye mask, her cheekbones were high, the line of her jaw daintily carved. He longed to tear it away, to see the whole of her face, to appreciate every last feature.

Their eyes met. Alec moved so that their sleeves touched. Her smell drifted to his nostrils. Warm, sweet flesh and the merest hint of perfume.

He wanted her. He was not a rogue. Not a man for whom lust struck quickly and blindly. He was not a man to trespass where he should not. He was discreet in his relationships. He was not a man to take a tumble simply for the sake of slaking passion.

Never had he experienced a wash of such passion so quickly. He'd wanted women before, but not like this. Never like this. Never had Alec desired a woman the way he desired this one. What he felt was immediate. Intoxicating. A little overwhelming, even. Not that he shouldn't desire her. She was, after all, a woman who would turn any man's eye. It was simply that the strength of his desire caught him by surprise.

Perhaps it was this masquerade. Her suggestion that they remain anonymous.

He cupped his palm beneath her elbow. "There are too many people. The air grows stale. Shall we walk?"

Laughing green eyes turned up to his. "I thought you should never ask."

A stone terrace ran the length of the house. They passed a few other couples, strolling arm in arm. All at once, she stumbled. Quite deliberately, Alec knew. Not that he was disinclined to play the rescuer.

He caught her by the waist and brought her around to face him. "Careful, Irish."

"Thank you, Scotsman." She gazed up at him, her fingertips poised on his chest, moist lips raised to his.

Alec's gut tightened. She was so tempting. Too tempting to resist. Too tempting to even *try*.

A smile played about his lips. Behind her mask, invitation glimmered in her eyes. "Is it a kiss you're wanting, Irish?" He knew very well that she did.

"Are you asking permission, Scotsman?"

The smoldering inside him deepened. "No, but I have a confession to make." He lowered his head so that their lips almost touched. "I've never kissed an Irish lass before."

"And I've never kissed a Scotsman before."

"So once again it seems we are evenly matched, are we not?"

"Mmmm . . ."

Alec could stand no more. That was as far as she got. His mouth trapped hers. He felt a jolt go through her the instant their lips touched. It was the same for him, and he knew then just how much she returned his passion. His mouth opened over hers. He'd wanted women before. But not like he wanted this one. It was as if she'd cast a spell over him.

And he kissed her the way he'd desired all evening, with a heady thoroughness, delving into the far corners of her mouth with the heat of his tongue. Tasting the promise inside her. Harder, until he was almost mindless with need.

She tore her mouth away. She was panting softly. "Scotsman!" she whispered.

Alec's eyes opened. His breathing was labored. It took a moment for him to focus, for her words to penetrate his consciousness.

"I . . . what if we should be seen?"

So his Irish lady-pirate was willing—and he was quite wanting. Oh yes, definitely wanting.

"I agree, Irish. I quite agree." He tugged at her hand and started to lead her toward the next set of double doors.

"Where are you taking me?"

He stopped short. "What! I thought you knew, Irish."

"Tell me."

He slid his hand beneath her hair and turned her face up to his. "Why, I'm about to kidnap you, Irish." He smiled against her lips. "I fear it is the pirate in me."

Coming April 2009

Confessions of a Little Black Gown

Elizabeth Boyle

When Thalia Langley spies a handsome stranger in the shadows of her brother-in-law's study, she knows in an instant she's found the dangerous, rakish sort of man she's always dreamt of. But Tally suspects there is more to Lord Larken than meets the eye, and she has the perfect weapon to help tempt the truth from him: a little black gown she's found mysteriously in a trunk.

"Oh, Thatcher, there you are," Tally said, coming to a stop in the middle of her brother-in-law's study, having not even bothered to knock. She supposed if he were any other duke, not the man who'd once been their footman, she'd have to view him as the toplofty and unapproachable Duke of Hollindrake as everyone else did.

Thankfully, Thatcher never expected *her* to stand on formality.

"One of the maids said she saw a carriage arrive, some wretchedly poor contraption that couldn't be one of Felicity's guests and I thought it might be my missing . . ."

Her voice trailed off as Brutus came trotting up behind her, having stopped on the way down the stairs to give a footman's boot a bit of a chew. Her ever-present companion had paused for only a second before he let out a little growl, then launched himself toward a spot in a shadowed corner, as if he'd spied a rat.

No, make that a very ill-looking pair of boots.

Oh, dear! She didn't know Thatcher had company. She tamped down the blush that started to rise on her cheeks, remembering that she'd just insulted this unknown visitor's carriage.

Oh, dash it all! What had she called it?

Some wretchedly poor contraption . . .

Tally shot a glance at Thatcher, who nodded toward the shadows, even as a man rose up from the chair, coming to life like one of the Greek sculptures Lord Hamilton had been forever collecting in Naples.

Yet this one lived and breathed.

Thatcher's study was a dark room, sitting on the northeast side of the house, and with the sun now on the far side, the room was all but dark, except for the slanting bit of light coming in from the narrow casement. But darkness aside, Tally didn't really need to see the man, whose boot Brutus had attached himself to, to *know* him.

A shiver ran down her spine, like a forebear of something momentous. She couldn't breath, she couldn't move, and she knew, just knew, her entire life was about to change.

It made no sense, but then again, Tally had never put much stock in sense, common or otherwise.

Perhaps it was because her heart thudded to a halt just by the way he stood, so tall and erect, even with a devilish little affenpinscher affixed to his boot.

Heavens! With Brutus thus, how could this man ever move forward?

"Oh, dear! Brutus, you rag-mannered mutt, come away from there," she said, pasting her best smile on her face and wishing that she wasn't wearing one of Felicity's old hand-me-down gowns. And blast Felicity's tiresome meddling, for if she'd just left well enough alone and not insisted the trunks be changed around, her own trunk wouldn't have become lost.

"You wretched little dog, are you listening to me? Come here!" She snapped her fingers, and after one last, great growling chew, Brutus let go of his prize and returned to his usual place, at the hem of her gown, his black eyes fixed on the man, or rather his boots, as if waiting for any sign that he could return for another good bite.

"I am so sorry, sir," Tally began. "I fear his manners are terrible, but I assure you his pedigree is impeccable. His grandsire belonged to Marie Antoinette." She snapped her lips shut even as she realized she was rambling like a fool. Going on about Brutus's royal connections like the worst sort of pandering mushroom.

"No offense taken, miss," he said.

Oh, yes. His simple apology swept over her in rich, masculine tones.

Then to her delight, he came closer, moving toward Thatcher's desk with a cat-like grace, making her think of the men she'd imagined in her plays: prowling pirates and secretive spies. It was almost as if he was used to moving through shadows, aloof and confident in his own power.

Tally tamped down another shiver and leaned over to pick up Brutus, holding him tightly as if he could be the anchor she suddenly felt she needed.

Whatever was it about this man that had her feeling as if she were about to be swept away? That he was capable of catching her up in his arms and stealing her away to some secluded room where he'd lock them both away? Then he'd toss her atop the bed and he'd strip away his jacket, his shirt, his . . .

Tally gulped back her shock.

What the devil is wrong with me? She hadn't even seen the man yet, and here she was imagining him nearly in his altogether.

Oh, dear heavens, she prayed silently, *please say he is here for the house party. Please . . .*

"I daresay we have met," she continued on, trying to lure him forward, force him to speak again, "but you'll have to excuse me, I'm a terrible widgeon when it comes to remembering names."

The man stepped closer, but stopped his progress when the door opened and Staines arrived, a brace of candles in hand, and making a *tsk, tsk* sound over the lack of light in the room. The butler shot the duke a withering glance that seemed to say, *You are supposed to ring for more light.*

Poor Thatcher, Tally thought. He still had yet to find his footing as the Duke of Hollindrake and all that it entailed.

"Have we met?" she asked, and to further her cause, she shifted Brutus to one hip and stuck out her hand, which must compel the man, if he was a gentleman, to take it.

"No, I don't believe we have ever met, Miss—"

Oh, heavens, his voice was as smooth as the French brandy she and Felicity used to steal from their teacher's wine cabinet. And it would be even better if he were whispering into her ear.

Tally, my love, what is it you desire most . . . ?

Oh, now you are being a complete widgeon, she chided herself, closing her eyes, for she couldn't believe she was having such thoughts over a perfect stranger. A man she'd never seen. She only hoped this ridiculous tumult he was causing on her insides wasn't showing on her face.

Taking a deep breath, she unshuttered her lashes and, much to her horror, found herself staring at a complete stranger.

Certainly not the man she'd imagined.

Whoever was this ordinary, rather dowdy-looking fellow blinking owlishly at her from behind a pair of dirty spectacles, his shoulders stooped over as if he'd carried the burden of the world upon them?

Where had he come from? She leaned over to peer past him, searching for any sign of the man she'd expected, but there was no one there.

Tally swayed a bit. Heavens, she was seeing things. If she didn't know better, she'd say she was as jug-bitten as their London housekeeper, Mrs. Hutchinson.

But no, all the evidence was before her, for instead of some rakish character in a Weston jacket and perfectly polished boots, stood a gentleman (well, she hoped he was at least a gentleman) in a coat that could best be described as lumpy, cut of some poorly dyed wool, with sleeves too short for his arms. Far too short, for his cuffs stuck out a good six inches. Then to her horror, she glanced at his cravat, or rather where his cravat should be.

For in its place sat a vicar's collar.

A vicar?